THE WORLD'S CLASSICS

PUDD'NHEAD WILSON

AND OTHER TALES

MARK TWAIN, the pen-name for Samuel Langhorne Clemens (1835–1910), drew his identity from life along the Mississippi River during the years immediately preceding the Civil War, which inspired the characters and incidents in his best-known works, including *The Adventures of Tom Sawyer* (1876) and *The Adventures of Huckleberry Finn* (1884). Born in Florida, Missouri, but raised in Hannibal, Clemens first trained as a printer, but in 1857 he became an apprentice pilot on the great river. At the start of the Civil War, he went to Nevada with his brother Orion, and was briefly involved in mining ventures before taking up a journalistic career (under the name Mark Twain) which eventually carried him to California and Hawaii, experiences recounted in *Roughing It* (1872). He next travelled to Europe and the Holy Land with an excursion party, the basis for *The Innocents Abroad* (1869), a humorous narrative that quickly established his reputation and launched his career as a comic lecturer. After marrying Olivia Langdon in 1870, Clemens abandoned the lecture circuit and moved to Hartford, Connecticut, where he wrote most of the books by which he is known, in a period of great prosperity that was ended in 1894 by bankruptcy resulting from incautious investments. Returning to the lecture circuit, Clemens recovered his fortune but his later life was darkened by tragedy, including the deaths of his favourite daughter, Susy, and his wife. Another daughter, Jean, suffered from epilepsy and died in 1909, followed shortly by her father.

R. D. GOODER is a fellow of Clare College, Cambridge, and an editor of *The Cambridge Quarterly*. He has also edited *The Bostonians* for the World's Classics.

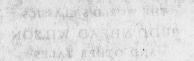

MARK TWAIN, the pen-name for Samuel Langhorne Clemens (1835-1910), drew his early life along the Mississippi River during the years of his teenage preceding the Civil War, which inspired the characters and problems in his best-known works, including *The Adventures of Tom Sawyer* (1876) and *The Adventures of Huckleberry Finn* (1884). Born in Florida, Missouri, but raised in Hannibal, Clemens first trained as a printer, but in 1857 he became an apprentice pilot on the great river. In 1861, at the start of the Civil War, he went to Nevada with his brother, and was largely engaged in mining ventures before taking on a phonetic career under the name Mark Twain, which he signed to his first California articles. Flawed experiences accounted for *The Innocents Abroad* (1869) ... his travels in Europe and the Holy Land ...

R. D. Gooder is a Fellow of Clare College, Cambridge, and an editor of *The Cambridge Quarterly*. He has also edited *The Scarlet Letter* for the World's Classics.

THE WORLD'S CLASSICS

MARK TWAIN

Pudd'nhead Wilson

Those Extraordinary Twins
The Man that Corrupted Hadleyburg

Edited by
R. D. GOODER

Oxford   New York
OXFORD UNIVERSITY PRESS
1992

Oxford University Press, Walton Street, Oxford OX2 6DP

Oxford New York Toronto
Delhi Bombay Calcutta Madras Karachi
Petaling Jaya Singapore Hong Kong Tokyo
Nairobi Dar es Salaam Cape Town
Melbourne Auckland

and associated companies in
Berlin Ibadan

Oxford is a trade mark of Oxford University Press

British Library Cataloguing in Publication Data
Data available

Library of Congress Cataloging in Publication Data
Twain, Mark, 1835–1910.
Pudd'nhead Wilson and other tales/ Mark Twain: edited by R.D. Gooder.
p. cm. — (The World's classics).
Includes bibliographical references (p.   ).
I. Gooder. R. D. II. Title. III. Series.
PS1317. A2G66 1992 813'.4—dc20 91–39011
ISBN 0–19–281806–6

Typeset by Pure Tech Corporation, India
Printed in Great Britain by
BPCC Hazells Ltd.

CONTENTS

CONTENTS

INTRODUCTION

ALTHOUGH Mark Twain, like most of his predecessors in America, has proved to be a one-book author (and that book is of course not *Pudd'nhead Wilson*), the forces limiting his creative development were not those that affected Hawthorne, for example, or Melville. Reviewing a history of American literature many years ago in the *Athenaeum*, T. S. Eliot wrote: 'The great figures of American literature are peculiarly isolated, and their isolation is an element, if not of their greatness, certainly of their originality.' But isolation, estrangement, and the burden of puritan tradition were not decisive elements for Mark Twain. On the contrary, he was a daylight writer, open to experience, and to a marked degree sympathetic to the prevailing ethos of his time. He was genuinely the product of his world and his age, and was willingly merged in it as no other American writer of comparable distinction. It was not self-doubt, want of material, or want of an audience and want of sympathy with it, that undermined Mark Twain's creative powers, but the very reverse of these things, and it is in *Pudd'nhead Wilson*, and 'The Man That Corrupted Hadleyburg', that the unhappy consequences of this oneness with the ethos of his time upon his art may best be studied.

Mark Twain was raised in Hannibal, Missouri, on the banks of the Mississippi River, half a day's steamboat journey above St Louis. The river was then, in the three decades prior to the Civil War, the main artery of trade, and, to a degree, of communication, in the rapidly expanding United States. In the heyday of the steamboats—from 1835 to 1855, a period roughly coinciding with Mark Twain's childhood—it would have been possible to get from New Orleans in the south to Pittsburgh in the east, a distance of 2,000 miles, in just under a week. Under the pressure of trade, travel, and westward expansion, Hannibal trebled its population during the time that Mark Twain lived there. So the little provincial village which prompts nostalgia in every reader of *Tom Sawyer* and feels somehow like the secure and innocent birthplace of half the population of America, was already under strain from the gathering forces of commercial expansion and exploitation. Mark Twain's earliest employment was (like Ben Franklin's) as a printer, first in his home town, then in other river ports from Keokuk to St Louis to Cincinnati, and then in New York and Philadelphia. In 1857 he himself became a cub pilot on a Mississippi steamboat, was licensed in 1859, and continued on the river until the middle of 1861, when the Civil War disrupted its traffic. The pastoral tranquillity of St Petersburg in *Tom Sawyer*, and the immense variety of life along the Mississippi in *Huckleberry Finn*, are generated not from idea or nightmare or historical reconstruction, but from an imagination richly nourished by memory. It is difficult for a great writer not to love the force of even the more rascally forms of life. The indulgence extended to the 'king' and the 'duke', like the indulgence extended to Falstaff, is not a matter of condoning rascality, but of a sympathy with reality. Mark Twain *knows* his best characters as Hawthorne and Melville can never know theirs. Mark Twain was steeped in reality.

In 1861 Mark Twain served for approximately two weeks with a Confederate militia group in Missouri, but he was neither physically brave nor much in sympathy with the Confederate cause, and he sloped out of the war and went west to Nevada, where he prospected for silver, speculated in mining stocks, and in the course of time became a popular journalist. By the end of 1866, when he left San Francisco for New York, he had learned something of the raw western world of the 'territory',[1] mastered the forms of serious and facetious journalism, started a career as a public lecturer, and gained a reputation as the best of the 'western humorists'. He was a writer who had material—however crude—that he was willing to use, and an audience, however popular, that

---

[1] If Huck Finn really does 'light out for the Territory', it will not be a flight to an innocent or pastoral world, but to a world of primitive violence and licentiousness.

he was happy to address. Moreover, he was a writer upon whom, in Hawthorne's phrase, 'the damned shadow of Europe' had not fallen.

But in 1867 Mark Twain positively embraced that shadow, travelling with a group of early 'package tourists' on board a steamship called the *Quaker City* to Europe and the Holy Land, and writing back a series of articles for his San Francisco paper, the *Alta California*, which show clearly what a different view of Europe he would take from either the solemn and overawed writers of the pre-War years, or from his cultivated contemporary Henry James. *The Innocents Abroad* is a satire upon the pretensions and mendacities of his fellow travellers, and at the same time a very sceptical account of the sights and attractions of Europe. It is deliberately and self-confidently philistine, and was an enormous commercial success. In *The Innocents Abroad* the mind of the true westerner[2] comes face to face with the old civilization of Europe.

In the following year, 1868, Mark Twain went to Washington, serving as private secretary to the senator from Nevada, and in the year after that he bought—with the help of a loan from his prospective father-in-law—a one-third interest in a Buffalo, New York, newspaper. In 1870 he married Olivia Langdon, daughter of a man made newly rich by coal mining, and he and his wife were installed by Olivia's father in sumptuous circumstances in Buffalo. In 1871 he set up house in Hartford, Connecticut, where he and his family were to live for the next twenty-one years; he built a grandiose mansion in the vulgarest possible taste, and entered upon the most successful period of his life. During the following years Mark Twain very nearly exemplified the spirit of the age. Able to live lavishly on his wife's wealth and the proceeds of his popularity as a lecturer and writer, his fortunes nevertheless fluctuated violently as he entered wholeheartedly into the speculative enterprises that characterized this first great age of American capitalism. But these were

---

[2] Cf. the attitude to Europe of, for example, the westerner Christopher Newman in Henry James's *The American*.

also the years of his most important work: *Roughing It* (1872), an account of his experience in the far West; *The Gilded Age* (1873), a satire, quite vicious in places, on entrepreneurial dreams of riches and the corruptions of Washington; *Tom Sawyer* (1876); *A Tramp Abroad* (1880); *The Prince and the Pauper* (1882); *Life on the Mississippi* (1883); *Huckleberry Finn* (1884); and *A Connecticut Yankee in King Arthur's Court* (1889). But Mark Twain's literary and speculative pursuits were not separate enterprises, for these books were among the world's first 'blockbusters', conceived and composed with a large popular audience in mind. *Innocents Abroad*, for example, sold more that 100,000 copies in two years, and made Mark Twain more than \$200,000, and *Huckleberry Finn* had sold more than 50,000 copies within three months of publication. The books were sold by subscription, a new technique in American publishing, which allowed author and publisher to reach readers and buyers in the new and expanding communities of the west, where bookshops did not exist.[3] One of the demands of this audience was that books should represent value for money—not literary value, but entertainment value and quantitative value. To serve both these functions Mark Twain's early books were lavishly decorated with elaborate chapter *incipits* and summaries, and extensively illustrated with engravings. The summaries were sometimes used twice, set out once in the table of contents and repeated at the head of each chapter, and even the list of illustrations swelled the number of pages. But the padding was also literary. In the cases of both *Roughing It* and *Life on the Mississippi* the first half of the book is a succinct, well-organized, and efficiently written account of its subject, and the second half is padded out with old newspaper copy and anecdotes. Every reader of *Huckleberry Finn* feels that the end of the novel is artistically ill managed, that the serious point underlying Tom Sawyer's conscienceless trifling with Jim could have been brought off

[3] 'Anything but subscription publishing is printing for private circulation.' MT to Howells, quoted in Justin Kaplan, *Mr Clemens and Mark Twain* (New York, 1966), 62.

in a fraction of the space given it. But commercial considerations—the proven popularity of *Tom Sawyer*, and the fact that even with Kemble's nearly 200 illustrations *Huckleberry Finn* is not a very long novel—induced Mark Twain to pad his closing episode to the point that it occupies well over a quarter of the whole text.

There is no question that Mark Twain profited, not only commercially but artistically, from a deep sympathy with the underlying currents of his age. He enjoyed its speculative spirit and loved even its mendacities. The greatness of some writers—Mark Twain is one, Dickens is another, so is Shakespeare—lies in their ability to feel what their contemporaries feel, and to express it so clearly and completely that judgement is the natural consequence of fullness of creation. Mark Twain does not *judge* Colonel Sellers, or Pap Finn, but he creates them in such complexity that the *reader* has all the evidence for judgement. They are altogether different in this respect from, say, Judge Pyncheon in *The House of Seven Gables*. Of the 'classic' American writers, Mark Twain is the only one who had a thorough, practical knowledge of the whole society and culture to which he was addressing himself, the only one to have in some sense loved it, and the only one really to have been wholly part of it. Like Shakespeare, Mark Twain was a provincial boy who made good in the capital by entertaining his contemporaries—rich and poor—in their own idiom and by way of a set of values in which they all could share. Yet a writer so thoroughly merged in his time is curiously at the mercy of his time, and when he comes to doubt its inherent virtue he will need other resources to save himself from failure. Shakespeare's resources were the resources of art, and art is what Mark Twain lacked. His connivance with the market flawed all his books, even his greatest, but the consequences were to become more far reaching still.

Mark Twain's next important book was *A Connecticut Yankee in King Arthur's Court*, which he published in 1894. This had begun life as a mere sketch, a spoof upon the romantic medievalism engendered by Tennyson's *Idylls of the King*, and the consequent taste for Malory's *Morte d'Arthur* (immensely popularized by the southern writer, Sidney Lanier, as *The Boy's King Arthur* in 1880). The original idea had been to set chivalric military methods and equipment against modern armour and scientific warfare, and at the same time to send up the aristocratic manners supposed to have been associated with chivalry. The best writing in the book is very much in line with what Mark Twain had already perfected, in the descriptions of a supposed Arthurian England which have all the nostalgic power of his earlier descriptions of St Petersburg and the topography of the Mississippi valley familiar from *Tom Sawyer* and *Huckleberry Finn*, and in the brilliant burlesque of the Yankee's 'Grailing expedition'. But the book quickly caught up in itself a great deal more than Mark Twain's usual sharp and fluent exposition. The generous scepticism of *Huckleberry Finn* gives way in *A Connecticut Yankee* to a more explicit set of ideas and prejudices. What started as a joke is carried on in earnest. Hank Morgan, the 'Yankee', grows into a representative of all that side of American life that seemed most to distinguish it from the older civilizations of Europe: he is a technocrat, a liberal democrat, a mercantilist, a philistine, self-confidently brash and given to notions of 'progress'. Intellectually and morally intact, he is perfectly confident that he has the future in his bones. Over against him is set, not so much 'King Arthur', as a constellation of morals, customs, attitudes, and arrangements vaguely supposed to represent the past, or Europe, or even the ante-bellum South. In Hank Morgan are to be found the Tenderfoot from *Roughing It*, the Cub Pilot from *Life on the Mississippi*, the sceptical tourist in Europe from *The Innocents Abroad*, not to say touches of both Tom Sawyer and Huck Finn—everything, that is to say, that showed Mark Twain most optimistic, most at ease with himself and his world. And on the other side are all those things which liberal, democratic, progressive America seemed set upon the earth to confound and destroy—feudalism, slavery, prejudice, tradition, hierarchy, 'art'. Hence Merlin is no match for Hank Morgan; nor agrarian feudalism for mercantilism; nor horses for bicycles, nor chain mail for Gatling guns. Hank Morgan emerges at the end a triumphant philistine in the midst of superstition laid waste.

But there are two forces at work in the book of which this summary does not take account, but which contribute to its ultimate disastrous failure. The first is that Mark Twain could no longer write with the innocence of his early manhood. The East, and Europe, were no longer the easy targets of frontier humour that they had once been. By the early 1890s Mark Twain had long been living permanently in the East, and had travelled extensively in Europe, indeed had spent extended periods of time there. He was under no illusion that Europe could be written off as expressing nothing but the values of a corrupt aristocracy. The second is that Mark Twain's own speculations in modern technology had (by the time he finished the book) gone disastrously wrong. In 1880 he had been persuaded to invest $5,000 in a machine that was just then being built at the Colt Arms Factory, a mechanical typesetting machine that even at this early stage of development was capable of doing the work of four men. The machine's inventor was James W. Paige, a man of great charm and persuasion, and over the next fifteen years or so Mark Twain was induced to invest nearly $200,000—and a great deal of emotional capital as well—in this mechanical marvel which, he claimed, would make all the other great modern inventions (the telephone, the telegraph, the steam engine, the cotton gin, the sewing machine, and so on) seem commonplace. And for a time he confidently believed that this speculative investment would lead to the foundation of a fortune comparable with that of the great plutocrats like Carnegie and Rockefeller. Mark Twain began serious work on *A Connecticut Yankee* early in 1886, at almost exactly the moment when he himself was most seriously engaged in organizing the company which would 'perfect, manufacture, and market all over the world' the Paige typesetter. The hero of *A Connecticut Yankee*, Hank Morgan, is a Hartford master mechanic and a superintendent at the Colt Arms Factory in Hartford, Connecticut, and his fictional fate, as well as that of the civilization he represents and that into which he intrudes, were entirely bound up with the fortunes of the machine which was engaging more and more of his creator's attention. The genial burlesque is left behind as the actual plot of the novel partakes more and more in the fantasy of wealth and power which Mark Twain was himself indulging in his own commercial speculations. And the novel demonstrates nothing so well as Mark Twain's own innocence in the face of modern speculative capitalism, and his ignorance of technology and its possibilities. The failure of the Paige typesetter, the failure of Mark Twain's speculation, and the simultaneous failure of his own publishing house, all of which left him financially and emotionally bankrupt, are translated into the novel in its incipient and ultimately explicit violence. The Battle of the Sand Belt, which is the climax of the novel, is won by Morgan with the help of electric fences and Gatling guns (such as were manufactured at the Colt Arms Factory in Hartford), but the 50,000 rotting corpses piled outside his bunker cut the hero off from the pastoral Arthurian world of which he is now nominally ruler. The victory is pyrrhic: the technological violence separates the hero from all that he has learned to care for. The hero is obliged to inhabit a dehumanized commercial and technological present, cut off from the innocent agrarian past of an Arthurian England which is in fact no more than a fictional revision of the ante-bellum Missouri of Mark Twain's childhood which he had already exploited in *Tom Sawyer* and *Huckleberry Finn*. The failure of *A Connecticut Yankee* reveals not only a deep split in its author's imagination, but also the very frail foundations that Mark Twain's earlier writing provided for the more serious subjects he now wished to engage. There was no ready route from burlesque to tragedy, and the meaning of Matthew Arnold's assertion that 'the funny man' was a 'national misfortune' is made manifest in *A Connecticut Yankee*. Everything Mark Twain cared about is bound up in it, but he hadn't the art to control his material.

After his financial misfortunes most of what Mark Twain wrote was—as now it *had* to be—written for money. Under the instruction of his friend, H. H. Rogers, a vice-president and one of the principal tycoons of the rapacious Standard Oil Trust, he reorganized his financial affairs, took an increasingly sharp interest in the value of the copyrights on work already in print, and published subsequently with an eye firmly cocked on a supposed 'market'. *Tom Sawyer, Detective* was a deliberate attempt to cash in on the vogue for Sherlock Holmes, and for detective fiction in general (the fingerprint plot in *Pudd'nhead Wilson* derives from the same source), and *How to Tell a Story* and *Following the Equator* were contrived out of material got up for a barnstorming, world-wide lecture tour undertaken for the sole purpose of raising money to satisfy his creditors. During the period when Mark Twain had confidently expected the success of his speculations to make it possible for him to write 'sage and serious' works without reference to any need to earn a living, he found himself bound to exploit his reputation as a 'funny man' and turn out hack-work which, by now, he himself could respect only in so far as it contributed to the relief of his financial distress. Amongst this mass of inferior stuff lie several works of a different kind which arose from Mark Twain's desire to recover a more serious note, to say something of the America which had so seduced and disappointed him. These pieces are mostly stunted and bitter fragments, like 'Was It Heaven or Hell?', or 'The Five Boons of Life', or mistakenly solemn tracts, like *What Is Man?*, or were too intractable in their material for Mark Twain to finish, like 'The Mysterious Stranger'. They all express the mood of bitterness, melancholy, and failure which overtook him in the closing years of his life. Two of these works, however, have the real stamp of his genius, *Pudd'nhead Wilson* and 'The Man That Corrupted Hadleyburg', in one of which Mark Twain plays the notes of *Tom Sawyer* and *Huckleberry Finn* in quite another key, and in the other he for once directs his bitterness to real artistic purpose.

The reason that Mark Twain didn't write novels was in the first place simply that he never felt he had to, and so never tried. The literary environment that he inhabited, and the audience to which he addressed himself, made it easy for him to prosper by running anecdotes together, telling stories, yarning, firing off outrageous opinions, making wise cracks and jokes, and generally just 'going on his nerves' in order to entertain a readership whose attention was easily distracted. Mark Twain's literary background was indeed as close to the American popular idiom as it could have been, that is, it was in south-western humour, the tall tale, the newspaper column, and the popular lecture. Nevertheless, his books are full of ideas, ideas about equality, democracy, liberty, and progress, such as exercised Americans with increasing urgency as the nineteenth century unfolded.[4] Mark Twain's work is thus the meeting-point of popular culture and national ideals as that of no other American writer is. However, there is always a certain uneasiness, as of potential conflict, between these two sides of Mark Twain, between, that is, the easy, pointed fluency of his style and an almost bumptious eagerness to exercise his ideological and moral prejudices. The problem is *least* in evidence in *Huckleberry Finn*, where a whole series of political and moral questions is subsumed in the realities so convincingly dramatized in Huck's bewildered description of the societies he encounters as he descends the Mississippi. On the other hand, it literally explodes in Mark Twain's hands in *A Connecticut Yankee at King Arthur's Court*, where the burlesque on Tennyson, nostalgia for his Missouri boyhood, and patriotic ideas about American progress cannot be made to cohere. *Pudd'nhead Wilson* is an attempt to control these ideas within a more consciously articulated literary form.

Pudd'nhead Wilson is the only serious attempt Mark Twain ever made to write a sustained, adult novel. It, too, *began* as a burlesque. 'Originally,' Mark Twain writes,

---

[4] Mark Twain is thus the opposite of Henry James, of whom T. S. Eliot said: 'James' critical genius comes out most tellingly in his mastery over, his baffling escape from Ideas; a mastery and an escape which are perhaps the last test of a superior intelligence. He had a mind so fine that no idea could violate it.' (Repr. by Edmund Wilson in *The Shock of Recognition*, 856.)

the story was called 'Those Extraordinary Twins'. I meant to make it very short. I had seen a picture of a youthful Italian 'freak'—or 'freaks'—which was—or which were—on exhibition in our cities—a combination consisting of two heads and four arms joined to a single body and a single pair of legs—and I thought I would write an extravagantly fantastic little story with this freak of nature for a hero—or heroes—a silly young miss for a heroine, and two old ladies and two boys for the minor parts.

But then, he continues:

Among them [the characters of 'Those Extraordinary Twins'] came a stranger named Pudd'nhead Wilson and a woman named Roxana: and presently the doings of those two pushed up into prominence a young fellow named Tom Driscoll, whose proper place was away in the obscure background. Before the book was half finished those three were taking things almost entirely into their own hands and working the whole tale as a private venture of their own—a tale which they had nothing at all to do with, by rights. (*Writings*, xiv. 209.)

Thus Mark Twain's imagination was working at a level deeper than the superficial, catchpenny mode of 'Those Extraordinary Twins', and generating material more consonant with the sombre mood into which his failing affairs had precipitated him. Pudd'nhead, Roxy, and Tom Driscoll are not figures of fun, or burlesque, or even satire. Tom is a villain, cruel, threatening, and banal; Wilson is a kind of grown-up, failing Tom Sawyer; and Roxy is the only fully conceived female character in the whole of Mark Twain, a woman deeply and tragically compromised not only socially, but morally, by her life of slavery. To introduce figures of such potency into a landscape that had invariably provided Mark Twain with the greatest stimulus to his imagination, and deliberately engage them in serious and consequential themes is a remarkable development. It is as though Mark Twain were trying to put back together what had been separated in the composition of *A Connecticut Yankee*, that is, his early, innocent experience, and his more recent worldly trials. A great deal of Mark Twain's experience is present in *Pudd'nhead Wilson*, but in a form sufficiently abstract, sufficiently detached from himself, to hold out the promise of a more finished work of art than he had ever before achieved. *Pudd'nhead Wilson* is not just another large draft upon the imagination in which Mark Twain sets off hoping he'll be able to make something good of whatever turns up; it is a conscious attempt to address a serious subject. Nevertheless, the novel never quite escapes its origins. The burlesque tale out of which *Pudd'nhead Wilson* developed concerned a pair of Siamese twins with two heads, four arms, one body, one pair of legs, and utterly differing characters. The humour depends entirely upon our being willing to find such deformity funny, and it is therefore deeply unpleasant. The deformity has gone from *Pudd'nhead Wilson*[5] and with it the sick humour, but the novel remains redolent of the severe disaffection from which it was germinated. The twins lose their potency in the plot, but they retain it in the tone.

At the centre of *Pudd'nhead Wilson* is the story of Roxy, the majestic mulatto slave who in herself gives the novel its real distinction. If for the moment we forget Henry James, we may accept the observation that she is the first seriously created female character in American fiction after Hester Prynne. At any rate, the comparisons with Hester Prynne are apt: a beautiful woman who conceives a child before the story opens, who has to live under a kind of curse, whose child turns out to be difficult, and from whom she is in the end permanently separated. Roxy has a force of character, and a depth of nature, similar to Hester's. She is more real than Hester in her early insouciance and gaiety, and in the economic, political, and moral circumstances of her life, which Mark Twain handles with deft conviction. She is a formidable woman fighting a losing battle in a world where all the odds are stacked against her, and she elicits Mark Twain's loathing of human oppression in general, of slavery in particular, and—in the Dawson's Landing community where her story is played out—of the complacency and false gentility that

---

[5] Except in those places—marked in the Notes—where Mark Twain failed to edit it out.

allowed the institution of slavery to survive.[6] Hers is the only tragedy Mark Twain ever wrote, and it is impressively conceived: Roxana, 20 years of age, strikingly beautiful, of strong character, fifteen parts white and one part black, is seduced by Cecil Burleigh Essex, the most distinguished citizen of Dawson's Landing, as she says, 'a real gentleman'. She bears his child, thirty-one parts white and one part black, and therefore condemned to a future of slavery. Force of circumstance brings the fear that her child may one day be 'sold down the river'; Wilson's intelligence accidentally suggests to her a remedy; her master's distraction and lack of interest in his own child (who happens to have been born at precisely the same time as Roxy's) provides the occasion. Able thus to act for the first time in her life as a free agent, and with the backing of religion, superstition, fear, confusion, and hope, she releases her child from its fate by substituting it for her master's child. But the child, though he takes on the superficial characteristics of white behaviour, and becomes into the bargain his mother's young 'master', has a flaw, his 'nigger blood' (which of course he shares with his mother). Thus he can't after all become what he isn't, and turns out a silly wastrel, selfish, cowardly, and cruel. (In the meantime the other changeling child, the true aristocrat, despite his condition as slave, manifests all the signs of innate nobility.) Thus Roxy in the end gets nothing. Her son's selfish cruelty hasn't even the justification that he's a proud gentleman. His unwillingness to fight in a duel arises from cowardice, not from principle, and elicits from Roxy the most striking moment of the novel:

Whatever has come o' yo' Essex blood? Dat's what I can't understan'. En it ain't on'y jist Essex blood dat's in you, not by a long sight—'deed it ain't! My great-great-great-gran'father en yo' great-

---

[6] To suggest, as some critics have done, that slavery was an irrelevant target so many years after its abolition, is to misconceive the nature of the book: *Pudd'nhead Wilson* is a novel, not a political tract. Recent attempts to assimilate the novel to the debates about reconstruction and 'Jim Crow' legislation seem to me equally irrelevant. (See E. J. Sundquist in Gillman and Robinson.)

great-great-great-gran'father was ole Cap'n John Smith, de highest blood dat Ole Virginny ever turned out, en *his* great-great-gran'mother or somers along back dah, was Pocahantas de Injun queen, en her husban' was a nigger king outen Africa—en yit here you is, a slinkin' outen a duel in disgracin' our whole line like a ornery low-down hound! Yes, it's de nigger in you! (p. 89)

It never occurs to Roxy that her son's failure may derive not from his ancestry, but from his pampered circumstances. Isolated and desperate, even with all her inventiveness and courage, she is unable to circumvent the traditions in which she has grown up, and accepts the white man's analysis of the character of her own child, attributing its failings to his 'nigger blood'. Tom is in the final irony sold down the river, inheriting the fate from which Roxy had tried to protect him, and precisely because of a sequence of events that she had herself set in train. No more complete defeat could be imagined.

So far, so good. In the Roxy plot Mark Twain was working with the grain of his own nature, and his sympathy with Roxy's travail is as deep as his sympathy with nigger Jim's. Roxy is, indeed, a *more* impressive figure than Jim because she is taken more seriously from the start, and because her story is never trivialized, as is Jim's at the end of *Huckleberry Finn*. But with the other two principal characters to which his imagination gave birth in the reworking of the material of 'Those Extraordinary Twins' Mark Twain was less comfortable. Tom Driscoll is a cardboard villain who will invariably and predictably do the nastiest thing available to him whatever the options; he is the very incarnation of the values and vices most detested by any sound-hearted schoolboy, and he is apparently allowed to behave as he does because he is the spoilt idle rich boy of popular legend, behaving as his elders behave—but (rather importantly) not quite. So deeply does Mark Twain dislike Tom that it is hard to believe that he hasn't actually himself forgotten that he's a changeling, for he allows the reader to infer that Tom behaves as he does *because he's black*. It is indeed part of Roxy's tragedy that this is what *she* thinks, but an unfortunate development of the plot that when (in Chapter 10) Tom discovers the truth about himself he immediately falls into the caricature behaviour of the 'low-down nigger', unable, for example, to face up to the challenge of a duel because he has been able to assume the external attributes, but not to assimilate the essential honour and courage, of a Virginia gentleman. The reverse of this, one might note in passing, is that the other changeling, the legitimate heir—despite his upbringing as a slave—behaves (whenever we see him) with dignity, selflessness, courage, and so on. As a matter of fact Mark Twain did believe that there was such a thing as a 'natural aristocracy', a belief which he had exploited with great force in *Huckleberry Finn*, where the handling of the Shepherdsons, the Grangerfords, and of Colonel Sherburn, amount to an analysis (rather terrifying in the case of Sherburn) of the very idea. But it is as impossible to conclude that Mark Twain believed that there was a natural southern gentleman, and a natural nigger slave, as it is impossible to avoid the conclusion that for the sake of short-term narrative profit he has inadvertently fallen into that moral solecism in his development of Tom Driscoll. At the end, Tom is 'sold down the river' to pay his 'master's' debts, not because this is the tough- minded conclusion to the artistic necessities of Mark Twain's analysis of the evils of slavery,[7] but because it is consonant with the animus with which his character is drawn.[8] Mark Twain ships him off with cruel relish, not because he hates slavery, but because he hates Tom, and does not scruple to use the institution of slavery to sweeten his revenge.

Mark Twain's difficulties in writing the fully articulated novel consonant with the mood into which his mature experience had precipitated him are most evident in the

---

[7] This line is argued by De Voto and Leavis. See *Mark Twain's America*, 293 f., and Leavis's Introduction, 30 f.

[8] Indeed, Mark Twain had to fiddle the plot to arrive at this disagreeable conclusion, for the arguments brought to bear by Percy Driscoll's creditors would at the time of his death have applied to Valet de Chambers.

construction of his eponymous hero. Much though he is committed to Pudd'nhead, whom he burdens with the full weight of his own ideals, Mark Twain cannot render him into a convincing adult. Shorn (unlike Hank Morgan) of the youthful energies of Tom or Huck, yet touched by no adult temptations or sorrows, Pudd'nhead becomes less and less a character and more and more a passive agent of the plot. Why does a bright young man like Wilson arrive, like another sort of 'mysterious stranger', from an eastern law school, and attempt to establish a practice in Dawson's Landing? Why does he fail? Why, having failed, does he stick around for more than twenty years doing almost nothing (apart from collecting fingerprints)? Why does he go on living as a bachelor? Why does his long period of isolation seem not to affect him, nor ever to bring him the force and respect that comes to, for example, Hester Prynne in *her* isolation? The answer is that, as with Tom, the character of Wilson is sacrificed to the exigencies of the plot, and particularly Wilson's part in first the duel and then the trial. How could a rational sceptic like Wilson give every appearance of supporting the absurd, pseudo-aristocratic pretensions of the 'code duello'—which Mark Twain anywhere else would have himself deplored—and why, if he knew what his friend Judge Driscoll's reaction would be, does he take on Luigi's case? (pp. 78 ff.) Worse, why is Wilson's defence of the twins so inept? There is a murder weapon, with fingerprints in blood upon its handle. The most interesting thing about Wilson is that he is an expert in the science of fingerprinting, yet it fails to occur to him—until presented with a blindingly obvious reason to do so—publicly to take the fingerprints of the twins and demonstrate that they are not the ones on the dagger. The reason that it does not occur to him is not really that he's stupid, but that by the end of the novel the weight of the plot is toward exposing Tom, and the theatricality of that denouement forces every other consideration out of focus. Mark Twain fails to find a way of underlining the cowardice and the lack of honour in Tom's character that does not undermine the consistency of his hero's.

That is not the end of the matter, however. The style in which Pudd'nhead Wilson is presented, indeed the fundamental style of the whole novel (outside the Roxy plot), is in Mark Twain's mature manner, direct, sharp, clear, and dry, disabused, if not actually disillusioned. It is a doubtful style for imaginative fiction because, though it can deliver information efficiently, it is wanting in resonance, and it deprives Mark Twain of imaginative patience. He is everywhere eager to get on, eager to wrap up his point. Here is Tom, for example, following the crisis of his discovery that he is in fact a mulatto:

In several ways his opinions were totally changed, and would never go back to what they were before, but the main structure of his character was not changed and could not be changed. One or two very important features of it were altered, and in time effects would result from this if opportunity offered—effects of a quite serious nature too. Under the influence of a great mental and moral upheaval his character and habits had taken on the appearance of complete change, but after a while, with the subsidence of the storm both began to settle toward their former places. (pp. 57 f.)

which is telling, not showing. But this hard-edged style is the style of Pudd'nhead Wilson himself, not the character of the plot, but the Pudd'nhead of Pudd'nhead Wilson's Calendar.

Apart from the figure of Roxy, it is for the Calendar that readers remember *Pudd'nhead Wilson*. In response to a recommendation of Howells's that he carry Tom Sawyer into manhood, Mark Twain replied that Tom Sawyer grown up 'would just be like all the other one horse men in literature.'[9] Mark Twain never did (despite the promise at the end of *Tom Sawyer*) take Tom Sawyer into adult life, but Pudd'nhead Wilson is a near enough approximation to an adult Tom, and true enough, he is a character of very little inward depth or force—'one horse', as Mark Twain had predicted. Shorn of his naughtiness and exuberance, but educated, and with his self-confidence still intact, Tom's imagination and wit have not deepened or expanded his character, rather they have fermented into Pudd'nhead's irony. Like Mark Twain's, Tom's

[9] James M. Cox, *The Fate of Humor* (Princeton, NJ, 1966), 148.

adult experience as it is lived out by Pudd'nhead Wilson is
of failure and disaffection, but the deep and disillusioned
irony which flows from such compromising experience, and
which is the ground note of Mark Twain's late style, never
finds its way into the plot of the novel. Wilson has two
characters, the one that functions in the plot, and is unam-
bitious, acquiescent, and benign (though of course observant),
and the other, which is expressed in the Calendar and is sharp
and sceptical to the point of cynicism. The defeat which is
Wilson's principal experience in Dawson's Landing is confined to the Calendar—a sour descendent of the virtuous
maxims of Poor Richard's *Almanac* (which Mark Twain had
loathed)—where Wilson sets down the more or less corrosive
ironies of a man who has been disappointed by life, has little
connection with it, and who expresses his frustration in
irritable verbal violence. Pudd'nhead's maxims are aimed
either at himself:

April 1.—This is the day upon which we are reminded of what we
are on the other three hundred and sixty-four. (Chapter 21)

Why is it that we rejoice at a birth and grieve at a funeral? It is
because we are not the person involved. (Chapter 9)

October. This is one of the peculiarly dangerous months to speculate
in stocks in. The others are July, January, September, April, November, May, March, June, December, August and February. (Chapter 13)

Or at America:

July 4. Statistics show that we lose more fools on this day than in
all the other days of the year put together. This proves, by the
number left in stock, that one Fourth of July per year is now
inadequate, the country has grown so. (Chapter 17)

October 12.—*The Discovery.*—It was wonderful to find America, but
it would have been more wonderful to miss it. (Conclusion)

Or at what Mark Twain called 'the damned human race':

The holy passion of Friendship is of so sweet and steady and loyal
and enduring a nature it will last through a whole lifetime, if not
asked to lend money. (Chapter 8)

If you pick up a starving dog and make him prosperous, he will not bite you. This is the principal difference between a dog and a man. (Chapter 16)

Or they express the world-weariness that increasingly infected Mark Twain's later years:

Gratitude and treachery are merely the two extremities of the same procession. You have seen all of it worth staying for when the band and the gaudy officials have gone by. (Chapter 18)

Whoever has lived long enough to find out what life is, knows how deep a debt of gratitude we owe to Adam, the first great benefactor of our race. He brought death into the world. (Chapter 3)

All say, 'How hard it is to die'—a strange complaint to come from the mouths of people who have had to live. (Chapter 10)

Few of Pudd'nhead Wilson's maxims are pleasant and the humour, which is sometimes very sharp, is never generous; yet, together with Roxy's tragedy, they represent the mind of Mark Twain more accurately than the uncertain plot that they embellish. Two sides of Mark Twain's genius are quite distinctly present in *Pudd'nhead Wilson*, whose flaws arise precisely because they were not easily knit together. Roxy's story, dark though it is, remains within the charmed circle of early Mark Twain, the part of the world that Mark Twain knew and loved, which nourished his imagination in the writing of his best books. Pudd'nhead Wilson, a modern man, trained in the law and partial to modern technology, comes into that world as an outsider. Try as he might, he can never accommodate himself to its provincial limitations and complacencies. Being unable to take root in Dawson's Landing, he remains imaginatively undernourished and but half created, expressing his irritation in the verbal violence of his Calendar. Leavis wrote that Wilson is 'the poised and pre-eminently civilised moral centre of the drama, whom we take to be very close in point of view to Mark Twain.' We may accept the latter part of this assertion, so long as we recognize that the point of view at issue is that of a man who feels alienated, betrayed, and frustrated, and whose principal interest in the world is to expose its hypocrisies, cruelties, and complacencies. Or, to put it another way, if the author of Pudd'nhead Wilson's Calendar had taken up fiction, 'The Man That Corrupted Hadleyburg' is the story he would have written.

Like Dawson's Landing, like St Petersburg, Hadleyburg is a fictionalized version of Mark Twain's native Hannibal, Missouri, but it is a Hannibal recreated on entirely different principles. Untapped is the vein of rich nostalgia that gave life to St Petersburg and Dawson's Landing, and was transposed scarcely altered for the Arthurian England of *A Connecticut Yankee* or the late medieval Austria of 'The Mysterious Stranger'. As a location Hadleyburg itself is so sparely evoked that it remains an abstraction, the mere symbol of any provincial American small town. It has houses, streets, a bank, a newspaper, a telegraph office, a postal service, two churches, a public square, and a town hall, none more than merely denominated. Hadleyburg has no climate, no geography, no weather, no atmosphere, no features, no *presence* whatsoever. But it does have citizens, divided into three classes: an aristocracy of bankers, lawyers, doctors, property owners, and politicians (the Nineteen), a middle class represented by the Hatter and the Tanner, and a democratic mob. Of these citizens three are individuated: the deceased Barclay Goodson, who had a fierce and disillusioned integrity reminiscent of Col. Sherburn; Jack Halliday, a Huck Finn grown up and disenchanted; and the mysteriously compromised Rev. Burgess. The rest represent a community only in the most negative sense. They all live together in the same town, and wonderfully share among themselves all of those human failings which Mark Twain most cordially detested—hypocrisy, greed, vanity, envy, selfishness, snobbery, complacency, racial prejudice, self-righteousness, cowardice, lying, meanness, humbug, mystification, cruelty. Hadleyburg has not a single redeeming quality, its only virtue exposed, when tested, as worse than no virtue at all. An outsider, a 'mysterious stranger', has at some time in the past come into this community and been sorely offended, injured as, one might suppose, David Wilson had been injured by the stupid complacencies of Dawson's Landing. But the Hadleyburg stranger does not contain his anger as Wilson does, venting his rage only in the pages of a diary. He resolves to be revenged upon the whole community in which he had suffered his wrong, and the hero whom Mark Twain represses in *Pudd'nhead Wilson* is allowed full rein in 'The Man That Corrupted Hadleyburg'.

The story is a brilliantly sustained attack upon the whole system of values and ambitions that Mark Twain believed to be characteristic of American society at the end of the nineteenth century, values and ambitions with which he had connived, and which had ruined him. It revolves round fairy-tale riches, the attraction of unearned wealth which had been part of Mark Twain's imaginative material from the first, and which modern speculative capitalism seemed to him able to deliver in reality. Of course the bitter warning that is expressed in 'The Man That Corrupted Hadleyburg' had been often sounded by Mark Twain before, but always in an indulgent style, or in a humorous narrative, or with that fund of optimism that could find common humanity in the worst villains. Almost everywhere Mark Twain's narrative prose is nourished by atmosphere and image drawn from the memory of his Hannibal boyhood, but not here. The keynote of Mark Twain's style is comedy, but no longer. This story is, indeed, founded upon a joke, but the joke is not, and is not intended to be, funny. It is the bitter jest of a wounded and disappointed man, told in that unsparing and unadorned language which would not work in *Pudd'nhead Wilson*, but is perfect here. No character in the tale escapes its sharp edge. The analysis of motive is unsparingly sceptical, and the moral isolation which is the profoundest consequence of Hadleyburg's vanity is sketched with ruthless efficiency and clarity. For once standing aside from the community he knew so well the better to meditate upon its follies, Mark Twain gave the fullest rein to the growing misanthropy which overtook his last years. 'The Man That Corrupted Hadleyburg' represents the perfect expression of a side of his genius which he seemed nowhere else quite willing to release, and the result is a bleak moral fable of extraordinary power and penetration, comparable with 'Young Goodman Brown', 'Bartleby', 'A Diamond as Big as the Ritz', or 'The Bear'.

NOTE ON THE TEXTS

The text of *Pudd'nhead Wilson* is unusually difficult to establish. There are two manuscript texts (and typescripts of each), the text of the serialization in *The Century Magazine* (1893–4), the text of the first English edition, published by Chatto & Windus in November 1894, and the text of the first American edition, published by the American Publishing Company at the same time (and including 'Those Extraordinary Twins'). The reader interested in the text should consult the Norton Critical Edition of *Pudd'nhead Wilson* and *Those Extraordinary Twins*, edited by Sidney E. Berger, where the problems are fully discussed, and a complete list of variants supplied. The text used for this edition is taken from the Chatto & Windus first edition of 1894. This has been carefully checked against Prof. Berger's critical edition and silently emended accordingly. There are many variations between these texts, but all are insignificant.

The text of 'Those Extraordinary Twins' is taken from the Author's National of Mark Twain's Works, New York and London (Harper & Brothers, 1899–1900). The text of 'The Man That Corrupted Hadleyburg' is taken from *The Man That Corrupted Hadleyburg and Other Stories and Essays*, New York and London (Harper & Bros., 1904).

SELECT BIBLIOGRAPHY

I. Mark Twain's Writings

The standard editions of Mark Twain's works are the Author's National Edition of *The Writings of Mark Twain*, 22 vols., New York and London, 1899–1900; and *The Writings of Mark Twain*, ed. Albert Bigelow Paine, 37 vols., New York, 1922–5. The Works and Papers of Mark Twain, in a projected 70 volumes, is currently forthcoming, edited by the Mark Twain Project at the Bancroft Library, Berkeley, California. The Mark Twain Library offers popular editions of some of the California scholarly texts. Two of a projected six volumes of the works of Mark Twain are now available in Library of America texts.

Most relevant to a reading of *Pudd'nhead Wilson* are the 'Mississippi Writings', i.e. *The Adventures of Tom Sawyer* (1876), *Life on the Mississippi* (1883), and *The Adventures of Huckleberry Finn* (1885). Equally important is *A Connecticut Yankee in King Arthur's Court* (1889). See also *The Celebrated Jumping Frog of Calaveras County, and Other Sketches* (1867), *The Innocents Abroad* (1869), *Roughing It* (1872), *The Gilded Age* (with Charles Dudley Warner) (1874), *Sketches, New and Old* (1875), *The Prince and the Pauper* (1882), *The Stolen White Elephant etc.* (1882), *The £1,000,000 Bank-Note and Other New Stories* (1893), and *The Man That Corrupted Hadleyburg and Other Stories and Essays* (1904). Of two deeply disaffected works of Mark Twain's last years, *What is Man?* was published privately in 1906, and *The Mysterious Stranger*, unfinished at Mark Twain's death, was published posthumously in 1916. *The Portable Mark Twain*, ed. Bernard De Voto (New York, 1968) is a useful selection from Mark Twain's works, some not easily found elsewhere.

II. Autobiography

Mark Twain's Autobiography, ed. A. B. Paine, 2 vols. (New York, 1924).
Mark Twain in Eruption, ed. Bernard De Voto (New York, 1940).
The Autobiography of Mark Twain, ed. Charles Neider (New York, 1959).
Mark Twain's Letters, ed. A. B. Paine (New York, 1917).
Mark Twain's Notebooks, ed. A. B. Paine (New York, 1935).

III. Biography

Howells, W. D., *My Mark Twain* (New York, 1910).

Kaplan, Justin, *Mr Clemens and Mark Twain* (New York, 1966).

Paine, A. B., *Mark Twain: A Biography*, 3 vols. (New York, 1912).

Wecter, Dixon, *Sam Clemens of Hannibal* (Boston, 1952).

IV. General Reference

Asselineau, Roger, *The Literary Reputation of Mark Twain from 1910 to 1950* (Paris, 1954).

Johnson, Merle, *A Bibliography of the Works of Mark Twain* (New York, 1935).

Long, E. Hudson, *Mark Twain Handbook* (New York, 1957).

Smith, Henry Nash, *Mark Twain: A Collection of Critical Essays* (Englewood Cliffs, NJ, 1963).

Frederick Anderson (ed.), *Mark Twain: The Critical Heritage* (London, 1971).

V. Criticism etc.

Barnum, P. T., *The Life of P. T. Barnum, Written by Himself* [1854], ed. G. S. Bryan (New York, 1927).

Berthoff, Warner, *The Ferment of Realism, American Literature, 1884–1919* (New York, 1965),

Blair, Walter, *Native American Humor, 1800–1900* (New York, 1960).

Brooks, Van Wyck, *The Ordeal of Mark Twain* (rev. edn., New York, 1933: London, 1934).

Canby, Henry S., *Turn West, Turn East: Mark Twain and Henry James* (Boston, 1951).

Carton, Evan, '*Pudd'nhead Wilson* and the Fiction of Law and Custom', in *American Realism: New Essays*, ed. E. J. Sundquist (Baltimore, 1982).

Cash, Wilbur J., *The Mind of the South* (New York, 1969).

Cox, James M., *Mark Twain: The Fate of Humor* (Princeton, NJ, 1966).

Debouzy, Marianne, *La Genèse de l'esprit de révolte dans le roman américain, 1875–1915* (Paris, 1968).

DeVoto, Bernard, *Mark Twain at Work* (Cambridge, Mass., 1942).

DeVoto, Bernard, *Mark Twain's America* (Boston, 1935).

Dreiser, Theodore, 'Mark the Double Twain', *English Journal*, 24 (1935).

Fiedler, Leslie, ' "As Free as Any Cretur . . . " ', The *New Republic*, 133/7–8 (15 and 22 Aug. 1955).

Fiedler, Leslie, *Love and Death in the American Novel* (New York, 1960).

Foner, Philip S., *Mark Twain: Social Critic* (New York, 1958).

Gabrilowitsch, Clara (Clemens), *My Father, Mark Twain* (New York, 1931).

Geismar, Maxwell, *Mark Twain: An American Prophet* (Boston, 1970).

Gillman, Susan K., and Patten, Robert L., 'Dickens : Doubles :: Twain : Twins', *Nineteenth Century Fiction*, 39/4 (March 1985).

Gillman, Susan, and Robinson, Forrest G. (eds.), *Mark Twain's Pudd'nhead Wilson: Race, Conflict, and Culture* (Durham, NC, and London, 1990).

Gross, S. L., and Hardy, J. E. (eds.), *Images of the Negro in American Literature* (Chicago and London, 1966).

Hubbell, Jay B., *The South in American Literature* (Durham, NC, 1954).

Jones, Maldwyn, *The Limits of Liberty* (Oxford, 1983).

Leacock, Stephen, *Mark Twain* (New York, 1933).

Leavis, F. R., Introduction to *Pudd'nhead Wilson* (London, 1955).

Lynn, Kenneth, *Mark Twain and Southwestern Humor* (Boston, 1959).

McElderry, Bruce R., Jun., *Contributions to 'The Galaxy', 1868–1871 by Mark Twain* (Gainesville, G., 1961).

McKeithan, Daniel M., 'The Morgan Manuscripts of Mark Twain's *Pudd'nhead Wilson*', *Essays and Studies on American Language and Literature*, 12 (1961).

Pettit, Arthur G., *Mark Twain and the South* (Lexington, Ky., 1974).

Rourke, Constance, *American Humor: A Study of the National Character* (New York, 1931).

Scott, Arthur L., (ed.), *Mark Twain: Selected Criticism* (Dallas, 1955).

Smith, Henry Nash, *Mark Twain: The Development of a Writer* (Cambridge, Mass., 1962).

Tanner, Tony, *The Reign of Wonder* (Cambridge, 1965).

Webster, Samuel C., *Mark Twain, Business Man* (New York, 1946).

Wigger, Anne P., 'The Composition of Mark Twain's *Pudd'nhead Wilson* and *Those Extraordinary Twins*: Chronology and Development', *Modern Philology*, 55 (Nov. 1957).

A CHRONOLOGY OF MARK TWAIN

1835   Samuel Langhorne Clemens born 30 November to John Marshall and Jane Lampton Clemens in Florida, Missouri, a third child and second son.

1839   Clemens family moves to Hannibal, Missouri, the St Petersburg of Mark Twain's recollected childhood.

1847   John Clemens dies, leaving his family unencumbered by wealth but endowing his sons with an hereditary propensity for engaging in optimistic schemes for acquiring sudden riches.

1848–52 Sam Clemens is forced to leave school and become a printer in the local newspaper office, from which, two years later, he moves to the paper printed by his older brother, Orion. During this period he begins to write occasional humorous sketches for newspaper publication.

1853–6 Becoming a 'jour' (journeyman) printer, Clemens works on newspapers in eastern (New York and Philadelphia) and western (St Louis and Keokuk) cities. While in Philadelphia, he makes a pious visit to Franklin's grave, whose life at this point his own somewhat resembles.

1857   Embarking on a South American venture, intending to get rich marketing coca (the raw stuff of cocaine), Clemens leaves St Louis but gets no further than Cincinnati, where he works briefly on a newspaper before signing on with Horace Bixby as an apprentice pilot.

1861   The Civil War and Union blockades severely restrain river traffic. Clemens enlists briefly as a Confederate guerrilla, then signs up to accompany Orion, who has been appointed secretary to the territorial governor of Nevada, on a trip west by stagecoach, an ordeal of nineteen days.

1862–3 Following a brief period exploring the region and labouring in various mining operations, Clemens returns to newspaper work, this time as a reporter for the Virginia City *Enterprise*, where he adopts the pen-name Mark Twain, occasionally reports on the legislature in Carson City, and begins to practise the craft of humorous writing as inspired by free-wheeling life in mining country. He is encouraged by the praise of Artemus Ward (Charles Farrar Browne), Yankee humorist and comic lecturer (1834–67), who visited Virginia City in 1863.

1864   Leaves for the San Francisco area, where he works panning for gold before returning to journalism. Meets Bret Harte (1836–1902), editor of *The Californian* and author of western regional stories, who assists Mark Twain in polishing his talents.

1866   Visits the Sandwich Islands (Hawaii), an experience recorded in humorous letters to the California newspapers which had sponsored the trip. Returns to California and begins career as a humorous lecturer, drawing on his Hawaiian material.

1867   Having sailed to New York via the isthmus of Panama, Twain takes ship for the Holy Land with a company of pilgrims aboard the *Quaker City*, sending letters back to Californian newspapers that will become the raw material for *The Innocents Abroad* (1869). He returns to New York to find himself famous, thanks to the reprinting of the *Quaker City* letters in the *Tribune* and *Herald*. His first book, *The Celebrated Jumping Frog of Calaveras County and Other Sketches*, is published, further promoting his reputation as a humorist, which he exploits by continuing his career as a comic lecturer.

1870   Marries Olivia Langdon, daughter of a wealthy coal magnate of Elmira, New York, who buys his son-in-law part ownership in a Buffalo newspaper, the *Express*. As Mark Twain, he is a contributing editor also to *Galaxy*, a monthly periodical, and works up his mining experiences as *Roughing It*, published in 1871.

1872   Sells his interest in the *Express*, relocates to Hartford, Connecticut, because of its proximity to the publishing centers of New York and Boston. Builds an extravagant mansion in the 'Nook Farm' section where his neighbours are Harriet Beecher Stowe and Charles Dudley Warner, a newspaper editor and belletrist (1829–1900) with whom Twain will collaborate on *The Gilded Age*, a satiric treatment of contemporary corruption (1873). During this period, Twain travels twice to England, pursuing his lecturing career, and develops a self-pasting scrapbook, his only successful invention.

1874   Writes *Old Times on the Mississippi,* a fictionalized account of his piloting days, for the *Atlantic Monthly,* the most influential of eastern literary magazines, edited by William Dean Howells, Ohio-born literary critic and novelist (1837–1920) who will become Twain's close friend and champion, shepherding his transition from a 'mere' humorist to a practitioner of the new literary realism, of which *The Adventures of Tom Sawyer* (1876) is a good example.

1876   Collaborates with Bret Harte on a stage comedy, *Ah Sin,* whose success is of short duration, as will be his relationship with Harte, whom he comes to detest.

1877   Delivers a humorous speech on the occasion of John Greenleaf Whittier's seventieth birthday, the main point of which turns on a mining-camp poker game in which the disreputable players assume the names of Longfellow, Emerson, and Oliver Wendell Holmes. Boston is not amused. However, Twain will remain, virtually to the end of his life, a popular after-dinner speaker.

1878–9   Though he has given up the lecture circuit, which he came to loathe, Twain continues to travel abroad, visiting Germany and Italy with his family and with his friend and pastor, Joseph H. Twichell, gathering experiences for his next travel narrative, *A Tramp Abroad* (1879).

1880   Seeking to reach a more genteel audience, Twain writes his first medieval tale, *The Prince and the Pauper,* tested on his daughters for its appeal. As in *The Gilded Age,* Twain reveals a social consciousness, albeit one aroused by the enormities of the feudal, not the capitalistic system.

1882   Encouraged to expand *Old Times on the Mississippi,* Twain returns to the river of his youth, a trip taken with his publisher so as to draw comparisons between 'Old Times' and new. His enthusiasm for improvements in navigational aids expressed in *Life on the Mississippi* (1883), is of a piece with his not always well-informed investments in inventions, the most notorious failure of which was the Paige Typesetter, a Rube–Goldberg contraption easily beaten out by the Linotype process, and contributing to Clemens's financial difficulties.

1884   Embarks on a lecture tour with the New Orleans writer
        George Washington Cable (1844–1925), each man reading
        from his works, including *The Adventures of Huckleberry Finn*,
        published this year. Cable was a champion of civil rights
        for blacks, an issue indirectly raised in his novel *The
        Grandissimes* (1880), a covert exposure of southern attitudes
        toward Reconstruction, though set in Louisiana at the time
        of the Purchase (1803). Twain accomplishes something
        similar in his story of a boy and an escaped slave descend-
        ing the river in the ante-bellum years.

1885   Having successfully served as his own publisher with *The
        Adventures of Huckleberry Finn*, Clemens contracts to publish
        the *Personal Memoirs of U. S. Grant*, reminiscences of the
        dying and disgraced President. This too is a great financial
        success, inspiring ventures that are much less so.

1889   Continues to attack the sins of the feudal system (i.e., the
        ante-bellum South) in *A Connecticut Yankee in King Arthur's
        Court*, in which Hank Morgan destroys 'the flower of
        chivalry' by means of modern technology.

1891–4 Repeatedly returns to Europe during these years, as his
        financial situation worsens, ending in the bankruptcy of
        his publishing company. At the urging of his wife and
        with the help of the Standard Oil executive Henry Hud-
        dleston Rogers (1840–1909), Twain vows to pay off his
        debtors rather than take refuge in bankruptcy court.

1894   Publishes *The Tragedy of Pudd'nhead Wilson*, a melodramatic
        tale of mistaken identity with a strong racial theme, the
        plot of which turns on the new 'science' of fingerprinting.

1895   Begins a lecture tour that will take him around the globe
        along the path of the Equator, raising money to pay off
        his debts and gathering material for his next travel book.
        While he is abroad his favourite daughter, Susy, left behind
        in Hartford, dies suddenly of meningitis. She is memo-
        rialized in Twain's sentimental historical novel *Joan of Arc*
        (1896).

1897–9 During his extended stay in Europe, Twain becomes
        increasingly pessimistic, signalled by his later books *What
        Is Man?* (1906), a dialogue promoting a mechanistic, deter-
        ministic world view, *The Man Who Corrupted Hadleyburg*
        (1899), and the unfinished *Mysterious Stranger* (1916).

1900   Twain returns to the United States but not to Hartford. He is given a warm welcome home and in 1901 is awarded a Litt.D. from Yale. During this period his writings attack various forms of imperialism, from outrages in the Belgian Congo to American military adventures in the Philippines. In 1903, he mounts a savage attack on the 'cult' of Christian Science.

1903   In the hope of repairing Mrs Clemens's declining health, Twain returns to Europe with his wife. She dies in Florence in 1904.

1904–8 Returning to the United States, Twain moves restlessly from one rented address to another, continuing in interviews and occasional pieces to protest against American imperialism abroad sponsored by the Roosevelt administration. Begins dictating his *Autobiography*, not to be published until after his death, along with other pieces intended for posthumous publication because of their presumed libelousness. In 1907, he is awarded a coveted D.Litt. from Oxford, and on this last trip to Europe he is lionized to the point of gratification.

1908–10 Builds his last mansion, Stormfield, a Florentine palace in Redding, Connecticut. His final years are clouded by paranoia and depression, though his personal popularity continues, associated with his flamboyant white suit, which during this period becomes year-round wear. Daughter Jean dies in 1909; Clemens follows her on 21 April 1910.

Pudd'nhead Wilson

A Tale

There is no character, howsoever good and fine, but it can be destroyed by ridicule, howsoever poor and witless. Observe the ass, for instance: his character is about perfect, he is the choicest spirit among all the humbler animals, yet see what ridicule has brought him to. Instead of feeling complimented when we are called an ass, we are left in doubt.

—PUDD'NHEAD WILSON'S CALENDAR

A Whisper to the Reader

A PERSON who is ignorant of legal matters is always liable to make mistakes when he tries to photograph a court scene with his pen; and so I was not willing to let the law chapters in this book go to press without first subjecting them to rigid and exhausting revision and correction by a trained barrister—if that is what they are called. These chapters are right, now, in every detail, for they were rewritten under the immediate eye of William Hicks, who studied law part of a while in south-west Missouri thirty-five years ago and then came over here to Florence for his health and is still helping for exercise and board in Macaroni and Vermicelli's horse-feed shed which is up the back alley as you turn around the corner out of the Piazza del Duomo just beyond the house where that stone that Dante used to sit on six hundred years ago is let into the wall when he let on to be watching them build Giotto's campanile and yet always got tired looking as soon as Beatrice passed along on her way to get a chunk of chestnut cake to defend herself with in case of a Ghibelline outbreak before she got to school, at the same old stand where they sell the same old cake to this day and it is just as light and good as it was then, too, and this is not flattery, far from it. He was a little rusty on his law, but he rubbed up for this book, and those two or three legal chapters are right and straight, now. He told me so himself.

Given under my hand this second day of January, 1893, at the Villa Viviani,* village of Settignano, three miles back of Florence, on the hills—the same certainly affording the most charming view to be found on this planet, and with it the most dream-like and enchanting sunsets to be found in any planet or even in any solar system—and given, too, in the swell room of the house, with the busts of Cerretani senators and other grandees of this line looking approvingly down upon me as they used to look down upon Dante, and mutely asking me to adopt them into my family, which I do with pleasure, for my remotest ancestors are but spring chickens compared with these robed and stately antiques, and it will be a great and satisfying lift for me, that six hundred years will.

MARK TWAIN

1

Tell the truth or trump—but get the trick.
— PUDD'NHEAD WILSON'S CALENDAR*

THE scene of this chronicle is the town of Dawson's*
Landing, on the Missouri side of the Mississippi, half a day's
journey, per steamboat, below St Louis.*

In 1830* it was a snug little collection of modest one-and
two-storey frame dwellings whose whitewashed exteriors were
almost concealed from sight by climbing tangles of rose-vines,
honeysuckles, and morning-glories. Each of these pretty
homes had a garden in front, fenced with white palings and
opulently stocked with hollyhocks, marigolds, touch-me-nots,
prince's-feathers and other old-fashioned flowers; while
on the window-sills of the houses stood wooden boxes
containing moss-rose plants and terracotta pots in which
grew a breed of geranium whose spread of intensely red
blossoms accented the prevailing pink tint of the rose-clad
house-front like an explosion of flame. When there was room
on the ledge outside of the pots and boxes for a cat, the cat
was there—in sunny weather—stretched at full length, asleep
and blissful, with her furry belly to the sun and a paw
curved over her nose. Then that home was complete, and its
contentment and peace were made manifest to the world by
this symbol, whose testimony is infallible. A home without
a cat—and a well-fed, well-petted, and properly revered
cat—may be a perfect home, perhaps, but how can it prove
title?

All along the streets, on both sides, at the outer edge of
the brick sidewalks,* stood locust-trees with trunks protected
by wooden boxing, and these furnished shade for summer
and a sweet fragrance in spring when the clusters of buds
came forth. The main street, one block back from the river
and running parallel with it, was the sole business street. It

was six blocks long, and in each block two or three brick stores three storeys high towered above interjected bunches of little frame shops. Swinging signs creaked in the wind, the street's whole length. The candy-striped pole which indicates nobility proud and ancient along the palace-bordered canals of Venice indicated merely the humble barber-shop along the main street of Dawson's Landing. On a chief corner stood a lofty unpainted pole wreathed from top to bottom with tin pots and pans and cups, the chief tinmonger's noisy notice to the world (when the wind blew) that his shop was on hand for business at that corner.

The hamlet's front was washed by the clear waters* of the great river; its body stretched itself rearward up a gentle incline; its most rearward border fringed itself out and scattered its houses about the base-line of the hills; the hills rose high, inclosing the town in a halfmoon curve, clothed with forests from foot to summit.

Steamboats passed up and down every hour or so. Those belonging to the little Cairo line and the little Memphis line always stopped; the big Orleans liners stopped for hails only, or to land passengers or freight; and this was the case also with the great flotilla of 'transients'. These latter came out of a dozen rivers—the Illinois, the Missouri, the Upper Mississippi, the Ohio, the Monongahela, the Tennessee, the Red River, the White River, and so on; and were bound every whither and stocked with every imaginable comfort or necessity which the Mississippi's communities could want, from the frosty Falls of St Anthony* down through nine climates* to torrid New Orleans.

Dawson's Landing was a slaveholding town,* with a rich, slave-worked grain and pork country back of it. The town was sleepy and comfortable and contented. It was fifty years old, and was growing slowly—very slowly, in fact, but still it was growing.

The chief citizen was York Leicester Driscoll, about forty years old, judge of the county court. He was very proud of his old Virginian ancestry,* and in his hospitalities and his rather formal and stately manners he kept up its traditions.

He was fine and just and generous. To be a gentleman—a gentleman without stain or blemish—was his only religion, and to it he was always faithful. He was respected, esteemed, and beloved by all the community. He was well off, and was gradually adding to his store. He and his wife were very nearly happy, but not quite, for they had no children. The longing for the treasure of a child had grown stronger and stronger as the years slipped away, but the blessing never came—and was never to come.

With this pair lived the Judge's widowed sister, Mrs Rachel Pratt, and she also was childless—childless, and sorrowful for that reason, and not to be comforted. The women were good and commonplace people, and did their duty and had their reward in clear consciences and the community's approbation. They were Presbyterians, the Judge was a free-thinker.*

Pembroke Howard, lawyer and bachelor, aged about forty, was another old Virginian grandee with proved descent from the First Families.* He was a fine, brave, majestic creature, a gentleman according to the nicest requirements of the Virginian rule, a devoted Presbyterian, an authority on the 'code',* and a man always courteously ready to stand up before you in the field if any act or word of his had seemed doubtful or suspicious to you, and explain it with any weapon you might prefer from bradawls to artillery. He was very popular with the people, and was the Judge's dearest friend.

Then there was Colonel Cecil Burleigh Essex, another F. F. V. of formidable calibre; however, with him we have no concern.

Percy Northumberland Driscoll,* brother to the Judge, and younger than he by five years, was a married man, and had had children around his hearthstone; but they were attacked in detail by measles, croup, and scarlet fever, and this had given the doctor a chance with his effective antediluvian methods; so the cradles were empty. He was a prosperous man, with a good head for speculations, and his fortune was growing. On the 1st of February, 1830, two boy babes were born in his house: one to him, the other to one of his slave girls, Roxana* by name. Roxana was twenty years old. She was up and around the same day, with her hands full, for she was tending both babies.

Mrs Percy Driscoll died within the week. Roxy remained in charge of the children. She had her own way, for Mr Driscoll soon absorbed himself in his speculations and left her to her own devices.

In that same month of February Dawson's Landing gained a new citizen. This was Mr David Wilson, a young fellow of Scotch parentage. He had wandered to this remote region from his birthplace in the interior of the State of New York to seek his fortune. He was twenty-five years old, college-bred, and had finished a post-college course in an Eastern law school* a couple of years before.

He was a homely, freckled, sandy-haired young fellow, with an intelligent blue eye that had frankness and comradeship in it and a covert twinkle of a pleasant sort. But for an unfortunate remark of his, he would no doubt have entered at once upon a successful career at Dawson's Landing. But he made his fatal remark the first day he spent in the village, and it 'gaged' him. He had just made the acquaintance of a group of citizens when an invisible dog began to yelp and snarl and howl and make himself very comprehensively disagreeable, whereupon young Wilson said, much as one who is thinking aloud—

'I wish I owned half of that dog.'*

'Why?' somebody asked.

'Because I would kill my half.'

The group searched his face with curiosity, with anxiety even, but found no light there, no expression that they could read. They fell away from him as from something uncanny, and went into privacy to discuss him. One said:

' 'Pears to be a fool.'

' 'Pears?' said another. '*Is*, I reckon you better say.'

'Said he wished he owned *half* of the dog, the idiot,' said a third. 'What did he reckon would become of the other half if he killed his half? Do you reckon he thought it would live?'

'Why, he must have thought it, unless he *is* the downrightest fool in the world; because, if he hadn't thought it, he would have wanted to own the whole dog, knowing that if he killed his half and the other half died, he would be responsible for that half just the same as if he had killed that half instead of his own. Don't it look that way to you, gents?'

'Yes, it does. If he owned one half of the general dog, it would be so; if he owned one end of the dog and another person owned the other end, it would be so, just the same; particularly in the first case, because if you kill one half of a general dog there ain't any man that can tell whose half it was, but if he owned one end of the dog, maybe he could kill his end of it and——'

'No, he couldn't either; he couldn't and not be responsible if the other end died, which it would. In my opinion the man ain't in his right mind.'

'In my opinion he hain't *got* any mind.'

No. 3 said: 'Well, he's a lummox,* any way.'

'That's what he is,' said No. 4; 'he's a labrick*—just a Simon-pure labrick, if ever there was one.'

'Yes, sir, he's a dam fool, that's the way I put him up,' said No. 5. 'Anybody can think different that wants to, but those are my sentiments.'

'I'm with you, gentlemen,' said No. 6. 'Perfect jackass—yes, and it ain't going too far to say he is a pudd'nhead. If he ain't a pudd'nhead, I ain't no judge, that's all.'

Mr Wilson stood elected. The incident was told all over the town, and gravely discussed by everybody. Within a week he had lost his first name; Pudd'nhead took its place. In time he came to be liked, and well liked, too; but by that time the nickname had got well stuck on, and it stayed. That first day's verdict made him a fool, and he was not able to get it set aside, or even modified. The nickname soon ceased to carry any harsh or unfriendly feeling with it, but it held its place, and was to continue to hold its place for twenty long years.

2

*Adam was but human—this explains it all. He did not want the apple
for the apple's sake; he only wanted it because it was forbidden. The
mistake was in not forbidding the serpent; then he would have eaten the
serpent.*

—PUDD'NHEAD WILSON'S CALENDAR

PUDD'NHEAD WILSON had a trifle of money when he
arrived, and he bought a small house on the extreme western
verge of the town. Between it and Judge Driscoll's house
there was only a grassy yard, with a paling fence dividing the
properties in the middle. He hired a small office down in the
town, and hung out a tin sign with these words on it:

DAVID WILSON,
ATTORNEY AND COUNSELLOR-AT-LAW,
SURVEYING, CONVEYANCING, ETC.

But his deadly remark had ruined his chance—at least in
the law. No clients came. He took down his sign after a
while, and put it up on his own house with the law features
knocked out of it. It offered his services now in the humble
capacities of land-surveyor and expert accountant. Now and
then he got a job of surveying to do, and now and then a
merchant got him to straighten out his books. With Scotch
patience and pluck he resolved to live down his reputation
and work his way into the legal field yet. Poor fellow, he
could not foresee that it was going to take him such a weary
long time to do it.

He had a rich abundance of idle time, but it never hung
heavy on his hands, for he interested himself in every new
thing that was born into the universe of ideas, and studied
it and experimented upon it at his house. One of his pet
fads was palmistry. To another one he gave no name, neither
would he explain to anybody what its purpose was, but merely

said it was an amusement. In fact, he had found that his fads added to his reputation as a pudd'nhead; therefore he was growing chary of being too communicative about them. The fad without a name was one which dealt with people's finger-marks.* He carried in his coat pocket a shallow box with grooves in it, and in the grooves strips of glass five inches long and three inches wide. Along the lower edge of each strip was pasted a slip of white paper. He asked people to pass their hands through their hair (thus collecting upon them a thin coating of the natural oil), and then make a thumb-mark on a glass strip, following it with the mark of the ball of each finger in succession. Under this row of faint grease-prints he would write a record on the strip of white paper, thus:

JOHN SMITH, *right hand*—

and add the day of the month and the year, and then take Smith's left hand on another glass strip, and add name and date and the words 'left hand'. The strips were now returned to the grooved box, and took their place among what Wilson called his 'records'.

He often studied his records, examining and poring over them with absorbing interest until far into the night; but what he found there, if he found anything, he revealed to no one. Sometimes he copied on paper the involved and delicate pattern left by the ball of a finger, and then vastly enlarged it with a pantograph, so that he could examine its web of curving lines with ease and convenience.

One sweltering afternoon—it was the first day of July, 1830—he was at work over a set of tangled account-books in his workroom, which looked westward over a stretch of vacant lots, when a conversation outside disturbed him. It was carried on in yells, which showed that the people engaged in it were not close together.

'Say, Roxy, how does yo' baby come on?' This from the distant voice.

'Fust-rate; how do *you* come on, Jasper?' This yell was from close by.

'Oh, I's middlin'; hain't got noth'n' to complain of. I's gwine to come a-court'n' you bimeby, Roxy.'

'*You* is, you black mud-cat! Yah—yah—yah! I got somep'n' better to do den 'sociat'n' wid niggers as black as you is. Is ole Miss Cooper's Nancy done give you de mitten?' Roxy followed this sally with another discharge of care-free laughter.

'You's jealous, Roxy; dat's what's de matter wid *you*, you hussy—yah—yah—yah! Dat's de time I got you!'

'Oh, yes, *you* got me, hain't you? 'Clah to goodness if dat conceit o' yo'n strikes in, Jasper, it gwine to kill you sho'. If you b'longed to me I'd sell you down de river 'fo' you git too fur gone. Fust time I runs acrost yo' marster I's gwine to tell him so.'

This idle and aimless jabber went on and on, both parties enjoying the friendly duel, and each well satisfied with his own share of the wit exchanged—for wit they considered it.

Wilson stepped to the window to observe the combatants; he could not work while their chatter continued. Over in the vacant lots was Jasper, young, coal-black, and of magnificent build, sitting on a wheelbarrow in the pelting sun—at work, supposably, whereas he was in fact only preparing for it by taking an hour's rest before beginning. In front of Wilson's porch stood Roxy, with a local hand-made baby-wagon, in which sat her two charges—one at each end, and facing each other. From Roxy's manner of speech a stranger would have expected her to be black, but she was not. Only one sixteenth of her was black, and that sixteenth did not show. She was of majestic form and stature; her attitudes were imposing and statuesque, and her gestures and movements distinguished by a noble and stately grace. Her complexion was very fair, with the rosy glow of vigorous health in the cheeks, her face was full of character and expression, her eyes were brown and liquid, and she had a heavy suit of fine soft hair which was also brown, but the fact was not apparent because her head was bound about with a chequered handkerchief and the hair was concealed under it. Her face was shapely, intelligent, and comely—even beautiful. She had an easy, independent carriage—when she was among her own caste—and a high and 'sassy' way withal; but, of course, she was meek and humble enough where white people were.

To all intents and purposes Roxy was as white as anybody, but the one sixteenth of her which was black outvoted the other fifteen parts and made her a negro. She was a slave, and saleable as such. Her child was thirty-one parts white, and he, too, was a slave and, by a fiction of law and custom, a negro. He had blue eyes and flaxen curls like his white comrade; but even the father of the white child was able to tell the children apart—little as he had commerce with them—by their clothes: for the white babe wore ruffled soft muslin and a coral necklace, while the other wore merely a coarse tow-linen shirt which barely reached to its knees, and no jewellery.

The white child's name was Thomas à Becket Driscoll; the other's name was Valet de Chambre: no surname—slaves hadn't the privilege. Roxana had heard that phrase somewhere; the fine sound of it had pleased her ear, and, as she had supposed it was a name, she loaded it on to her darling. It soon got shortened to 'Chambers', of course.

Wilson knew Roxy by sight, and when the duel of wit began to play out, he stepped outside to gather in a record or two. Jasper went to work energetically, at once, perceiving that his leisure was observed. Wilson inspected the children and asked—

'How old are they, Roxy?'

'Bofe de same age, sir—five months. Bawn de fust o' Feb'uary.'

'They're handsome little chaps. One's just as handsome as the other, too.'

A delighted smile exposed the girl's white teeth and she said:

'Bless yo' soul, Misto Wilson, it's pow'ful nice o'you to say dat, 'ca'se one of 'em ain't on'y a nigger. Mighty prime little nigger, *I* al'ays says, but dat's 'ca'se it's mine, o'course.'

'How do you tell them apart, Roxy, when they haven't any clothes on?'

Roxy laughed a laugh proportioned to her size, and said:

'Oh, *I* kin tell 'em 'part, Misto Wilson, but I bet Marse Percy couldn't, not to save his life.'

Wilson chatted along for a while, and presently got Roxy's finger-prints for his collection—right hand and left—on a couple of his glass strips; then labelled and dated them, and took the 'records' of both children, and labelled and dated them also.

Two months later, on the 3rd of September, he took this trio of finger-marks again. He liked to have a 'series', two or three 'takings' at intervals during the period of child-hood, these to be followed by others at intervals of several years.

The next day—that is to say, on the 4th of September—something occurred which profoundly impressed Roxana. Mr Driscoll missed another small sum of money—which is a way of saying that this was not a new thing, but had happened before. In truth it had happened three times before. Driscoll's patience was exhausted. He was a fairly humane man towards slaves and other animals; he was an exceedingly humane man toward the erring of his own race. Theft he could not abide, and plainly there was a thief in his house. Necessarily the thief must be one of his negroes. Sharp measures must be taken. He called his servants before him. There were three of these, besides Roxy: a man, a woman, and a boy twelve years old. They were not related. Mr Driscoll said:

'You have all been warned before. It has done no good. This time I will teach you a lesson. I will sell the thief. Which of you is the guilty one?'

They all shuddered at the threat, for here they had a good home, and a new one was likely to be a change for the worse. The denial was general. None had stolen anything—not money, anyway—a little sugar, or cake, or honey, or some-thing like that, that 'Marse Percy wouldn't mind or miss', but not money—never a cent of money. They were eloquent in their protestations, but Mr Driscoll was not moved by them. He answered each in turn with a stern 'Name the thief!'

The truth was, all were guilty but Roxana; she suspected that the others were guilty, but she did not know them to be so. She was horrified to think how near she had come to being guilty herself; she had been saved in the nick of time by a revival in the coloured Methodist Church, a fortnight before, at which time and place she 'got religion'. The very next day after that gracious experience, while her change of style was fresh upon her and she was vain of her purified condition, her master left a couple of dollars lying unprotected on his desk, and she happened upon that temptation when she was polishing around with a dust-rag. She looked at the money awhile with a steadily rising resentment, then she burst out with—

'Dad blame dat revival, I wisht it had 'a' be'n put off till to-morrow!'

Then she covered the tempter with a book, and another member of the kitchen cabinet got it. She made this sacrifice as a matter of religious etiquette; as a thing necessary just now, but by no means to be wrested into a precedent; no, a week or two would limber up her piety, then she would be rational again, and the next two dollars that got left out in the cold would find a comforter—and she could name the comforter.

Was she bad? Was she worse than the general run of her race? No. They had an unfair show in the battle of life, and they held it no sin to take military advantage of the enemy—in a small way; in a small way, but not in a large one. They would smouch provisions from the pantry whenever they got a chance; or a brass thimble, or a cake of wax, or an emery-bag, or a paper of needles, or a silver spoon, or a dollar bill, or small articles of clothing, or any other property of light value; and so far were they from considering such reprisals sinful, that they would go to church and shout and pray their loudest and sincerest with their plunder in their pockets. A farm smoke-house had to be kept heavily padlocked, for even the coloured deacon himself could not resist a ham when Providence showed him in a dream, or otherwise, where such a thing hung lonesome and longed for some one to love. But with a hundred hanging before him the deacon would not take two—that is, on the same night. On frosty nights the humane negro prowler would warm the end of a plank* and put it up under the cold claws of chickens roosting in a tree; a drowsy hen would step on to the comfortable board, softly clucking her gratitude, and the prowler would dump her into his bag, and later into his stomach, perfectly sure that in taking this trifle from the man who daily robbed him of an inestimable treasure—his liberty—he was not committing any sin that God would remember against him in the Last Great Day.

'Name the thief!'

For the fourth time Mr Driscoll had said it, and always in the same hard tone. And now he added these words of awful import:

'I give you one minute'—he took out his watch. 'If at the end of that time you have not confessed, I will not only sell all four of you, *but*—I will sell you DOWN THE RIVER!'

It was equivalent to condemning them to hell! No Missouri negro doubted this. Roxy reeled in her tracks and the colour vanished out of her face; the others dropped to their knees as if they had been shot; tears gushed from their eyes, their supplicating hands went up, and three answers came in the one instant:

'I done it!'

'I done it!'

'I done it!—have mercy, marster—Lord have mercy on us po' niggers!'

'Very good,' said the master, putting up his watch, 'I will sell you *here*, though you don't deserve it. You ought to be sold down the river.'

The culprits flung themselves prone, in an ecstasy of gratitude, and kissed his feet, declaring that they would never forget his goodness and never cease to pray for him as long as they lived. They were sincere, for like a god he had stretched forth his mighty hand and closed the gates of hell against them. He knew, himself, that he had done a noble and gracious thing, and was privately well pleased with his magnanimity; and that night he set the incident down in his diary, so that his son might read it in after years, and be thereby moved to deeds of gentleness and humanity himself.

3

Whoever has lived long enough to find out what life is, knows how deep a debt of gratitude we owe to Adam, the first great benefactor of our race. He brought death into the world.

—PUDD'NHEAD WILSON'S CALENDAR

PERCY DRISCOLL slept well the night he saved his house-minions from going down the river, but no wink of sleep visited Roxy's eyes. A profound terror had taken possession of her. Her child could grow up and be sold down the river! The thought crazed her with horror. If she dozed and lost herself for a moment, the next moment she was on her feet and flying to her child's cradle to see if it was still there. Then she would gather it to her heart and pour out her love upon it in a frenzy of kisses, moaning, crying, and saying 'Dey sha'n't, oh, dey *sha'n't!* yo' po' mammy will kill you fust!'

Once, when she was tucking it back in its cradle again, the other child nestled in its sleep and attracted her attention. She went and stood over it a long time, communing with herself:

'What has my po' baby done, dat he couldn't have yo' luck? He hain't done noth'n'. God was good to you; why warn't he good to him? Dey can't sell *you* down de river. I hates yo' pappy; he ain't got no heart—for niggers he ain't, anyways. I hates him, en I could kill him!' She paused awhile, thinking; then she burst into wild sobbings again, and turned away, saying, 'Oh, I got to kill my chile, dey ain't no yuther way,—killin' *him* wouldn't save de chile fum goin' down de river. Oh, I got to do it, yo' po' mammy's got to kill you to save you, honey'—she gathered her baby to her bosom, now, and began to smother it with caresses—'Mammy's got to kill you—how *kin* I do it? But yo' mammy ain't gwine to desert you,—no, no; *dah*, don't cry—she gwine *wid* you, she gwine to kill herself too. Come along, honey, come along wid mammy; we gwine to jump in de river, den de troubles o' dis worl' is all over—dey don't sell po' niggers down the river over *yonder*.'

She started toward the door, crooning to the child and hushing it; midway she stopped, suddenly. She had caught sight of her new Sunday gown—a cheap curtain-calico thing, a conflagration of gaudy colours and fantastic figures. She surveyed it wistfully, longingly.

'Hain't ever wore it yet,' she said, 'en it's jist lovely.' Then she nodded her head in response to a pleasant idea, and added, 'No, I ain't gwine to be fished out, wid everybody lookin' at me, in dis mis'able ole linsey-woolsey.'

She put down the child and made the change. She looked in the glass and was astonished at her beauty. She resolved to make her death-toilet perfect. She took off her handkerchief-turban and dressed her glossy wealth of hair 'like white folks'; she added some odds and ends of rather lurid ribbon and a spray of atrocious artificial flowers; finally she threw over her shoulders a fluffy thing called a 'cloud' in that day, which was of a blazing red complexion. Then she was ready for the tomb.

She gathered up her baby once more; but when her eye fell upon its miserably short little gray tow-linen shirt and noted the contrast between its pauper shabbiness and her own volcanic irruption of infernal splendours, her mother-heart was touched, and she was ashamed.

'No, dolling, mammy ain't gwine to treat you so. De angels is gwine to 'mire you jist as much as dey does yo' mammy. Ain't gwine to have 'em putt'n' dey han's up 'fo' dey eyes en sayin' to David en Goliah en dem yuther prophets, 'Dat chile is dress' too indelicate fo' dis place.''

By this time she had stripped off the shirt. Now she clothed the naked little creature in one of Thomas à Becket's snowy long baby-gowns, with its bright blue bows and dainty flummery of ruffles.

'Dah—now you's fixed.' She propped the child in a chair and stood off to inspect it. Straightway her eyes began to widen with astonishment and admiration, and she clapped her hands and cried out, 'Why, it do beat all! I *never* knowed you was so lovely. Marse Tommy ain't a bit puttier—not a single bit.'

She stepped over and glanced at the other infant; she flung a glance back at her own; then one more at the heir of the house. Now a strange light dawned in her eyes, and in a moment she was lost in thought. She seemed in a trance; when she came out of it she muttered, 'When I 'uz a-washin' 'em in de tub, yistiddy, his own pappy asked me which of 'em was his'n.'

She began to move about like one in a dream. She undressed Thomas à Becket, stripping him of everything, and put the tow-linen shirt on him. She put his coral necklace on her own child's neck. Then she placed the children side by side, and after earnest inspection she muttered—

'Now who would b'lieve clo'es could do de like o' dat? Dog my cats if it ain't all *I* kin do to tell t'other fum which, let alone his pappy.'

She put her cub in Tommy's elegant cradle and said:

'You's young Marse *Tom* fum dis out, en I got to practise and git used to 'memberin' to call you dat, honey, or I's gwine to make a mistake some time en git us bofe into trouble. Dah—now you lay still en don't fret no mo', Marse Tom—oh, thank de good Lord in heaven, you's saved, you's saved!—dey ain't no man kin ever sell mammy's po' little honey down de river now!'

She put the heir of the house in her own child's unpainted pine cradle, and said, contemplating its slumbering form uneasily:

'I's sorry for you, honey; I's sorry, God knows I is—but what *kin* I do, what *could* I do? Yo' pappy would sell him to somebody, some time, en den he'd go down de river, sho', en I couldn't, couldn't, *couldn't* stan' it.'

She flung herself on her bed and began to think and toss, toss and think. By-and-by she sat suddenly upright, for a comforting thought had flown through her worried mind:

''Tain't no sin—*white* folks has done it! It ain't no sin, glory to goodness it ain't no sin! *Dey's* done it—yes, en dey was de biggest quality in de whole bilin',* too—*kings!*'

She began to muse; she was trying to gather out of her memory the dim particulars of some tale she had heard some time or other. At last she said:

'Now I's got it; now I 'member. It was dat ole nigger preacher dat tole it, de time he come over here fum Illinois en preached in de nigger church. He said dey ain't nobody kin save his own self—can't do it by faith, can't do it by works, can't do it no way at all. Free grace is de _on'y_ way, en dat don't come fum nobody but jis' de Lord; en _he_ kin give it to anybody he please, saint or sinner—_he_ don't kyer. He do jis' as he's a mineter. He s'lect out anybody dat suit him, en put another one in his place, en make de fust one happy for ever en leave t'other one to burn wid Satan. De preacher said it was jist like dey done in Englan' one time, long time ago.* De queen she lef' her baby layin' aroun' one day, en went out callin'; en one o' de niggers roun' 'bout de place dat was 'mos' white, she come in en see de chile layin' aroun', en tuck en put her own chile's clo'es on de queen's chile, and put de queen's chile's clo'es on her own chile, en den lef' her own chile layin' aroun' en tuck and toted de queen's chile home to de nigger-quarter, en nobody ever foun' it out, en her chile was de king bimeby, en sole de queen's chile down de river one time when dey had to settle up de estate. Dah, now—de preacher said it his own self, en it ain't no sin, 'ca'se white folks done it. _Dey_ done it—yes, _dey_ done it; en not on'y jis' common white folks nuther, but de biggest quality dey is in de whole bilin'. Oh, I's _so_ glad I 'member 'bout dat!'

She got up light-hearted and happy, and went to the cradles and spent what was left of the night 'practising'. She would give her own child a light pat and say humbly, 'Lay still, Marse Tom,' then give the real Tom a pat and say with severity, 'Lay _still_, Chambers!—does you want me to take somep'n' _to_ you?'

As she progressed with her practice, she was surprised to see how steadily and surely the awe which had kept her tongue reverent and her manner humble toward her young master was transferring itself to her speech and manner toward the usurper, and how similarly handy she was becoming in transferring her motherly curtness of speech and peremptoriness of manner to the unlucky heir of the ancient house of Driscoll.

She took occasional rests from practising, and absorbed herself in calculating her chances.

'Dey'll sell dese niggers to-day fo' stealin' de money, den dey'll buy some mo' dat don't know de chillen—so *dat's* all right. When I takes de chillen out to git de air, de minute I'se roun' de corner I'se gwine to gaum dey mouths all roun' wid jam, den dey can't *nobody* notice dey's changed. Yes, I gwineter do dat till I's safe, if it takes a year.

'Dey ain't but one man dat I's afeared of, en dat's dat Pudd'nhead Wilson. Dey calls him a pudd'nhead, en says he's a fool. My lan', dat man ain't no mo' fool den I is! He's de smartes' man in dis town, less'n it's Jedge Driscoll or maybe Pem Howard. Blame dat man, he worries me wid dem ornery glasses o' hisn; *I* b'lieve he's a witch. But nemmine, I's gwine to happen aroun' dah one o' dese days en let on dat I reckon he wants to print de chillen's fingers ag'in; en if *he* don't notice dey's changed, I bound dey ain't nobody gwine to notice it, en den I's safe, sho'. But I reckon I'll tote along a hoss-shoe to keep off de witch-work.'

The new negroes gave Roxy no trouble, of course. The master gave her none, for one of his speculations was in jeopardy, and his mind was so occupied that he hardly saw the children when he looked at them, and all Roxy had to do was to get them both into a gale of laughter when he came about; then their faces were mainly cavities exposing gums, and he was gone again before the spasm passed and the little creatures resumed a human aspect.

Within a few days the fate of the speculation became so dubious that Mr Percy went away with his brother the Judge, to see what could be done with it. It was a land speculation as usual, and it had gotten complicated with a lawsuit. The men were gone seven weeks. Before they got back, Roxy had paid her visit to Wilson, and was satisfied. Wilson took the finger-prints, labelled them with the names and with the

date—October the first—put them carefully away and continued his chat with Roxy, who seemed very anxious that he
should admire the great advance in flesh and beauty which
the babies had made since he took their finger-prints a month
before. He complimented their improvement to her content-
ment; and as they were without any disguise of jam or other
stain, she trembled all the while and was miserably frightened
lest at any moment he—

But he didn't. He discovered nothing; and she went home
jubilant, and dropped all concern about the matter permanently out of her mind.

4

*Adam and Eve had many advantages, but the principal one was that
they escaped teething.*
                              —PUDD'NHEAD WILSON'S CALENDAR

*There is this trouble about special providences—namely, there is so often a
doubt as to which party was intended to be the beneficiary. In the case of
the children,* the bears, and the prophet, the bears got more real satisfaction
out of the episode than the prophet did, because they got the children.*
                              —PUDD'NHEAD WILSON'S CALENDAR

THIS history must henceforth accommodate itself to the
change which Roxana has consummated, and call the real
heir 'Chambers' and the usurping little slave 'Thomas à
Becket'—shortening this latter name to 'Tom', for daily use,
as the people about him did.

'Tom' was a bad baby, from the very beginning of his
usurpation. He would cry for nothing; he would burst into
storms of devilish temper without notice, and let go scream
after scream and squall after squall, then climax the thing
with 'holding his breath'—that frightful specialty of the
teething nursling, in the throes of which the creature exhausts
its lungs, then is convulsed with noiseless squirmings and
twistings and kickings in the effort to get its breath, while
the lips turn blue and the mouth stands wide and rigid,
offering for inspection one wee tooth set in the lower rim

of a hoop of red gums; and when the appalling stillness has endured until one is sure the lost breath will never return, a nurse comes flying, and dashes water in the child's face, and—presto! the lungs fill, and instantly discharge a shriek, or a yell, or a howl which bursts the listening ear and surprises the owner of it into saying words which would not go well with a halo if he had one. The baby Tom would claw anybody who came within reach of his nails, and pound anybody he could reach with his rattle. He would scream for water until he got it, and then throw cup and all on the floor and scream for more. He was indulged in all his caprices, howsoever troublesome and exasperating they might be; he was allowed to eat anything he wanted, particularly things that would give him the stomach-ache.

When he got to be old enough to begin to toddle about and say broken words and get an idea of what his hands were for, he was a more consummate pest than ever. Roxy got no rest while he was awake. He would call for anything and everything he saw, simply saying 'Awnt it!' (want it), which was a command. When it was brought, he said in a frenzy, and motioning it away with his hands, 'Don't awnt it! don't awnt it!' and the moment it was gone he set up frantic yells of 'Awnt it! awnt it! awnt it!' and Roxy had to give wings to her heels to get that thing back to him again before he could get time to carry out his intention of going into convulsions about it.

What he preferred above all other things was the tongs. This was because his 'father' had forbidden him to have them lest he break windows and furniture with them. The moment Roxy's back was turned he would toddle to the presence of the tongs and say 'Like it!' and cock his eye to one side to see if Roxy was observing; then, 'Awnt it!' and cock his eye again; then, 'Hab it!' with another furtive glance; and finally, 'Take it!'—and the prize was his. The next moment the heavy implement was raised aloft; the next, there was a crash and a squall, and the cat was off on three legs to meet an engagement; Roxy would arrive just as the lamp or a window went to irremediable smash.

Tom got all the petting, Chambers got none. Tom got all the delicacies, Chambers got mush* and milk, and clabber* without sugar. In consequence Tom was a sickly child and Chambers wasn't. Tom was 'fractious', as Roxy called it, and overbearing; Chambers was meek and docile.

With all her splendid common sense and practical everyday ability, Roxy was a doting fool of a mother. She was this toward her child—and she was also more than this: by the fiction created by herself, he was become her master; the necessity of recognising this relation outwardly and of perfecting herself in the forms required to express the recognition, had moved her to such diligence and faithfulness in practising these forms that this exercise soon concreted itself into habit; it became automatic and unconscious; then a natural result followed: deceptions intended solely for others gradually grew practically into self-deceptions as well; the mock reverence became real reverence, the mock obsequiousness real obsequiousness, the mock homage real homage; the little counterfeit rift of separation between imitation-slave and imitation-master widened and widened, and became an abyss, and a very real one—and on one side of it stood Roxy, the dupe of her own deceptions, and on the other stood her child, no longer a usurper to her, but her accepted and recognised master. He was her darling, her master, and her deity all in one, and in her worship of him she forgot who she was and what he had been.

In babyhood Tom cuffed and banged and scratched Chambers unrebuked, and Chambers early learned that between meekly bearing it and resenting it, the advantage all lay with the former policy. The few times that his persecutions had moved him beyond control and made him fight back had cost him very dear at head-quarters; not at the hands of Roxy, for if she ever went beyond scolding him sharply for 'forgitt'n' who his young marster was', she at least never extended her punishment beyond a box on the ear. No, Percy Driscoll was the person. He told Chambers that under no provocation whatever was he privileged to lift his hand against his little master. Chambers overstepped the line three times, and got three such convincing canings from the man who was his father and didn't know it, that he took Tom's cruelties in all humility after that, and made no more experiments.

Outside of the house the two boys were together all through their boyhood. Chambers was strong beyond his years, and a good fighter; strong because he was coarsely fed and hard worked about the house, and a good fighter because Tom furnished him plenty of practice—on white boys whom he hated and was afraid of. Chambers was his constant bodyguard, to and from school; he was present on the playground at recess to protect his charge. He fought himself into such a formidable reputation, by-and-by, that Tom could have changed clothes with him and 'ridden in peace', like Sir Kay* in Launcelot's armour.

He was good at games of skill, too. Tom staked him with marbles to play 'keeps' with, and then took all the winnings away from him. In the winter season Chambers was on hand, in Tom's worn-out clothes, with 'holy' red mittens, and 'holy' shoes, and pants 'holy' at the knees and seat, to drag a sled up the hill for Tom, warmly clad, to ride down on; but he never got a ride himself. He built snow men and snow fortifications under Tom's directions. He was Tom's patient target when Tom wanted to do some snowballing, but the target couldn't fire back. Chambers carried Tom's skates to the river and strapped them on him, then trotted around after him on the ice, so as to be on hand when wanted; but he wasn't ever asked to try the skates himself.

In summer the pet pastime of the boys of Dawson's Landing was to steal apples, peaches, and melons from the farmers' fruit-waggons—mainly on account of the risk they ran of getting their heads laid open with the butt of the farmer's whip. Tom was a distinguished adept at these thefts—by proxy. Chambers did his stealing, and got the peach-stones, apple-cores, and melon-rinds for his share.

Tom always made Chambers go in swimming with him, and stay by him as a protection. When Tom had had enough, he would slip out and tie knots in Chambers's shirt, dip the knots in the water to make them hard to undo, then dress himself and sit by and laugh while the naked shiverer tugged at the stubborn knots with his teeth.

Tom did his humble comrade these various ill turns partly out of his native viciousness, and partly because he hated him for his superiorities of physique and pluck, and for his manifold clein his clevernesses. Tom couldn't dive, for it gave him splitting headaches. Chambers could dive without inconvenience, and was fond of doing it. He excited so much admiration, one day, among a crowd of white boys, by throwing back somersaults from the stern of a canoe, that it wearied Tom's spirit, and at last he shoved the canoe underneath Chambers while he was in the air—so he came down on his head in the canoe-bottom; and while he lay unconscious, several of Tom's ancient adversaries saw that their long-desired opportunity was come, and they gave the false heir such a drubbing that with Chambers's best help he was hardly able to drag himself home afterward.

When the boys were fifteen and upward, Tom was 'showing off' in the river one day, when he was taken with a cramp, and shouted for help. It was a common trick with the boys—particularly if a stranger was present—to pretend a cramp and howl for help; then when the stranger came tearing hand over hand to the rescue, the howler would go on struggling and howling till he was close at hand, and then replace the howl with a sarcastic smile and swim blandly away, while the town boys assailed the dupe with a volley of jeers and laughter. Tom had never tried this joke as yet, but was supposed to be trying it now, so the boys held warily back; but Chambers believed his master was in earnest, therefore he swam out, and arrived in time, unfortunately, and saved his life.

This was the last feather. Tom had managed to endure everything else, but to have to remain publicly and permanently under such an obligation as this to a nigger, and to this nigger of all niggers—this was too much. He heaped insults upon Chambers for 'pretending' to think he was in earnest in calling for help, and said that anybody but a blockheaded nigger would have known he was funning and left him alone.

Tom's enemies were in strong force here, so they came out with their opinions quite freely. They laughed at him, and called him coward, liar, sneak, and other sorts of pet names, and told him they meant to call Chambers by a new name after this, and make it common in the town—'Tom Driscoll's niggerpappy',—to signify that he had had a second birth into this life, and that Chambers was the author of his new being. Tom grew frantic under these taunts, and shouted:

'Knock their heads off, Chambers! knock their heads off! What do you stand there with your hands in your pockets for?'

Chambers expostulated, and said: 'But, Marse Tom, dey's too many of 'em—dey's——'

'Do you hear me?'

'Please, Marse Tom, don't make me! Dey's so many of 'em dat——'

Tom sprang at him and drove his pocket-knife into him two or three times before the boys could snatch him away and give the wounded lad a chance to escape. He was considerably hurt, but not seriously. If the blade had been a little longer his career would have ended there.

Tom had long ago taught Roxy 'her place'. It had been many a day now since she had ventured a caress or a fondling epithet in his quarter. Such things, from a 'nigger', were repulsive to him, and she had been warned to keep her distance and remember who she was. She saw her darling gradually cease from being her son, she saw *that* detail perish utterly; all that was left was master—master, pure and simple, and it was not a gentle mastership either. She saw herself sink from the sublime height of motherhood to the sombre deeps of unmodified slavery. The abyss of separation between her and her boy was complete. She was merely his chattel, now, his convenience, his dog, his cringing and helpless slave, the humble and unresisting victim of his capricious temper and vicious nature.

Sometimes she could not go to sleep, even when worn out with fatigue, because her rage boiled so high over the day's experiences with her boy. She would mumble and mutter to herself:

'He struck me, en I warn't no way to blame—struck me in de face, right before folks. En he's al'ays callin' me nigger-wench, en hussy, en all dem mean names, when I's doin' de very bes' I kin. Oh, Lord, I done so much for him—I lift' him away up to what he is—en dis is what I git for it.'

Sometimes when some outrage of peculiar offensiveness stung her to the heart, she would plan schemes of vengeance and revel in the fancied spectacle of his exposure to the world as an impostor and a slave; but in the midst of these joys fear would strike her: she had made him too strong; she could prove nothing, and—heavens, she might get sold down the river for her pains! So her schemes always went for nothing, and she laid them aside in impotent rage against the fates, and against herself for playing the fool on that fatal September day in not providing herself with a witness for use in the day when such a thing might be needed for the appeasing of her vengeance-hungry heart.

And yet the moment Tom happened to be good to her, and kind—and this occurred every now and then—all her sore places were healed, and she was happy; happy and proud, for this was her son, her nigger son, lording it among the whites and securely avenging their crimes against her race.

There were two grand funerals in Dawson's Landing that fall—the fall of 1845. One was that of Colonel Cecil Burleigh Essex, the other that of Percy Driscoll.

On his death-bed Driscoll set Roxy free and delivered his idolised ostensible son solemnly into the keeping of his brother the Judge and his wife. Those childless people were glad to get him. Childless people are not difficult to please.

Judge Driscoll had gone privately to his brother, a month before, and bought Chambers. He had heard that Tom had been trying to get his father to sell the boy down the river, and he wanted to prevent the scandal—for public sentiment did not approve of that way of treating family servants for light cause or for no cause.

Percy Driscoll had worn himself out in trying to save his great speculative landed estate, and had died without succeeding. He was hardly in his grave before the boom collapsed and left his hitherto envied young devil of an heir a pauper. But that was nothing; his uncle told him he should be his heir and have all his fortune when he died; so Tom was comforted.

Roxy had no home now; so she resolved to go around and say good-bye to her friends and then clear out and see the world—that is to say, she would go chamber-maiding on a steamboat, the darling ambition of her race and sex.

Her last call was on the black giant, Jasper. She found him chopping Pudd'nhead Wilson's winter provision of wood. Wilson was chatting with him when Roxy arrived. He asked her how she could bear to go off chambermaiding and leave her boys; and chaffingly offered to copy off a series of their finger-prints, reaching up to their twelfth year, for her to remember them by; but she sobered in a moment, wondering if he suspected anything; then she said she believed she didn't want them. Wilson said to himself, 'The drop of black blood in her is superstitious; she thinks there's some deviltry, some witch-business about my glass mystery somewhere; she used to come here with an old horseshoe in her hand; it could have been an accident, but I doubt it.'

5

Training is everything. The peach was once a bitter almond; cauliflower is nothing but cabbage with a college education.

—PUDD'NHEAD WILSON'S CALENDAR

Remark of Dr Baldwin's, concerning upstarts: We don't care to eat toadstools that think they are truffles.

—PUDD'NHEAD WILSON'S CALENDAR

MRS YORK DRISCOLL enjoyed two years of bliss with that prize, Tom—bliss that was troubled a little at times, it is true, but bliss nevertheless; then she died, and her husband and his childless sister, Mrs Pratt, continued the bliss-business at the old stand. Tom was petted and indulged and spoiled to his entire content—or nearly that. This went on till he was nineteen, then he was sent to Yale. He went handsomely equipped with 'conditions',* but otherwise he was not an object of distinction there. He remained at Yale two years, and then threw up the struggle. He came home with his manners a good deal improved; he had lost his surliness and brusqueness, and was rather pleasantly soft and smooth now; he was furtively, and sometimes openly, ironical of speech, and given to gently touching people on the raw, but he did it with a good-natured semiconscious air that carried it off safely, and kept him from getting into trouble. He was as indolent as ever and showed no very strenuous desire to hunt up an occupation. People argued from this that he preferred to be supported by his uncle until his uncle's shoes should become vacant. He brought back one or two new habits with him, one of which he rather openly practised—tippling—but concealed another, which was gambling. It would not do to gamble where his uncle could hear of it; he knew that quite well.

Tom's Eastern polish was not popular among the young people. They could have endured it, perhaps, if Tom had stopped there; but he wore gloves, and that they couldn't stand, and wouldn't; so he was mainly without society. He brought home with him a suit of clothes of such exquisite style and cut and fashion—Eastern fashion, city fashion—that it filled everybody with anguish, and was regarded as a peculiarly wanton affront. He enjoyed the feeling which he was exciting, and paraded the town serene and happy all day; but the young fellows set a tailor to work that night, and when Tom started out on his parade next morning he found the old deformed negro bell-ringer straddling along in his wake tricked out in a flamboyant curtain-calico exaggeration of his finery, and imitating his fancy Eastern graces as well as he could.*

Tom surrendered, and after that clothed himself in the local fashion. But the dull country town was tiresome to him, since his acquaintanceship with livelier regions, and it grew daily

more and more so. He began to make little trips to St Louis*
for refreshment. There he found companionship to suit him,
and pleasures to his taste, along with more freedom, in some
particulars, than he could have at home. So during the next
two years his visits to the city grew in frequency and his
tarryings there grew steadily longer in duration.

He was getting into deep waters. He was taking chances,
privately, which might get him into trouble some day—in
fact *did*.

Judge Driscoll had retired from the bench and from all
business activities in 1850, and had now been comfortably
idle three years. He was President of the Freethinkers' Society, and Pudd'nhead Wilson was the other member. The
society's weekly discussions were now the old lawyer's main
interest in life. Pudd'nhead was still toiling in obscurity at
the bottom of the ladder, under the blight of that unlucky
remark which he had let fall twenty-three years before about
the dog.

Judge Driscoll was his friend, and claimed that he had a
mind above the average, but that was regarded as one of the
Judge's whims, and it failed to modify the public opinion.
Or rather, that was one of the reasons why it failed, but there
was another and better one. If the Judge had stopped with
bare assertion, it would have had a good deal of effect; but
he made the mistake of trying to prove his position. For
some years Wilson had been privately at work on a whimsical
almanac, for his amusement—a calendar, with a little dab of
ostensible philosophy, usually in ironical form, appended to
each date; and the Judge thought that these quips and fancies
of Wilson's were neatly turned and cute; so he carried a
handful of them around, one day, and read them to some of
the chief citizens. But irony was not for those people; their
mental vision was not focussed for it. They read those playful
trifles in the solidest earnest, and decided without hesitancy
that if there had ever been any doubt that Dave Wilson was
a pudd'nhead—which there hadn't—this revelation removed
that doubt for good and all. That is just the way in this
world; an enemy can partly ruin a man, but it takes a

good-natured injudicious friend to complete the thing and make it perfect. After this the Judge felt tenderer than ever toward Wilson, and surer than ever that his calendar had merit.

Judge Driscoll could be a freethinker and still hold his place in society because he was the person of most consequence in the community, and therefore could venture to go his own way and follow out his own notions. The other member of his pet organisation was allowed the like liberty because he was a cipher in the estimation of the public, and nobody attached any importance to what he thought or did. He was liked, he was welcome enough all around, but he simply didn't count for anything.

The widow Cooper—affectionately called 'aunt Patsy' by everybody—lived in a snug and comely cottage with her daughter Rowena, who was nineteen, romantic, amiable, and very pretty, but otherwise of no consequence. Rowena had a couple of young brothers—also of no consequence.

The widow had a large spare room which she let to a lodger, with board, when she could find one, but this room had been empty for a year now, to her sorrow. Her income was only sufficient for the family support, and she needed the lodging-money for trifling luxuries. But now, at last, on a flaming June day, she found herself happy; her tedious wait was ended; her year-worn advertisement had been answered; and not by a village applicant, oh, no!—this letter was from away off yonder in the dim great world to the North: it was from St Louis. She sat on her porch gazing out with unseeing eyes upon the shining reaches of the mighty Mississippi, her thoughts steeped in her good fortune. Indeed it was specially good fortune, for she was to have two lodgers instead of one.

She had read the letter to the family, and Rowena had danced away to see to the cleaning and airing of the room by the slave woman Nancy, and the boys had rushed abroad in the town to spread the great news, for it was matter of public interest, and the public would wonder and not be pleased if not informed. Presently Rowena returned, all aflush

with joyous excitement, and begged for a re-reading of the
letter. It was framed thus:

'HONOURED MADAM,—My brother and I have seen your
advertisement, by chance, and beg leave to take the room
you offer. We are twenty-four years of age and twins.* We
are Italians by birth, but have lived long in the various
countries of Europe, and several years in the United States.
Our names are Luigi and Angelo Capello. You desire but one
guest; but, dear madam, if you will allow us to pay for two,
we will not <u>incommode</u> you. We shall be down Thursday.'

'Italians! How romantic! Just think, ma—there's never been
one in this town, and everybody will be dying to see them,
and they're all *ours*! Think of that!'

'Yes, I reckon they'll make a grand stir.'

'Oh, indeed they will! The whole town will be on its head!
Think—they've been in Europe and everywhere! There's
never been a traveller in this town before. Ma, I shouldn't
wonder if they've seen kings!'

'Well, a body can't tell; but they'll make stir enough,
without that.'

'Yes, that's of course. Luigi—Angelo. They're lovely names;
and so grand and foreign—not like Jones and Robinson and
such. Thursday they are coming, and this is only Tuesday;
it's a cruel long time to wait. Here comes Judge Driscoll in
at the gate. He's heard about it. I'll go and open the door.'

The Judge was full of congratulations and curiosity. The
letter was read and discussed. Soon Justice Robinson arrived
with more congratulations, and there was a new reading and
a new discussion. This was the beginning. Neighbour after
neighbour, of both sexes, followed, and the procession drifted
in and out all day and evening and all Wednesday and
Thursday. The letter was read and re-read until it was nearly
worn out; everybody admired its courtly and gracious tone,
and smooth and practised style, everybody was sympathetic
and excited, and the Coopers were steeped in happiness all
the while.

The boats were very uncertain in low water,* in these
primitive times. This time the Thursday boat had not arrived

at ten at night—so the people had waited at the landing all day for nothing; they were driven to their homes by a heavy storm without having had a view of the illustrious foreigners.

Eleven o'clock came; then twelve, and the Cooper house was the only one in the town that still had lights burning. The rain and thunder were booming yet, and the anxious family were still waiting, still hoping. At last there was a knock at the door and the family jumped to open it. Two negro men entered, each carrying a trunk, and proceeded upstairs toward the guest-room. Then entered the twins—the handsomest, the best dressed, the most distinguished-looking pair of young fellows the West* had ever seen. One was a little fairer than the other, but otherwise they were exact duplicates.

6

Let us endeavour so to live that when we come to die even the undertaker will be sorry.

—PUDD'NHEAD WILSON'S CALENDAR

Habit is habit, and not to be flung out of the window by any man, but coaxed downstairs a step at a time.

—PUDD'NHEAD WILSON'S CALENDAR

AT breakfast in the morning the twins' charm of manner and easy and polished bearing made speedy conquest of the family's good graces. All constraint and formality quickly disappeared, and the friendliest feeling succeeded. Aunt Patsy called them by their Christian names almost from the beginning. She was full of the keenest curiosity about them, and showed it; they responded by talking about themselves, which pleased her greatly. It presently appeared that in their early youth they had known poverty and hardship. As the talk wandered along the old lady watched for the right place to drop in a question or two concerning that matter, and when she found it she said to the blonde twin, who was now doing the biographies in his turn while the brunette one rested:

'If it ain't asking what I ought not to ask, Mr Angelo, how did you come to be so friendless and in such trouble when you were little? Do you mind telling? But don't if you do.'

'Oh, we don't mind at all, madam; in our case it was merely misfortune, and nobody's fault. Our parents were well to do, there in Italy, and we were their only child.* We were of the old Florentine nobility'—Rowena's heart gave a great bound, her nostrils expanded, and a fine light played in her eyes— 'and when the war* broke out my father was on the losing side and had to fly for his life. His estates were confiscated, his personal property seized, and there we were, in Germany, strangers, friendless, and in fact paupers. My brother and I were ten years old, and well educated for that age, very studious, very fond of our books, and well grounded in the German, French, Spanish, and English languages. Also, we were marvellous musical prodigies—if you will allow me to say it, it being only the truth.

'Our father survived his misfortunes only a month, our mother soon followed him, and we were alone in the world. Our parents could have made themselves comfortable by exhibiting us as a show, and they had many and large offers; but the thought revolted their pride, and they said they would starve and die first. But what they wouldn't consent to do we had to do without the formality of consent. We were seized for the debts occasioned by their illness and their funerals, and placed among the attractions of a cheap museum* in Berlin to earn the liquidation money. It took us two years to get out of that slavery. We travelled all about Germany, receiving no wages, and not even our keep. We had to exhibit for nothing, and beg our bread.

'Well, madam, the rest is not of much consequence. When we escaped from that slavery at twelve years of age, we were in some respects men. Experience had taught us some valuable things; among others, how to take care of ourselves, how to avoid and defeat sharks and sharpers, and how to conduct our own business for our own profit and without other people's help. We travelled everywhere—years and years—picking up smatterings of strange tongues, familiarising ourselves with strange sights and strange customs, accumulating an education of a wide and varied and curious sort. It was a pleasant life. We went to Venice—to London, Paris, Russia, India, China, Japan——'

At this point Nancy the slave woman thrust her head in at the door and exclaimed:

'Ole Missus, de house is plum' jam full o' people, en dey 's jes a-spi'lin' to see de gen'lemen!' She indicated the twins with a nod of her head, and tucked it back out of sight again.

It was a proud occasion for the widow, and she promised herself high satisfaction in showing off her fine foreign birds before her neighbours and friends—simple folk who had hardly ever seen a foreigner of any kind, and never one of any distinction or style. Yet her feeling was moderate indeed when contrasted with Rowena's. Rowena was in the clouds, she walked on air; this was to be the greatest day, the most romantic episode, in the colourless history of that dull country town. She was to be familiarly near the source of its glory and feel the full flood of it pour over her and about her; the other girls could only gaze and envy, not partake.

The widow was ready, Rowena was ready, so also were the foreigners.

The party moved along the hall, the twins in advance, and entered the open parlour door, whence issued a low hum of conversation. The twins took a position near the door, the widow stood at Luigi's side, Rowena stood beside Angelo, and the march-past and the introductions began. The widow was all smiles and contentment. She received the procession and passed it on to Rowena.

'Good mornin', Sister Cooper'—hand-shake.

'Good morning, Brother Higgins—Count Luigi Capello, Mr Higgins'—hand-shake, followed by a devouring stare and 'I'm glad to see ye,' on the part of Higgins, and a courteous inclination of the head and a pleasant 'Most happy!' on the part of Count Luigi.

'Good morning', Roweny'—hand-shake.

'Good morning, Mr. Higgins—present you to Count Angelo Capello.' Hand-shake, admiring stare, 'Glad to see ye,'—courteous nod, smily 'Most happy!' and Higgins passes on.

None of these visitors was at ease, but, being honest people, they didn't pretend to be. None of them had ever seen a person bearing a title of nobility before, and none had been expecting to see one now, consequently the title came upon them as a kind of pile-driving surprise, and caught them unprepared. A few tried to rise to the emergency, and got out an awkward 'My lord', or 'Your lordship', or something of that sort, but the great majority were overwhelmed by the unaccustomed word and its dim and awful associations with gilded courts and stately ceremony and anointed kingship, so they only fumbled through the hand-shake and passed on, speechless. Now and then, as happens at all receptions everywhere, a more than ordinarily friendly soul* blocked the procession and kept it waiting while he inquired how the brothers liked the village, and how long they were going to stay, and if their families were well, and dragged in the weather, and hoped it would get cooler soon, and all that sort of thing, so as to be able to say, when they got home, 'I had quite a long talk with them'; but nobody did or said anything of a regrettable kind, and so the great affair went through to the end in a creditable and satisfactory fashion.

General conversation followed, and the twins drifted about from group to group, talking easily and fluently and winning approval, compelling admiration and achieving favour from all. The widow followed their conquering march with a proud eye, and every now and then Rowena said to herself with deep satisfaction, 'And to think they are ours—all ours!'

There were no idle moments for mother or daughter. Eager inquiries concerning the twins were pouring into their enchanted ears all the time; each was the constant centre of a group of breathless listeners; each recognised that she knew now for the first time the real meaning of that great word Glory, and perceived the stupendous value of it, and understood why men in all ages had been willing to throw away meaner happinesses, treasure, life itself, to get a taste of its sublime and supreme joy. Napoleon and all his kind stood accounted for—and justified.

When Rowena had at last done all her duty by the people in the parlour, she went upstairs to satisfy the longings of an overflow-meeting there, for the parlour was not big enough to hold all the comers. Again she was besieged by eager questioners, and again she swam in sunset seas of glory.* When the forenoon was nearly gone, she recognised with a pang that this most splendid episode of her life was almost over, that nothing could prolong it, that nothing quite its equal could ever fall to her fortune again. But never mind, it was sufficient unto itself; the grand occasion had moved on an ascending scale from the start, and was a noble and memorable success. If the twins could but do some crowning act, now, to climax it, something unusual, something startling, something to concentrate upon themselves the company's loftiest admiration, something in the nature of an electric surprise——

Here a prodigious slam-banging broke out below, and everybody rushed down to see. It was the twins knocking out a classic four-handed piece on the piano in great style. Rowena was satisfied—satisfied down to the bottom of her heart.

The young strangers were kept long at the piano. The villagers were astonished and enchanted with the magnificence of their performance, and could not bear to have them stop. All the music that they had ever heard before seemed spiritless prentice-work and barren of grace or charm when compared with these intoxicating floods of melodious sound. They realised that for once in their lives they were hearing masters.

7

One of the most striking differences between a cat and a lie is that a cat has only nine lives.

—PUDD'NHEAD WILSON'S CALENDAR

THE company broke up reluctantly, and drifted toward their several homes, chatting with vivacity, and all agreeing that it would be many a long day before Dawson's Landing would see the equal of this one again. The twins had accepted several invitations while the reception was in progress, and had also volunteered to play some duets at an amateur entertainment for the benefit of a local charity. Society was eager to receive them to its bosom. Judge Driscoll had the good fortune to secure them for an immediate drive, and to be the first to display them in public. They entered his buggy with him, and were paraded down the main street, everybody flocking to the windows and sidewalks to see.

The Judge showed the strangers the new graveyard, and the gaol, and where the richest man lived, and the Freemasons' Hall, and the Methodist Church, and the Presbyterian Church, and where the Baptist Church was going to be when they got some money to build it with, and showed them the town hall and the slaughter-house, and got out the independent fire company in uniform and had them put out an imaginary fire; then he let them inspect the muskets of the militia company, and poured out an exhaustless stream of enthusiasm over all these splendours, and seemed very well satisfied with the responses he got, for the twins admired his admiration, and paid him back the best they could, though they could have done better if some fifteen or sixteen hundred thousand previous experiences of this sort in various countries had not already rubbed off a considerable part of the novelty of it.

The Judge laid himself hospitably out to make them have a good time, and if there was a defect anywhere it was not his fault. He told them a good many humorous anecdotes, and always forgot the nub, but they were always able to furnish it, for these yarns were of a pretty early vintage, and they had had many a rejuvenating pull at them before. And he told them all about his several dignities, and how he had held this and that and the other place of honour or profit, and had once been to the legislature, and was now president of the Society of Freethinkers. He said the society had been in existence four years, and already had two members, and was firmly established. He would call for the brothers in the evening if they would like to attend a meeting of it.

Accordingly he called for them, and on the way he told them all about Pudd'nhead Wilson, in order that they might get a favourable impression of him in advance, and be prepared to like him. This scheme succeeded—the favourable impression was achieved. Later it was confirmed and solidified when Wilson proposed that out of courtesy to the strangers the usual topics be put aside and the hour be devoted to conversation upon ordinary subjects and the cultivation of friendly relations and goodfellowship—a proposition which was put to vote and carried.

The hour passed quickly away in lively talk, and when it was ended the lonesome and neglected Wilson was richer by two friends than he had been when it began. He invited the twins to look in at his lodgings, presently, after disposing of an intervening engagement, and they accepted with pleasure.

Towards the middle of the evening they found themselves on the road to his house. Pudd'nhead was at home waiting for them, and putting in his time puzzling over a thing which had come under his notice that morning. The matter was this: He happened to be up very early—at dawn in fact; and he crossed the hall, which divided his cottage through the centre, and entered a room to get something there. The window of the room had no curtains, for that side of the house had long been unoccupied, and through this window he caught sight of something which surprised and interested him. It was a young woman—a young woman where properly no young woman belonged; for she was in Judge Driscoll's house, and in the bedroom over the Judge's private study or sitting-room. This was young Tom Driscoll's bedroom. He and the Judge, the Judge's widowed sister Mrs Pratt, and three negro servants were the only people who belonged in the house. Who, then, might this young lady be? The two houses were separated by an ordinary yard, with a low fence running back through its middle from the street in front to the lane in the rear. The distance was not great, and Wilson was able to see the girl very well, the window-shades of the room she was in being up, and the window also. The girl had on a neat and trim summer dress, patterned in broad stripes of pink and white, and her bonnet was equipped with a pink veil. She was practising steps, gaits, and attitudes, apparently; she was doing the thing gracefully, and was very much absorbed in her work. Who could she be, and how came she to be in young Tom Driscoll's room?

Wilson had quickly chosen a position from which he could watch the girl without running much risk of being seen by her, and he remained there hoping she would raise her veil and betray her face. But she disappointed him. After a matter of twenty minutes she disappeared, and although he stayed at his post half an hour longer, she came no more.

Toward noon he dropped in at the Judge's, and talked with Mrs Pratt about the great event of the day, the levee of the distinguished foreigners at Aunt Patsy Cooper's. He asked after her nephew Tom, and she said he was on his way home, and that she was expecting him to arrive a little before night; and added that she and the Judge were gratified to gather from his letters that he was conducting himself very nicely and credit-ably—at which Wilson winked to himself privately. Wilson did not ask if there was a new-comer in the house, but he asked questions that would have brought light-throwing answers as to that matter if Mrs Pratt had had any light to throw; so he went away satisfied that he knew of things that were going on in her house of which she herself was not aware.

He was now waiting for the twins, and still puzzling over the problem of who that girl might be, and how she happened to be in that young fellow's room at daybreak in the morning.

8

The holy passion of Friendship is of so sweet and steady and loyal and enduring a nature that it will last through a whole lifetime, if not asked to lend money.

—PUDD'NHEAD WILSON'S CALENDAR

Consider well the proportions of things. It is better to be a young June-bug than an old bird of paradise.

—PUDD'NHEAD WILSON'S CALENDAR

IT is necessary now to hunt up Roxy.

At the time she was set free and went away chamber-maiding, she was thirty-five. She got a berth as second chambermaid on a Cincinnati boat in the New Orleans trade, the *Grand Mogul.** A couple of trips made her wonted and easy-going at the work, and infatuated her with the stir and adventure and independence of steamboat life. Then she was promoted and became head chambermaid. She was a favourite with the officers, and exceedingly proud of their joking and friendly ways with her.

During eight years she served three parts of the year on that boat, and the winters on a Vicksburg packet.* But now for two months she had had rheumatism in her arms, and was obliged to let the wash-tub alone. So she resigned. But she was well fixed—rich, as she would have described it; for she had lived a steady life, and had banked four dollars every month in New Orleans as a provision for her old age. She said in the start that she had 'put shoes on one bar'footed nigger to tromple on her with', and that one mistake like that was enough; she would be independent of the human race thenceforth for evermore if hard work and economy could accomplish it. When the boat touched the levee at New Orleans she bade goodbye to her comrades on the *Grand Mogul* and moved her kit ashore.

But she was back in an hour. The bank had gone to smash and carried her four hundred dollars with it. She was a pauper, and homeless. Also disabled bodily, at least for the present. The officers were full of sympathy for her in her trouble, and made up a little purse for her. She resolved to go to her birthplace; she had friends there among the negroes, and the unfortunate always help the unfortunate, she was well aware of that; those lowly comrades of her youth would not let her starve.

She took the little local packet at Cairo, and now she was on the home-stretch. Time had worn away her bitterness against her son, and she was able to think of him with serenity. She put the vile side of him out of her mind, and dwelt only on recollections of his occasional acts of kindness to her. She gilded and otherwise decorated these, and made them very pleasant to contemplate. She began to long to see him. She would go and fawn upon him, slave-like—for this would have to be her attitude, of course—and maybe she would find that time had modified him, and that he would be glad to see his long-forgotten old nurse and treat her gently. That would be lovely; that would make her forget her woes and her poverty.

Her poverty! That thought inspired her to add another castle to her dream: maybe he would give her a trifle now and then—maybe a dollar, once a month, say; any little thing like that would help, oh, ever so much.

By the time she reached Dawson's Landing she was her old self again; her blues were gone, she was in high feather. She would get along, surely; there were many kitchens where the servants would share their meals with her, and also steal sugar and apples and other dainties for her to carry home—or give her a chance to pilfer them herself, which would answer just as well. And there was the church. She was a more rabid and devoted Methodist than ever, and her piety was no sham, but was strong and sincere. Yes, with plenty of creature comforts and her old place in the amen corner* in her possession again, she would be perfectly happy and at peace thenceforward to the end.

She went to Judge Driscoll's kitchen first of all. She was received there in great form and with vast enthusiasm. her wonderful travels, and the strange countries she had seen and the adventures she had had, made her a marvel, and a heroine of romance. The negroes hung enchanted upon the great story of her experiences, interrupting her all along with eager questions, with laughter, exclamations of delight and expressions of applause; and she was obliged to confess to herself that if there was anything better in this world than steam-boating, it was the glory to be got by telling about it. The audience loaded her stomach with their dinners and then stole the pantry bare to load up her basket.

Tom was in St Louis. The servants said he had spent the best part of his time there during the previous two years. Roxy came every day, and had many talks about the family and its affairs. Once she asked why Tom was away so much. The ostensible 'Chambers' said:

'De fac' is, ole marster kin git along better when young marster's away den he kin when he's in de town; yes, en he love him better, too; so he gives him fifty dollahs a month——'

'No, is dat so? Chambers, you's a jokin', ain't you?'

''Clah to goodness I ain't, mammy; Marse Tom tole me so his own self. But nemmine, 't ain't enough.'

'My lan', what de reason 't ain't enough?'

'Well, I 's gwine to tell you, if you gimme a chanst, mammy. De reason it ain't enough is 'ca'se Marse Tom gambles.'

Roxy threw up her hands in astonishment and Chambers went on:

'Ole marster found it out, 'ca'se he had to pay two hundred dollahs for Marse Tom's gamblin' debts, en dat's true, mammy, jes as dead certain as you's bawn.'

'Two—hund'd—dollahs! Why, what is you talkin' 'bout? Two—hund'd—dollahs. Sakes alive, it's 'most enough to buy a tol'able good secondhand nigger wid. En you ain't lying', honey?—you wouldn't lie to yo' ole mammy?'

'It's God's own truth, jes as I tell you—two hund'd dollahs—I wisht I may never stir outen my tracks if it ain't so. En, oh, my lan', ole Marse was jes a-hoppin'! he was b'ilin' mad, I tell you! He tuck 'n' dissenhurrit him.'

He licked his chops with relish after that stately word. Roxy struggled with it a moment, then gave it up and said:

'Dissen*whiched* him?'

'Dissenhurrit him.'

'What's dat? What do it mean?'

'Means he bu'sted de will.'

'Bu's—ted de will! He wouldn't *ever* treat him so! Take it back, you mis'able imitation nigger dat I bore in sorrow en tribbilation.'

Roxy's pet castle—an occasional dollar from Tom's pocket—was tumbling to ruin before her eyes. She could not abide such a disaster as that; she couldn't endure the thought of it. Her remark amused Chambers:

'Yah-yah-yah! jes listen to dat! If I's imitation, what is you? Bofe of us is imitation *white*—dat's what we is——en pow'ful good imitation too—yah-yah-yah!—we don't 'mount to noth'n' as imitation *niggers*; en as for——'

'Shet up yo' foolin', 'fo' I knock you side de head, en tell me 'bout de will. Tell me 'tain't bu'sted—do, honey, en I'll never forgit you.'

'Well, *'tain't*—'ca'se dey's a new one made, en Marse Tom's all right ag'in. But what is you in sich a sweat 'bout it for, mammy? 'Tain't none o' your business I don't reckon.'

' 'Tain't none o' my business? Whose business is it den, I'd like to know? Wuz I his mother tell he was fifteen years old, or wusn't I?—you answer me dat. En you speck I could see him turned out po' en ornery on de worl' en never care noth'n' 'bout it? I reckon if you'd ever be'n a mother yo'self, Valet de Chambers, you wouldn't talk sich foolishness as dat.'

'Well, den, ole Marse forgive him en fixed up de will ag'in—do dat satisfy you?'

Yes, she was satisfied now, and quite happy and sentimental over it. She kept coming daily, and at last she was told that Tom had come home. She began to tremble with emotion, and straightway sent to beg him to let his 'po' ole nigger mammy have jes one sight of him en die for joy'.

Tom was stretched at his lazy ease on a sofa when Chambers brought the petition. Time had not modified his ancient detestation of the humble drudge and protector of his boyhood; it was still bitter and uncompromising. He sat up and bent a severe gaze upon the fair face of the young fellow whose name he was unconsciously using and whose family rights he was enjoying. He maintained the gaze until the victim of it had become satisfactorily pallid with terror, then he said:

'What does the old rip want with me?'

The petition was meekly repeated.

'Who gave you permission to come and disturb me with the social attentions of niggers?'

Tom had risen. The other young man was trembling now, visibly. He saw what was coming, and bent his head sideways, and put up his left arm to shield it. Tom rained cuffs upon the head and its shield, saying no word: the victim received each blow with a beseeching 'Please, Marse Tom!—oh, please, Marse Tom!' Seven blows—then Tom said, 'Face the door—march!' He followed behind with one, two, three solid kicks. The last one helped the pure-white slave over the door sill, and he limped away mopping his eyes with his old ragged sleeve. Tom shouted after him, 'Send her in!'

Then he flung himself panting on the sofa again, and rasped out the remark, 'He arrived just at the right moment; I was full to the brim with bitter thinkings, and nobody to take it out of. How refreshing it was! I feel better.'

Tom's mother entered now, closing the door behind her, and approached her son with all the wheedling and suppli-cating servilities that fear and interest can impart to the words and attitudes of the born slave. She stopped a yard from her boy and made two or three admiring exclamations over his manly stature and general handsomeness, and Tom put an arm under his head and hoisted a leg over the sofa-back in order to look properly indifferent.

'My lan', how you is growed, honey! 'Clah to goodness, I wouldn't a-knowed you, Marse Tom! 'deed I wouldn't! Look at me good; does you 'member old Roxy?—does you know yo' old nigger mammy, honey? Well, now, I kin lay down en die in peace, 'ca'se I's seed——'

'Cut it short,—damn it,—cut it short! What is it you want?'

'You heah dat? Jes de same old Marse Tom, al'ays so gay and funnin' wid de ole mammy. I'uz jes as shore——'

'Cut it short, I tell you, and get along! What do you want?'

This was a bitter disappointment. Roxy had for so many days nourished and fondled and petted her notion that Tom would be glad to see his old nurse, and would make her proud and happy to the marrow with a cordial word or two, that it took two rebuffs to convince her that he was not funning, and that her beautiful dream was a fond and foolish vanity, a shabby and pitiful mistake. She was hurt to the heart, and so ashamed that for a moment she did not quite know what to do or how to act. Then her breast began to heave, the tears came, and in her forlornness she was moved to try that other dream of hers—an appeal to her boy's charity; and so, upon the impulse, and without reflection, she offered her supplication:

'Oh, Marse Tom, de po' ole mammy is in sich hard luck dese days; en she's kinder crippled in de arms en can't work, en if you could gimme a dollah—on'y jes one little dol——'

Tom was on his feet so suddenly that the supplicant was startled into a jump herself.

'A dollar!—give you a dollar! I've a notion to strangle you. Is *that* your errand here? Clear out! and be quick about it!'

Roxy backed slowly toward the door. When she was half-way she stopped, and said mournfully:

'Marse Tom, I nussed you when you was a little baby, en I raised you all by myself tell you was 'most a young man; en now you is young en rich, en I is po' en gitt'n' ole, en I come heah b'lievin' dat you would he'p de ole mammy 'long down de little road dat's lef' 'twix' her en de grave, en——'

Tom relished this tune less than any that had preceded it, for it began to wake up a sort of echo in his conscience; so he interrupted and said with decision, though without asperity, that he was not in a situation to help her, and wasn't going to do it.

'Ain't you ever gwine to he'p me, Marse Tom?'

'No! Now go away and don't bother me any more.'

Roxy's head was down, in an attitude of humility. But now the fires of her old wrongs flamed up in her breast and began to burn fiercely. She raised her head slowly, till it was well up, and at the same time her great frame unconsciously assumed an erect and masterful attitude, with all the majesty and grace of her vanished youth in it. She raised her finger and punctuated with it:

'You has said de word. You has had yo' chance, en you has trompled it under yo' foot. When you git another one, you'll git down on yo' knees en *beg* for it!'

A cold chill went to Tom's heart, he didn't know why; for

he did not reflect that such words, from such an incongruous source, and so solemnly delivered, could not easily fail of that effect. However, he did the natural thing: he replied with bluster and mockery:

'*You'll* give me a chance—*you!* Perhaps I'd better get down on my knees now! But in case I don't—just for argument's sake—what's going to happen, pray?'

'Dis is what is gwine to happen. I'se gwine as straight to yo' uncle as I kin walk, en tell him every las' thing I knows 'bout you.'

Tom's cheek blenched, and she saw it. Disturbing thoughts began to chase each other through his head. 'How can she know? And yet she must have found out—she looks it. I've had the will back only three months, and am already deep in debt again, and moving heaven and earth to save myself from exposure and destruction, with a reasonably fair show of getting the thing covered up if I'm let alone, and now this fiend has gone and found me out somehow or other. I wonder how much she knows? Oh, oh, oh, it's enough to break a body's heart! But I've got to humour her—there's no other way.'

Then he worked up a rather sickly sample of a gay laugh and a hollow chipperness of manner, and said:

'Well, well, Roxy dear, old friends like you and me mustn't quarrel. Here's your dollar—now tell me what you know.'

He held out the wild-cat bill; she stood as she was, and made no movement. It was her turn to scorn persuasive foolery now, and she did not waste it. She said, with a grim implacability in voice and manner which made Tom almost realise that even a former slave can remember for ten minutes insults and injuries returned for compliments and flatteries received, and can also enjoy taking revenge for them when the opportunity offers.

'What does I know? I'll tell you what I knows. I knows enough to bu'st dat will to flinders—en more, mind you, *more!*'

Tom was aghast.

'More?' he said. 'What do you call more? Where's there

any room for more?'

Roxy laughed a mocking laugh, and said scoffingly, with a toss of her head, and her hands on her hips:

'Yes!—oh, I reckon! *Co'se* you'd like to know—wid yo' po' little ole rag dollah. What you reckon I'se gwine to tell *you* for?—you ain't got no money. I'se gwine to tell yo' uncle—en I'll do it dis minute, too—he'll gimme *five* dollahs for de news, en mighty glad, too.'

She swung herself around disdainfully, and started away. Tom was in a panic. He seized her skirts, and implored her to wait. She turned and said, loftily:

'Look-a-heah, what 'uz it I tole you?'

'You—you—I don't remember anything. What was it you told me?'

'I tole you dat de next time I give you a chance you'd git down on yo' knees en beg for it.'

Tom was stupefied for a moment. He was panting with excitement. Then he said:

'Oh, Roxy, you wouldn't require your young master to do such a horrible thing. You can't mean it.'

'I'll let you know mighty quick whether I means it or not! You call me names, en as good as spit on me when I comes here po' en ornery en 'umble, to praise you for bein' growed up so fine en handsome, en tell you how I used to nuss you en tend you en watch you when you 'uz sick en hadn't no mother but me in de whole worl', en beg you to give de po' ole nigger a dollah for to git her sum'n' to eat, en you call me names—*names*, dad blame you! Yassir, I gives you jes one chance mo', and dat's *now*, en it las' on'y a half a second—you hear?'

Tom slumped to his knees and began to beg, saying:

'You see I'm begging, and it's honest begging, too! Now tell me, Roxy, tell me.'

The heir of two centuries of unatoned insult and outrage looked down on him and seemed to drink in deep draughts of satisfaction. Then she said:

'Fine nice young white gen'l'man kneelin' down to a nigger-wench! I'se wanted to see dat jes once befo' I'se called. Now,

Gabr'el, blow de hawn, I'se ready.... Git up!'

Tom did it. He said, humbly:

'Now, Roxy, don't punish me any more. I deserved what I've got, but be good and let me off with that. Don't go to uncle. Tell me—I'll give you the five dollars.'

'Yes, I bet you will; en you won't stop dah, nuther. But I ain't gwine to tell you heah——'

'Good gracious, no!'

'Is you 'feared o' de ha'nted house?'

'N—no.'

'Well, den, you come to de ha'nted house 'bout ten or 'leven to-night, en climb up de ladder, 'ca'se de sta'r-steps is broke down, en you'll fine me. I'se a-roostin' in de ha'nted house 'ca'se I can't 'ford to roos' nowher's else.' She started toward the door, but stopped and said, 'Gimme de dollah bill!' He gave it to her. She examined it and said, 'H'm—like enough de bank's bu'sted.' She started again, but halted again. 'Has you got any whisky?'

'Yes, a little.'

'Fetch it!'

He ran to his room overhead and brought down a bottle which was two-thirds full. She tilted it up and took a drink. Her eyes sparkled with satisfaction, and she tucked the bottle under her shawl, saying, 'It's prime. I'll take it along.'

Tom humbly held the door for her, and she marched out as grim and erect as a grenadier.

9

Why is it that we rejoice at a birth and grieve at a funeral? It is because we are not the person involved.

—PUDD'NHEAD WILSON'S CALENDAR

It is easy to find fault, if one has that disposition. There was once a man who, not being able to find any other fault with his coal, complained that there were too many prehistoric toads in it.

—PUDD'NHEAD WILSON'S CALENDAR

TOM flung himself on the sofa, and put his throbbing head in his hands, and rested his elbows on his knees. He rocked himself back and forth and moaned.

'I've knelt to a nigger-wench!' he muttered. 'I thought I had struck the deepest deeps of degradation before, but oh, dear, it was nothing to this.... Well, there is one consolation, such as it is—I've struck bottom this time; there's nothing lower.'

But that was a hasty conclusion.

At ten that night he climbed the ladder in the haunted house, pale, weak, and wretched. Roxy was standing in the door of one of the rooms, waiting, for she had heard him.

This was a two-storey log house which had acquired the reputation a few years before of being haunted, and that was the end of its usefulness. Nobody would live in it afterward, or go near it by night, and most people even gave it a wide berth in the daytime. As it had no competition, it was called *the* haunted house. It was getting crazy and ruinous, now, from long neglect. It stood three hundred yards beyond Pudd'nhead Wilson's house, with nothing between but vacancy. It was the last house in the town at that end.

Tom followed Roxy into the room. She had a pile of clean straw in the corner for a bed, some cheap but well-kept clothing was hanging on the wall, there was a tin lantern freckling the floor with little spots of light, and there were various soap- and candle-boxes scattered about, which served for chairs. The two sat down. Roxy said:

'Now den, I'll tell you straight off, en I'll begin to k'leck de money later on; I ain't in no hurry. What does you reckon I'se gwine to tell you?'

'Well, you—you—oh, Roxy, don't make it too hard for me! Come right out and tell me you've found out somehow what a shape I'm in on account of dissipation and foolishness.'

'Disposition en foolishness! *No*, sir, dat ain't it. Dat jist ain't nothin' at all, 'longside o' what *I* knows.'

Tom stared at her, and said:

'Why—Roxy, what do you mean?'

She rose, and gloomed above him like a Fate.

'I mean dis—en it's de Lord's truth. You ain't no more kin to ole Marse Driscoll den I is—*dat's* what I mean!' and her eyes flamed with triumph.

'What?'

'Yassir, en *dat* ain't all! You's a *nigger!*—*bawn* a nigger en a *slave!*—en you's a nigger en a slave dis minute; en if I opens my mouf ole Marse Driscoll 'll sell you down de river befo' you is two days older den what you is now.'

'It's a thundering lie, you miserable old blatherskite!'

'It ain't no lie, nuther. It's jes de truth, en nothin' *but* de truth, so he'p me. Yassir—you's my *son*——'

'You devil!'

'En dat po' boy dat you's be'n a-kickin' en a-cuffing to-day is Percy Driscoll's son en yo' *marster*——'

'You beast!'

'En *his* name's Tom Driscoll, en yo' name's Valet de Chambers, en you ain't *got* no fambly name, beca'se niggers don't *have* 'em!'

Tom sprang up and seized a billet of wood and raised it; but his mother only laughed at him, and said:

'Set down, you pup! Does you think you kin skyer me? It ain't in you, nor de likes of you. I reckon you'd shoot me in de back, maybe, if you got a chance, for dat's jist yo' style—*I* knows you, thoo en thoo—but I don't mind gitt'n' killed, beca'se all dis is down in writin', en it's in safe hands, too, en de man dat's got it knows whah to look for de right man when I gits killed. Oh, bless yo' soul, if you puts yo' mother up for as big a fool as *you* is, you's pow'ful mistaken, I kin tell you! Now den, you sit still en behave yo'self; en don't you git up ag'in till I tell you!'

Tom fretted and chafed awhile in a whirlwind of disorganising sensations and emotions, and finally said, with something like settled conviction:

'The whole thing is moonshine; now then, go ahead and do your worst; I'm done with you.'

Roxy made no answer. She took the lantern and started toward the door. Tom was in a cold panic in a moment.

'Come back, come back!' he wailed. 'I didn't mean it, Roxy; I take it all back, and I'll never say it again! Please come back, Roxy!'

The woman stood a moment, then she said gravely:

'Dah's one thing yo's got to stop, Valet de Chambers. You can't call me *Roxy*, same as if you was my equal. Chillen don't speak to dey mammies like dat. You'll call me ma or mammy, dat's what you'll call me—leastways when dey ain't nobody aroun'. *Say* it!'

It cost Tom a struggle, but he got it out.

'Dat's all right. Don't you ever forgit it ag'in, if you knows what's good for you. Now den, you has said you wouldn't ever call it lies en moonshine ag'in. I'll tell you dis, for a warnin': if you ever does say it ag'in, it's de *las'* time you'll ever say it to me; I'll tramp as straight to de Judge as I kin walk, en tell him who you is, en *prove* it. Does you b'lieve me when I says dat?'

'Oh,' groaned Tom, 'I more than believe it; I *know* it.'

Roxy knew her conquest was complete. She could have proved nothing to anybody, and her threat about the writings was a lie; but she knew the person she was dealing with, and had made both statements without any doubt as to the effect they would produce.

She went and sat down on her candle-box, and the pride and pomp of her victorious attitude made it a throne. She said:

'Now den, Chambers, we's gwine to talk business, en dey ain't gwine to be no mo' foolishness. In de fust place, you gits fifty dollahs a month; you's gwine to han' over half of it to yo' ma. Plank it out!'

But Tom had only six dollars in the world. He gave her that, and promised to start fair on next month's pension.

'Chambers, how much is you in debt?'

Tom shuddered, and said:

'Nearly three hundred dollars.'

'How is you gwine to pay it?'

Tom groaned out:

'Oh, I don't know; don't ask me such awful questions.'

But she stuck to her point until she wearied a confession out of him: he had been prowling about in disguise, stealing small valuables from private houses; in fact, had made a good deal of a raid on his fellow-villagers a fortnight before, when he was supposed to be in St Louis; but he doubted if he had sent away enough stuff to realise the required amount, and was afraid to make a further venture in the present excited state of the town. His mother approved of his conduct, and offered to help, but this frightened him. He tremblingly ventured to say that if she would retire from the town he should feel better and safer, and could hold his head higher— and was going on to make an argument, but she interrupted and surprised him pleasantly by saying she was ready; it didn't make any difference to her where she stayed, so that she got her share of the pension regularly. She said she would not go far, and would call at the haunted house once a month for her money. Then she said:

'I don't hate you so much now, but I've hated you a many a year—and anybody would. Didn't I change you off, en give you a good fambly en a good name, en made you a white gen'l'man en rich, wid store clothes on—en what did I git for it? You despised me all de time, en was al'ays sayin' mean hard things to me befo' folks, en wouldn't ever let me forgit I's a nigger—en—en——'

She fell to sobbing, and broke down. Tom said:

'But you know I didn't know you were my mother; and besides——'

'Well, nemmine 'bout dat, now; let it go. I'se gwine to fo'git it.' Then she added fiercely, 'En don't you ever make me remember it ag'in, or you'll be sorry, *I* tell you.'

When they were parting, Tom said, in the most persuasive way he could command:

'Ma, would you mind telling me who was my father?'

He had supposed he was asking an embarrassing question. He was mistaken. Roxy drew herself up with a proud toss of her head, and said:

'Does I mine tellin' you? No, dat I don't! You ain't got no 'casion to be shame' o' yo' father, *I* kin tell you. He wuz

de highest quality in dis whole town—ole Virginny stock.
Fust famblies, he wuz. Jes as good stock as de Driscolls en
de Howards, de bes' day dey ever seed.' She put on a little
prouder air, if possible, and added impressively: 'Does you
'member Cunnel Cecil Burleigh Essex, dat died de same year
yo' young Marse Tom Driscoll's pappy died, en all de Masons
en Odd Fellers en Churches turned out en give him de bigges'
funeral dis town ever seed? Dat's de man.'

Under the inspiration of her soaring complacency the
departed graces of her earlier days returned to her, and her
bearing took to itself a dignity and state that might have
passed for queenly if her surroundings had been a little more
in keeping with it.

'Dey ain't another nigger in dis town dat's as high-bawn
as you is. Now den, go 'long! En jes you hold yo' head up
as high as you want to—you has de right, en dat I kin swah.'

10

All say, 'How hard it is that we have to die'—a strange complaint to
come from the mouths of people who have had to live.
                                —PUDD'NHEAD WILSON'S CALENDAR

When angry, count four; when very angry, swear.
                                —PUDD'NHEAD WILSON'S CALENDAR

EVERY now and then, after Tom went to bed, he had sudden
wakings out of his sleep, and his first thought was, 'Oh, joy,
it was all a dream!' Then he laid himself heavily down again,
with a groan and the muttered words, 'A nigger! I am a
nigger! Oh, I wish I was dead!'

He woke at dawn with one more repetition of this horror,
and then he resolved to meddle no more with that treacher-
ous sleep. He began to think. Sufficiently bitter thinkings they
were. They wandered along something after this fashion:

'Why were niggers *and* whites made? What crime did the
uncreated first nigger commit that the curse of birth was
decreed for him? And why is this awful difference made

between white and black?... How hard the nigger's fate seems, this morning!—yet until last night such a thought never entered my head.'

He sighed and groaned an hour or more away. Then 'Chambers' came humbly in to say that breakfast was nearly ready. 'Tom' blushed scarlet to see this aristocratic white youth cringe to him, a nigger, and call him 'Young Marster'. He said roughly:

'Get out of my sight!' and when the youth was gone, he muttered: 'He has done me no harm, poor wretch, but he is an eyesore to me now, for he is Driscoll the young gentleman, and I am a—oh, I wish I was dead!'

A gigantic irruption, like that of Krakatoa* a few years ago, with the accompanying earthquakes, tidal waves, and clouds of volcanic dust, changes the face of the surrounding land-scape beyond recognition, bringing down the high lands, elevating the low, making fair lakes where deserts had been, and deserts where green prairies had smiled before. The tremendous catastrophe which had befallen Tom had changed his moral landscape in much the same way. Some of his low places he found lifted to ideals, some of his ideals had sunk to the valleys, and lay there with the sackcloth and ashes of pumice-stone and sulphur on their ruined heads.

For days he wandered in lonely places, thinking, thinking, thinking—trying to get his bearings. It was new work. If he met a friend, he found that the habit of a lifetime had in some mysterious way vanished—his arm hung limp, instead of involuntarily extending the hand for a shake. It was the 'nigger' in him asserting its humility, and he blushed and was abashed. And the 'nigger' in him was surprised when the white friend put out his hand for a shake with him. He found the 'nigger' in him involuntarily giving the road, on the sidewalk, to the white rowdy and loafer. When Rowena, the dearest thing his heart knew, the idol of his secret worship, invited him in, the 'nigger' in him made an embarrassed excuse and was afraid to enter and sit with the dread white folks on equal terms. The 'nigger' in him went shrinking and skulking here and there and yonder, and fancying it saw suspicion and maybe detection in all faces, tones, and gestures. So strange and uncharacteristic was Tom's conduct that people noticed it, and turned to look after him when he passed on; and when he glanced back—as he could not help doing, in spite of his best resistance—and caught that puzzled expression in a person's face, it gave him a sick feeling, and he took himself out of view as quickly as he could. He presently came to have a hunted sense and a hunted look, and then he fled away to the hill-tops and the solitudes. He said to himself that the curse of Ham* was upon him.

He dreaded his meals; the 'nigger' in him was ashamed to sit at the white folks' table, and feared discovery all the time; and once when Judge Driscoll said, 'What's the matter with you? You look as meek as a nigger,' he felt as secret murderers are said to feel when the accuser says, 'Thou art the man!' Tom said he was not well, and left the table.

His ostensible 'aunt's' solicitudes and endearments were become a terror to him, and he avoided them.

And all the time hatred of his ostensible 'uncle' was steadily growing in his heart; for he said to himself, 'He is white; and I am his chattel, his property, his goods, and he can sell me, just as he could his dog.'

For as much as a week after this Tom imagined that his character had undergone a pretty radical change. But that was because he did not know himself.

In several ways his opinions were totally changed, and would never go back to what they were before, but the main structure of his character was not changed and could not be changed. One or two very important features of it were altered, and in time effects would result from this if opportunity offered—effects of a quite serious nature too. Under the influence of a great mental and moral upheaval his character and habits had taken on the appearance of complete change, but after a while, with the subsidence of the storm both began to settle toward their former places. He dropped gradually back into his old frivolous and easy-going ways and conditions of feeling and manner of speech, and no familiar of his could have detected anything in him that differentiated him from the weak and careless Tom of other days.

The theft-raid which he had made upon the village turned out better than he had ventured to hope. It produced the sum necessary to pay his gaming-debts, and saved him from exposure to his uncle and another smashing of the will. He and his mother learned to like each other fairly well. She couldn't love him as yet, because there 'warn't nothing *to* him', as she expressed it, but her nature needed something or somebody to rule over, and he was better than nothing. Her strong character and aggressive and commanding ways compelled Tom's admiration in spite of the fact that he got more illustrations of them than he needed for his comfort. However, as a rule, her conversation was made up of racy tattle about the privacies of the chief families of the town (for she went harvesting among their kitchens every time she came to the village), and Tom enjoyed this. It was just in his line. She always collected her half of his pension punctually, and he was always at the haunted house to have a chat with her on these occasions. Every now and then she paid him a visit there on between-days also.

Occasionally he would run up to St Louis for a few weeks, and at last temptation caught him again. He won a lot of money, but lost it, and with it a deal more besides, which he promised to raise as soon as possible.

For this purpose he projected a new raid on his town. He never meddled with any other town, for he was afraid to venture into houses whose ins and outs he did not know and the habits of whose households he was not acquainted with. He arrived at the haunted house in disguise on the Wednesday before the advent of the twins—after writing his aunt Pratt that he would not arrive until two days later—and lay in hiding there with his mother until toward daylight Friday morning, when he went to his uncle's house and entered by the back way with his own key, and slipped up to his room, where he could have the use of mirror and toilet articles. He had a suit of girl's clothes with him in a bundle as a disguise for his raid, and was wearing a suit of his mother's clothing, with black gloves and veil. By dawn he was tricked out for his raid, but he caught a glimpse of Pudd'nhead Wilson through the window over the way, and knew that Pudd'nhead had caught a glimpse of him. So he entertained Wilson with some airs and graces and attitudes for a while, then stepped out of sight and resumed the other disguise, and by-and-by went out the back way and started down town to reconnoitre the scene of his intended labours.

But he was ill at ease. He had changed back to Roxy's dress, with the stoop of age added to the disguise, so that Wilson would not bother himself about a humble old woman leaving a neighbour's house by the back way in the early morning, in case he was still spying. But supposing Wilson had seen him leave, and had thought it suspicious, and had also followed him? The thought made Tom cold. He gave up the raid for the day, and hurried back to the haunted house by the obscurest route he knew. His mother was gone; but she came back by-and-by with the news of the grand reception at Patsy Cooper's, and soon persuaded him that the opportunity was like a special providence, it was so inviting and perfect. So he went raiding after all, and made a nice success of it while everybody was gone to Patsy Cooper's. Success gave him nerve and even actual intrepidity; insomuch, indeed, that after he had conveyed his harvest to his mother in a back alley he went to the reception himself, and added several of the valuables of that house to his takings.

After this long digression we have now arrived once more at the point where Pudd'nhead Wilson, while waiting for the arrival of the twins on that same Friday evening, sat puzzling over the strange apparition of that morning—a girl in young Tom Driscoll's bedroom; fretting, and guessing, and puzzling over it, and wondering who the shameless creature might be.

11

*There are three infallible ways of pleasing an author, and the three form
a rising scale of compliment: 1, to tell him you have read one of his
books; 2, to tell him you have read all of his books; 3, to ask him to
let you read the manuscript of his forthcoming book. No. 1 admits you
to his respect; No. 2 admits you to his admiration; No. 3 carries you
clear into his heart.*

—PUDD'NHEAD WILSON'S CALENDAR

As to the Adjective: when in doubt, strike it out.

—PUDD'NHEAD WILSON'S CALENDAR

THE twins arrived presently, and talk began. It flowed along
chattily and sociably, and under its influence the new friendship gathered ease and strength. Wilson got out his Calendar,
by request, and read a passage or two from it, which the
twins praised quite cordially. This pleased the author so much
that he complied gladly when they asked him to lend them
a batch of the work to read at home. In the course of their
wide travels they had found out that there are three sure
ways of pleasing an author; they were now working the best
of the three.

There was an interruption now. Young Tom Driscoll appeared and joined the party. He pretended to be seeing the
distinguished strangers for the first time when they rose to
shake hands; but this was only a blind, as he had already had
a glimpse of them at the reception, while robbing the house.
The twins made mental note that he was smooth-faced and
rather handsome, and smooth and undulatory in his movements—graceful, in fact. Angelo thought he had a good eye;
Luigi thought there was something veiled and sly about it.
Angelo thought he had a pleasant free-and-easy way of
talking; Luigi thought it was more so than was agreeable.
Angelo thought he was a sufficiently nice young man; Luigi
reserved his decision. Tom's first contribution to the conversation was a question which he had put to Wilson a hundred

times before. It was always cheerily and good-naturedly put, and always inflicted a little pang, for it touched a secret sore; but this time the pang was sharp, since strangers were present.

'Well, how does the law come on? Had a case yet?'

Wilson bit his lip, but answered, 'No—not yet,' with as much indifference as he could assume. Judge Driscoll had generously left the law feature out of the Wilson biography which he had furnished to the twins. Young Tom laughed pleasantly, and said:

'Wilson's a lawyer, gentlemen, but he doesn't practise now.'

The sarcasm bit, but Wilson kept himself under control, and said without passion:

'I don't practise, it is true. It is true that I have never had a case, and have had to earn a poor living for twenty years as an expert accountant in a town where I can't get hold of a set of books to untangle as often as I should like. But it is also true that I did fit myself well for the practice of the law. By the time I was your age, Tom, I had chosen a profession, and was soon competent to enter upon it.' Tom winced. 'I never got a chance to try my hand at it, and I may never get a chance; and yet if I ever do get it I shall be found ready, for I have kept up my law-studies all these years.'

'That's it; that's good grit! I like to see it. I've a notion to throw all my business your way. My business and your law-practice ought to make a pretty gay team, Dave,' and the young fellow laughed again.

'If you will throw——' Wilson had thought of the girl in Tom's bedroom, and was going to say, 'If you will throw the surreptitious and disreputable part of your business my way it may amount to something,' but thought better of it, and said: 'However, this matter doesn't fit well in a general conversation.'

'All right, we'll change the subject; I guess you were about to give me another dig, anyway, so I'm willing to change. How's the Awful Mystery flourishing these days? Wilson's got a scheme for driving plain window-glass out of the market by decorating it with greasy finger-marks, and getting rich by selling it at famine prices to the crowned heads over in Europe to outfit their palaces with. Fetch it out, Dave.'

Wilson brought three of his glass strips, and said,

'I get the subject to pass the fingers of his right hand through his hair, so as to get a little coating of the natural oil on them, and then press the balls of them on the glass. A fine and delicate print of the lines in the skin results, and is permanent if it doesn't come in contact with something able to rub it off. You begin, Tom.'

'Why, I think you took my finger-marks once or twice before.'

'Yes; but you were a little boy the last time, only about twelve years old.'

'That's so. Of course, I've changed entirely since then, and variety is what the crowned heads want, I guess.'

He passed his fingers through his crop of short hair, and pressed them one at a time on the glass. Angelo made a print of his fingers on another glass, and Luigi followed with a third. Wilson marked the glasses with names and date, and put them away. Tom gave one of his little laughs, and said:

'I thought I wouldn't say anything, but if variety is what you are after, you have wasted a piece of glass. The hand-print of one twin is the same as the hand-print of the fellow-twin.'

'Well, it's done now, and I like to have them both, anyway,' said Wilson, returning to his place.

'But look here, Dave,' said Tom, 'you used to tell people's fortunes, too, when you took their finger-marks. Dave's just an all-round genius—a genius of the first water, gentlemen; a great scientist running to seed here in this village, a prophet with the kind of honour that prophets generally get at home—for here they don't give shucks for his scientifics, and they call his skull a notion factory—hey, Dave, ain't it so? But never mind; he'll make his mark some day—finger-mark, you know—he-he! But really, you want to let him take a shy at your palms once; it's worth twice the price of admission, or your money's returned at the door. Why, he'll read your wrinkles as easy as a book, and not only tell you fifty or sixty things that's going to happen to you but fifty or sixty thousand that ain't. Come, Dave, show the gentlemen what an inspired Jack-at-all-science we've got in this town and don't know it.'

Wilson winced under this nagging and not very courteous chaff, and the twins suffered with him and for him. They rightly judged now that the best way to relieve him would be to take the thing in earnest and treat it with respect, ignoring Tom's rather overdone raillery; so Luigi said:

'We have seen something of palmistry in our wanderings, and know very well what astonishing things it can do. If it isn't a science, and one of the greatest of them, too, I don't know what it's other name ought to be. In the Orient——'

Tom looked surprised and incredulous. He said—

'That jugglery a science? But, really, you ain't serious, are you?'

'Yes, entirely so. Four years ago we had our hands read out to us as if our palms had been covered with print.'

'Well, do you mean to say there was actually anything in it?' asked Tom, his incredulity beginning to weaken a little.

'There was this much in it,' said Angelo: 'what was told us of our characters was minutely exact—we could not have bettered it ourselves. Next, two or three memorable things that had happened to us were laid bare—things which no one present but ourselves could have known about.'

'Why, it's rank sorcery!' exclaimed Tom, who was now becoming very much interested. 'And how did they make out with what was going to happen to you in the future?'

'On the whole, quite fairly,' said Luigi. 'Two or three of the most striking things foretold have happened since; much the most striking one of all happened within that same year. Some of the minor prophecies have come true; some of the minor and some of the major ones have not been fulfilled yet, and, of course, may never be—still, I should be more surprised if they failed to arrive than if they didn't.'

Tom was entirely sobered and profoundly impressed. He said, apologetically:

'Dave, I wasn't meaning to belittle that science; I was only chaffing—chattering, I reckon I'd better say. I wish you would look at their palms. Come, won't you?'

'Why, certainly, if you want me to; but you know I've had no chance to become an expert, and don't claim to be one. When a past event is somewhat prominently recorded in the palm I can generally detect that, but minor ones often escape me—not always, of course, but often—but I haven't much confidence in myself when it comes to reading the future. I am talking as if palmistry was a daily study with me, but that is not so. I haven't examined half a dozen hands in the last half-dozen years; you see, the people got to joking about it, and I stopped to let the talk die down. I'll tell you what we'll do, Count Luigi: I'll make a try at your past, and if I have any success there—no, on the whole, I'll let the future alone; that's really the affair of an expert.'

He took Luigi's hand. Tom said:

'Wait—don't look yet, Dave! Count Luigi, here's paper and pencil. Set down that thing that you said was the most striking one that was foretold to you, and happened less than a year afterward, and give it to me so I can see if Dave finds it in your hand.'

Luigi wrote a line privately, and folded up the piece of paper and handed it to Tom, saying—

'I'll tell you when to look at it, if he finds it.'

Wilson began to study Luigi's palm, tracing life-lines, heart-lines, head-lines, and so on, and noting carefully their relations with the cobweb of finer and more delicate marks and lines that enmeshed them on all sides; he felt of the fleshy cushion at the base of the thumb, and noted its shape; he felt of the fleshy side of the hand between the wrist and the base of the little finger, and noted its shape also; he painstakingly examined the fingers, observing their form, proportions, and natural manner of disposing themselves when in repose. All this process was watched by the three spectators with absorbing interest, their heads bent together over Luigi's palm, and nobody disturbing the stillness with a word. Wilson now entered upon a close survey of the palm again, and his revelations began.

He mapped out Luigi's character and disposition, his tastes, aversions, proclivities, ambitions, and eccentricities in a way which sometimes made Luigi wince and the others laugh, but both twins declared that the chart was artistically drawn and was correct.

Next, Wilson took up Luigi's history. He proceeded cautiously and with hesitation now, moving his fingers slowly along the great lines of the palm, and now and then halting it at a 'star' or some such landmark, and examining that neighbourhood minutely. He proclaimed one or two past events; Luigi confirmed his correctness, and the search went on. Presently Wilson glanced up suddenly with a surprised expression.

'Here is a record of an incident which you would perhaps not wish me to——'

'Bring it out,' said Luigi, good-naturedly; 'I promise you it sha'n't embarrass me.'

But Wilson still hesitated, and did not seem quite to know what to do. Then he said:

'I think it is too delicate a matter to—to—I believe I would rather write it or whisper it to you and let you decide for yourself whether you want it talked out or not.'

'That will answer,' said Luigi; 'write it.'

Wilson wrote something on a slip of paper and handed it to Luigi, who read it to himself and said to Tom:

'Unfold your slip and read it, Mr Driscoll.'

Tom read:

'*It was prophesied that I would kill a man. It came true before the year was out.*'

Tom added, 'Great Scott!'

Luigi handed Wilson's paper to Tom, and said:

'Now read this one.'

Tom read:

'*You have killed some one, but whether man, woman, or child, I do not make out.*'

'Cæsar's ghost!' commented Tom, with astonishment. 'It beats anything that was ever heard of! Why, a man's own hand is his deadliest enemy! Just think of that—a man's own hand keeps a record of the deepest and fatalest secrets of his life, and is treacherously ready to expose him to any black-magic stranger that comes along. But what do you let a person look at your hand for, with that awful thing printed in it?'

'Oh,' said Luigi, reposefully, 'I don't mind it. I killed the man for good reasons, and I don't regret it.'

'What were the reasons?'

'Well, he needed killing.'

'I'll tell you why he did it, since he won't say himself,' said Angelo, warmly. 'He did it to save my life, that's what he did it for. So it was a noble act, and not a thing to be hid in the dark.'

'So it was, so it was,' said Wilson; 'to do such a thing to save a brother's life is a great and fine action.'

'Now come,' said Luigi, 'it is very pleasant to hear you say these things, but for unselfishness, or heroism, or magnanimity, the circumstances won't stand scrutiny. You overlook one detail: suppose I hadn't saved Angelo's life, what would have become of mine? If I had let the man kill him, wouldn't he have killed me too? I saved my own life,* you see.'

'Yes, that is your way of talking,' said Angelo; 'but I know you—I don't believe you thought of yourself at all. I keep that weapon yet that Luigi killed the man with, and I'll show it to you some time. That incident makes it interesting, and it had a history before it came into Luigi's hands which adds to its interest. It was given to Luigi by a great Indian prince, the Gaikowar of Baroda,* and it had been in his family two or three centuries. It killed a good many disagreeable people who troubled that hearthstone at one time and another. It isn't much to look at, except that it isn't shaped like other knives, or dirks, or whatever it may be called. Here, I'll draw it for you.' He took a sheet of paper and made a rapid sketch. 'There it is—a broad and murderous blade, with edges like a razor for sharpness. The devices engraved on it are the ciphers or names of its long line of possessors. I had Luigi's name added in Roman letters myself with our coat of arms, as you see. You notice what a curious handle the thing has.

It is solid ivory, polished like a mirror, and is four or five inches long—round, and as thick as a large man's wrist, with the end squared off flat, for your thumb to rest on; for you grasp it, with your thumb resting on the blunt end—so—and lift it aloft and strike downwards. The Gaikowar showed us how the thing was done when he gave it to Luigi, and before that night was ended Luigi had used the knife, and the Gaikowar was a man short by reason of it. The sheath is magnificently ornamented with gems of great value. You will find the sheath more worth looking at than the knife itself, of course.'

Tom said to himself:

'It's lucky I came here. I would have sold that knife for a song; I supposed the jewels were glass.'

'But go on; don't stop,' said Wilson. 'Our curiosity is up now, to hear about the homicide. Tell us about that.'

'Well, briefly, the knife was to blame for that, all round. A native servant slipped into our room in the palace in the night, to kill us and steal the knife on account of the fortune incrusted on its sheath, without a doubt. Luigi had it under his pillow; we were in bed together. There was a dim night-light burning. I was asleep; but Luigi was awake, and he thought he detected a vague form nearing the bed. He slipped the knife out of the sheath and was ready and unembarrassed by hampering bed-clothes, for the weather was hot and we hadn't any. Suddenly that native rose at the bedside, and bent over me with his right hand lifted and a dirk in it aimed at my throat; but Luigi grabbed his wrist, pulled him downward, and drove his own knife into the man's neck. That is the whole story.'

Wilson and Tom drew deep breaths, and after some general chat about the tragedy, Pudd'nhead said, taking Tom's hand:

'Now, Tom, I've never had a look at your palms, as it happens; perhaps you've got some little questionable privacies that need—hel-lo!'

Tom had snatched away his hand, and was looking a good deal confused.

'Why, he's blushing!' said Luigi.

Tom darted an ugly look at him, and said sharply:

'Well, if I am, it ain't because I'm a murderer!' Luigi's dark face flushed, but before he could speak or move, Tom added with anxious haste: 'Oh, I beg a thousand pardons. I didn't mean that; it was out before I thought, and I'm very, very sorry—you must forgive me!'

Wilson came to the rescue, and smoothed things down as well as he could; and in fact was entirely successful as far as the twins were concerned, for they felt sorrier for the affront put upon him by his guest's outburst of ill-manners than for the insult offered to Luigi. But the success was not so pronounced with the offender. Tom tried to seem at his ease, and he went through the motions fairly well, but at bottom he felt resentful toward all the three witnesses of his exhibition; in fact, he felt so annoyed at them for having witnessed it and noticed it, that he almost forgot to feel annoyed at himself for placing it before them. However, something presently happened which made him almost comfortable, and brought him nearly back to a state of charity and friendliness. This was a little spat between the twins; not much of a spat, but still a spat; and before they got far with it they were in a decided condition of irritation with each other. Tom was charmed; so pleased, indeed, that he cautiously did what he could to increase the irritation while pretending to be actuated by more respectable motives. By his help the fire got warmed up to the blazing-point, and he might have had the happiness of seeing the flames show up in another moment, but for the interruption of a knock on the door—an interruption which fretted him as much as it gratified Wilson. Wilson opened the door.

The visitor was a good-natured, ignorant, energetic, middle-aged Irishman named John Buckstone, who was a great politician in a small way, and always took a large share in public matters of every sort. One of the town's chief excitements, just now, was over the matter of rum. There was a strong rum party and a strong anti-rum party. Buckstone was training with the rum party, and he had been sent to hunt up the twins and invite them to attend a mass-meeting of that faction. He delivered his errand, and said the clans were already gathering in the big hall over the market-house. Luigi accepted the invitation cordially, Angelo less cordially, since he disliked crowds, and did not drink the powerful intoxicants of America.* In fact, he was even a teetotaler sometimes— when it was judicious to be one.

The twins left with Buckstone, and Tom Driscoll joined company with them uninvited.

In the distance one could see a long wavering line of torches drifting down the main street, and could hear the throbbing of the bass drum, the clash of cymbals, the squeaking of a fife or two, and the faint roar of remote hurrahs. The tail-end of this procession was climbing the market-house stairs when the twins arrived in its neighbour-hood; when they reached the hall it was full of people, torches, smoke, noise, and enthusiasm. They were conducted to the platform by Buckstone—Tom Driscoll still following— and were delivered to the chairman in the midst of a prodigious explosion of welcome. When the noise had moderated a little, the chair proposed that 'our illustrious guests be at once elected, by complimentary acclamation, to membership in our ever-glorious organisation, the paradise of the free, and the perdition of the slave.'

This eloquent discharge opened the floodgates of enthusi-asm again, and the election was carried with thundering unanimity. Then arose a storm of cries:

'Wet them down! Wet them down! Give them a drink!'

Glasses of whisky were handed to the twins. Luigi waved his aloft, then brought it to his lips; but Angelo set his down. There was another storm of cries:

'What's the matter with the other one?' 'What is the blonde one going back on us for?' 'Explain! Explain!'

The chairman inquired and then reported:

'We have made an unfortunate mistake, gentlemen. I find that the Count Angelo Capello is opposed to our creed—is a teetotaler, in fact, and was not intending to apply for membership with us. He desires that we reconsider the vote by which he was elected. What is the pleasure of the house?'

There was a general burst of laughter, plentifully accented with whistlings and cat-calls, but the energetic use of the gavel presently restored something like order. Then a man spoke from the crowd, and said that while he was very sorry that the mistake had been made, it would not be possible to rectify it at the present meeting. According to the by-laws it must go over to the next regular meeting for action. He would not offer a motion, as none was required. He desired to apologise to the gentleman in the name of the house, and begged to assure him that, as far as it might lie in the power of the Sons of Liberty, his temporary membership in the order would be made pleasant to him.

This speech was received with great applause, mixed with cries of—

'That's the talk!' 'He's a good fellow, anyway, if he *is* a teetotaler!' 'Drink his health!' 'Give him a rouser, and no heel-taps!'*

Glasses were handed round, and everybody on the platform drank Angelo's health, while the house bellowed forth in song:

> *For he's a jolly good fel-low,*
> *For he's a jolly good fel-low,*
> *For he's a jolly good fe-el-low,*
> *Which nobody can deny.*

Tom Driscoll drank. It was his second glass, for he had drunk Angelo's the moment that Angelo had set it down. The two drinks made him very merry—almost idiotically so—and he began to take a most lively and prominent part in the proceedings, particularly in the music and cat-calls and side-remarks.

The chairman was still standing at the front, the twins at his side. The extraordinarily close resemblance of the brothers to each other suggested a witticism to Tom Driscoll, and just as the chairman began a speech he skipped forward and said with an air of tipsy confidence to the audience:

'Boys, I move that he keeps still and lets this human philopena snip* you out a speech.'

The descriptive aptness of the phrase caught the house, and a mighty burst of laughter followed.

Luigi's southern blood leaped to the boiling-point in a moment under the sharp humiliation of this insult delivered in the presence of four hundred strangers. It was not in the young man's nature to let the matter pass, or to delay the squaring of the account. He took a couple of strides and halted behind the unsuspecting joker. Then he drew back and delivered a kick of such titanic vigour that it lifted Tom clear over the footlights and landed him on the heads of the front row of the Sons of Liberty.

Even a sober person does not like to have a human being emptied on him when he is not doing any harm; a person who is not sober cannot endure such an attention at all. The nest of Sons of Liberty that Driscoll landed in had not a sober bird in it: in fact, there was probably not an entirely sober one in the auditorium. Driscoll was promptly and indignantly flung on to the heads of Sons in the next row, and these Sons passed him on toward the rear, and then immediately began to pummel the front-row Sons who had passed him to them. This course was strictly followed by bench after bench as Driscoll travelled in his tumultuous and airy flight toward the door; so he left behind him an ever lengthening wake of raging and plunging and fighting and swearing humanity. Down went group after group of torches, and presently above the deafening clatter of the gavel, roar of angry voices, and crash of succumbing benches, rose the paralysing cry of—'FIRE!'

The fighting ceased instantly; the cursing ceased; for one distinctly defined moment there was a dead hush, a motionless calm, where the tempest had been; then with one impulse the multitude awoke to life and energy again, and went surging and struggling and swaying this way and that, its outer edges melting away through windows and doors, and gradually lessening the pressure and relieving the mass.

The fire-boys were never on hand so suddenly before; for there was no distance to go, this time, their quarters being in the rear end of the market-house. There was an engine company and a hook-and-ladder company. Half of each was composed of rummies and the other half of anti-rummies, after the moral and political share-and-share-alike fashion of the frontier town of the period. Enough anti-rummies were loafing in quarters to man the engine and the ladders. In two minutes they had their red shirts and helmets on—they never stirred officially in unofficial costume—and as the mass meeting overhead smashed through the long row of windows and poured out upon the roof of the arcade, the deliverers were ready for them with a powerful stream of water, which washed some of them off the roof and nearly drowned the rest. But water was preferable to fire, and still the stampede from the windows continued, and still the pitiless drenchings assailed it until the building was empty; then the fire-boys mounted to the hall and flooded it with water enough to annihilate forty times as much fire as there was there; for a village fire-company does not often get a chance to show off, and so when it does get a chance it makes the most of it. Such citizens of that village as were of a thoughtful and judicious temperament did not insure against fire; they insured against the fire-company.

12

Courage is resistance to fear, mastery of fear—not absence of fear. Except a creature be part coward it is not a compliment to say it is brave; it is merely a loose misapplication of the word. Consider the flea!—incomparably the bravest of all the creatures of God, if ignorance of fear were courage. Whether you are asleep or awake he will attack you, caring nothing for the fact that in bulk and strength you are to him as are the massed armies of the earth to a sucking child; he lives both day and night and all days and nights in the very lap of peril and the immediate presence of death, and yet is no more afraid than is the man who walks the streets of a city that was threatened by an earthquake ten centuries before. When we speak of Clive, Nelson, and Putnam as men who 'didn't know what fear was', we ought always to add the flea—and put him at the head of the procession.

—PUDD'NHEAD WILSON'S CALENDAR

JUDGE DRISCOLL was in bed and asleep by ten o'clock on Friday night, and he was up and gone a-fishing before daylight in the morning with his friend Pembroke Howard. These two had been boys together in Virginia when the State still ranked as the chief and most imposing member of the Union, and they still coupled the proud and affectionate adjective 'Old' with her name when they spoke of her. In Missouri a recognised superiority attached to any person who hailed from Old Virginia;* and this superiority was exalted to supremacy when a person of such nativity could also prove descent from the First Families of that great commonwealth. The Howards and Driscolls were of this aristocracy. In their eyes it was a nobility. It had its unwritten laws, and they were as clearly defined and as strict as any that could be found among the printed statutes of the land. The F. F. V. was born a gentleman; his highest duty in life was to watch over that great inheritance and keep it unsmirched. He must keep his honour spotless. Those laws were his chart; his course was marked out on it; if he swerved from it by so much as half a point of the compass it meant shipwreck to his honour; that is to say, degradation from his rank as a gentleman. These laws required certain things of him which his religion might forbid: then his religion must yield—the laws could not be relaxed to accommodate religion or anything else. Honour stood first; and the laws defined what it was and wherein it differed in certain details from honour as defined by church creeds and by the social laws and customs of some of the minor divisions of the globe that had got crowded out when the sacred boundaries of Virginia were staked out.

If Judge Driscoll was the recognised first citizen of Dawson's Landing, Pembroke Howard was easily its recognised second citizen. He was called 'the great lawyer'—an earned title. He and Driscoll were of the same age—a year or two past sixty.

Although Driscoll was a Freethinker and Howard a strong and determined Presbyterian, their warm intimacy suffered no impairment in consequence. They were men whose opinions were their own property and not subject to revision and amendment, suggestion or criticism, by anybody, even their friends.

The day's fishing finished, they came floating down stream in their skiff, talking national politics and other high matters, and presently met a skiff coming up from town, with a man in it, who said:

'I reckon you know one of the new twins gave your nephew a kicking last night, Judge?'

'Did *what*?'

'Gave him a kicking.'

The old Judge's lips paled, and his eyes began to flame. He choked with anger for a moment, then he got out what he was trying to say.

'Well—well—go on! Give me the details.'

The man did it. At the finish the Judge was silent a minute, turning over in his mind the shameful picture of Tom's flight over the footlights; then he said, as if musing aloud:

'H'm—I don't understand it. I was asleep at home. He didn't wake me. Thought he was competent to manage his affair without my help, I reckon.' His face lit up with pride and pleasure at that thought, and he said with a cheery complacency, 'I like that—it's the true old blood—hey, Pembroke?'

Howard smiled an iron smile, and nodded his head approvingly. Then the news-bringer spoke again.

'But Tom beat the twin on the trial.'

The Judge looked at the man wonderingly, and said:

'The trial? What trial?'

'Why, Tom had him up before Judge Robinson for assault and battery.'

The old man shrank suddenly together like one who has received a death-stroke. Howard sprang for him as he sank forward in a swoon, and took him in his arms, and bedded him on his back in the boat. He sprinkled water in his face, and said to the startled visitor:

'Go, now—don't let him come to and find you here. You see what an effect your heedless speech has had; you ought to have been more considerate than to blurt out such a cruel piece of slander as that.'

'I'm right down sorry I did it now, Mr Howard, and I wouldn't have done it if I had thought: but it ain't a slander; it's perfectly true, just as I told him.'

He rowed away. Presently the old Judge came out of his faint and looked up piteously into the sympathetic face that was bent over him.

'Say it ain't true, Pembroke; tell me it ain't true!' he said in a weak voice.

There was nothing weak in the deep organ-tones that responded:

'You know it's a lie as well as I do, old friend. He is of the best blood of the Old Dominion.'

'God bless you for saying it!' said the old gentleman fervently. 'Ah, Pembroke, it was such a blow!'

Howard stayed by his friend, and saw him home, and entered the house with him. It was dark, and past supper-time, but the Judge was not thinking of supper; he was eager to hear the slander refuted from head-quarters, and as eager to have Howard hear it too. Tom was sent for, and he came immediately. He was bruised and lame, and was not a happy-looking object. His uncle made him sit down, and said:

'We have been hearing about your adventure, Tom, with a handsome lie added to it for embellishment. Now pulverise that lie to dust! What measures have you taken? How does the thing stand?'

Tom answered guilelessly: 'It don't stand at all; it's all over. I had him up in court and beat him. Pudd'nhead Wilson defended him—first case he ever had, and lost it. The Judge fined the miserable hound five dollars for the assault.'

Howard and the Judge sprang to their feet with the opening sentence—why, neither knew; then they stood gazing vacantly at each other. Howard stood a moment, then sat mournfully down without saying anything. The Judge's wrath began to kindle, and he burst out:

'You cur! You scum! You vermin! Do you mean to tell me that blood of my race has suffered a blow and crawled to a court of law about it? Answer me!'

Tom's head drooped, and he answered with an eloquent silence. His uncle stared at him with a mixed expression of amazement and shame and incredulity that was sorrowful to see. At last he said:

'Which of the twins was it?'

'Count Luigi.'

'You have challenged him?'*

'N—no,' hesitated Tom, turning pale.

'You will challenge him to-night. Howard will carry it.'

Tom began to turn sick, and to show it. He turned his hat round and round in his hand, his uncle glowering blacker and blacker upon him as the heavy seconds drifted by; then at last he began to stammer, and said piteously:

'Oh, please don't ask me to do it, uncle! I never could. He is a murderous devil. I—I'm afraid of him!'

Old Driscoll's mouth opened and closed three times before he could get it to perform its office; then he stormed out:

'A coward in my family! A Driscoll a coward! Oh, what have I done to deserve this infamy!' He tottered to his secretary in the corner repeating that lament again and again in heartbreaking tones, and got out of a drawer a paper, which he slowly tore to bits, scattering the bits absently in his track as he walked up and down the room, still grieving and lamenting. At last he said:

'There it is, shreds and fragments once more—my will. Once more you have forced me to disinherit you, you base son of a most noble father! Leave my sight! Go—before I spit on you!'

The young man did not tarry. Then the Judge turned to Howard:

'You will be my second, old friend?'

'Of course.'

'There is pen and paper. Draft the cartel,* and lose no time.'

'The Count shall have it in his hands in fifteen minutes,' said Howard.

Tom was very heavy-hearted. His appetite was gone with his property and his self-respect. He went out the back way and wandered down the obscure lane grieving, and wondering if any course of future conduct, however discreet and carefully perfected and watched over, could win back his uncle's favour and persuade him to reconstruct once more that generous will which had just gone to ruin before his eyes. He finally concluded that it could. He said to himself that he had accomplished this sort of triumph once already, and that what had been done once could be done again. He would set about it. He would bend every energy to the task, and he would score that triumph once more, cost what it might to his convenience, limit as it might his frivolous and liberty-loving life.

'To begin,' he said to himself, 'I'll square up with the proceeds of my raid, and then gambling has got to be stopped—and stopped short off. It's the worst vice I've got—from my standpoint, anyway, because it's the one he can most easily find out, through the impatience of my creditors. He thought it expensive to have to pay two hundred dollars to them for me once. Expensive—*that*! Why, it cost me the whole of his fortune—but of course he never thought of that; some people can't think of any but their own side of a case. If he had known how deep I am in, now, the will would have gone to pot without waiting for a duel to help. Three hundred dollars! It's a pile! But he'll never hear of it, I'm thankful to say. The minute I've cleared it off, I'm safe; and I'll never touch a card again. Anyway, I won't while he lives, I make oath to that. I'm entering on my last reform—I know it—yes, and I'll win; but after that, if I ever slip again I'm gone.'

13

When I reflect upon the number of disagreeable people who I know have gone to a better world, I am moved to lead a different life.

—PUDD'NHEAD WILSON'S CALENDAR

October. This is one of the peculiarly dangerous months to speculate in stocks in. The others are July, January, September, April, November, May, March, June, December, August, and February.
—PUDD'NHEAD WILSON'S CALENDAR

THUS mournfully communing with himself Tom moped along the lane past Pudd'nhead Wilson's house, and still on and on between fences inclosing vacant country on each hand till he neared the haunted house, then he came moping back again, with many sighs and heavy with trouble. He sorely wanted cheerful company. Rowena! His heart gave a bound at the thought, but the next thought quieted it—the detested twins would be there.

He was on the inhabited side of Wilson's house, and now as he approached it he noticed that the sitting-room was lighted. This would do; others made him feel unwelcome sometimes, but Wilson never failed in courtesy toward him, and a kindly courtesy does at least save one's feelings, even if it is not professing to stand for a welcome. Wilson heard footsteps at his threshold, then the clearing of a throat.

'It's that fickle-tempered, dissipated young goose—poor devil, he finds friends pretty scarce to-day, likely, after the disgrace of carrying a personal-assault case into a law-court.'

A dejected knock. 'Come in!'

Tom entered, and drooped into a chair, without saying anything. Wilson said kindly:

'Why, my boy, you look desolate. Don't take it so hard. Try and forget you have been kicked.'

'Oh, dear,' said Tom, wretchedly, 'it's not that, Pudd'nhead—it's not that. It's a thousand times worse than that—oh, yes, a million times worse.'

'Why, Tom, what do you mean? Has Rowena——'

'Flung me? No, but the old man has.'

Wilson said to himself, 'Aha!' and thought of the mysterious girl in the bedroom. 'The Driscolls have been making discoveries!' Then he said aloud, gravely:

'Tom, there are some kinds of dissipation which——'

'Oh, shucks, this hasn't got anything to do with dissipation. He wanted me to challenge that derned Italian savage, and I wouldn't do it.'

'Yes, of course he would do that,' said Wilson in a meditative matter-of-course way; 'but the thing that puzzled me was, why he didn't look to that last night, for one thing, and why he let you carry such a matter into a court of law at all, either before the duel or after it. It's no place for it. It was not like him. I couldn't understand it. How did it happen?'

'It happened because he didn't know anything about it. He was asleep when I got home last night.'

'And you didn't wake him? Tom, is that possible?'

Tom was not getting much comfort here. He fidgeted a moment, then said:

'I didn't choose to tell him—that's all. He was going a-fishing before dawn, with Pembroke Howard, and if I got the twins into the common calaboose—and I thought sure I could—I never dreamed of their slipping out on a paltry fine for such an outrageous offence—well, once in the calaboose they would be disgraced, and uncle wouldn't want any duels with that sort of characters, and wouldn't allow any.'

'Tom, I am ashamed of you! I don't see how you could treat your good old uncle so. I am a better friend of his than you are; for if I had known the circumstances I would have kept that case out of court until I got word to him and let him have a gentleman's chance.'

'You would?' exclaimed Tom, with lively surprise. 'And it your first case! And you know perfectly well there never would have *been* any case if he had got that chance, don't you? And you'd have finished your days a pauper nobody, instead of being an actually launched and recognised lawyer to-day. And you would really have done that, would you?'

'Certainly.'

Tom looked at him a moment or two, then shook his head sorrowfully and said:

'I believe you—upon my word I do. I don't know why I do, but I do. Pudd'nhead Wilson, I think you're the biggest fool I ever saw.'

'Thank you.'

'Don't mention it.'

'Well, he has been requiring you to fight the Italian and you have refused. You degenerate remnant of an honourable line! I'm thoroughly ashamed of you, Tom!'

'Oh, that's nothing! I don't care for anything, now that the will's torn up again.'

'Tom, tell me squarely—didn't he find any fault with you for anything but those two things—carrying the case into court and refusing to fight?'

He watched the young fellow's face narrowly, but it was entirely reposeful, and so also was the voice that answered:

'No, he didn't find any other fault with me. If he had had any to find, he would have begun yesterday, for he was just in the humour for it. He drove that jack-pair* around town and showed them the sights, and when he came home he couldn't find his father's old silver watch that don't keep time and he thinks so much of, and couldn't remember what he did with it three of four days ago when he saw it last; and so when I arrived he was all in a sweat about it, and when I suggested that it probably wasn't lost but stolen, it put him in a regular passion and he said I was a fool—which convinced me, without any trouble, that that was just what he was afraid *had* happened, himself, but did not want to believe it, because lost things stand a better chance of being found again than stolen ones.'

'Whe-ew!' whistled Wilson; 'score another on the list.'

'Another what?'

'Another theft!'

'Theft?'

'Yes, theft. That watch isn't lost, it's stolen. There's been another raid on the town—and just the same old mysterious sort of thing that has happened once before, as you remember.'

'You don't mean it!'

'It's as sure as you are born! Have you missed anything yourself?'

'No. That is, I did miss a silver pencil-case that Aunt Mary Pratt gave me last birthday——'

'You'll find it's stolen—that's what you'll find.'

'No, I sha'n't; for when I suggested theft about the watch, and got such a rap, I went and examined my room, and the pencil-case was missing, but it was only mislaid, and I found it again.'

'You are sure you missed nothing else?'

'Well, nothing of consequence. I missed a small plain gold ring worth two or three dollars, but that will turn up. I'll look again.'

'In my opinion you'll not find it. There's been a raid, I tell you. Come *in*!'

Mr Justice Robinson entered, followed by Buckstone and the town-constable, Jim Blake. They sat down, and after some wandering and aimless weather-conversation Wilson said:

'By the way, we've just added another to the list of thefts, maybe two. Judge Driscoll's old silver watch is gone, and Tom here has missed a gold ring.'

'Well, it is a bad business,' said the Justice, 'and gets worse the further it goes. The Hankses, the Dobsons, the Pilligrews, the Ortons, the Grangers, the Hales, the Fullers, the Holcombs, in fact everybody that lives around about Patsy Cooper's has been robbed of little things like trinkets and teaspoons and suchlike small valuables that are easily carried off. It's perfectly plain that the thief took advantage of the reception at Patsy Cooper's, when all the neighbours were in her house and all their niggers hanging around her fence for a look at the show, to raid the vacant houses undisturbed. Patsy is miserable about it; miserable on account of the neighbours, and particularly miserable on account of her foreigners, of course; so miserable on their account that she hasn't any room to worry about her own little losses.'

'It's the same old raider,' said Wilson. 'I suppose there isn't any doubt about that.'

'Constable Blake doesn't think so.'

'No, you're wrong there,' said Blake; 'the other times it was a man; there was plenty of signs of that, as we know, in the profession, though we never got hands on him; but this time it's a woman.'

Wilson thought of the mysterious girl straight off. She was always in his mind now. But she failed him again. Blake continued:

'She's a stoop-shouldered old woman with a covered basket on her arm, in a black veil, dressed in mourning. I saw her going aboard the ferry-boat yesterday. Lives in Illinois, I reckon; but I don't care where she lives, I'm going to get her—she can make herself sure of that.'

'What makes you think she's the thief?'

'Well, there ain't any other, for one thing; and for another, some of the nigger draymen that happened to be driving along saw her coming out of or going into houses, and told me so—and it just happens that they was *robbed* houses, every time.'

It was granted that this was plenty good enough circumstantial evidence. A pensive silence followed, which lasted some moments, then Wilson said:

'There's one good thing, anyway. She can't either pawn or sell Count Luigi's costly Indian dagger.'

'My!' said Tom, 'is *that* gone?'

'Yes.'

'Well, that was a haul! But why can't she pawn it or sell it?'

'Because when the twins went home from the Sons of Liberty meeting last night, news of the raid was sifting in from everywhere, and Aunt Patsy was in distress to know if they had lost anything. They found that the dagger was gone, and they notified the police and pawnbrokers everywhere. It was a great haul, yes, but the old woman won't get anything out of it, because she'll get caught.'

'Did they offer a reward?' asked Buckstone.

'Yes; five hundred dollars for the knife, and five hundred more for the thief.'

'What a leather-headed idea!' exclaimed the constable. 'The thief da'sn't go near them, nor send anybody. Whoever goes is going to get himself nabbed, for there ain't any pawnbroker that's going to lose the chance to——'

If anybody had noticed Tom's face at that time, the grey-green colour of it might have provoked curiosity; but nobody did. He said to himself: 'I'm gone! I never can square up; the rest of the plunder won't pawn or sell for half of the bill. Oh, I know it—I'm gone, I'm gone—and this time it's for good. Oh, this is awful—I don't know what to do, nor which way to turn!'

'Softly, softly,' said Wilson to Blake. 'I planned their scheme for them at midnight last night, and it was all finished up shipshape by two this morning. They'll get their dagger back, and then I'll explain to you how the thing was done.'

There were strong signs of a general curiosity, and Buckstone said:

'Well, you have whetted us up pretty sharp, Wilson, and I'm free to say that if you don't mind telling us in confidence——'

'Oh, I'd as soon tell as not, Buckstone, but as long as the twins and I agree to say nothing about it, we must let it stand so. But you can take my word for it you won't be kept waiting three days. Somebody will apply for that reward pretty promptly, and I'll show you the thief and the dagger both very soon afterward.'

The constable was disappointed, and also perplexed. He said:

'It may all be—yes, and I hope it will, but I'm blamed if I can see my way through it. It's too many for yours truly.'

The subject seemed about talked out. Nobody seemed to have anything further to offer. After a silence the justice of the peace informed Wilson that he and Buckstone and the constable had come as a committee, on the part of the Democratic party, to ask him to run for mayor—for the little town was about to become a city and the first charter election was approaching. It was the first attention which Wilson had ever received at the hands of any party; it was a sufficiently humble one, but it was a recognition of his *début* into the town's life and activities at last; it was a step upward, and he was deeply gratified. He accepted, and the committee departed, followed by young Tom.

14

The true Southern watermelon is a boon apart, and not to be mentioned
with commoner things. It is chief of this world's luxuries, king by the
grace of God over all the fruits of the earth. When one has tasted it,
he knows what the angels eat. It was not a Southern watermelon that
Eve took: we know it because she repented.

—PUDD'NHEAD WILSON'S CALENDAR

ABOUT the time that Wilson was bowing the committee out,
Pembroke Howard was entering the next house to report. He
found the old Judge sitting grim and straight in his chair, waiting.

'Well, Howard—the news?'

'The best in the world.'

'Accepts, does he?' and the light of battle gleamed joyously
in the Judge's eye.

'Accepts? Why, he jumped at it.'

'Did, did he? Now that's fine—that's very fine. I like that.
When is it to be?'

'Now! Straight off! To-night! An admirable fellow—admirable!'

'Admirable? He's a darling! Why, it's an honour as well as
a pleasure to stand up before such a man. Come—off with
you! Go and arrange everything—and give him my heartiest
compliments. A rare fellow, indeed; an admirable fellow, as
you have said!'

Howard hurried away, saying:

'I'll have him in the vacant stretch between Wilson's and
the haunted house within the hour, and I'll bring my own
pistols.'

Judge Driscoll began to walk the floor in a state of pleased
excitement; but presently he stopped and began to think—
began to think of Tom. Twice he moved toward the secretary,
and twice he turned away again; but finally he said:

'This may be my last night in the world—I must not take
the chance. He is worthless and unworthy, but it is largely

my fault. He was entrusted to me by my brother on his dying bed, and I have indulged him to his hurt, instead of training him up severely, and making a man of him. I have violated my trust, and I must not add the sin of desertion to that. I have forgiven him once already, and would subject him to a long and hard trial before forgiving him again, if I could live; but I must not run that risk. No, I must restore the will. But if I survive the duel, I will hide it away, and he will not know, and I will not tell him until he reforms and I see that his reformation is going to be permanent.'

He re-drew the will, and his ostensible nephew was heir to a fortune again. As he was finishing his task, Tom, wearied with another brooding tramp, entered the house, and went tip-toeing past the sitting-room door. He glanced in, and hurried on, for the sight of his uncle had nothing but terrors for him to-night. But his uncle was writing! That was unusual at this late hour. What could he be writing? A chill anxiety settled down upon Tom's heart. Did that writing concern him? He was afraid so. He reflected that when ill luck begins, it does not come in sprinkles, but in showers. He said he would get a glimpse of that document or know the reason why. He heard some one coming, and stepped out of sight and hearing. It was Pembroke Howard. What could be hatching?

Howard said, with great satisfaction—

'Everything's right and ready. He's gone to the battle-ground with his second and the surgeon—also with his brother. I've arranged it all with Wilson—Wilson's his second. We are to have three shots apiece.'

'Good! How is the moon?'

'Bright as day, nearly. Perfect for the distance—fifteen yards. No wind—not a breath; hot and still.'

'All good; all first-rate. Here, Pembroke, read this, and witness it.'

Pembroke read and witnessed the will, then gave the old man's hand a hearty shake and said:

'Now that's right, York—but I knew you would do it. You couldn't leave that poor chap to fight along without means or profession, with certain defeat before him, and I knew you wouldn't, for his father's sake if not for his own.'

'For his dead father's sake I couldn't, I know; for poor Percy—but you know what Percy was to me. But mind— Tom is not to know of this unless I fall to-night.'

'I understand. I'll keep the secret.'

The Judge put the will away, and the two started for the battle-ground. In another minute the will was in Tom's hands. His misery vanished, his feelings underwent a tremendous revulsion. He put the will carefully back in its place, and spread his mouth and swung his hat once, twice, three times around his head, in imitation of three rousing huzzas, no sound issuing from his lips. He fell to communing with himself excitedly and joyously, but every now and then he let off another volley of dumb hurrahs.

He said to himself: 'I've got the fortune again, but I'll not let on that I know about it. And this time I'm going to hang on to it. I take no more risks. I'll gamble no more, I'll drink no more, because—well, because I'll not go where there is any of that sort of thing going on, again. It's the sure way, the only sure way; I might have thought of that sooner—well, yes, if I had wanted to. But now—dear me, I've had a bad scare this time, and I'll take no more chances. Not a single chance more. Land! I persuaded myself this evening that I could fetch him around without any great amount of effort, but I've been getting more and more heavy-hearted and doubtful straight along, ever since. If he tells me about this thing, all right; but if he doesn't, I sha'n't let on. I—well, I'd like to tell Pudd'nhead Wilson, but—no, I'll think about that; perhaps I won't.' He whirled off another dead huzza, and said: 'I'm reformed, and this time I'll stay so, sure!'

He was about to close with a final grand silent demonstration, when he suddenly recollected that Wilson had put it out of his power to pawn or sell the Indian knife, and that he was once more in awful peril of exposure by his creditors for that reason. His joy collapsed utterly, and he turned away and moped toward the door, moaning and lamenting over the bitterness of his luck. He dragged himself upstairs, and brooded in his room a long time disconsolate and forlorn, with Luigi's Indian knife for a text. At last he sighed and said:

'When I supposed these stones were glass and this ivory bone, the thing hadn't any interest for me because it hadn't any value, and couldn't help me out of my trouble. But now—why, now it is full of interest; yes, and of a sort to break a body's heart. It's a bag of gold that has turned to dirt and ashes in my hands. It could save me, and save me so easily, and yet I've got to go to ruin. It's like drowning with a life-preserver in my reach. All the hard luck comes to me, and all the good luck goes to other people—Puddn'head Wilson, for instance; even his career has got a sort of a little start at last, and what has he done to deserve it, I should like to know? Yes, he has opened his own road, but he isn't content with that, but must block mine. It's a sordid, selfish world, and I wish I was out of it.' He allowed the light of the candle to play upon the jewels of the sheath, but the flashings and sparklings had no charm for his eye; they were only just so many pangs to his heart. 'I must not say anything to Roxy about this thing,' he said, 'she is too daring. She would be for digging these stones out and selling them, and then—why, she would be arrested and the stones traced, and then——' The thought made him quake, and he hid the knife away, trembling all over and glancing furtively about, like a criminal who fancies that the accuser is already at hand.

Should he try to sleep? Oh no, sleep was not for him; his trouble was too haunting, too afflicting for that. He must have somebody to mourn with. He would carry his despair to Roxy.

He had heard several distant gunshots, but that sort of thing was not uncommon, and they had made no impression upon him. He went out at the back door, and turned westward. He passed Wilson's house and proceeded along the lane, and presently saw several figures approaching Wilson's place through the vacant lots. These were the duellists returning from the fight; he thought he recognised them, but

as he had no desire for white people's company, he stooped
down behind the fence until they were out of his way.

Roxy was feeling fine. She said:

'Whah was you, child? Warn't you in it?'

'In what?'

'In de duel.'

'Duel? Has there been a duel?'

''Co'se dey has. De ole Jedge has be'n havin' a duel wid
one o' dem twins.'

'Great Scott!' Then he added to himself: 'That's what made
him re-make the will; he thought he might get killed, and it
softened him toward me. And that's what he and Howard
were so busy about.... Oh dear, if the twin had only killed
him, I should be out of my——'

'What is you mumblin' 'bout, Chambers? Whah was you?
Didn't yo know dey was gwyne to be a duel?'

'No, I didn't. The old man tried to get me to fight one
with Count Luigi, but he didn't succeed, so I reckon he
concluded to patch up the family honour himself.'

He laughed at the idea, and went rambling on with a
detailed account of his talk with the Judge, and how shocked
and ashamed the Judge was to find that he had a coward in
his family. He glanced up at last, and got a shock himself.
Roxana's bosom was heaving with supressed passion, and she
was glowering down upon him with measureless contempt
written in her face.

'En you refuse' to fight a man dat kicked you, 'stid o'
jumpin' at de chance! En you ain't got no mo' feelin' den to
come en tell me, dat fetched sich a po' low-down ornery
rabbit into de worl'! Pah! it make me sick! It's de nigger in
you, dat's what it is. Thirty-one parts o' you is white, en on'y
one part nigger, en dat po' little one part is yo' *soul*. Tain't
wuth savin'; tain't wuth totin' out on a shovel en throwin'
in de gutter. You has disgraced yo' birth. What would yo' pa
think o' you? It's enough to make him turn in his grave.'

The last three sentences stung Tom into a fury, and he
said to himself that if his father were only alive and in reach
of assassination his mother would soon find that he had a

very clear notion of the size of his indebtedness to that man, and was willing to pay it up in full, and would do it too, even at risk of his life; but he kept his thought to himself; that was safest in his mother's present state.

'Whatever has come o' yo' Essex blood? Dat's what I can't understan'. En it ain't on'y jist Essex blood dat's in you, not by a long sight—'deed it ain't! My great-great-great-gran'father en yo' great-great-great-great-gran'-father was ole Cap'n John Smith,* de highest blood dat Ole Virginny ever turned out, en *his* great-great-gran'mother or somers along back dah, was Pocahontas de Injun queen, en her husbun' was a nigger king outen Africa—en yit here you is, a slinkin' outen a duel en disgracin' our whole line like a ornery low-down hound! Yes, it's de nigger in you!'

She sat down on her candle-box and fell into a reverie. Tom did not disturb her; he sometimes lacked prudence, but it was not in circumstances of this kind. Roxana's storm went gradually down, but it died hard, and even when it seemed to be quite gone, it would now and then break out in a distant rumble, so to speak, in the form of muttered ejaculations. One of these was, 'Ain't nigger enough in him to show in his finger-nails,* en dat takes mighty little—yit dey's enough to paint his soul.'

Presently she muttered, 'Yassir, enough to paint a whole thimbleful of 'em.' At last her ramblings ceased altogether, and her countenance began to clear—a welcome sign to Tom, who had learned her moods, and knew she was on the threshold of good-humour, now. He noticed that from time to time she unconsciously carried her finger to the end of her nose. He looked closer and said:

'Why, mammy, the end of your nose is skinned. How did that come?'

She sent out the sort of whole-hearted peal of laughter which God has vouchsafed in its perfection to none but the happy angels in heaven and the bruised and broken black slave on the earth, and said:

'Dad fetch dat duel, I be'n in it myself.'

'Gracious! did a bullet do that?'

'Yassir, you bet it did!'

'Well, I declare! Why, how did that happen?'

'Happen dis-away. I 'uz a-sett'n' here kinder dozin' in de dark, en *che-bang*! goes a gun, right out dah. I skips along out towards t'other end o' de house to see what's gwyne on, en stops by de ole winder on de side towards Pudd'nhead Wilson's house dat ain't got no sash in it—but dey ain't none of 'em got any sashes, fur as dat's concerned,—en I stood dah in de dark en look out, en dar in de moonlight, right down under me 'uz one o' de twins a-cussin'—not much, but jist a-cussin' soft—it 'uz de brown one dat 'uz cussin', 'ca'se he 'uz hit in de shoulder. En Doctor Claypool he 'uz a-workin' at him, en Pudd'nhead Wilson he 'uz a-he'pin', en ole Jedge Driscoll en Pem Howard 'uz a-standin' out yonder a little piece waitin' for 'em to git ready agin. En treckly dey squared off en give de word, en *bang-bang* went de pistols, en de twin he say, 'Ouch!'—hit him on de han' dis time—en I hear dat same bullet go *spat*! ag'in' de logs under de winder; en de nex' time dey shoot, de twin say, 'Ouch!' ag'in, en I done it too, 'ca'se de bullet glance on his cheek-bone en skip up here en glance on de side o' de winder en whiz right acrost my face en tuck de hide off'n my nose—why, if I'd 'a' be'n jist a inch or a inch en a half furder 'twould 'a' tuck de whole nose en disfigger me. Here's de bullet; I hunted her up.'

'Did you stand there all the time?'

'Dat's a question to ask, ain't it! What else would I do? Does I git a chance to see a duel every day?'

'Why, you were right in range! Weren't you afraid?'

The woman gave a sniff of scorn.

"Fraid! De Smith-Pocahontases ain't 'fraid o' nothin', let alone bullets.'

'They've got pluck enough, I suppose; what they lack is judgment. *I* wouldn't have stood there.'

'Nobody's accusin' you!'

'Did anybody else get hurt?'

'Yes, we all got hit 'cep' de blon' twin en de doctor en de seconds. De Jedge didn't git hurt, but I hear Pudd'nhead say de bullet snip some o' his ha'r off.'

' 'George!' said Tom to himself, 'to come so near being out of my trouble, and miss it by an inch. Oh dear, dear, he will live to find me out and sell me to some nigger-trader yet—yes, and he would do it in a minute.' Then he said aloud, in a grave tone:

'Mother, we are in an awful fix.'

Roxana caught her breath with a spasm, and said:

'Chile! What you hit a body so sudden for, like dat? What's be'n en gone en happen'?'

'Well, there's one thing I didn't tell you. When I wouldn't fight, he tore up the will again, and——'

Roxana's face turned a dead white, and she said:

'Now you's *done*!—done for ever! Dat's de end. Bofe un us is gwyne to starve to——'

'Wait and hear me through, can't you? I reckon that when he resolved to fight, himself, he thought he might get killed and not have a chance to forgive me any more in this life, so he made the will again, and I've seen it, and it's all right. But——'

'Oh, thank goodness, den we's safe ag'in!—safe! en so what did you want to come here en talk sich dreadful——'

'Hold *on*, I tell you, and let me finish. The swag I gathered won't half square me up, and the first thing we know, my creditors—well, you know what'll happen.'

Roxana dropped her chin, and told her son to leave her alone—she must think this matter out. Presently she said impressively:

'You got to go mighty keerful now, I tell you! En here's what you got to do. He didn't git killed, en if you gives him de least reason, he'll bust de will a'gin, en dat's de *las'* time, now you hear me! So—you's got to show him what you kin do in de nex' few days. You's got to be pison good, en let him see it; you got to do everything dat'll make him b'lieve in you, en you got to sweeten aroun' ole Aunt Pratt, too— she's pow'ful strong wid de Jedge, en de bes' frien' you got. Nex', you'll go 'long away to Sent Louis, en dat'll *keep* him in yo' favour. Den you go en make a bargain wid dem people. You tell 'em he ain't gwyne to live long—en dat's de fac',

too—en tell 'em you'll pay 'em intrust, en big intrust, too—
ten per—what you call it?'

'Ten per cent. a month?'

'Dat's it. Den you take and sell yo' truck aroun', a little at
a time, en pay de intrust. How long will it las'?'

'I think there's enough to pay the interest five or six
months.'

'Den you's all right. If he don't die in six months, dat
don't make no diff'rence—Providence'll provide. You's
gwyne to be safe—if you behaves.' She bent an austere eye
on him and added, 'En you *is* gwyne to behave—does you
know dat?'

He laughed and said he was going to try, anyway. She did
not unbend. She said gravely:

'Tryin' ain't de thing. You's gwyne to *do* it. You ain't gwyne
to steal a pin—'ca'se it ain't safe no mo'; en you ain't gwyne
into no bad comp'ny—not even once, you understand; en
you ain't gwyne to drink a drop—nary single drop; en you
ain't gwyne to gamble one single gamble—not one! Dis ain't
what you's gwyne to *try* to do, it's what you's gwyne to *do*.
En I'll tell you how I knows it. Dis is how. I's gwyne to
foller along to Sent Louis my own self; en you's gwyne to
come to me every day o' yo' life, en I'll look you over; en
if you fails in one single one o' dem things—jist *once*—I take
my oath I'll come straight down to dis town en tell de Jedge
you's a nigger en a slave—en *prove* it!' She paused to let her
words sink home. Then she added: 'Chambers, does you
b'lieve me when I say dat?'

Tom was sober enough now. There was no levity in his
voice when he answered:

'Yes, mother. I know, now, that I am reformed—and
permanently. Permanently—and beyond the reach of any
human temptation.'

'Den g' long home en begin!'

15

Nothing so needs reforming as other people's habits.

—PUDD'NHEAD WILSON'S CALENDAR

Behold, the fool saith, 'Put not all thine eggs in the one basket'—which is but a manner of saying, 'Scatter your money and your attention'; but the wise man saith, 'Put all your eggs in the one basket and—WATCH THAT BASKET.'

—PUDD'NHEAD WILSON'S CALENDAR

WHAT a time of it Dawson's Landing was having! All its life it had been asleep, but now it hardly got a chance for a nod, so swiftly did big events and crashing surprises come along in one another's wake: Friday morning, first glimpse of Real Nobility, also grand reception at Aunt Patsy Cooper's, also great robber-raid; Friday evening, dramatic kicking of the heir of the chief citizen in presence of four hundred people; Saturday morning, emergence as practising lawyer of the long-submerged Pudd'nhead Wilson; Saturday night, duel between chief citizen and titled stranger.

The people took more pride in the duel than in all the other events put together, perhaps. It was a glory to their town to have such a thing happen there. In their eyes the principals had reached the summit of human honour. Everybody paid homage to their names; their praises were in all mouths. Even the duellists' subordinates came in for a handsome share of the public approbation: wherefore Pudd'nhead Wilson was suddenly become a man of consequence. When asked to run for the mayoralty Saturday night he was risking defeat, but Sunday morning found him a made man and his success assured.

The twins were prodigiously great now; the town took them to its bosom with enthusiasm. Day after day, and night after night, they went dining and visiting from house to house, making friends, enlarging and solidifying their popularity, and charming and surprising all with their musical prodigies, and now and then heightening the effects with samples of what they could do in other directions, out of their stock of rare and curious accomplishments. They were so pleased that they gave the regulation thirty days' notice, the required preparation for citizenship, and resolved to finish their days in this pleasant place. That was the climax. The delighted community rose as one man and applauded; and when the twins were asked to stand for seats in the forth-coming aldermanic board, and consented, the public content-ment was rounded and complete.

Tom Driscoll was not happy over these things; they sunk deep, and hurt all the way down. He hated the one twin for kicking him, and the other one for being the kicker's brother.

Now and then the people wondered why nothing was heard of the raider, or of the stolen knife or the other plunder, but nobody was able to throw any light on that matter. Nearly a week had drifted by, and still the thing remained a vexed mystery.

On Saturday Constable Blake and Pudd'nhead Wilson met on the street, and Tom Driscoll joined them in time to open their conversation for them. He said to Blake:

'You are not looking well, Blake; you seem to be annoyed about something. Has anything gone wrong in the detective business? I believe you fairly and justifiably claim to have a pretty good reputation in that line, isn't it so?'—which made Blake feel good and look it; but Tom added, 'for a country detective'—which made Blake feel the other way, and not only look it, but betray it in his voice.

'Yes, sir, I *have* got a reputation; and it's as good as anybody's in the profession, too, country or no country.'

'Oh, I beg pardon; I didn't mean any offence. What I started out to ask was only about the old woman that raided the town—the stoop-shouldered old woman, you know, that you said you were going to catch; and I knew you would, too, because you have the reputation of never boasting, and—well, you—you've caught the old woman?'

'D——the old woman!'

'Why, sho! you don't mean to say you haven't caught her?'

'No; I haven't caught her. If anybody could have caught her, I could; but nobody couldn't, I don't care who he is.'

'I am sorry, real sorry—for your sake; because when it gets around that a detective has expressed himself so confidently, and then——'

'Don't you worry, that's all—don't you worry; and as for the town, the town needn't worry either. She's my meat—make yourself easy about that. I'm on her track; I've got clues that——'

'That's good! Now if you could get an old veteran detective down from St Louis to help you find out what the clues mean, and where they lead to, and then——'

'I'm plenty veteran enough myself, and I don't need anybody's help. I'll have her inside of a we—inside of a month. That I'll swear to!'

Tom said carelessly:

'I suppose that will answer—yes, that will answer. But I reckon she is pretty old, and old people don't often outlive the cautious pace of the professional detective when he has got his clues together and is out on his still-hunt.'*

Blake's dull face flushed under this gibe, but before he could set his retort in order Tom had turned to Wilson, and was saying, with placid indifference of manner and voice:

'Who got the reward, Pudd'nhead?'

Wilson winced slightly, and saw that his own turn was come.

'What reward?'

'Why, the reward for the thief, and the other one for the knife.'

Wilson answered—and rather uncomfortably, to judge by his hesitating fashion of delivering himself:

'Well, the—well, in fact, nobody has claimed it yet.'

Tom seemed surprised.

'Why, is that so?'

Wilson showed a trifle of irritation when he replied:

'Yes, it's so. And what of it?'

'Oh, nothing. Only I thought you had struck out a new idea, and invented a scheme that was going to revolutionise the time-worn and ineffectual methods of the——' He stopped, and turned to Blake, who was happy now that another had taken his place on the gridiron: 'Blake, didn't you understand him to intimate that it wouldn't be necessary for you to hunt the old woman down?'

'B'George, he said he'd have thief and swag both inside of three days—he did, by hokey! and that's just about a week ago. Why, I said at the time that no thief and no thief's pal was going to try to pawn or sell a thing where he knowed the pawnbroker could get both rewards by taking _him_ into camp _with_ the swag. It was the blessedest idea that ever _I_ struck!'

'You'd change your mind,' said Wilson, with irritated bluntness, 'if you knew the entire scheme instead of only part of it.'

'Well,' said the constable, pensively, 'I had the idea that it wouldn't work, and up to now I'm right, anyway.'

'Very well, then, let it stand at that, and give it a further show. It has worked at least as well as your own methods, you perceive.'

The constable hadn't anything handy to hit back with, so he discharged a discontented sniff, and said nothing.

After the night that Wilson had partly revealed his scheme at his house, Tom had tried for several days to guess out the secret of the rest of it, but had failed. Then it occurred to him to give Roxana's smarter head a chance at it. He made up a suppositious case, and laid it before her. She thought it over, and delivered her verdict upon it. Tom said to himself, 'She's hit it, sure!' He thought he would test that verdict, now, and watch Wilson's face; so he said reflectively:

'Wilson, you're not a fool—a fact of recent discovery. Whatever your scheme was, it had sense in it, Blake's opinion to the contrary notwithstanding. I don't ask you to reveal it, but I will suppose a case—a case which will answer as a starting-point for the real thing I am going to come at, and that's all I want. You offered five hundred dollars for the knife, and five hundred for the thief. We will suppose, for argument's sake, that the first reward is *advertised*, and the second offered by *private letter* to pawn-brokers and——'

Blake slapped his thigh, and cried out:

'By Jackson, he's got you, Pudd'nhead! Now why couldn't I or *any* fool have thought of that?'

Wilson said to himself, 'Anybody with a reasonably good head would have thought of it. I am not surprised that Blake didn't detect it; I am only surprised that Tom did. There is more to him than I supposed.' He said nothing aloud, and Tom went on:

'Very well. The thief would not suspect that there was a trap, and he would bring or send the knife, and say he bought it for a song, or found it in the road, or something like that, and try to collect the reward, and be arrested—wouldn't he?'

'Yes,' said Wilson.

'I think so,' said Tom. 'There can't be any doubt of it. Have you ever seen that knife?'

'No.'

'Has any friend of yours?'

'Not that I know of.'

'Well, I begin to think I understand why your scheme failed.'

'What do you mean, Tom? What are you driving at?' asked Wilson, with a dawning sense of discomfort.

'Why, that there *isn't* any such knife.'

'Look here, Wilson,' said Blake, 'Tom Driscoll's right, for a thousand dollars—if I had it.'

Wilson's blood warmed a little, and he wondered if he had been played upon by those strangers; it certainly had something of that look. But what could they gain by it? He threw out that suggestion. Tom replied:

'Gain. Oh, nothing that you would value, maybe. But they are strangers making their way in a new community. Is it nothing to them to appear as pets of an Oriental prince—at no expense? Is it nothing to them to be able to dazzle this poor little town with thousand-dollar rewards—at no expense? Wilson, there isn't any such knife, or your scheme would have fetched it to light. Or if there is any such knife, they've got it yet. I believe, myself, that they've seen such a knife, for Angelo pictured it out with his pencil too swiftly and handily for him to have been inventing it, and of course I can't swear that they've never had it; but this I'll go bail for—if they had it when they came to this town, they've got it yet.'

Blake said:

'It looks mighty reasonable, the way Tom puts it; it most certainly does.'

Tom responded, turning to leave:

'You find the old woman, Blake, and if she can't furnish the knife, go and search the twins!'

Tom sauntered away. Wilson felt a good deal depressed. He hardly knew what to think. He was loth to withdraw his faith from the twins, and was resolved not to do it on the present indecisive evidence; but—well, he would think, and then decide how to act.

'Blake, what do you think of this matter?'

'Well, Pudd'nhead, I'm bound to say I put it up the way Tom does. They hadn't the knife; or if they had it, they've got it yet.'

The men parted. Wilson said to himself:

'I believe they had it; if it had been stolen, the scheme would have restored it, that is certain. And so I believe they've got it yet.'

Tom had no purpose in his mind when he encountered those two men. When he began his talk he hoped to be able to gall them a little and get a trifle of malicious entertainment out of it. But when he left, he left in great spirits, for he perceived that just by pure luck and no troublesome labour he had accomplished several delightful things: he had touched both men on a raw spot and seen them squirm; he had modified Wilson's sweetness for the twins with one small bitter taste that he wouldn't be able to get out of his mouth right away; and, best of all, he had taken the hated twins down a peg with the community; for Blake would gossip around freely, after the manner of detectives, and within a week the town would be laughing at them in its sleeve for offering a gaudy reward for a bauble which they either never possessed or hadn't lost. Tom was very well satisfied with himself.

Tom's behaviour at home had been perfect during the entire week. His uncle and aunt had seen nothing like it before. They could find no fault with him anywhere.

Saturday evening he said to the Judge:

'I've had something preying on my mind, uncle, and as I am going away, and might never see you again, I can't bear it any longer. I made you believe I was afraid to fight that Italian adventurer. I had to get out of it on some pretext or other, and maybe I chose badly, being taken unawares, but no honourable person could consent to meet him in the field, knowing what I knew about him.'

'Indeed. What was that?'

'Count Luigi is a confessed assassin.'

'Incredible!'

'It is perfectly true. Wilson detected it in his hand, by palmistry, and charged him with it, and cornered him up so close that he had to confess; but both twins begged us on their knees to keep the secret, and swore they would lead straight lives here; and it was all so pitiful that we gave our word of honour never to expose them while they kept that promise. You would have done it yourself, uncle.'

'You are right, my boy, I would. A man's secret is still his own property, and sacred, when it has been surprised out of him like that. You did well, and I am proud of you.' Then he added mournfully: 'But I wish I could have been saved the shame of meeting an assassin on the field of honour.'

'It couldn't be helped, uncle. If I had known you were going to challenge him I should have felt obliged to sacrifice my pledged word in order to stop it, but Wilson couldn't be expected to do otherwise than keep silent.'

'Oh no; Wilson did right, and is in no way to blame. Tom, Tom, you have lifted a heavy load from my heart; I was stung to the very soul when I seemed to have discovered that I had a coward in my family.'

'You may imagine what it cost *me* to assume such a part, uncle.'

'Oh, I know it, poor boy, I know it. And I can understand how much it has cost you to remain under that unjust stigma to this time. But it is all right now, and no harm is done. You have restored my comfort of mind, and with it your own; and both of us had suffered enough.'

The old man sat awhile plunged in thought; then he looked up with a satisfied light in his eye, and said: 'That this assassin should have put the affront upon me of letting me meet him on the field of honour as if he were a gentleman is a matter which I will presently settle—but not now. I will not shoot him until after election. I see a way to ruin them both before; I will attend to that first. Neither of them shall be elected, that I promise. You are sure that the fact that he is an assassin has not got abroad?'

'Perfectly certain of it, sir.'

'It will be a good card. I will fling a hint at it from the stump on the polling-day. It will sweep the ground from under both of them.'

'There's not a doubt of it. It will finish them.'

'That and outside work among the voters will, to a certainty. I want you to come down here by-and-by and work privately among the rag-tag and bob-tail. You shall spend money among them; I will furnish it.'

Another point scored against the detested twins! Really it was a great day for Tom. He was encouraged to chance a parting shot, now, at the same target, and did it.

'You know that wonderful Indian knife that the twins have been making such a to-do about? Well, there's no track or trace of it yet; so the town is beginning to sneer and gossip and laugh. Half the people believe they never had any such knife, the other half believe they had it and have got it still. I've heard twenty people talking like that to-day.'

Yes, Tom's blemishless week had restored him to the favour of his aunt and uncle.

His mother was satisfied with him, too. Privately, she believed she was coming to love him, but she did not say so. She told him to go along to St Louis, now, and she would get ready and follow. Then she smashed her whisky bottle and said:

'Dah now! I's a-gwyne to make you walk as straight as a string, Chambers, en so I's bown' you ain't gwyne to git no bad example out o' yo' mammy. I tole you you couldn't go into no bad comp'ny. Well, you's gwyne into my comp'ny, en I's gwyne to fill de bill. Now, den, trot along, trot along!'

Tom went aboard one of the big transient boats that night with his heavy satchel of miscellaneous plunder, and slept the sleep of the unjust, which is serener and sounder than the other kind, as we know by the hanging-eve history of a million rascals. But when he got up in the morning, luck was against him again: a brother-thief had robbed him while he slept, and gone ashore at some intermediate landing.

16

If you pick up a starving dog and make him prosperous, he will not bite you. This is the principal difference between a dog and a man.
—PUDD'NHEAD WILSON'S CALENDAR

We know all about the habits of the ant, we know all about the habits of the bee, but we know nothing at all about the habits of the oyster. It seems almost certain that we have been choosing the wrong time for studying the oyster.
—PUDD'NHEAD WILSON'S CALENDAR

WHEN Roxana arrived, she found her son in such despair and misery that her heart was touched and her motherhood rose up strong in her. He was ruined past hope, now; his destruction would be immediate and sure, and he would be an outcast and friendless. That was reason enough for a mother to love a child; so she loved him, and told him so. It made him wince, secretly—for she was a 'nigger'. That he was one himself was far from reconciling him to that despised race.

Roxana poured out endearments upon him, to which he responded uncomfortably, but as well as he could. And she

tried to comfort him, but that was not possible. These
intimacies quickly became horrible to him, and within the
hour he began to try to get up courage enough to tell her
so, and require that they be discontinued or very considerably
modified. But he was afraid of her; and besides, there came
a lull, now, for she had begun to think. She was trying to
invent a saving plan. Finally she started up, and said she had
found a way out. Tom was almost suffocated by the joy of
this sudden good news. Roxana said:

'Here is de plan, en she'll win, sure. I's a nigger, en nobody
ain't gwyne to doubt it dat hears me talk. I's wuth six hund'd
dollahs. Take en sell me, en pay off dese gamblers.'

Tom was dazed. He was not sure he had heard aright. He
was dumb for a moment; then he said:

'Do you mean that you would be sold into slavery to save
me?'

'Ain't you my chile?* En does you know anything dat a
mother won't do for her chile? Dey ain't nothin' a white mother
won't do for her chile. Who made 'em so? De Lord done it.
En who made de niggers? De Lord made 'em. In de inside,
mothers is all de same. De good Lord he made 'em so. I's
gwyne to be sole into slavery, en in a year you's gwyne to buy
yo' ole mammy free ag'in. I'll show you how. Dat's de plan.'

Tom's hopes began to rise, and his spirits along with them.
He said:

'It's lovely of you, mammy—it's just——'

'Say it ag'in! En keep on sayin' it! It's all de pay a body
kin want in dis worl', en it's mo' den enough. Laws bless
you, honey, when I's slavin' aroun', en dey 'buses me, if I
knows you's a-sayin' dat, 'way off yonder somers, it'll heal
up all de sore places, en I kin stan' 'em.'

'I *do* say it again, mammy, and I'll keep on saying it, too.
But how am I going to sell you? You're free, you know.'

'Much diff'rence dat make! White folks ain't partic'lar. De
law kin sell me now if dey tell me to leave de State in six
months en I don't go. You draw up a paper—bill o' sale—en
put it 'way off yonder, down in de middle o' Kaintuck somers,
en sign some names to it, en say you'll sell me cheap 'ca'se

you's hard up; you'll fine you ain't gwyne to have no trouble.
You take me up de country a piece, en sell me on a farm;
dem people ain't gwyne to ask no questions if I's a bargain.'

Tom forged a bill of sale and sold his mother to an
Arkansas* cotton-planter for a trifle over six hundred dollars.
He did not want to commit this treachery, but luck threw
the man in his way, and this saved him the necessity of going
up country to hunt up a purchaser, with the added risk of
having to answer a lot of questions, whereas this planter was
so pleased with Roxy that he asked next to none at all.
Besides, the planter insisted that Roxy wouldn't know where
she was at first, and that by the time she found out she
would already have become contented. And Tom argued with
himself that it was an immense advantage for Roxy to have
a master who was so pleased with her, as this planter
manifestly was. In almost no time his flowing reasonings
carried him to the point of even half believing he was doing
Roxy a splendid surreptitious service in selling her 'down the
river'. And then he kept diligently saying to himself all the
time: 'It's for only a year. In a year I buy her free again;
she'll keep that in mind, and it'll reconcile her.' Yes; the little
deception could do no harm, and everything would come out
right and pleasant in the end, anyway. By agreement, the
conversation in Roxy's presence was all about the man's 'up-
country' farm, and how pleasant a place it was, and how
happy the slaves were there; so poor Roxy was entirely
deceived, and easily, for she was not dreaming that her own
son could be guilty of treason to a mother who, by voluntarily
going into slavery—slavery of any kind, mild or severe, or
of any duration, brief or long—was making a sacrifice for
him compared with¹ which death would have been a poor
and commonplace one. She lavished tears and loving caresses
upon him privately, and then went away with her owner—
went away broken-hearted, and yet proud of what she was
doing, and glad that it was in her power to do it.

Tom squared his accounts, and resolved to keep to the
very letter of his reform, and never to put that will in
jeopardy again. He had three hundred dollars left. According

to his mother's plan, he was to put that safely away, and add her half of his pension to it monthly. In one year this fund would buy her free again.

For a whole week he was not able to sleep well, so much the villainy which he had played upon his trusting mother preyed upon his rag of a conscience; but after that he began to get comfortable again, and was presently able to sleep like any other miscreant.

The boat bore Roxy away from St Louis at four in the afternoon, and she stood on the lower guard abaft the paddle-box and watched Tom through a blur of tears until he melted into the throng of people and disappeared; then she looked no more, but sat there on a coil of cable crying till far into the night. When she went to her foul steerage-bunk at last, between the clashing engines, it was not to sleep but only to wait for the morning, and, waiting, grieve.

It had been imagined that she 'would not know', and would think she was travelling up stream. She! Why, she had been steamboating for years. At dawn she got up and went listlessly and sat down on the cable-coil again. She passed many a snag whose 'break' could have told her a thing to break her heart, for it showed a current moving in the same direction that the boat was going; but her thoughts were elsewhere, and she did not notice. But at last the roar of a bigger and nearer break than usual brought her out of her torpor, and she looked up, and her practised eye fell upon that tell-tale rush of water. For one moment her petrified gaze fixed itself there. Then her head dropped upon her breast, and she said:

'Oh, de good Lord God have mercy on po' sinful me—*I's sole down de river!*'

17

Even popularity can be overdone. In Rome, alone at first, you are full of regrets that Michelangelo died; but by-and-by you only regret that you didn't see him do it.*

—PUDD'NHEAD WILSON'S CALENDAR

*July 4.—Statistics show that we lose more fools on this day than in all
the other days of the year put together. This proves, by the number left
in stock, that one Fourth of July per year is now inadequate, the country
has grown so.*

—PUDD'NHEAD WILSON'S CALENDAR

THE summer weeks dragged by, and then the political campaign opened—opened in pretty warm fashion, and waxed
hotter and hotter daily. The twins threw themselves into it
with their whole heart, for their self-love was engaged. Their
popularity, so general at first, had suffered afterward; mainly
because they had been *too* popular, and so a natural reaction
had followed. Besides, it had been diligently whispered
around that it was curious—indeed, *very* curious—that that
wonderful knife of theirs did not turn up—*if* it was so
valuable, or *if* it had ever existed. And with the whisperings
went chucklings and nudgings and winks, and such things
have an effect. The twins considered that success in the
election would reinstate them, and that defeat would work
them irreparable damage. Therefore they worked hard, but
not harder than Judge Driscoll and Tom worked against them
in the closing days of the canvas. Tom's conduct had remained so letter-perfect during two whole months now that
his uncle not only trusted him with money with which to
persuade voters, but trusted him to go and get it himself out
of the safe in the private sitting-room.

The closing speech of the campaign was made by Judge
Driscoll, and he made it against both of the foreigners. It
was disastrously effective. He poured out rivers of ridicule
upon them, and forced the big mass-meeting to laugh and
applaud. He scoffed at them as adventurers, mountebanks,
side-show riff-raff, dime-museum freaks;* he assailed their
showy titles with measureless derision; he said they were
back-alley barbers disguised as nobilities,* pea-nut pedlers
masquerading as gentlemen, organ-grinders bereft of their
brother-monkey. At last he stopped and stood still. He waited
until the place had become absolutely silent and expectant,
then he delivered his deadliest shot; delivered it with ice-cold

seriousness and deliberation, with a significant emphasis upon the closing words: he said he believed that the reward offered for the lost knife was humbug and buncombe, and that its owner would know where to find it whenever he should have occasion *to assassinate somebody.*

Then he stepped from the stand, leaving a startled and impressive hush behind him instead of the customary explosion of cheers and party cries.

The strange remark flew far and wide over the town and made an extraordinary sensation. Everybody was asking, 'What could he mean by that?' And everybody went on asking that question, but in vain; for the Judge only said he knew what he was talking about, and stopped there; Tom said he hadn't any idea what his uncle meant, and Wilson, whenever he was asked what he thought it meant, parried the question by asking the questioner what *he* thought it meant.

Wilson was elected, the twins were defeated—crushed, in fact, and left forlorn and substantially friendless. Tom went back to St Louis happy.

Dawson's Landing had a week of repose, now, and it needed it. But it was in an expectant state, for the air was full of rumours of a new duel. Judge Driscoll's election labours had prostrated him, but it was said that as soon as he was well enough to entertain a challenge he would get one from Count Luigi.

The brothers withdrew entirely from society, and nursed their humiliation in privacy. They avoided the people, and went out for exercise only late at night, when the streets were deserted.

18

Gratitude and treachery are merely the two extremities of the same procession. You have seen all of it that is worth staying for when the band and the gaudy officials have gone by.

—PUDD'NHEAD WILSON'S CALENDAR

Thanksgiving Day.—Let all give humble, hearty, and sincere thanks,
now, but the turkeys. In the island of Fiji they do not use turkeys, they
use plumbers. It does not become you and me to sneer at Fiji.
                                    —PUDD'NHEAD WILSON'S CALENDAR

THE Friday after the election was a rainy one in St Louis.
It rained all day long, and rained hard, apparently trying its
best to wash that soot-blackened town white, but of course
not succeeding. Toward midnight Tom Driscoll arrived at his
lodgings from the theatre in the heavy downpour, and closed
his umbrella and let himself in; but when he would have shut
the door, he found that there was another person entering—
doubtless another lodger; this person closed the door and
tramped upstairs behind Tom. Tom found his door in the
dark, and entered it and turned up the gas. When he faced
about, lightly whistling, he saw the back of a man. The man
was closing and locking his door for him. His whistle faded
out and he felt uneasy. The man turned round, a wreck of
shabby old clothes sodden with rain and all a-drip, and
showed a black face under an old slouch hat. Tom was
frightened. He tried to order the man out but the words
refused to come, and the other man got the start. He said,
in a low voice:

'Keep still—I's yo' mother!'

Tom sunk in a heap on a chair, and gasped out:

'It was mean of me, and base—I know it; but I meant it
for the best, I did indeed—I can swear it.'

Roxana stood awhile looking mutely down on him while
he writhed in shame and went on incoherently babbling self-
accusations mixed with pitiful attempts at explanation and
palliation of his crime; then she seated herself and took off
her hat, and her unkempt masses of long brown hair tumbled
down about her shoulders.

'It ain't no fault o' yo'n dat dat ain't grey,' she said sadly,
noticing the hair.

'I know it, I know it! I'm a scoundrel. But I swear I meant
for the best. It was a mistake, of course, but I thought it
was for the best, I truly did.'

Roxy began to cry softly, and presently words began to find their way out between her sobs. They were uttered lamentingly, rather than angrily—

'Sell a pusson down de river—*down de river!*—for de bes'! I wouldn't treat a dog so! I is all broke down en wore out, now, en so I reckon it ain't in me to storm aroun' no mo', like I used to when I 'uz trompled on en 'bused. I don't know—but maybe it's so. Leastways, I's suffered so much dat mournin' seem to come mo' handy to me now den stormin'.'

These words should have touched Tom Driscoll, but if they did, that effect was obliterated by a stronger one—one which removed the heavy weight of fear which lay upon him, and gave his crushed spirit a most grateful rebound, and filled all his small soul with a deep sense of relief. But he kept prudently still, and ventured no comment. There was a voiceless interval of some duration, now, in which no sounds were heard but the beating of the rain upon the panes, the sighing and complaining of the winds, and now and then a muffled sob from Roxana. The sobs became more and more infrequent, and at last ceased. Then the refugee began to talk again:

'Shet down dat light a little. More. More yit. A pusson dat is hunted don't like de light. Dah—dat'll do. I kin see whah you is, en dat's enough. I's gwyne to tell you de tale, en cut it jes' as short as I kin, en den I'll tell you what you's got to do. Dat man dat bought me ain't a bad man, he's good enough, as planters goes; en if he could a had his way I'd a ben a house servant in his fambly en ben comfortable; but his wife she was a Yank, en not right down good-lookin', en she riz up ag'in me straight off; so den dey sent me out to de quarter 'mongst de common fiel' han's. Dat woman warn't satisfied, even wid dat, but she worked up the overseer ag'in me, she 'uz dat jealous en hateful; so de overseer he had me out befo' day in de mawnins en worked me de whole long day as long as dey 'uz any light to see by; en many's de lashins I got 'ca'se I couldn't come up to de work o' de stronges'. Dat overseer wuz a Yank, too, outen New Eng-lan',* en anybody down South kin tell you what dat mean.

Dey knows how to work a nigger to death, en dey knows how to whale 'em, too—whale 'em till dey backs is welted like a washboard. 'Long at fust my marster say de good word for me to de overseer, but dat 'uz bad for me; for de mistis she fine it out, an' arter dat I jes' ketched it at every turn—dey warn't no mercy for me no mo'.'

Tom's heart was fired—with fury against the planter's wife; and he said to himself, 'But for that meddlesome fool, everything would have gone all right.' He added a deep and bitter curse against her.

The expression of this sentiment was fiercely written in his face, and stood thus revealed to Roxana by a white glare of lightning which turned the sombre dusk of the room into dazzling day at that moment. She was pleased—pleased and grateful; for did not that expression show that her child was capable of grieving for his mother's wrongs and of feeling resentment toward her persecutors?—a thing which she had been doubting. But her flash of happiness was only a flash, and went out again and left her spirit dark; for she said to herself, 'He sole me down de river—he can't feel for a body long; dis'll pass en go.' Then she took up her tale again.

' 'Bout ten days ago I 'uz sayin' to myself dat I could not las' many mo' weeks I 'uz so wore out wid de awful work en de lashins, en so down-hearted en misable. En I didn't care no mo', nuther—life warn't wuth noth'n to me if I got to go on like dat. Well, when a body is in a frame o' mine like dat, what do a body care what a body do? Dey was a little sickly nigger wench 'bout ten year ole dat 'uz good to me, en hadn't no mammy, po' thing, en I loved her en she loved me; en she come out whah I 'uz workin' en she had a roasted tater, en tried to slip it to me—robbin' herself, you see, 'ca'se she knowed de overseer didn't gimme enough to eat—en he ketched her at it, en give her a lick acrost de back wid his stick which 'uz as thick as a broom-handle, en she drop' screamin' on de groun', en squirmin' en wallerin' aroun' in de dust like a spider dat 's got crippled. I couldn't stan' it. All de hell-fire dat 'uz ever in my heart flame' up, en I snatch de stick outen his han' en laid him flat. He laid dah moanin' en cussin', en all out of his head, you know, en de niggers 'uz plum sk'yerd to death. Dey gathered 'roun' him to he'p him, en I jumped on his hoss en took out for de river as tight as I could go. I knowed what dey would do wid me. Soon as he got well he would start en work me to death if marster let him; en if dey didn't do dat they'd sell me furder down de river, en dat's de same thing. So I 'lowed to drown myself en git out o' my troubles. It 'uz gitt'n toward dark. I 'uz at de river in two minutes. Den I see a canoe, en I says dey ain't no use to drown myself tell I got to; so I ties de hoss in de edge o' de timber en shove out down de river, keepin' in under de shelter o' de bluff bank en prayin' for de dark to shet down quick. I had a pow'ful good start, 'ca'se de big house 'uz three mile back fum de river en on'y de work-mules to ride dah on, en on'y niggers to ride 'em, en *dey* warn't gwyne to hurry—dey'd gimme all de chance dey could. Befo' a body could go to de house en back it would be long pas' dark, en dey couldn't track de hoss en fine out which way I went tell mawnin', en de niggers would tell 'em all de lies dey could 'bout it.

'Well, de dark come, en I went on a-spinnin' down de river. I paddled mo'n two hours, den I warn't worried no mo', so I quit paddlin', en floated down de current, considerin' what I 'uz gwyne to do if I didn't have to drown myself. I made up some plans, en floated along, turnin' 'em over in my mind. Well, when it 'uz a little pas' midnight as I reckoned, en I had come fifteen or twenty mile, I see de lights o' a steamboat layin' at de bank, whah dey warn't no town en no woodyard, en putty soon I ketched de shape o' de chimbly-tops ag'in de stars, en den good gracious me, I most jumped out o' my skin for joy! It 'uz de *Grand Mogul*—I 'uz chambermaid on her for eight seasons in de Cincinnati en Orleans trade. I slid 'long pas'—don't see nobody stirrin' nowhah—hear 'em a-hammerin' away in de engine-room, den I knowed what de matter was—some o' de machinery's broke. I got asho' below de boat and turn' de canoe loose, den I goes 'long up, en dey 'uz jes' one plank out, en I step' board de boat. It 'uz pow'ful hot, deckhan's en roustabouts 'uz sprawled aroun' asleep on de fo'cas'l; de second mate, Jim Bangs, he sot dah on the bitts* wid his head down, asleep—'ca'se dat's de way de second mate stan' de cap'n's watch!—en de ole watchman, Billy Hatch, he 'uz a-noddin' on de companion way;—en I knowed 'em all; en lan', but dey did look good! I says to myself, I wisht old marster'd come along *now* en try to take me—bless yo' heart, I's 'mong frien's, I is. So I tromped right along 'mongst 'em, en went up on de biler deck en 'way back aft to de ladies' cabin guard, en sot down dah in de same cheer dat I'd sot in mos' a hund'd million times, I reckon; en it 'uz jist home agin, I tell you!

'In 'bout an hour I heard de ready-bell jingle, en den de racket begin. Putty soon I hear de gong strike. 'Set her back on de outside,' I says to myself—'I reckon I knows dat music!' I hear de gong ag'in. 'Come ahead on de inside,' I says. Gong ag'in. 'Stop de outside.' Gong ag'in. 'Come ahead on de outside—now we's pinted for Sent Louis, en I's outer de woods en ain't got to drown myself at all.' I knowed de *Mogul* 'uz in de Sent Louis trade now, you see. It 'uz jes' fair daylight when we passed our plantation, en I seed a gang o' niggers en white folks huntin' up en down de sho', en troublin' deyselves a good deal 'bout me, but I warn't troublin' myself none 'bout dem.

' 'Bout dat time Sally Jackson, dat used to be my second chambermaid, en 'uz head chambermaid now, she come out on de guard, en 'uz pow'ful glad to see me, en so 'uz all de officers; en I tole 'em I'd got kidnapped en sole down de river, en dey made me up twenty dollahs en give it to me, en Sally she rigged me out wid good clo'es, en when I got here I went straight to whah you used to wuz, en den I come to dis house en dey say you's away, but 'spected back every day; so I didn't dast to go down to de river to Dawson's, 'ca'se I might miss you.

'Well, las' Monday I 'uz pass'n by one o' dem places in Fourth Street whah dey sticks up runaway-nigger bills, en he'ps to ketch 'em, en I seed my marster! I 'most flopped down on de groun', I felt so gone. He had his back to me, en 'uz talkin' to de man en givin' him some bills—nigger-bills, I reckon, en I's de nigger. He's offerin' a reward—dat's it. Ain't I right, don't you reckon?'

Tom had been gradually sinking into a state of ghastly terror, and he said to himself, now, 'I'm lost, no matter what turn things take! This man has said to me that he thinks there was something suspicious about that sale. He said he had a letter from a passenger on the *Grand Mogul* saying that Roxy came here on that boat and that everybody on board knew all about the case; so he says that her coming here instead of flying to a free state looks bad for me, and that if I don't find her for him, and that pretty soon, he will make trouble for me. I never believed that story; I couldn't believe she would be so dead to all motherly instincts as to come here, knowing the risk she would run of getting me into irremediable trouble. And after all, here she is! And I stupidly swore I would help him find her, thinking it was a perfectly safe thing to promise. If I venture to deliver her up, she—she—but how can I help myself? I've got to do that or pay the money, and where's the money to come from? I—I—well, I should think that if he would swear to treat her kindly hereafter—and she says, herself, that he is a good man—and if he would swear to never allow her to be over-worked, or ill fed, or——'

A flash of lightning exposed Tom's pallid face, drawn and rigid with these worrying thoughts. Roxana spoke up sharply now, and there was apprehension in her voice:

'Turn up dat light! I want to see yo' face better. Dah now—lemme look at you. Chambers, you's as white as yo' shirt! Has you seen dat man? Has he ben to see you?'

'Ye—s.'

'When?'

'Monday noon.'

'Monday noon! Was he on my track?'

'He—well, he thought he was. That is, he hoped he was. This is the bill you saw.' He took it out of his pocket.

'Read it to me!'

She was panting with excitement, and there was a dusky glow in her eyes that Tom could not translate with certainty, but there seemed to be something threatening about it. The handbill had the usual rude woodcut of a turbaned negro woman running, with the customary bundle on a stick over her shoulder, and the heading in bold type, '$100 REWARD'. Tom read the bill aloud—at least the part that described Roxana and named the master and his St Louis address and the address of the Fourth Street agency; but he left out the item that applicants for the reward might also apply to Mr Thomas Driscoll.

'Gimme de bill!'

Tom had folded it and was putting it in his pocket. He felt a chilly streak creeping down his back, but said, as carelessly as he could:

'The bill? Why, it isn't any use to you, you can't read it. What do you want with it?'

'Gimme de bill!' Tom gave it to her, but with a reluctance which he could not entirely disguise. 'Did you read it *all* to me?'

'Certainly I did.'

'Hole up yo' han' en swah to it.'

Tom did it. Roxana put the bill carefully away in her pocket, with her eyes fixed upon Tom's face all the while, then she said—

'You's lyin'!'

'What would I want to lie about it for?'

'I don't know—but you is. Dat's my opinion, anyways. But nemmine 'bout dat. When I seed dat man, I 'uz dat sk'yerd dat I could scasely wobble home. Den I give a nigger man a dollar for dese clo'es, en I ain't ben in a house sence, night ner day, till now. I blacked my face en laid hid in de cellar of a ole house dat's burnt down, daytimes, en robbed de sugar hogsheads en grain sacks on de wharf, nights, to git somethin' to eat, en never dast to try to buy noth'n, en I's mos' starved. En I never dast to come near dis place till dis rainy night, when dey ain't no people roun' scasely. But to-night I ben a stannin' in de dark alley ever sence night come, waitin' for you to go by. En here I is.'

She fell to thinking. Presently she said:

'You seed dat man at noon, las' Monday?'

'Yes.'

'I seed him de middle o' dat arternoon. He hunted you up, didn't he?'

'Yes.'

'Did he give you de bill dat time?'

'No, he hadn't got it printed yet.'

Roxana darted a suspicious glance at him.

'Did you he'p him fix up de bill?'

Tom cursed himself for making that stupid blunder, and tried to rectify it by saying he remembered, now, that it *was* at noon Monday that the man gave him the bill. Roxana said:

'You's lyin' agin, sho'.' Then she straightened up and raised her finger:

'Now den! I's gwyne to ast you a question, en I wants to know how you's gwyne to git aroun' it. You knowed he 'uz arter me; en if you runs off, 'stid o' stayin' here to he'p him, he'd know dey 'uz somethin' wrong 'bout dis business, en den he would inquire 'bout you, en dat would take him to yo' uncle, en yo' uncle would read de bill en see dat you ben sellin' a free nigger down de river, en you know *him*, I reckon! He'd tar up de will en kick you outen de house. Now, den, you answer me dis question: hain't you tole dat man dat I would be sho' to come here, en den you would fix it so he could set a trap en ketch me?'

Tom recognised that neither lies nor arguments could help him any longer—he was in a vice, with the screw turned on, and out of it there was no budging. His face began to take on an ugly look, and presently he said, with a snarl:

'Well, what could I do? You see, yourself, that I was in his grip and couldn't get out.'

Roxy scorched him with a scornful gaze awhile, then she said:

'What could you do? You could be Judas to yo' own mother to save yo' wuthless hide! Would anybody b'lieve it? No—a dog couldn't! You is de low-downest orneriest hound dat was ever pupp'd into dis worl'—en I's 'sponsible for it!' And she spat on him.

He made no effort to resent this. Roxy reflected a moment, then she said:

'Now I'll tell you what you's gwyne to do. You's gwyne to give dat man de money dat you's got laid up, en make him wait till you kin go to de Jedge en git de res' en buy me free ag'in.'

'Thunder! what are you thinking of? Go and ask him for three hundred dollars and odd? What would I tell him I want with it, pray?'

Roxy's answer was delivered in a serene and level voice:

'You'll tell him you's sole me to pay yo' gambling debts, en dat you lied to me en was a villain, en dat I 'quires you to git dat money en buy me back ag'in.'

'Why, you've gone stark mad! He would tear the will to shreds in a minute—don't you know that?'

'Yes, I does.'

'Then you don't believe I'm idiot enough to go to him, do you?'

'I don't b'lieve nothin' 'bout it—I *knows* you's a-goin'. I knows it beca'se you knows dat if you don't raise dat money I'll go to him myself, en den he'll sell *you* down the river, en you kin see how you like it!'

Tom rose trembling, and excited, and there was an evil light in his eye. He strode to the door and said he must get out of this suffocating place for a moment and clear his brain in the fresh air so that he could determine what to do. The door wouldn't open. Roxy smiled grimly, and said:

'I's got the key, honey—set down. You needn't cle'r up yo' brain none to fine out what you gwyne to do—*I* knows what you's gwyne to do.' Tom sat down and began to pass his hands through his hair with a helpless and desperate air. Roxy said: 'Is dat man in dis house?'

Tom glanced up with a surprised expression and asked:

'What gave you such an idea?'

'You done it. Gwyne out to cle'r yo' brain! In de fust place you ain't got none to cle'r, en in de second place yo' ornery eye tole on you. You's de low-downest hound dat ever—but I done tole you dat befo'. Now, den, dis is Friday. You can fix it up wid dat man, en tell him you's gwyne away to git de res 'o 'de money, en dat you'll be back wid it nex' Tuesday, or maybe Wednesday. You understan'?'

Tom answered sullenly: 'Yes.'

'En when you gets de new bill o' sale dat sells me to my own self, take en send it in de mail to Mr Pudd'nhead Wilson, en write on de back dat he's to keep it till I come. You understan'?'

'Yes.'

'Dat's all, den. Take yo' umbreller, en put on yo' hat.'

'Why?'

'Beca'se you's gwyne to see me home to de wharf. You see dis knife? I's totted it aroun' sence de day I seed dat man en bought dese clo'es en it. If he ketched me, I 'uz gwyne to kill myself wid it. Now start along, en go sof', en lead de way; en if you gives a sign in dis house, or if anybody comes up to you in de street, I's gwyne to jam it into you. Chambers, does you b'lieve me when I says dat?'

'It's no use to bother me with that question. I know your word's good.'

'Yes, it's diff'rent fom yo'n! Shet de light out en move along—here's de key.'

They were not followed. Tom trembled every time a late straggler brushed by them on the street, and half expected to feel the cold steel in his back. Roxy was right at his heels and always in reach. After tramping a mile they reached a wide vacancy on the deserted wharves, and in this dark and rainy desert they parted.

As Tom trudged home his mind was full of dreary thoughts and wild plans; but at last he said to himself, wearily—

'There is but the one way out. I must follow her plan. But with a variation—I will not ask for the money and ruin myself, I will *rob* the old skinflint.'

19

Few things are harder to put up with than the annoyance of a good example.

—PUDD'NHEAD WILSON'S CALENDAR

It were not best that we should all think alike; it is difference of opinion that makes horse-races.

—PUDD'NHEAD WILSON'S CALENDAR

DAWSON'S LANDING was comfortably finishing its season of dull repose and waiting patiently for the duel. Count Luigi was waiting too; but not patiently, rumour said. Sunday came, and Luigi insisted on having his challenge conveyed. Wilson carried it. Judge Driscoll declined to fight with an assassin— 'that is,' he added, significantly, 'in the field of honour.'

Elsewhere, of course, he would be ready. Wilson tried to convince him that if he had been present himself when Angelo told about the homicide committed by Luigi, he would not have considered the act discreditable to Luigi; but the obstinate old man was not to be moved.

Wilson went back to his principal and reported the failure of his mission. Luigi was incensed, and asked how it could be that the old gentleman, who was by no means dull-witted, held his trifling nephew's evidence and inferences to be of more value than Wilson's. But Wilson laughed, and said:

'That is quite simple; that is easily explicable. I am not his doll—his baby—his infatuation: his nephew is. The Judge and his late wife never had any children. The Judge and his wife were past middle age when this treasure fell into their lap. One must make allowances for a parental instinct that has been starving for twenty-five or thirty years. It is famished, it is crazed with hunger by that time, and will be entirely satisfied with anything that comes handy; its taste is atrophied, it can't tell mud-cat from shad. A devil born to a young couple is measurably recognisable by them as a devil before long, but a devil adopted by an old couple is an angel to them, and remains so, through thick and thin. Tom is this old man's angel; he is infatuated with him. Tom can persuade him into things which other people can't—not all things, I don't mean that, but a good many—particularly one class of things: the things that create or abolish personal partialities or prejudices in the old man's mind. The old man liked both of you. Tom conceived a hatred for you. That was enough; it turned the old man around at once. The oldest and strongest friendship must go to the ground when one of these late-adopted darlings throws a brick at it.'

'It's a curious philosophy,' said Luigi.

'It ain't a philosophy at all—it's a fact. And there is something pathetic and beautiful about it, too. I think there is nothing more pathetic than to see one of these poor old childless couples taking a menagerie of yelping little worthless dogs to their hearts; and then adding some cursing and squawking parrots and a jackass-voiced macaw; and next a couple of hundred screeching song-birds, and presently some fœtid guinea-pigs and rabbits, and a howling colony of cats. It is all a groping and ignorant effort to construct out of base metal and brass filings, so to speak, something to take the place of that golden treasure denied them by Nature—a child. But this is a digression. The unwritten law of this region requires you to kill Judge Driscoll on sight, and he and the community will expect that attention at your hands—though of course your own death by his bullet will answer every purpose. Look out for him! Are you heeled—that is, fixed?'

'Yes; he shall have his opportunity. If he attacks me I will respond.'

As Wilson was leaving he said—

'The Judge is still a little used up by his campaign work, and will not get out for a day or so, but when he does get out, you want to be on the alert.'

About eleven at night the twins went out for exercise, and started on a long stroll in the veiled moonlight.

Tom Driscoll had landed at Hackett's Store, two miles below Dawson's, just about half an hour earlier, the only passenger for that lonely spot, and had walked up the shore road and entered Judge Driscoll's house without having encountered any one either on the road or under the roof.

He pulled down his window-blinds and lighted his candle. He laid off his coat and hat and began his preparations. He unlocked his trunk and got his suit of girl's clothes out from under the male attire in it and laid it by. Then he blacked his face with burnt cork and put the cork in his pocket. His plan was to slip down to his uncle's private sitting-room below, pass into the bedroom, steal the safe-key from the old gentleman's clothes, and then go back and rob the safe. He took up his candle to start. His courage and confidence were high, up to this point, but both began to waver a little now. Suppose he should make a noise, by some accident, and get caught—say, in the act of opening the safe? Perhaps it would be well to go armed. He took the Indian knife from its hiding-place, and felt a pleasant return of his waning courage. He slipped stealthily down the narrow stair, his hair rising and his pulses halting at the slightest creak. When he was half-way down, he was disturbed to perceive that the landing below was touched by a faint glow of light. What could that mean? Was his uncle still up? No, that was not likely; he must have left his night-taper there when he went to bed. Tom crept on down, pausing at every step to listen. He found the door standing open, and glanced in. What he saw pleased him beyond measure. His uncle was asleep on the sofa; on a small table at the head of the sofa a lamp was burning low, and by it stood the old man's small tin cash-box, closed. Near the box was a pile of bank-notes and a piece of paper covered with figures in pencil. The safe-door was not open. Evidently the sleeper had wearied himself with work upon his finances and was taking a rest.

Tom set his candle on the stairs, and began to make his way toward the pile of notes, stooping low as he went. When he was passing his uncle, the old man stirred in his sleep, and Tom stopped instantly—stopped, and softly drew the knife from its sheath, with his heart thumping and his eyes fastened upon his benefactor's face. After a moment or two he ventured forward again—one step—reached for his prize and seized it, dropping the knife-sheath. Then he felt the old man's strong grip upon him, and a wild cry of 'Help! help!' rang in his ear. Without hesitation he drove the knife home— and was free. Some of the notes escaped from his left hand and fell in the blood on the floor. He dropped the knife and snatched them up and started to fly; transferred them to his left hand and seized the knife again, in his fright and confusion, but remembered himself and flung it from him, as being a dangerous witness to carry away with him.

He jumped for the stair-foot, and closed the door behind him; and as he snatched his candle and fled upward, the stillness of the night was broken by the sound of urgent footsteps approaching the house. In another moment he was in his room and the twins were standing aghast over the body of the murdered man!

Tom put on his coat, buttoned his hat under it, threw on his suit of girl's clothes, dropped the veil, blew out his light, locked the room door by which he had just entered, taking the key, passed through his other door into the back hall, locked that door and kept the key, then worked his way along in the dark and descended the back-stairs. He was not expecting to meet anybody, for all interest was centred in the other part of the house now. His calculation proved correct. By the time he was passing through the back-yard, Mrs Pratt, her servants, and a dozen half-dressed neighbours had joined the twins and the dead, and accessions were still arriving at the front door.

As Tom, quaking as with a palsy, passed out at the gate, three women came flying from the house on the opposite side of the lane. They rushed by him and in at the gate, asking him what the trouble was there, but not waiting for an answer. Tom said to himself, 'Those old maids waited to dress; they did the same thing the night Stevens's house burned down next door.' In a few minutes he was in the haunted house. He lit a candle and took off his girl-clothes. There was blood on him all down his left side, and his right hand was red with the stains of the blood-soaked notes which he had crushed in it; but otherwise he was free from this sort of evidence. He cleansed his hand on the straw, and cleaned the most of the smut from his face. Then he burned his male and female attire to ashes, scattered the ashes, and put on a disguise proper for a tramp. He blew out his light, went below, and was soon loafing down the river road with the intent to borrow and use one of Roxy's devices. He found a canoe and paddled off down stream, setting the canoe adrift as dawn approached, and making his way by land to the next village, where he kept out of sight till a transient steamer came along, and then took deck passage for St Louis. He was ill at ease until Dawson's Landing was behind him; then he said to himself: 'All the detectives on earth couldn't trace me now; there's not a vestige of a clue left in the world; that homicide will take its place with the permanent mysteries, and people won't get done trying to guess out the secret of it for fifty years.'

In St Louis, next morning, he read this brief telegram* in the papers—dated at Dawson's Landing:

'Judge Driscoll, an old and respected citizen, was assassinated here about midnight by a profligate Italian nobleman or barber, on account of a quarrel growing out of the recent election. The assassin will probably be lynched.'*

'One of the twins!' soliloquised Tom; 'how lucky! It is the knife that has done him this grace. We never know when fortune is trying to favour us. I actually cursed Pudd'nhead Wilson in my heart for putting it out of my power to sell that knife. I take it back now.'

Tom was now rich and independent. He arranged with the planter, and mailed to Wilson the new bill of sale which sold Roxana to herself; then he telegraphed his Aunt Pratt:

'Have seen the awful news in the papers and am almost prostrate with grief. Shall start by packet to-day. Try to bear up till I come.'

When Wilson reached the house of mourning, and had gathered such details as Mrs Pratt and the rest of the crowd could tell him, he took command as mayor, and gave orders that nothing should be touched, but everything left as it was until Justice Robinson should arrive and take the proper measures as coroner. He cleared everybody out of the room but the twins and himself. The sheriff soon arrived and took the twins away to jail. Wilson told them to keep heart, and promised to do his best in their defence when the case should come to trial. Justice Robinson came presently, and with him Constable Blake. They examined the room thoroughly. They found the knife and the sheath. Wilson noticed that there were finger-prints on the knife-handle. That pleased him, for the twins had required the earliest comers to make a scrutiny of their hands and clothes, and neither these people nor Wilson himself had found any blood-stains upon them. Could there be a possibility that the twins had spoken the truth when they said they found the man dead when they ran into the house in answer to the cry for help? He thought of that mysterious girl at once. But this was not the sort of work for a girl to be engaged in. No matter, Tom Driscoll's room must be examined.

After the coroner's jury had viewed the body and its surroundings, Wilson suggested a search upstairs, and he went along. The jury forced an entrance to Tom's room, but found nothing, of course.

The coroner's jury found that the homicide was committed by Luigi, and that Angelo was accessory to it.

The town was bitter against the unfortunates, and for the first few days after the murder they were in constant danger of being lynched. The grand jury presently indicted Luigi for murder in the first degree, and Angelo as accessory before the fact. The twins were transferred from the city gaol to the county prison to await trial.

Wilson examined the finger-marks on the knife-handle, and said to himself: 'Neither of the twins made those marks.' Then manifestly there was another person concerned, either in his own interest or as hired assassin.

But who could it be? That, he must try to find out. The safe was not open, the cash-box was closed, and had three thousand dollars in it. Then robbery was not the motive, and revenge was. Where had the murdered man an enemy except

Luigi? There was but that one person in the world with a
deep grudge against him.

The mysterious girl! The girl was a great trial to Wilson.
If the motive had been robbery, the girl might answer, but
there wasn't any girl that would want to take this old man's
life for revenge. He had no quarrels with girls; he was a
gentleman.

Wilson had perfect tracings of the finger-marks of the
knife-handle; and among his glass-records he had a great array
of the finger-prints of women and girls, collected during the
last fifteen or eighteen years, but he scanned them in vain,
they successfully withstood every test; among them were no
duplicates of the prints on the knife.

The presence of the knife on the stage of the murder was
a worrying circumstance for Wilson. A week previously he
had as good as admitted to himself that he believed Luigi
had possessed such a knife, and that he still possessed it,
notwithstanding his pretence that it had been stolen. And
now here was the knife, and with it the twins. Half the town
had said the twins were humbugging when they claimed that
they had lost their knife, and now these people were joyful,
and said, 'I told you so.'

If their finger-prints had been on the handle—but it was
useless to bother any further about that; the finger-prints on
the handle were *not* theirs—that he knew perfectly.

Wilson refused to suspect Tom; for firstly, Tom couldn't
murder anybody—he hadn't character enough; secondly if he
could murder a person he wouldn't select his doting benefactor and nearest relative; thirdly, self-interest was in the
way; for while the uncle lived, Tom was sure of a free support
and a chance to get the destroyed will revived again, but with
the uncle gone that chance was gone too. It was true the
will had really been revived, as was now discovered, but Tom
could not have been aware of it, or he would have spoken
of it, in his native, talky, unsecretive way. Finally, Tom was
in St Louis when the murder was done, and got the news
out of the morning journals, as was shown by his telegram
to his aunt. These speculations were unemphasised sensations

rather than articulated thoughts, for Wilson would have laughed at the idea of seriously connecting Tom with the murder.

Wilson regarded the case of the twins as desperate—in fact, about hopeless. For he argued that if a confederate was not found, an enlightened Missouri jury would hang them, sure; if a confederate was found, that would not improve the matter, but simply furnish one more person for the sheriff to hang. Nothing could save the twins but the discovery of a person who did the murder on his sole personal account— an undertaking which had all the aspect of the impossible. Still, the person who made the finger-prints must be sought. The twins might have no case *with* him, but they certainly would have none without him.

So Wilson mooned around, thinking, thinking, guessing, guessing, day and night, and arriving nowhere. Whenever he ran across a girl or woman he was not acquainted with, he got her finger-prints, on one pretext or another; and they always cost him a sigh when he got home, for they never tallied with the finger-marks on the knife-handle.

As to the mysterious girl, Tom swore he knew no such girl, and did not remember ever seeing a girl wearing a dress like the one described by Wilson. He admitted that he did not always lock his room, and that sometimes the servants forgot to lock the house-doors; still, in his opinion the girl must have made but few visits, or she would have been discovered. When Wilson tried to connect her with the stealing-raid, and thought she might have been the old woman's confederate, if not the very thief herself disguised as an old woman, Tom seemed struck, and also much interested, and said he would keep a sharp eye out for this person or persons, although he was afraid that she or they would be too smart to venture again into a town where everybody would now be on the watch for a good while to come.

Everybody was pitying Tom, he looked so quiet and sorrowful, and seemed to feel his great loss so deeply. He was playing a part, but it was not all a part. The picture of his alleged uncle, as he had last seen him, was before him in the dark pretty frequently, when he was awake, and called again in his dreams, when he was asleep. He wouldn't go into the room where the tragedy had happened. This charmed the doting Mrs Pratt, who 'realised now, as she had never done before', she said, what a sensitive and delicate nature her darling had, and how he adored his poor uncle.

20

Even the clearest and most perfect circumstantial evidence is likely to be at fault, after all, and therefore ought to be received with great caution. Take the case of any pencil, sharpened by any woman: if you have witnesses you will find she did it with a knife; but if you take simply the aspect of the pencil you will say she did it with her teeth.
—PUDD'NHEAD WILSON'S CALENDAR

THE weeks dragged along, no friend visiting the gaoled twins but their counsel and Aunt Patsy Cooper, and the day of trial came at last—the heaviest day in Wilson's life; for with all his tireless diligence he had discovered no sign or trace of the missing confederate. 'Confederate' was the term he had long ago privately accepted for that person—not as being unquestionably the right term, but as being at least possibly the right one, though he was never able to understand why the twins didn't vanish and escape, as the confederate had done, instead of remaining by the murdered man and getting caught there.

The court-house was crowded, of course, and would remain so to the finish, for not only in the town itself, but in the country for miles around the trial was the one topic of conversation among the people. Mrs Pratt, in deep mourning, and Tom with a weed on his hat, had seats near Pembroke Howard, the public prosecutor, and back of them sat a great array of friends of the family. The twins had but one friend present to keep their counsel in countenance, their poor old sorrowing landlady. She sat near Wilson, and looked her friendliest. In the 'nigger corner' sat Chambers; also Roxy, with good clothes on, and her bill of sale in her pocket. It was her most precious possession, and she never parted with it, day or night. Tom had allowed her thirty-five dollars a month ever since he came into his property, and had said that he and she ought to be grateful to the twins for making them rich; but had roused such a temper in her by this speech that he did not repeat the argument afterward. She said the old Judge had treated her child a thousand times better than he deserved, and had never done her an unkindness in his life; so she hated these outlandish devils for killing him, and shouldn't ever sleep satisfied till she saw them hanged for it. She was here to watch the trial now, and was going to lift up just one 'hooraw' over it if the County Judge put her in gaol a year for it. She gave her turbaned head a toss and said, 'When dat verdic' comes, I'se gwyne to lif' dat *roof*, now, I *tell* you.'

Pembroke Howard briefly sketched the State's case. He said he would show by a chain of circumstantial evidence, without break or fault in it anywhere, that the principal prisoner at the bar committed the murder; that the motive was partly revenge, and partly a desire to take his own life out of jeopardy, and that his brother, by his presence, was a consenting accessory to the crime; a crime which was the basest known to the calendar of human misdeeds—assassination; that it was conceived by the blackest of hearts and consummated by the cowardliest of hands; a crime which had broken a loving sister's heart, blighted the happiness of a young nephew who was as dear as a son, brought inconsolable grief to many friends, and sorrow and loss to the whole community. The utmost penalty of the outraged law would be exacted, and upon the accused, now present at the bar, that penalty would unquestionably be executed. He would reserve further remark until his closing speech.

He was strongly moved, and so also was the whole house; Mrs Pratt and several other women were weeping when he sat down; and many an eye that was full of hate was riveted upon the unhappy prisoners.

Witness after witness was called by the State, and questioned at length; but the cross-questioning was brief. Wilson knew they could furnish nothing valuable for his side. People were sorry for Pudd'nhead; his budding career would get hurt by this trial.

Several witnesses swore they heard Judge Driscoll say in his public speech that the twins would be able to find their lost knife again when they needed it to assassinate somebody with. This was not news, but now it was seen to have been sorrowfully prophetic, and a profound sensation quivered through the hushed court-room when those dismal words were repeated.

The public prosecutor rose and said that it was within his knowledge, through a conversation held with Judge Driscoll on the last day of his life, that counsel for the defence had brought him a challenge from the person charged at this bar with murder; that he had refused to fight with a confessed assassin—'that is, on the field of honour', but had added significantly, that he would be ready for him elsewhere. Presumably the person here charged with murder was warned that he must kill or be killed the first time he should meet Judge Driscoll. If counsel for the defence chose to let the statement stand so, he would not call him to the witness stand. Mr Wilson said he would offer no denial. (Murmurs in the house—'It is getting worse and worse for Wilson's case.')

Mrs Pratt testified that she heard no outcry, and did not know what woke her up, unless it was the sound of rapid footsteps approaching the front door. She jumped up and ran out in the hall just as she was, and heard the footsteps flying up the front steps and then following behind her as she ran to the sitting-room. There she found the accused standing over her murdered brother. (Here she broke down and sobbed. Sensation in the court.) Resuming, she said the persons entering behind her were Mr Rogers and Mr Buckstone.

Cross-examined by Wilson, she said the twins proclaimed their innocence; declared that they had been taking a walk, and had hurried to the house in response to a cry for help which was so loud and strong that they had heard it at a considerable distance; that they begged her and the gentlemen just mentioned to examine their hands and clothes—which was done, and no blood stains found.

Confirmatory evidence followed, from Rogers and Buckstone.

The finding of the knife was verified, the advertisement minutely describing it and offering a reward for it was put in evidence, and its exact correspondence with that description proven. Then followed a few minor details, and the case for the State was closed.

Wilson said that he had three witnesses, the Misses Clarkson, who would testify that they met a veiled young woman leaving Judge Driscoll's premises by the back gate a few minutes after the cries for help were heard, and that their evidence, taken with certain circumstantial evidence which he would call the court's attention to, would in his opinion convince the court that there was still one person concerned in this crime who had not yet been found, and also that a stay of proceedings ought to be granted, in justice to his clients, until that person should be discovered. As it was late, he would ask leave to defer the examination of his three witnesses until the next morning.

The crowd poured out of the place and went flocking away in excited groups and couples, talking the events of the session over with vivacity and consuming interest, and everybody seemed to have had a satisfactory and enjoyable day except the accused, their counsel, and their old-lady friend. There was no cheer among these, and no substantial hope.

In parting with the twins Aunt Patsy did attempt a good-night with a gay pretence of hope and cheer in it, but broke down without finishing.

Absolutely secure as Tom considered himself to be, the opening solemnities of the trial had nevertheless oppressed him with a vague uneasiness, his being a nature sensitive to even the smallest alarms; but from the moment that the poverty and weakness of Wilson's case lay exposed to the court, he was comfortable once more, even jubilant. He left the courtroom sarcastically sorry for Wilson. 'The Clarksons met an unknown woman in the back lane,' he said to himself—'*that* is his case! I'll give him a century to find her in—a couple of them if he likes. A woman who doesn't exist any longer, and the clothes that gave her her sex burnt up, and the ashes thrown away—oh, certainly he'll find *her* easy enough!' This reflection set him to admiring, for the hundredth time, the shrewd ingenuities by which he had insured himself against detection—more, against even suspicion.

'Nearly always in cases like this there is some little detail or other overlooked, some wee little track or trace left behind, and detection follows; but here there's not even the faintest suggestion of a trace left. No more than a bird leaves when it flies through the air—yes, through the night, you may say. The man that can track a bird through the air in the dark and find that bird is the man to track me out and find the Judge's assassin—no other need apply. And that is the job that has been laid out for poor Pudd'nhead Wilson, of all people in the world! Lord, it will be pathetically funny to see him grubbing and groping after that woman that don't exist, and the right person sitting under his very nose all the time!' The more he thought the situation over, the more the humour of it struck him. Finally he said: 'I'll never let him hear the last of that woman. Every time I catch him in company, to his dying day, I'll ask him, in the guileless, affectionate way that used to gravel him so when I inquired how his unborn law-business was coming along, "Got on her track yet—hey, Pudd'nhead?"' He wanted to laugh, but that would not have answered; there were people about, and he was mourning for his uncle. He made up his mind that it would be good entertainment to look in on Wilson that night and watch him worry over his barren law-case and goad him with an exasperating word or two of sympathy and commiseration now and then.

Wilson wanted no supper, he had no appetite. He got out all the finger-prints of girls and women in his collection of 'records', and pored gloomily over them an hour or more, trying to convince himself that that troublesome girl's marks were there somewhere and had been overlooked. But it was not so. He drew back his chair, clasped his hands over his head, and gave himself up to dull and arid musings.

Tom Driscoll dropped in, an hour after dark, and said with a pleasant laugh as he took a seat:

'Hello, we've gone back to the amusements of our days of neglect and obscurity for consolation, have we?' and he took up one of the glass strips and held it against the light to inspect it. 'Come, cheer up, old man, there's no use in losing your grip and going back to this child's-play merely because this big sun-spot is drifting across your shiny new disk. It'll pass, and you'll be all right again'—and he laid the glass down. 'Did you think you could win always?'

'Oh, no,' said Wilson with a sigh, 'I didn't expect that, but I can't believe Luigi killed your uncle, and I feel very sorry for him. It makes me blue. And you would feel as I do, Tom, if you were not prejudiced against those young fellows.'

'I don't know about that,' and Tom's countenance darkened, for his memory reverted to his kicking. 'I owe them no goodwill, considering the brunette one's treatment of me that night. Prejudice or no prejudice, Pudd'nhead, I don't like them, and when they get their deserts you're not going to find me sitting on the mourner's bench.'

He took up another strip of glass, and exclaimed:

'Why, here's old Roxy's label! Are you going to ornament the royal palaces with nigger paw-marks, too? By the date here, I was seven months old when this was done, and she was nursing me and her little nigger cub. There's a line straight across her thumb-print. How comes that?' And Tom held out the piece of glass to Wilson.

'That is common,' said the bored man, wearily. 'Scar of a cut or a scratch, usually.' And he took the strip of glass indifferently, and raised it toward the lamp.

All the blood sunk suddenly out of his face, his hand quaked, and he gazed at the polished surface before him with the glassy stare of a corpse.

'Great Heavens! what's the matter with you, Wilson? Are you going to faint?'

Tom sprang for a glass of water and offered it, but Wilson shrank shuddering from him, and said:

'No, no!—take it away!' His breast was rising and falling, and he moved his head about in a dull and wandering way, like a person who has been stunned. Presently he said, 'I shall feel better when I get to bed; I have been overwrought to-day—yes, and overworked for many days.'

'Then I'll leave you and let you get to your rest. Good-night, old man.' But as Tom went out he couldn't deny himself a small parting gibe: 'Don't take it so hard; a body can't win every time; you'll hang somebody yet.'

Wilson muttered to himself, 'It is no lie to say I am sorry I have to begin with you, miserable dog though you are!'

He braced himself up with a glass of cold whisky and went to work again. He did not compare the new fingermarks unintentionally left by Tom a few minutes before on Roxy's glass with the tracings of the marks left on the knife-handle, there being no need of that (for his trained eye), but busied himself with another matter, muttering from time to time, 'Idiot that I was!—Nothing but a *girl* would do me—a man in girl's clothes never occurred to me.' First, he hunted out the plate containing the finger-prints made by Tom when he was twelve years old, and laid it by itself; then he brought forth the marks made by Tom's baby fingers when he was a suckling of seven months, and placed these two plates with the one containing this subject's newly (and unconsciously) made record.

'Now the series is complete,' he said with satisfaction, and sat down to inspect these things and enjoy them.

But his enjoyment was brief. He stared a considerable time at the three strips, and seemed stupefied with astonishment. At last he put them down and said: 'I can't make it out at all. Hang it! the baby's don't tally with the others!'

He walked the floor for half an hour, puzzling over his enigma, then he hunted out two other glass plates.

He sat down and puzzled over these things a good while, but kept muttering, 'It's no use—I can't understand it. They don't tally right, and yet I'll swear the names and dates are right, and so of course they *ought* to tally. I never labelled one of these things carelessly in my life. There is a most extraordinary mystery here.'

He was tired out now, and his brains were beginning to clog. He said he would sleep himself fresh, and then see what he could do with this riddle. He slept through a troubled and unrestful hour, then unconsciousness began to shred away, and presently he rose drowsily to a sitting posture. 'Now what was that dream?' he said, trying to recall it. 'What was that dream? It seemed to unravel that puz——'

He landed in the middle of the floor at a bound, without finishing the sentence, and ran and turned up his light and seized his 'records'. He took a single swift glance at them and cried out—

'It's so! Heavens, what a revelation! And for twenty-three years no man has ever suspected it!'

21

He is useless on top of the ground; he ought to be under it, inspiring the cabbages.

——PUDD'NHEAD WILSON'S CALENDAR

April 1.——This is the day upon which we are reminded of what we are on the other three hundred and sixty-four.

——PUDD'NHEAD WILSON'S CALENDAR

WILSON put on enough clothes for business purposes and went to work under a high pressure of steam. He was awake all over. All sense of weariness had been swept away by the invigorating refreshment of the great and hopeful discovery which he had made. He made fine and accurate reproductions of a number of his 'records', and then enlarged them on a scale of ten to one with his pantagraph. He did these pantagraph enlargements on sheets of white cardboard, and made each individual line of the bewildering maze of whorls or curves or loops which constituted the 'pattern' of a 'record' stand out bold and black by reinforcing it with ink.

To the untrained eye the collection of delicate originals made by the human finger on the glass plates looked about alike; but when enlarged ten times they resembled the markings of a block of wood that has been sawed across the grain, and the dullest eye could detect at a glance, and at a distance of many feet, that no two of the patterns were alike. When Wilson had at last finished his tedious and difficult work, he arranged its results according to a plan in which a progressive order and sequence was a principal feature, then he added to the batch several pantagraph enlargements which he had made from time to time in bygone years.

The night was spent and the day well advanced now. By the time he had snatched a trifle of breakfast it was nine o'clock, and the court ready to begin its sitting. He was in his place twelve minutes later with his 'records'.

Tom Driscoll caught a slight glimpse of the 'records', and nudged his nearest friend and said, with a wink, 'Pudd'nhead's got a rare eye to business—thinks that as long as he can't win his case it's at least a noble good chance to advertise his palace-window decorations without any expense.' Wilson was informed that his witnesses had been delayed, but would arrive presently; but he rose and said he should probably not have occasion to make use of their testimony. (An amused murmur ran through the room—'It's a clean back-down! he gives up without hitting a lick!') Wilson continued—'I have other testimony—and better.' (This compelled interest, and evoked murmurs of surprise that had a detectable ingredient of disappointment in them.) 'If I seem to be springing this evidence upon the court, I offer as my justification for this, that I did not discover its existence until late last night, and have been engaged in examining and classifying it ever since, until half an hour ago. I shall offer it presently; but first I wish to say a few preliminary words.

'May it please the court, the claim given the front place, the claim most persistently urged, the claim most strenuously and I may even say aggressively and defiantly insisted upon by the prosecution, is this—that the person whose hand left the blood-stained finger-prints upon the handle of the Indian

knife is the person who committed the murder.' Wilson
paused, during several moments, to give impressiveness to
what he was about to say, and then added, tranquilly, '*We
grant that claim.*'

It was an electrical surprise. No one was prepared for such
an admission. A buzz of astonishment rose on all sides, and
people were heard to intimate that the over-worked lawyer
had lost his mind. Even the veteran Judge, accustomed as he
was to legal ambushes and masked batteries in criminal
procedure, was not sure that his ears were not deceiving him,
and asked counsel what it was he had said. Howard's im-
passive face betrayed no sign, but his attitude and bearing
lost something of their careless confidence for a moment.
Wilson resumed:

'We not only grant that claim, but we welcome it and
strongly endorse it. Leaving that matter for the present, we
will now proceed to consider other points in the case which
we propose to establish by evidence, and shall include that
one in the chain in its proper place.'

He had made up his mind to try a few hardy guesses, in
mapping out his theory of the origin and motive of the
murder—guesses designed to fill up gaps in it—guesses which
could help if they hit, and would probably do no harm if
they didn't.

'To my mind, certain circumstances of the case before the
court seem to suggest a motive for the homicide quite
different from the one insisted on by the State. It is my
conviction that the motive was not revenge, but robbery. It
has been urged that the presence of the accused brothers in
that fatal room, just after notification that one of them must
take the life of Judge Driscoll or lose his own the moment
the parties should meet, clearly signifies that the natural
instinct of self-preservation moved my clients to go there
secretly and save Count Luigi by destroying his adversary.

'Then why did they stay there, after the deed was done?
Mrs Pratt had time, although she did not hear the cry for
help, but woke up some moments later, to run to that
room—and there she found these men standing, and making

no effort to escape. If they were guilty, they ought to have been running out of the house at the same time that she was running to that room. If they had had such a strong instinct toward self-preservation as to move them to kill that unarmed man, what had become of it now, when it should have been more alert than ever? Would any of us have remained there? Let us slander not our intelligence to that degree.

'Much stress has been laid upon the fact that the accused offered a very large reward for the knife with which this murder was done; that no thief came forward to claim that extraordinary reward; that the latter fact was good circumstantial evidence that the claim that the knife had been stolen was a vanity and a fraud; that these details, taken in connection with the memorable and apparently prophetic speech of the deceased concerning that knife, and the final discovery of that very knife in the fatal room where no living person was found present with the slaughtered man but the owner of the knife and his brother, form an indestructible chain of evidence which fixes the crime upon those unfortunate strangers.

'But I shall presently ask to be sworn, and shall testify that there was a large reward offered for the *thief*, also; that it was offered secretly and not advertised; that this fact was indiscreetly mentioned—or at least tacitly admitted—in what was supposed to be safe circumstances, but may *not* have been. The thief may have been present himself.' (Tom Driscoll had been looking at the speaker, but dropped his eyes at this point.) 'In that case he would retain the knife in his possession, not daring to offer it for sale, or for pledge in a pawnshop.' (There was a nodding of heads among the audience by way of admission that this was not a bad stroke.) 'I shall prove to the satisfaction of the jury that there *was* a person in Judge Driscoll's room several minutes before the accused entered it.' (This produced a strong sensation; the last drowsyhead in the court-room roused up, now, and made preparation to listen.) 'If it shall seem necessary, I will prove by the Misses Clarkson that they met a veiled person—ostensibly a woman—coming out of the back gate a few minutes after the cry for help was heard. This person was not a woman, but a man dressed in woman's clothes.' (Another sensation. Wilson had his eye on Tom when he hazarded this guess, to see what effect it would produce. He was satisfied with the result, and said to himself, 'It was a success—he's hit!')

'The object of that person in that house was robbery, not murder. It is true that the safe was not open, but there was an ordinary tin cash-box on the table, with three thousand dollars in it. It is easily supposable that the thief was concealed in the house; that he knew of this box, and of its owner's habit of counting its contents and arranging his accounts at night—if he had that habit, which I do not assert, of course; that he tried to take the box while its owner slept, but made a noise and was seized, and had to use the knife to save himself from capture; and that he fled without his booty because he heard help coming.

'I have now done with my theory, and will proceed to the evidences by which I propose to try to prove its soundness.' Wilson took up several of his strips of glass. When the audience recognised these familiar mementoes of Pudd'nhead's old-time childish 'puttering' and folly, the tense and funereal interest vanished out of their faces, and the house burst into volleys of relieving and refreshing laughter, and Tom chirked up and joined in the fun himself; but Wilson was apparently not disturbed. He arranged his 'records' on the table before him, and said:

'I beg the indulgence of the court while I make a few remarks in explanation of some evidence which I am about to introduce, and which I shall presently ask to be allowed to verify under oath on the witness stand. Every human being carries with him from his cradle to his grave certain physical marks which do not change their character, and by which he can always be identified—and that without shade of doubt or question. These marks are his signature, his physiological autograph, so to speak, and this autograph cannot be counterfeited, nor can he disguise it or hide it away, nor can it become illegible by the wear and the mutations of time. This signature is not his face—age can change that beyond recognition; it is not his hair, for that can fall out; it is not his height, for duplicates of that exist; it is not his form, for duplicates of that exist also, whereas this signature is each man's very own—there is no duplicate of it among the swarming populations of the globe!' (The audience were interested once more.)

'This autograph consists of the delicate lines or corrugations with which Nature marks the insides of the hands and the soles of the feet. If you will look at the balls of your fingers—you that have very sharp eyesight—you will observe that these dainty curving lines lie close together, like those that indicate the borders of oceans in maps, and that they form various clearly defined patterns, such as arches, circles, long curves, whorls, &c., and that these patterns differ on the different fingers.' (Every man in the room had his hand up to the light, now, and his head canted to one side, and was minutely scrutinising the balls of his fingers; there were whispered ejaculations of 'Why, it's so—I never noticed that before!') 'The patterns on the right hand are not the same as those on the left.' (Ejaculations of 'Why, that's so, too!') 'Taken finger for finger, your patterns differ from your neighbour's.' (Comparisons were made all over the house— even the Judge and jury were absorbed in this curious work.) 'The patterns of a twin's right hand are not the same as those on his left. One twin's patterns are never the same as his fellow-twin's patterns—the jury will find that the patterns upon the finger-balls of the accused follow this rule.' (An examination of the twins' hands was begun at once.) 'You have often heard of twins who were so exactly alike that when dressed alike their own parents could not tell them apart. Yet there was never a twin born into this world that did not carry from birth to death a sure identifier in this mysterious and marvellous natal autograph. That once known to you, his fellow-twin could never personate him and deceive you.'

Wilson stopped* and stood silent. Inattention dies a quick and sure death when a speaker does that. The stillness gives warning that something is coming. All palms and finger-balls

went down, now, all slouching forms straightened, all heads
came up, all eyes were fastened upon Wilson's face. He waited
yet one, two, three moments, to let his pause complete and
perfect its spell upon the house; then, when through the
profound hush he could hear the ticking of the clock on the
wall, he put out his hand and took the Indian knife by the blade
and held it aloft where all could see the sinister spots upon its
ivory handle; then he said, in a level, passionless voice:

'Upon this haft stands the assassin's natal autograph, written in the blood of that helpless and unoffending old man
who loved you and whom you all loved. There is but one
man in the whole earth whose hand can duplicate that
crimson sign'—he paused and raised his eyes to the pendulum
swinging back and forth—'and please God we will produce
that man in this room before the clock strikes noon!'

Stunned, distraught, unconscious of its own movement, the
house half rose, as if expecting to see the murderer appear
at the door, and a breeze of muttered ejaculations swept the
place. 'Order in the court!—sit down!' This from the sheriff.
He was obeyed, and quiet reigned again. Wilson stole a glance
at Tom, and said to himself: 'He is flying signals of distress,
now; even people who despise him are pitying him; they think
this is a hard ordeal for a young fellow who has lost his
benefactor by so cruel a stroke—and they are right.' He
resumed his speech:

'For more than twenty years I have amused my compulsory
leisure with collecting these curious physical signatures in this
town. At my house I have hundreds upon hundreds of them.
Each and every one is labelled with name and date; not
labelled the next day, or even the next hour, but in the very
minute that the impression was taken. When I go upon the
witness stand I will repeat under oath the things which I am
now saying. I have the finger-prints of the court, the sheriff,
and every member of the jury. There is hardly a person in
this room, white or black, whose natal signature I cannot
produce, and not one of them can so disguise himself that
I cannot pick him out from a multitude of his fellow-crea-
tures and unerringly identify him by his hands. And if he and

I should live to be a hundred I could still do it!' (The interest of the audience was steadily deepening now.)

'I have studied some of these signatures so much that I know them as well as the bank cashier knows the autograph of his oldest customer. While I turn my back now, I beg that several persons will be so good as to pass their fingers through their hair, and then press them upon one of the panes of the window near the jury, and that among them the accused may set *their* finger-marks. Also, I beg that these experimenters, or others, will set their finger-marks upon another pane, and add again the marks of the accused, but not placing them in the same order or relation to the other signatures as before—for, by one chance in a million a person might happen upon the right marks by pure guess-work *once*, therefore I wish to be tested twice.'

He turned his back, and the two panes were quickly covered with delicately-lined oval spots, but visible only to such persons as could get a dark background for them—the foliage of a tree outside, for instance. Then, upon call, Wilson went to the window, made his examination, and said:

'This is Count Luigi's right hand; this one, three signatures below, is his left. Here is Count Angelo's right; down here is his left. Now for the other pane: here and here are Count Luigi's, here and here are his brother's.' He faced about. 'Am I right?'

A deafening explosion of applause was the answer. The Bench said:

'This certainly approaches the miraculous!'

Wilson turned to the window again and remarked, pointing with his finger:

'This is the signature of Mr Justice Robinson.' (Applause.) 'This, of Constable Blake.' (Applause.) 'This, of John Mason, juryman.' (Applause.) 'This, of the sheriff.' (Applause.) 'I cannot name the others, but I have them all at home, named and dated, and could identify them all by my finger-print records.'

He moved to his place through a storm of applause—which the sheriff stopped, and also made the people sit down, for they were all standing and struggling to see, of course. Court, jury, sheriff, and everybody had been too absorbed in observing Wilson's performance to attend to the audience earlier.

'Now then,' said Wilson, 'I have here the natal autographs of two children, thrown up to ten times the natural size by the pantagraph, so that anyone who can see at all can tell the markings apart at a glance. We will call the children *A* and *B*. Here are *A*'s finger-marks taken at the age of five months. Here they are again, taken at seven months.' (Tom started.) 'They are alike, you see. Here are *B*'s at five months, and also at seven months. They, too, exactly copy each other, but the patterns are quite different from *A*'s, you observe. I shall refer to these again presently, but we will turn them face down now.

'Here, thrown up ten sizes, are the natal autographs of the two persons who are here before you accused of murdering Judge Driscoll. I made these pantagraph copies last night, and will so swear when I go upon the witness stand. I ask the jury to compare them with the finger-marks of the accused upon the window-panes, and tell the court if they are the same.'

He passed a powerful magnifying-glass to the foreman.

One juryman after another took the cardboard and the glass and made the comparison. Then the foreman said to the Judge:

'Your honour, we are all agreed that they are identical.'

Wilson said to the foreman:

'Please turn that cardboard face down, and take this one, and compare it searchingly, by the magnifier, with the fatal signature upon the knife-handle, and report your finding to the court.'

Again the jury made minute examination, and again reported:

'We find them to be exactly identical, your honour.'

Wilson turned toward the counsel for the prosecution, and there was a clearly recognisable note of warning in his voice when he said:

'May it please the court, the State has claimed, strenuously and persistently, that the blood-stained finger-prints upon that knife-handle were left there by the assassin of Judge Driscoll. You have heard us grant that claim, and welcome it.' He turned to the jury. 'Compare the finger-prints of the accused with the finger-prints left by the assassin—and report.'

The comparison began. As it proceeded all movement and all sound ceased, and the deep silence of an absorbed and waiting suspense settled upon the house; and when at last the words came, '*They do not even resemble,*' a thundercrash of applause followed and the house sprang to its feet, but was quickly repressed by official force and brought to order again. Tom was altering his position every few minutes, now, but none of his changes brought repose nor any small trifle of comfort. When the house's attention was becoming fixed once more, Wilson said gravely, indicating the twins with a gesture:

'These men are innocent. I have no further concern with them.' (Another outbreak of applause began, but was promptly checked.) 'We will now proceed to find the guilty.' (Tom's eyes were starting from their sockets. Yes, it was a cruel day for the bereaved youth, everybody thought.) 'We will return to the infant autographs of *A* and *B*. I will ask the jury to take these large pantagraph facsimiles of *A*'s, marked five months and seven months. Do they tally?'

The foreman responded, 'Perfectly.'

'Now examine this pantagraph, taken at eight months, and also marked *A*. Does it tally with the other two?'

The surprised response was—

'*No—they differ widely.*'

'You are quite right. Now take these two pantagraphs of *B*'s autograph, marked five months and seven months. Do they tally with each other?'

'Yes—perfectly.'

'Take this third pantagraph marked *B*, eight months. Does it tally with *B*'s other two?'

'*By no means!*'

'Do you know how to account for those strange discrepancies? I will tell you. For a purpose unknown to us, but probably a selfish one, somebody changed those children in the cradle.'

This produced a vast sensation, naturally. Roxana was astonished at this admirable guess, but not disturbed by it. To guess the exchange was one thing, to guess who did it quite another. Pudd'nhead Wilson could do wonderful things, no doubt, but he couldn't do impossible ones. Safe? She was perfectly safe. She smiled privately.

'Between the ages of seven months and eight months those children were changed in the cradle'—he made one of his effect-collecting pauses, and added—'and the person who did it is in this house!'

Roxy's pulses stood still! The house was thrilled as with an electric shock, and the people half rose as if to seek a glimpse of the person who had made that exchange. Tom was growing limp; the life seemed oozing out of him. Wilson resumed:

'*A* was put into *B*'s cradle in the nursery; *B* was transferred to the kitchen and became a negro and a slave'—(Sensation—confusion of angry ejaculations)—'but within a quarter of an hour he will stand before you white and free!' (Burst of applause, checked by the officers.) 'From seven months onward until now, *A* has still been a usurper, and in my finger-records he bears *B*'s name. Here is his pantagraph at the age of twelve. Compare it with the assassin's signature upon the knife-handle. Do they tally?'

The foreman answered—

'*To the minutest detail!*'

Wilson said solemnly, 'The murderer of your friend and mine—York Driscoll of the generous hand and the kindly spirit—sits among you. Valet de Chambre, negro and slave—falsely called Thomas à Becket Driscoll—make upon the window the finger-prints that will hang you!'

Tom turned his ashen face imploringly towards the speaker, made some impotent movements with his white lips, then slid limp and lifeless to the floor.

Wilson broke the awed silence with the words:

'There is no need. He has confessed.'

Roxy flung herself upon her knees, covered her face with her hands, and out through her sobs the words struggled:

'De Lord have mercy on me, po' misable sinner dat I is!'

The clock struck twelve.

The court rose; the new prisoner, handcuffed, was removed.

Conclusion

It is often the case that the man who can't tell a lie thinks he is the best judge of one.

—PUDD'NHEAD WILSON'S CALENDAR

October 12.—The Discovery.—It was wonderful to find America, but it would have been more wonderful to miss it.

—PUDD'NHEAD WILSON'S CALENDAR

THE town sat up all night to discuss the amazing events of the day, and swop guesses as to when Tom's trial would begin. Troop after troop of citizens came to serenade Wilson, and require a speech, and shout themselves hoarse over every sentence that fell from his lips—for all his sentences were golden now, all were marvellous. His long fight against hard luck and prejudice was ended; he was a made man for good.

And as each of these roaring gangs of enthusiasts marched away, some remorseful member of it was quite sure to raise his voice and say:

'And this is the man the likes of us has called a pudd'nhead for more than twenty years. He has resigned from that position, friends.'

'Yes, but it isn't vacant—we're elected.'

The twins were heroes of romance now, and with rehabilitated reputations. But they were weary of Western adventure, and straightway retired to Europe.

Roxy's heart was broken. The young fellow upon whom she had inflicted twenty-three years of slavery continued the false heir's pension of thirty-five dollars a month to her, but her hurts were too deep for money to heal; the spirit in her eye was quenched, her martial bearing departed with it, and the voice of her laughter ceased in the land. In her church and its affairs she found her only solace.

The real heir suddenly found himself rich and free, but in a most embarrassing situation. He could neither read nor write, and his speech was the basest dialect of the negro quarter. His gait, his attitudes, his gestures, his bearing, his laugh—all were vulgar and uncouth; his manners were the manners of a slave. Money and fine clothes could not mend these defects or cover them up, they only made them the more glaring and the more pathetic. The poor fellow could not endure the terrors of the white man's parlour, and felt at home and at peace nowhere but in the kitchen. The family pew was a misery to him, yet he could nevermore enter into the solacing refuge of the 'nigger gallery'—that was closed to him for good and all. But we cannot follow his curious fate further—that would be a long story.

The false heir made a full confession and was sentenced to imprisonment for life. But now a complication came up. The Percy Driscoll estate was in such a crippled shape when its owner died that it could pay only sixty per cent. of its great indebtedness, and was settled at that rate. But the creditors came forward now, and complained that inasmuch as through an error for which *they* were in no way to blame the false heir was not inventoried at that time with the rest of the property, great wrong and loss had thereby been inflicted upon them. They rightly claimed that 'Tom' was lawfully their property and had been so for eight years; that they had already lost sufficiently in being deprived of his services during that long period, and ought not to be required to add anything to that loss; that if he had been delivered up to them in the first place, they would have sold him and he could not have murdered Judge Driscoll, therefore it was not he that had really committed the murder, the guilt lay with the erroneous inventory. Everybody saw that there was reason in this. Everybody granted that if 'Tom' were white and free it would be unquestionably right to punish him—it

would be no loss to anybody; but to shut up a valuable slave
for life—that was quite another matter.

As soon as the Governor understood the case, he pardoned
Tom at once, and the creditors sold him down the river.*

Those Extraordinary Twins

A MAN who is not born with the novel-writing gift has a troublesome time of it when he tries to build a novel. I know this from experience. He has no clear idea of his story; in fact he has no story. He merely has some people in his mind, and an incident or two, also a locality. He knows these people, he knows the selected locality, and he trusts that he can plunge those people into those incidents with interesting results. So he goes to work. To write a novel? No—that is a thought which comes later; in the beginning he is only proposing to tell a little tale; a very little tale; a six-page tale. But as it is a tale which he is not acquainted with, and can only find out what it is by listening as it goes along telling itself, it is more than apt to go on and on and on till it spreads itself into a book. I know about this, because it has happened to me so many times.

And I have noticed another thing: that as the short tale grows into the long tale, the original intention (or motif) is apt to get abolished and find itself superseded by a quite different one. It was so in the case of a magazine sketch which I once started to write—a funny and fantastic sketch about a prince and a pauper; it presently assumed a grave cast of its own accord, and in that new shape spread itself out into a book. Much the same thing happened with 'Pudd'nhead Wilson'. I had a sufficiently hard time with that tale, because it changed itself from a farce to a tragedy while I was going along with it—a most embarrassing circumstance. But what was a great deal worse was, that it was not one story, but two stories tangled together; and they obstructed and interrupted each other at every turn and created no end of confusion and annoyance. I could not offer the book for publication, for I was afraid it would unseat the reader's reason. I did not know what was the matter with it, for I had not noticed, as yet, that it was two stories in one. It took me months to make that discovery. I carried the manuscript back and forth across the Atlantic two or three times, and read it and studied over it on shipboard; and at last I saw where the difficulty lay. I had no further trouble. I pulled one of the stories out by the roots, and left the other one—a kind of literary Cæsarean operation.

Would the reader care to know something about the story which I pulled out? He has been told many a time how the born-and-trained novelist works. Won't he let me round and complete his knowledge by telling him how the jack-leg* does it?

Originally the story was called 'Those Extraordinary Twins'. I meant to make it very short. I had seen a picture of a youthful Italian 'freak'—or 'freaks'*—which was—or which were—on exhibition in our cities—a combination consisting of two heads and four arms joined to a single body and a single pair of legs—and I thought I would write an extravagantly fantastic little story with this freak of nature for hero—or heroes—a silly young miss for heroine, and two old ladies and two boys for the minor parts. I lavishly elaborated these people and their doings, of course. But the tale kept spreading along, and spreading along, and other people got to intruding themselves and taking up more and more room with their talk and their affairs. Among them came a stranger named Pudd'nhead Wilson, and a woman named Roxana; and presently the doings of these two pushed up into prominence a young fellow named Tom Driscoll, whose proper place was away in the obscure background. Before the book was half finished those three were taking things almost entirely into their own hands and working the whole tale as a private venture of their own—a tale which they had nothing at all to do with, by rights.

When the book was finished and I came to look around to see what had become of the team I had originally started out with—Aunt Patsy Cooper, Aunt Betsy Hale, the two boys, and Rowena the light-weight heroine—they were nowhere to be seen; they had disappeared from the story some time or other. I hunted about and found them—found them stranded, idle, forgotten, and permanently useless. It was very awkward. It was awkward all around; but more particularly in the case of Rowena, because there was a love-match on, between her and one of the twins that constituted the freak, and I had worked it up to a blistering heat and thrown in a quite dramatic love-quarrel, wherein Rowena scathingly denounced her betrothed for getting drunk, and scoffed at his explanation of how it had happened, and wouldn't listen to it, and had driven him from her in the usual 'forever' way; and now here she sat crying and broken-hearted; for she had found that he had spoken only the truth; that it was not he, but the other half of the freak, that had drunk the liquor that made him drunk; that her half was a prohibitionist and had never drunk a drop in his life, and, although tight as a brick three days in the week, was wholly innocent of blame; and indeed, when sober, was constantly doing all he could to reform his brother, the other half, who never got any satisfaction out of drinking, anyway, because liquor never affected him. Yes, here she was, stranded with that deep injustice of hers torturing her poor torn heart.

I didn't know what to do with her. I was as sorry for her as anybody could be, but the campaign was over, the book was finished, she was side-tracked, and there was no possible way of crowding her in, anywhere. I could not leave her there, of course; it would not do. After spreading her out so, and making such a to-do over her affairs, it would be absolutely necessary to account to the reader for her. I thought and thought and studied and studied; but I arrived at nothing. I finally saw plainly that there was really no way but one—I must simply give her the grand bounce. It grieved me to do it, for after associating with her so much I had come to kind of like her after a fashion, notwithstanding she was such an ass and said such stupid, irritating things and was so nauseatingly sentimental. Still it had to be done. So, at the top of Chapter XVII, I put a 'Calendar' remark concerning July the Fourth, and began the chapter with this statistic:

'Rowena went out in the back yard after supper to see the fireworks and fell down the well and got drowned.'

It seemed abrupt, but I thought maybe the reader wouldn't notice it, because I changed the subject right away to something else. Anyway it loosened up Rowena from where she was stuck and got her out of the way, and that was the main thing. It seemed a prompt good way of weeding out people that had got stalled, and a plenty good enough way for those others; so I hunted up the two boys and said 'they went out back one night to stone the cat and fell down the well and got drowned'. Next I searched around and found old Aunt Patsy Cooper and Aunt Betsy Hale where they were aground, and said 'they went out back one night to visit the sick and fell down the well and got drowned.' I was going to drown some of the others, but I gave up the idea, partly because I believed that if I kept that up it would arouse attention, and perhaps sympathy with those people, and partly because it was not a large well and would not hold any more anyway.

Still the story was unsatisfactory. Here was a set of new characters who were become inordinately prominent and who persisted in remaining so to the end; and back yonder was an older set who made a large noise and a great to-do for a little while and then suddenly played out utterly and fell down the well. There was a radical defect somewhere, and I must search it out and cure it.

The defect turned out to be the one already spoken of—two stories in one, a farce and a tragedy. So I pulled out the farce and left the tragedy. This left the original team in, but only as mere names, not as characters. Their prominence was wholly gone; they were not even worth drowning; so I removed that detail. Also I took those twins apart and made two separate men of them. They had no occasion to have foreign names now, but it was too much trouble to remove them all through, so I left them christened as they were and made no explanation.

1

THE conglomerate twins were brought on the stage in Chapter I of the original extravaganza. Aunt Patsy Cooper has received their letter applying for board and lodging, and

Rowena, her daughter, insane with joy, is begging for a hearing of it:

'Well, set down then, and be quiet a minute and don't fly around so; it fairly makes me tired to see you. It starts off so: "HONORED MADAM——"'

'I like that, ma, don't you? It shows they're high-bred.'

'Yes, I noticed that when I first read it. "My brother and I have seen your advertisement, by chance, in a copy of your local journal——"'

'It's so beautiful and smooth, ma—don't you think so?'

'Yes, seems so to me—"and beg leave to take the room you offer. We are twenty-four years of age, and twins——"'

'Twins! How sweet! I do hope they are handsome, and I just know they are! Don't you hope they are, ma?'

'Land, I ain't particular. "We are Italians by birth——"'

'It's so romantic! Just think—there's never been one in this town, and everybody will want to see them, and they're all *ours!* Think of that!'

'—"but have lived long in the various countries of Europe, and several years in the United States."'

'Oh, just think what wonders they've seen, ma! Won't it be good to hear them talk?'

'I reckon so; yes, I reckon so. "Our names are Luigi and Angelo Capello——"'

'Beautiful, perfectly beautiful! Not like Jones and Robinson and those horrible names.'

'"You desire but one guest, but dear madam, if you will allow us to pay for two we will not discommode you. We will sleep together in the same bed. We have always been used to this, and prefer it." And then he goes on to say they will be down Thursday.'

'And this is Tuesday—I don't know how I'm ever going to wait, ma! The time does drag along so, and I'm so dying to see them! Which of them do you reckon is the tallest, ma?'

'How do you s'pose I can tell, child? Mostly they are the same size—twins are.'

'Well then, which do you reckon is the best looking?'

'Goodness knows—I don't.'

'I think Angelo is; it's the prettiest name, anyway. Don't you think it's a sweet name, ma?'

'Yes, it's well enough. I'd like both of them better if I knew the way to pronounce them—the Eyetalian way, I mean. The Missouri way and the Eyetalian way is different, I judge.'

'Maybe—yes. It's Luigi that writes the letter. What do you reckon is the reason Angelo didn't write it?'

'Why, how can I tell? What's the difference who writes it, so long as it's done?'

'Oh, I hope it wasn't because he is sick! You don't think he is sick, do you, ma?'

'Sick your granny; what's to make him sick?'

'Oh, there's never any telling. These foreigners with that kind of names are so delicate, and of course that kind of names are not suited to our climate—you wouldn't expect it.'

[And so-on and so-on, no end. The time drags along; Thursday comes: the boat arrives in a pouring storm toward midnight.]

At last there was a knock at the door and the anxious family jumped to open it. Two negro men entered, each carrying a trunk, and proceeded upstairs toward the guest-room. Then followed a stupefying apparition—a double-headed human creature with four arms, one body, and a single pair of legs! It—or they, as you please—bowed with elaborate foreign formality, but the Coopers could not respond immediately; they were paralysed. At this moment there came from the rear of the group a fervent ejaculation—'My lan'!'—followed by a crash of crockery, and the slave-wench Nancy stood petrified and staring, with a tray of wrecked tea-things at her feet. The incident broke the spell, and brought the family to consciousness. The beautiful heads of the new-comer bowed again, and one of them said with easy grace and dignity:

'I crave the honor, madam and miss, to introduce to you my brother, Count Luigi Capello,' (the other head bowed) 'and myself—Count Angelo; and at the same time offer sincere apologies for the lateness of our coming, which was unavoidable,' and both heads bowed again.

The poor old lady was in a whirl of amazement and confusion, but she managed to stammer out:

'I'm sure I'm glad to make your acquaintance, sir—I mean, gentlemen. As for the delay, it is nothing, don't mention it. This is my daughter Rowena, sir—gentlemen. Please step into the parlor and sit down and have a bite and sup; you are dreadful wet and must be uncomfortable—both of you, I mean.'

But to the old lady's relief they courteously excused themselves, saying it would be wrong to keep the family out of their beds longer; then each head bowed in turn and uttered a friendly good-night, and the singular figure moved away in the wake of Rowena's small brothers, who bore candles, and disappeared up the stairs.

The widow tottered into the parlor and sank into a chair with a gasp, and Rowena followed, tongue-tied and dazed. The two sat silent in the throbbing summer heat unconscious of the million-voiced music of the mosquitoes, unconscious of the roaring gale, the lashing and thrashing of the rain along the windows and the roof, the white glare of the lightning, the tumultuous booming and bellowing of the thunder; conscious of nothing but that prodigy, that uncanny apparition that had come and gone so suddenly—that weird strange thing that was so soft-spoken and so gentle of manner and yet had shaken them up like an earthquake with the shock of its gruesome aspect. At last a cold little shudder quivered along down the widow's meager frame and she said in a weak voice:

'Ugh, it was awful—just the mere look of that phillipene!'

Rowena did not answer. Her faculties were still caked, she had not yet found her voice. Presently the widow said, a little resentfully:

'Always been *used* to sleeping together—in fact, *prefer* it. And I was thinking it was to accommodate me. I thought it was very good of them, whereas a person situated as that young man is—'

'Ma, you oughtn't to begin by getting up a prejudice against him. I'm sure he is good-hearted and means well. Both of his faces show it.'

'I'm not so certain about that. The one on the left—I mean the one on *its* left—hasn't near as good a face, in my opinion, as its brother.'

'That's Luigi.'

'Yes, Luigi; anyway it's the dark-skinned one; the one that was west of his brother when they stood in the door. Up to all kinds of mischief and disobedience when he was a boy, I'll be bound. I lay his mother had trouble to lay her hand on him when she wanted him. But the one on the right is as good as gold, I can see that.'

'That's Angelo.'

'Yes, Angelo, I reckon, though I can't tell t' other from which by their names, yet awhile. But it's the right-hand one—the blonde one. He has such kind blue eyes, and curly copper hair and fresh complexion—'

'And such a noble face!—oh, it *is* a noble face, ma, just royal, you may say! And beautiful—deary me, how beautiful! But both are that; the dark one's as beautiful as a picture. There's no such wonderful faces and handsome heads in this town—none that even begin. And such hands especially Angelo's—so shapely and—'

'Stuff, how could you tell which they belonged to?—they had gloves on.'

'Why, didn't I see them take off their hats?'

'That don't signify. They might have taken off each other's hats. Nobody could tell. There was just a wormy squirming of arms in the air—seemed to be a couple of dozen of them, all writhing at once, and it just made me dizzy to see them go.'

'Why, ma, I hadn't any difficulty. There's two arms on each shoulder—'

'There, now. One arm on each shoulder belongs to each of the creatures, don't it? For a person to have two arms on one shoulder wouldn't do him any good, would it? Of course not. Each has an arm on each shoulder. Now then, you tell me which of them belongs to which, if you can. *They* don't know, themselves—they just work whichever arm comes handy. Of course they do; especially if they are in a hurry and can't stop to think which belongs to which.'

The mother seemed to have the rights of the argument, so the daughter abandoned the struggle. Presently the widow rose with a yawn and said:

'Poor thing, I hope it won't catch cold; it was powerful wet, just drenched, you may say. I hope it has left its boots outside, so they can be dried.' Then she gave a little start, and looked perplexed. 'Now I remember I heard one of them ask Joe to call him at half after seven—I think it was the one on the left—no, it was the one to the east of the other one—but I didn't hear the other one say anything. I wonder if he wants to be called too. Do you reckon it's too late to ask?'

'Why, ma, it's not necessary. Calling one is calling both. If one gets up, the other's *got* to.'

'Sho, of course; I never thought of that. Well, come along, maybe we can get some sleep, but I don't know, I'm so shook up with what we've been through.'

The stranger had made an impression on the boys, too. They had a word of talk as they were getting to bed. Henry, the gentle, the humane, said:

'I feel ever so sorry for it, don't you, Joe?'

But Joe was a boy of this world, active, enterprising, and had a theatrical side to him:

'Sorry? Why, how you talk! It can't stir a step without attracting attention. It's just grand!'

Henry said, reproachfully:

'Instead of pitying it, Joe, you talk as if—'

'Talk as if *what?* I know one thing mighty certain: if you can fix me so I can eat for two and only have to stub toes for one, I ain't going to fool away no such chance just for sentiment.'

The twins were wet and tired, and they proceeded to undress without any preliminary remarks. The abundance of sleeve made the partnership-coat hard to get off, for it was like skinning a tarantula; but it came at last, after much tugging and perspiring. The mutual vest followed. Then the brothers stood up before the glass, and each took off his own cravat and collar. The collars were of the standing kind, and came high up under the ears, like the sides of a wheelbarrow, as required by the fashion of the day. The cravats were as broad as a bank bill, with fringed ends which stood far out to right and left like the wings of a dragon-fly, and this also was strictly in accordance with the fashion of the time. Each cravat, as to color, was in perfect taste, so far as its owner's complexion was concerned—a delicate pink, in the case of the blonde brother, a violent scarlet in the case of the brunette—but as a combination they broke all the laws of taste known to civilization. Nothing more fiendish and irreconcilable than those shrieking and blaspheming colors could have been contrived. The wet boots gave no end of trouble—to Luigi. When they were off at last, Angelo said, with bitterness:

'I wish you wouldn't wear such tight boots, they hurt my feet.'

Luigi answered with indifference:

'My friend, when I am in command of our body, I choose my apparel according to my own convenience, as I have remarked more than several times already. When you are in command, I beg you will do as you please.'

Angelo was hurt, and the tears came into his eyes. There was gentle reproach in his voice, but not anger, when he replied:

'Luigi, I often consult your wishes, but you never consult mine. When I am in command I treat you as a guest; I try to make you feel at home; when you are in command you treat me as an intruder, you make me feel unwelcome. It embarrasses me cruelly in company, for I can see that people notice it and comment on it.'

'Oh, damn the people,' responded the brother languidly, and with the air of one who is tired of the subject.

A slight shudder shook the frame of Angelo, but he said nothing and the conversation ceased. Each buttoned his own share of the night-shirt in silence; then Luigi, with Paine's

'Age of Reason'* in his hand, sat down in one chair and put his feet in another and lit his pipe, while Angelo took his 'Whole Duty of Man',* and both began to read. Angelo presently began to cough; his coughing increased and became mixed with gaspings for breath, and he was finally obliged to make an appeal to his brother's humanity:

'Luigi, if you would only smoke a little milder tobacco, I am sure I could learn not to mind it in time, but this is so strong, and the pipe is so rank that—'

'Angelo, I wouldn't be such a baby! I have learned to smoke in a week, and the trouble is already over with me; if you would try, you could learn too, and then you would stop spoiling my comfort with your everlasting complaints.'

'Ah, brother, that is a strong word—everlasting—and isn't quite fair. I only complain when I suffocate; you know I don't complain when we are in the open air.'

'Well, anyway, you could learn to smoke yourself.'

'But my *principles*, Luigi, you forget my principles. You would not have me do a thing which I regard as a sin?'

'Oh, bosh!'

The conversation ceased again, for Angelo was sick and discouraged and strangling; but after some time he closed his book and asked Luigi to sing 'From Greenland's Icy Mountains'* with him, but he would not, and when he tried to sing by himself Luigi did his best to drown his plaintive tenor with a rude and rollicking song delivered in a thundering bass.

After the singing there was silence, and neither brother was happy. Before blowing the light out Luigi swallowed half a tumbler of whisky, and Angelo, whose sensitive organization could not endure intoxicants of any kind, took a pill to keep it from giving him the headache.

2

THE family sat in the breakfast-room waiting for the twins to come down. The widow was quiet, the daughter was alive with happy excitement. She said:

'Ah, they're a boon, ma, just a boon! don't you think so?'

'Laws, I hope so, I don't know.'

'Why, ma, yes you do. They're so fine and handsome, and high-bred and polite, so every way superior to our gawks here in this village; why, they'll make life different from what it was—so humdrum and commonplace, you know—oh, you may be sure they're full of accomplishments, and knowledge of the world, and all that, that will be an immense advantage to society here. Don't you think so, ma?'

'Mercy on me, how should I know, and I've hardly set eyes on them yet.' After a pause she added, 'They made considerable noise after they went up.'

'Noise? Why, ma, they were singing! And it was beautiful, too.'

'Oh, it was well enough, but too mixed-up, seemed to me.'

'Now, ma, honor bright, did you ever hear "Greenland's Icy Mountains" sung sweeter—now did you?'

'If it had been sung by itself, it would have been uncommon sweet, I don't deny it; but what they wanted to mix it up with "Old Bob Ridley"* for, I can't make out. Why, they don't go together, at all. They are not of the same nature. "Bob Ridley" is a common rackety slam-bang secular song, one of the rippingest and rantingest and noisest there is. I am no judge of music, and I don't claim it, but in my opinion nobody can make those two songs go together right.'

'Why, ma, I thought—'

'It don't make any difference what you thought, it can't be done. They tried it, and to my mind it was a failure. I never heard such a crazy uproar; seemed to me, sometimes, the roof would come off; and as for the cats—well, I've lived a many a year, and seen cats aggravated in more ways than one, but I've never seen cats take on the way they took on last night.'

'Well, I don't think that that goes for anything, ma, because it is the nature of cats that any sound that is unusual—'

'Unusual! You may well call it so. Now if they are going to sing duets every night, I do hope they will both sing the same tune at the same time, for in my opinion a duet that is made up of two different tunes is a mistake; especially when the tunes ain't any kin to one another, that way.'

'But, ma, I think it must be a foreign custom; and it must be right too, and the best way, because they have had every opportunity to know what is right, and it don't stand to reason that with their education they would do anything but what the highest musical authorities have sanctioned. You can't help but admit that, ma.'

The argument was formidably strong; the old lady could not find any way around it; so, after thinking it over a while she gave in with a sigh of discontent, and admitted that the daughter's position was probably correct. Being vanquished, she had no mind to continue the topic at that disadvantage, and was about to seek a change when a change came of itself. A footstep was heard on the stairs, and she said:

'There—he's coming!'

'*They*, ma—you ought to say *they*—it's nearer right.'

The new lodger, rather shoutingly dressed but looking superbly handsome, stepped with courtly carriage into the trim little breakfast-room and put out all his cordial arms at once, like one of those pocket-knifes with a multiplicity of blades, and shook hands with the whole family simultaneously. He was so easy and pleasant and hearty that all embarrassment presently thawed away and disappeared, and a cheery feeling of friendliness and comradeship took its place. He—or preferably they—were asked to occupy the seat of honor at the foot of the table. They consented with thanks, and carved the beefsteak with one set of their hands while they distributed it at the same time with the other set.

'Will you have coffee, gentlemen, or tea?'

'Coffee for Luigi, if you please, madam, tea for me.'

'Cream and sugar?'

'For me, yes, madam; Luigi takes his coffee black. Our natures differ a good deal from each other, and our tastes also.'

The first time the negro girl Nancy appeared in the door and saw the two heads turned in opposite directions and both talking at once, then saw the commingling arms feed potatoes into one mouth and coffee into the other at the same time, she had to pause and pull herself out of a faintness that came over her; but after that she held her grip and was able to wait on the table with fair courage.

Conversation fell naturally into the customary grooves. It was a little jerky, at first, because none of the family could get smoothly through a sentence without a wobble in it here and a break there, caused by some new surprise in the way of attitude or gesture on the part of the twins. The weather suffered the most. The weather was all finished up and disposed of, as a subject, before the simple Missourians had gotten sufficiently wonted to the spectacle of one body feeding two heads to feel composed and reconciled in the presence of so bizarre a miracle. And even after everybody's mind became tranquilized there was still one slight distraction left: the hand that picked up a biscuit carried it to the wrong head, as often as any other way, and the wrong mouth devoured it. This was a puzzling thing, and marred the talk a little. It bothered the widow to such a degree that she presently dropped out of the conversation without knowing it, and fell to watching and guessing and talking to herself.

'Now that hand is going to take that coffee to—no, it's gone to the other mouth; I can't understand it; and now, here is the dark complected hand with a potato on its fork, I'll see what goes with it—there, the light complected head's got it, as sure as I live!' Finally Rowena said:

'Ma, what is the matter with you? Are you dreaming about something?'

The old lady came to herself and blushed; then she explained with the first random thing that came into her mind: 'I saw Mr Angelo take up Mr Luigi's coffee, and I thought maybe he—sha'n't I give *you* a cup, Mr Angelo?'

'Oh no, madam, I am very much obliged, but I never drink coffee, much as I would like to. You did see me take up Luigi's cup, it is true, but if you noticed, I didn't carry it to my mouth, but to his.'

'Y—es, I thought you did. Did you mean to?'

'How?'

The widow was a little embarrassed again. She said:

'I don't know but what I'm foolish, and you mustn't mind; but you see, he got the coffee I was expecting to see you drink, and you got a potato that I thought he was going to get. So I thought it might be a mistake all around, and everybody getting what wasn't intended for him.'

Both twins laughed and Luigi said:

'Dear madam, there wasn't any mistake. We are always helping each other that way. It is a great economy for us both; it saves time and labor. We have a system of signs which nobody can notice or understand but ourselves. If I am using both my hands and want some coffee, I make the sign and Angelo furnishes it to me; and you saw that when he needed a potato I delivered it.'

'How convenient!'

'Yes, and often of the extremest value. Take the Mississippi boats, for instance. They are always over-crowded. There is table-room for only half of the passengers, therefore they have to get a second table for the second half. The stewards rush both parties, they give them no time to eat a satisfying meal, both divisions leave the table hungry. It isn't so with us. Angelo books himself for the one table, I book myself for the other. Neither of us eats anything at the other's table, but just simply works—works. Thus, you see there are four hands to feed Angelo, and the same four to feed me. Each of us eats two meals.'

The old lady was dazed with admiration, and kept saying, 'It is *per*fectly wonderful, perfectly wonderful!' and the boy Joe licked his chops enviously, but said nothing—at least aloud.

'Yes,' continued Luigi, 'our construction may have its disadvantages—in fact, *has*—but it also has its compensations of one sort and another. Take travel, for instance. Travel is enormously expensive, in all countries; we have been obliged to do a vast deal of it—come, Angelo, don't put any more sugar in your tea, I'm just over one indigestion and don't want another right away—been obliged to do a deal of it, as

I was saying. Well, we always travel as one person, since we occupy but one seat; so we save half the fare.'

'How romantic!' interjected Rowena, with effusion.

'Yes, my dear young lady, and how practical too, and economical. In Europe, beds in the hotels are not charged with the board, but separately—another saving, for we stood to our rights and paid for the one bed only. The landlords often insisted that as both of us occupied the bed we ought—'

'No, they didn't,' said Angelo. 'They did it only twice, and in both cases it was a double bed—a rare thing in Europe—and the double bed gave them some excuse. Be fair to the landlords; twice doesn't constitute "often".'

'Well, that depends—that depends. I knew a man who fell down a well twice. He said he didn't mind the first time, but he thought the second time was once too often. Have I misused that word, Mrs Cooper?'

'To tell the truth, I was afraid you had, but it seems to look, now, like you hadn't.' She stopped, and was evidently struggling with the difficult problem a moment, then she added in the tone of one who is convinced without being converted, 'It seems so, but I can't somehow tell why.'

Rowena thought Luigi's retort was wonderfully quick and bright, and she remarked to herself with satisfaction that there wasn't any young native of Dawson's Landing that could have risen to the occasion like that. Luigi detected the applause in her face, and expressed his pleasure and his thanks with his eyes; and so eloquently withal, that the girl was proud and pleased, and hung out the delicate sign of it on her cheeks.

Luigi went on, with animation:

'Both of us get a bath for one ticket, theater seat for one ticket, pew-rent is on the same basis, but at peep-shows we pay double.'

'We have much to be thankful for,' said Angelo, impressively, with a reverent light in his eye and a reminiscent tone in his voice, 'we have been greatly blessed. As a rule, what one of us has lacked, the other, by the bounty of Providence, has been able to supply. My brother is hardy, I am not; he is very masculine, assertive, aggressive; I am much less so. I am subject to illness, he is never ill. I cannot abide medicines, and cannot take them, but he has no prejudice against them, and—'

'Why, goodness gracious,' interrupted the widow, 'when you are sick, does he take the medicine for you?'

'Always, madam.'

'Why, I never heard such a thing in my life! I think it's beautiful of you.'

'Oh, madam, it's nothing, don't mention it, it's really nothing at all.'

'But I say it's beautiful, and I stick to it!' cried the widow, with a speaking moisture in her eye. 'A well brother to take the medicine for his poor sick brother—I wish I had such a son,' and she glanced reproachfully at her boys. 'I declare I'll never rest till I've shook you by the hand,' and she scrambled out of her chair in a fever of generous enthusiasm, and made for the twins, blind with her tears, and began to shake. The boy Joe corrected her:

'You're shaking the wrong one, ma.'

This flurried her, but she made a swift change and went on shaking.

'Got the wrong one again, ma,' said the boy.

'Oh, shut up, can't you!' said the widow, embarrassed and irritated. 'Give me *all* your hands, I want to shake them all; for I know you are both just as good as you can be.'

It was a victorious thought, a master-stroke of diplomacy, though that never occurred to her and she cared nothing for diplomacy. She shook the four hands in turn cordially, and went back to her place in a state of high and fine exaltation that made her look young and handsome.

'Indeed I owe everything to Luigi,' said Angelo, affectionately. 'But for him I could not have survived our boyhood days, when we were friendless and poor—ah, so poor! We lived from hand to mouth—lived on the coarse fare of unwilling charity, and for weeks and weeks together not a morsel of food passed my lips, for its character revolted me and I could not eat it. But for Luigi I should have died. He ate for us both.'

'How noble!' sighed Rowena.

'Do you hear that?' said the widow, severely, to her boys. 'Let it be an example to you—I mean you, Joe.'

Joe gave his head a barely perceptible disparaging toss and said: 'Et for both. It ain't anything—I'd a done it.'

'Hush, if you haven't got any better manners than that. You don't see the point at all. It wasn't good food.'

'I don't care—it was food, and I'd a et it if it was rotten.'

'Shame! Such language! Can't you understand? They were starving—actually starving—and he ate for both, and—'

'Shucks! you gimme a chance and I'll—'

'There, now—close your head! and don't you open it again till you're asked.'

[Angelo goes on and tells how his parents the Count and Countess had to fly from Florence for political reasons, and died poor in Berlin bereft of their great property by confiscation; and how he and Luigi had to travel with a freak-show during two years and suffer semi-starvation.]

'That hateful black-bread! but I seldom ate anything during that time; that was poor Luigi's affair—'

'I'll never *Mister* him again!' cried the widow, with strong emotion, 'he's Luigi to me, from this out!'

'Thank you a thousand times, madam, a thousand times! though in truth I don't deserve it.'

'Ah, Luigi is always the fortunate one when honors are showering,' said Angelo, plaintively, 'now what have I done, Mrs Cooper, that you leave me out? Come, you must strain a point in my favor.'

'Call you Angelo? Why, certainly I will; what are you thinking of! In the case of twins, why—'

'But, ma, you're breaking up the story—do let him go on.'

'You keep still, Rowena Cooper, and he can go on all the better, I reckon. One interruption don't hurt, it's two that makes the trouble.'

'But you've added one, now, and that is three.'

'Rowena! I will not allow you to talk back at me when you have got nothing rational to say.'

3

[After breakfast the whole village crowded in, and there was a grand reception in honor of the twins; and at the close of it the gifted 'freak' captured everybody's admiration by sitting down at the piano and knocking out a classic four-handed piece in great style. Then the Judge took it—or them—driving in his buggy and showed off his village.]

ALL along the streets the people crowded the windows and stared at the amazing twins. Troops of small boys flocked after the buggy, excited and yelling. At first the dogs showed no interest. They thought they merely saw three men in a buggy—a matter of no consequence; but when they found out the facts of the case, they altered their opinion pretty radically, and joined the boys, expressing their minds as they came. Other dogs got interested; indeed, all the dogs. It was a spirited sight to see them come leaping fences, tearing around corners, swarming out of every by-street and alley. The noise they made was something beyond belief—or praise. They did not seem to be moved by malice but only by prejudice, the common human prejudice against lack of conformity. If the twins turned their heads, they broke and fled in every direction, but stopped at a safe distance and faced about; and then formed and came on again as soon as the strangers showed them their back. Negroes and farmers' wives took to the woods when the buggy came upon them suddenly, and altogether the drive was pleasant and animated, and a refreshment all around.

[It was a long and lively drive. Angelo was a Methodist, Luigi was a Freethinker. The Judge was very proud of his Freethinkers' Society, which was flourishing along in a most prosperous way and already had two members—himself and the obscure and neglected

Pudd'nhead Wilson. It was to meet that evening, and he invited Luigi to join; a thing which Luigi was glad to do, partly because it would please himself, and partly because it would gravel Angelo.]

They had now arrived at the widow's gate, and the excursion was ended. The twins politely expressed their obligations for the pleasant outing which had been afforded them; to which the Judge bowed his thanks, and then said he would now go and arrange for the Freethinkers' meeting, and would call for Count Luigi in the evening.

'For you also, dear sir,' he added hastily, turning to Angelo and bowing. 'In addressing myself particularly to your brother, I was not meaning to leave you out. It was an unintentional rudeness, I assure you, and due wholly to accident—accident and preoccupation. I beg you to forgive me.'

His quick eye had seen the sensitive blood mount into Angelo's face, betraying the wound that had been inflicted. The sting of the slight had gone deep, but the apology was so prompt, and so evidently sincere, that the hurt was almost immediately healed, and a forgiving smile testified to the kindly Judge that all was well again.

Concealed behind Angelo's modest and unassuming exterior, and unsuspected by any but his intimates, was a lofty pride, a pride of almost abnormal proportions, indeed, and this rendered him ever the prey of slights; and although they were almost always imaginary ones, they hurt none the less on that account. By ill fortune Judge Driscoll had happened to touch his sorest point, *i.e.*, his conviction that his brother's presence was welcomer everywhere than his own; that he was often invited, out of mere courtesy, where only his brother was wanted, and that in a majority of cases he would not be included in an invitation if he could be left out without offense. A sensitive nature like this is necessarily subject to moods; moods which traverse the whole gamut of feeling; moods which know all the climes of emotion, from the sunny heights of joy to the black abysses of despair. At times, in his seasons of deepest depressions, Angelo almost wished that he and his brother might become segregated from each other and be separate individuals, like other men. But of course as soon as his mind cleared and these diseased imaginings passed away, he shuddered at the repulsive thought, and earnestly prayed that it might visit him no more. To be separate, and as other men are! How awkward it would seem; how unendurable. What would he do with his hands, his arms? How would his legs feel? How odd, and strange, and grotesque every action, attitude, movement, gesture would be. To sleep by himself, eat by himself, walk by himself—how lonely, how unspeakably lonely! No, no, any fate but that. In every way and from every point, the idea was revolting.

This was of course natural; to have felt otherwise would have been unnatural. He had known no life but a combined one; he had been familiar with it from his birth; he was not able to conceive of any other as being agreeable, or even bearable. To him, in the privacy of his secret thoughts, all other men were monsters, deformities: and during three-fourths of his life their aspect had filled him with what promised to be an unconquerable aversion. But at eighteen his eye began to take note of female beauty; and little by little, undefined longings grew up in his heart, under whose softening influences the old stubborn aversion gradually diminished, and finally disappeared. Men were still monstrosities to him, still deformities, and in his sober moments he had no desire to be like them, but their strange and unsocial and uncanny construction was no longer offensive to him.

This had been a hard day for him, physically and mentally. He had been called in the morning before he had quite slept off the effects of the liquor which Luigi had drunk; and so, for the first half hour had had the seedy feeling, and languor, the brooding depression, the cobwebby mouth and druggy taste that come of dissipation and are so ill a preparation for bodily or intellectual activities; the long violent strain of the reception had followed; and this had been followed, in turn, by the dreary sight-seeing, the Judge's wearying explanations and laudations of the sights, and the stupefying clamor of the dogs. As a congruous conclusion, a fitting end, his feelings had been hurt, a slight had been put upon him. He would have been glad to forego dinner and betake himself to rest and sleep, but he held his peace and said no word, for he knew his brother, Luigi, was fresh, unweary, full of life, spirit, energy; he would have scoffed at the idea of wasting valuable time on a bed or a sofa, and would have refused permission.

4

ROWENA was dining out, Joe and Harry were belated at play, there were but three chairs and four persons that noon at the home dinner-table—the twins, the widow, and her chum, Aunt Betsy Hale. The widow soon perceived that Angelo's spirits were as low as Luigi's were high, and also that he had a jaded look. Her motherly solicitude was aroused, and she tried to get him interested in the talk and win him to a happier frame of mind, but the cloud of sadness remained on his countenance. Luigi lent his help, too. He used a form and a phrase which he was always accustomed to employ in these circumstances. He gave his brother an affectionate slap on the shoulder and said, encouragingly:

'Cheer up, the worst is yet to come!'

But this did no good. It never did. If anything, it made the matter worse, as a rule, because it irritated Angelo. This made it a favorite with Luigi. By and by the widow said:

'Angelo, you are tired, you've overdone yourself; you go right to bed after dinner, and get a good nap and a rest, then you'll be all right.'

'Indeed, I would give anything if I could do that, madam.'

'And what's to hender, I'd like to know? Land, the room's yours to do what you please with! The idea that you can't do what you like with your own!'

'But, you see, there's one prime essential—an essential of the very first importance—which isn't my own.'

'What is that?'

'My body.'

The old ladies looked puzzled, and Aunt Betsy Hale said: 'Why bless your heart, how is that?'

'It's my brother's.'

'Your brother's! I don't quite understand. I supposed it belonged to both of you.'

'So it does. But not to both at the same time.'

'That is mighty curious; I don't see how it can be. I shouldn't think it could be managed that way.'

'Oh, it's a good enough arrangement, and goes very well; in fact, it wouldn't do to have it otherwise. I find that the teetotalers and the anti-teetotalers hire the use of the same hall for their meetings. Both parties don't use it at the same time, do they?'

'You bet they don't!' said both old ladies in a breath.

'And, moreover,' said Aunt Betsy, 'the Freethinkers and the Baptist Bible class use the same room over the Market house, but you can take my word for it they don't mush up together and use it at the same time.'

'Very well,' said Angelo, 'you understand it now. And it stands to reason that the arrangement couldn't be improved. I'll prove it to you. If our legs tried to obey two wills, how could we ever get anywhere? I would start one way, Luigi would start another, at the same moment—the result would be a standstill, wouldn't it?'

'As sure as you are born! Now ain't that wonderful! A body would never have thought of it.'

'We should always be arguing and fussing and disputing over the merest trifles. We should lose worlds of time, for we couldn't go down stairs or up, couldn't go to bed, couldn't rise, couldn't wash, couldn't dress, couldn't stand up, couldn't sit down, couldn't even cross our legs, without calling a meeting first and explaining the case and passing resolutions, and getting consent. It wouldn't ever do—now would it?'

'Do? Why, it would wear a person out in a week! Did you ever hear anything like it, Patsy Cooper?'

'Oh, you'll find there's more than one thing about them that ain't commonplace,' said the widow, with the complacent air of a person with a property-right in a novelty that is under admiring scrutiny.

'Well, now, how ever do you manage it? I don't mind saying I'm suffering to know.'

'He who made us,' said Angelo reverently, 'and with us this difficulty, also provided a way out of it. By a mysterious law of our being, each of us has utter and indisputable command of our body a week at a time, turn and turn about.'

'Well, I never! Now ain't that beautiful!'

'Yes, it is beautiful!'

'Yes, it is beautiful and infinitely wise and just. The week ends every Saturday at midnight to the minute, to the second, to the last shade of a fraction of a second, infallibly, unerringly, and in that instant the one brother's power over the body vanishes and the other brother takes possession, asleep or awake.'

'How marvelous are His ways, and past finding out!'

Luigi said: 'So exactly to the instant does the change come, that during our stay in many of the great cities of the world, the public clocks were regulated by it; and as hundreds of thousands of private clocks and watches were set and corrected in accordance with the public clocks, we really furnished the standard time for the entire city.'

'Don't tell me that He don't do miracles any more! Blowing down the walls of Jericho with rams' horns wa'n't as difficult, in my opinion.'

'And that is not all,' said Angelo. 'A thing that is even more marvelous, perhaps, is the fact that the change takes note of longitude and fits itself to the meridian we are on. Luigi is in command this week. Now, if on Saturday night at a moment before midnight we could fly in an instant to a point fifteen degrees west of here, he would hold possession of the power another hour, for the change observes *local* time and no other.'

Betsy Hale was deeply impressed, and said with solemnity: 'Patsy Cooper, for *de*tail it lays over the Passage of the Red Sea.'

'Now, I shouldn't go as far as that,' said Aunt Patsy, 'but if you've a mind to say Sodom and Gomorrah, I am with you, Betsy Hale.'

'I am agreeable, then, though I do think I was right, and I believe Parson Maltby would say the same. Well, now, there's another thing. Suppose one of you wants to borrow the legs a minute from the one that's got them, could he let him?'

'Yes, but we hardly ever do that. There were disagreeable results, several times, and so we very seldom ask or grant the privilege, nowadays, and we never even think of such a thing unless the case is extremely urgent. Besides, a week's possession at a time seems so little that we can't bear to spare a minute of it. People who have the use of their legs all the time never think of what a blessing it is, of course. It never occurs to them; it's just their natural ordinary condition, and so it does not excite them at all. But when I wake up, on Sunday morning, and it's my week and I feel the power all through me, oh, such a wave of exultation and thanksgiving goes surging over me, and I want to shout "I can walk! I can walk!" Madam, do you ever, at your up-rising want to shout "I can walk! I can walk!"?'

'No, you poor unfortunate cretur', but I'll never get out of my bed again without *doing* it! Laws, to think I've had this unspeakable blessing all my long life and never had the grace to thank the good Lord that gave it to me!'

Tears stood in the eyes of both the old ladies and the widow said, softly:

'Betsy Hale, we have learned something, you and me.'

The conversation now drifted wide, but by and by floated back once more to that admired detail, the rigid and beautiful impartiality with which the possession of power had been distributed between the twins. Aunt Betsy saw in it a far finer justice than human law exhibits in related cases. She said:

'In my opinion it ain't right now, and never has been right, the way a twin born a quarter of a minute sooner than the other one gets all the land and grandeurs and nobilities in the old countries and his brother has to go bare and be a nobody. Which of you was born first?'

Angelo's head was resting against Luigi's; weariness had overcome him, and for the past five minutes he had been peacefully sleeping. The old ladies had dropped their voices to a lulling drone, to help him steal the rest his brother wouldn't take him up stairs to get. Luigi listened a moment to Angelo's regular breathing, then said in a voice barely audible:

'We were both born at the same time, but I am six months older than he is.'

'For the land's sake!'

' 'Sh! don't wake him up; he wouldn't like my telling this. It has always been kept secret till now.'

'But how in the world can it be? If you were both born at the same time, how can one of you be older than the other?'

'It is very simple, and I assure you it is true. I was born with a full crop of hair, he was as bald as an egg for six months. I could walk six months before he could make a step. I finished teething six months ahead of him. I began to take solids six months before he left the breast. I began to talk six months before he could say a word. Last, and absolutely unassailable proof, *the sutures in my skull closed six months ahead of his.* Always just that six months difference to a day. Was that accident? Nobody is going to claim that, I'm sure. It was ordained—it was law—it had its meaning, and we know what that meaning was. Now what does this overwhelming body of evidence establish? It establishes just one thing, and that thing it establishes beyond any peradventure whatever. Friends, we would not have it known for the world, and I must beg you to keep it strictly to yourselves, but the truth is, *we are no more twins than you are.*'

The two old ladies were stunned, paralyzed—petrified, one may almost say—and could only sit and gaze vacantly at each other for some moments; then Aunt Betsy Hale said impressively:

'There's no getting around proof like that. I do believe it's the most amazing thing I ever heard of.' She sat silent a moment or two and breathing hard with excitement, then she looked up and surveyed the strangers steadfastly a little while, and added: 'Well, it does beat me, but I would have took you for twins anywhere.'

'So would I, so would I,' said Aunt Patsy with the emphasis of a certainty that is not impaired by any shade of doubt.

'*Any*body would—anybody in the world, I don't care who he is,' said Aunt Betsy with decision.

'You won't tell,' said Luigi, appealingly.

'Oh, dear, no!' answered both ladies promptly, 'you can trust us, don't you be afraid.'

'That is good of you, and kind. Never let on; treat us always as if we were twins.'

'You can depend on us,' said Aunt Betsy, 'but it won't be easy, because now that I know you ain't you don't *seem* so.'

Luigi muttered to himself with satisfaction: 'That swindle has gone through without change of cars.'*

It was not very kind of him to load the poor things up with a secret like that, which would be always flying to their tongues' ends every time they heard any one speak of the strangers as twins, and would become harder and harder to hang on to with every recurrence of the temptation to tell it, while the torture of retaining it would increase with every new strain that was applied; but he never thought of that, and probably would not have worried much about it if he had.

A visitor was announced—some one to see the twins. They withdrew to the parlor, and the two old ladies began to discuss with interest the strange things which they had been listening to. When they had finished the matter to their satisfaction, and Aunt Betsy rose to go, she stopped to ask a question:

'How does things come on between Roweny and Tom Driscoll?'

'Well, about the same. He writes tolerable often, and she answers tolerable seldom.'

'Where is he?'

'In St Louis, I believe, though he's such a gadabout that a body can't be very certain of him, I reckon.'

'Don't Roweny know?'

'Oh, yes, like enough. I haven't asked her lately.'

'Do you know how him and the Judge are getting along now?'

'First-rate, I believe. Mrs Pratt says so; and being right in the house, and sister to the one and aunt to t'other, of course she ought to know. She says the Judge is real fond of him when he's away; but frets when he's around and is vexed with his ways, and not sorry to have him go again. He has been gone three weeks this time—a pleasant thing for both of them, I reckon.'

'Tom's ruther harum-scarum, but there ain't anything bad in him, I guess.'

'Oh, no, he's just young, that's all. Still, twenty-three is old, in one way. A young man ought to be earning his living by that time. If Tom were doing that, or was even trying to do it, the Judge would be a heap better satisfied with him. Tom's always going to begin, but somehow he can't seem to find just the opening he likes.'

'Well, now, it's partly the Judge's own fault. Promising the boy his property wasn't the way to set him to earning a fortune of his own. But what do you think—is Roweny beginning to lean any toward him, or ain't she?'

Aunt Patsy had a secret in her bosom; she wanted to keep it there, but nature was too strong for her. She drew Aunt Betsy aside, and said in her most confidential and mysterious manner:

'Don't you breathe a syllable to a soul—I'm going to tell you something. In my opinion Tom Driscoll's chances were considerable better yesterday than they are to-day.'

'Patsy Cooper, what *do* you mean?'

'It's so, as sure as you're born. I wish you could 'a' been at breakfast and seen for yourself.'

'You don't mean it!'

'Well, if I'm any judge, there's a leaning—there's a leaning, sure.'

'My land! Which one of 'em is it?'

'I can't say for certain, but I think it's the youngest one—Anjy.'

Then there were handshakings, and congratulations, and hopes, and so on, and the old ladies parted, perfectly happy—the one in knowing something which the rest of the town didn't, and the other in having been the sole person able to furnish that knowledge.

The visitor who had called to see the twins was the Rev. Mr Hotchkiss, pastor of the Baptist church. At the reception Angelo had told him he had lately experienced a change in his religious views, and was now desirous of becoming a Baptist, and would immediately join Mr Hotchkiss's church. There was no time to say more, and the brief talk ended at that point. The minister was much gratified, and had dropped in for a moment now, to invite the twins to attend his Bible class at eight that evening. Angelo accepted, and was expecting Luigi to decline, but he did not, because he knew that the Bible class and the Free-thinkers met in the same room, and he wanted to treat his brother to the embarrassment of being caught in free-thinking company.

5

[A long and vigorous quarrel follows, between the twins. And there is plenty to quarrel about, for Angelo was always seeking truth, and this obliged him to change and improve his religion with frequency, which wearied Luigi, and annoyed him too; for he had to be present at each new enlistment—which placed him in the false position of seeming to endorse and approve his brother's fickleness; moreover, he had to go to Angelo's prohibition meetings, and he hated them. On the other hand, when it was his week to command the legs he gave Angelo just cause of complaint, for he took him to circuses and horse-races and fandangoes, exposing him to all sorts of censure and criticism; and he drank, too; and whatever he drank went to Angelo's head instead of his own and made him act disgracefully. When the evening was come, the two attended the Freethinkers' meeting, where Angelo was sad and silent; then came the Bible-class and looked upon him coldly, finding him in such company. Then they went to Wilson's house and Chapter II of 'Pudd'nhead Wilson' follows, which tells of the girl seen in Tom Driscoll's room; and closes with the kicking of Tom by Luigi at the anti-temperance mass meeting of the Sons of Liberty; with the addition of some account of Roxy's adventures as a chambermaid on a Mississippi boat. Her exchange of the children had been flippantly and farcically described in an earlier chapter.]

NEXT morning all the town was a-buzz with great news; Pudd'nhead Wilson had a law case! The public astonishment was so great and the public curiosity so intense, that when the justice of the peace opened his court, the place was packed with people, and even the windows were full. Everybody was flushed and perspiring; the summer heat was almost unendurable.

Tom Driscoll had brought a charge of assault and battery against the twins. Robert Allen was retained by Driscoll, David Wilson by the defense. Tom, his native cheerfulness unannihilated by his back-breaking and bone-bruising passage across the massed heads of the Sons of Liberty the previous night, laughed his little customary laugh, and said to Wilson:

'I've kept my promise, you see; I'm throwing my business your way. Sooner than I was expecting, too.'

'It's very good of you—particularly if you mean to keep it up.'

'Well, I can't tell about that yet. But we'll see. If I find you deserve it I'll take you under my protection and make your fame and fortune for you.'

'I'll try to deserve it, Tom.'

A jury was sworn in; then Mr Allen said:

'We will detain your honor but a moment with this case. It is not one where any doubt of the fact of the assault can enter in. These gentlemen—the accused—kicked my client at the Market Hall last night; they kicked him with violence; with extraordinary violence; with even unprecedented violence, I may say; insomuch that he was lifted entirely off his feet and discharged into the midst of the audience. We can prove this by four hundred witnesses—we shall call but three. Mr Harkness will take the stand.'

Mr Harkness, being sworn, testified that he was chairman upon the occasion mentioned; that he was close at hand and saw the defendants in this action kick the plaintiff into the air and saw him descend among the audience.

'Take the witness,' said Allen.

'Mr Harkness,' said Wilson, 'you say you saw these gentlemen, my clients, kick the plaintiff. Are you sure—and please remember that you are on oath—are you perfectly sure that you saw *both* of them kick him, or only one? Now be careful.'

A bewildered look began to spread itself over the witness's face. He hesitated, stammered, but got out nothing. His eyes wandered to the twins and fixed themselves there with a vacant gaze.

'Please answer, Mr Harkness, you are keeping the court waiting. It is a very simple question.'

Counsel for the prosecution broke in with impatience:

'Your honor, the question is an irrelevant triviality. Necessarily, they both kicked him, for they have but the one pair of legs, and both are responsible for them.'

Wilson said, sarcastically:

'Will your honor permit this new witness to be sworn? He seems to possess knowledge which can be of the utmost value just at this moment—knowledge which would at once dispose of what every one must see is a very difficult question in this case. Brother Allen, will you take the stand?'

'Go on with your case!' said Allen, petulantly. The audience laughed, and got a warning from the court.

'Now, Mr Harkness,' said Wilson, insinuatingly, 'we shall have to insist upon an answer to that question.'

'I—er—well, of course, I do not absolutely *know*, but in my opinion—'

'Never mind your opinion, sir—answer the question.'

'I—why, I *can't* answer it.'

'That will do, Mr Harkness. Stand down.'

The audience tittered and the discomfited witness retired in a state of great embarrassment.

Mr Wakeman took the stand and swore that he saw the twins kick the plaintiff off the platform. The defense took the witness.

'Mr Wakeman, you have sworn that you saw these gentlemen kick the plaintiff. Do I understand you to swear that you saw them *both* do it?'

'Yes, sir,'—with decision.

'How do you know that both did it?'

'Because I *saw* them do it.'

The audience laughed, and got another warning from the court.

'But by what means do you know that both, and not one, did it?'

'Well, in the first place, the insult was given to both of them equally, for they were called a pair of scissors. Of course they would both want to resent it, and so—'

'Wait! You are theorizing now. Stick to facts—counsel will attend to the arguments. Go on.'

'Well, they both went over there—*that* I saw.'

'Very good. Go on.'

'And they both kicked him—I swear to it.'

'Mr Wakeman, was Count Luigi, here, willing to join the Sons of Liberty last night?'

'Yes, sir, he was. He did join, too, and drank a glass or two of whisky, like a man.'

'Was his brother willing to join?'

'No, sir, he wasn't. He is a teetotaler, and was elected through a mistake.'

'Was he given a glass of whisky?'

'Yes, sir, but of course that was another mistake, and not intentional. He wouldn't drink it. He set it down.' A slight pause, then he added, casually and quite simply: 'The plaintiff reached for it and hogged it.'

There was a fine outburst of laughter, but as the justice was caught out himself, his reprimand was not very vigorous.

Mr Allen jumped up and exclaimed: 'I protest against these foolish irrelevancies. What have they to do with the case?'

Wilson said: 'Calm yourself, brother, it was only an experiment. Now, Mr Wakeman, if one of these gentlemen chooses to join an association and the other doesn't; and if one of them enjoys whisky and the other doesn't, but sets it aside and leaves it unprotected' (titter from the audience), 'it seems to show that they have independent minds, and tastes, and preferences, and that one of them is able to approve of a thing at the very moment that the other is heartily disapproving of it. Doesn't it seem so to you?'

'Certainly it does. It's perfectly plain.'

'Now, then, it might be—I only say it might be—that one of these brothers wanted to kick the plaintiff last night, and that the other didn't want that humiliating punishment inflicted upon him in that public way and before all those people. Isn't that possible?'

'Of course it is. It's more than possible. I don't believe the blond one would kick anybody. It was the other one that—'

'Silence!' shouted the plaintiff's counsel, and went on with an angry sentence which was lost in the wave of laughter that swept the house.

'That will do, Mr Wakeman,' said Wilson, 'you may stand down.'

The third witness was called. He had seen the twins kick the plaintiff. Mr Wilson took the witness.

'Mr Rogers, you say you saw these accused gentlemen kick the plaintiff?'

'Yes, sir.'

'Both of them?'

'Yes, sir.'

'Which of them kicked him first?'

'Why—they—they both kicked him at the same time.'

'Are you perfectly sure of that?'

'Yes, sir.'

'What makes you sure of it?'

'Why, I stood right behind them, and *saw* them do it.'

'How many kicks were delivered?'

'Only one.'

'If two men kick, the result should be two kicks, shouldn't it?'

'Why—why—yes, as a rule.'

'Then what do you think went with the other kick?'

'I—well—the fact is, I wasn't thinking of two being necessary, this time.'

'What do you think now?'

'Well, I—I'm sure I don't quite know what to think, but I reckon that one of them did half of the kick and the other one did the other half.'

Somebody in the crowd sung out: 'It's the first sane thing that any of them has said.'

The audience applauded. The judge said: 'Silence! or I will clear the court.'

Mr Allen looked pleased, but Wilson did not seem disturbed. He said:

'Mr Rogers, you have favored us with what you think and what you reckon, but as thinking and reckoning are not evidence, I will now give you a chance to come out with something positive, one way or the other, and shall require you to produce it. I will ask the accused to stand up and repeat the phenomenal kick of last night.' The twins stood up. 'Now, Mr Rogers, please stand behind them.'

A Voice: 'No, stand in front!' (Laughter. Silenced by the court.) Another Voice: 'No, give Tommy another highst!' (Laughter. Sharply rebuked by the court.)

'Now, then, Mr Rogers, two kicks shall be delivered, one after the other, and I give you my word that at least one of the two shall be delivered by one of the twins alone, without the slightest assistance from his brother. Watch sharply, for you have got to render a decision without any if's and and's in it.' Rogers bent himself behind the twins with his palms just above his knees, in the modern attitude of the catcher at a base-ball match, and riveted his eyes on the pair of legs in front of him. 'Are you ready, Mr Rogers?'

'Ready, sir.'

'Kick!'

The kick was launched.

'Have you got that one classified, Mr Rogers?'

'Let me study a minute, sir.'

'Take as much time as you please. Let me know when you are ready.'

For as much as a minute Rogers pondered, with all eyes and a breathless interest fastened upon him. Then he gave the word: 'Ready, sir.'

'Kick!'

The kick that followed was an exact duplicate of the first one.

'Now, then, Mr Rogers, one of those kicks was an individual kick, not a mutual one. You will now state positively which was the mutual one.'

The witness said, with a crestfallen look:

'I've got to give it up. There ain't any man in the world that could tell t'other from which, sir.'

'Do you still assert that last night's kick was a mutual kick?'

'Indeed, I don't, sir.'

'That will do, Mr Rogers. If my brother Allen desires to address the court, your honor, very well; but as far as I am concerned I am ready to let the case be at once delivered into the hands of this intelligent jury without comment.'

Mr Justice Robinson had been in office only two months, and in that short time had not had many cases to try, of course. He had no knowledge of laws and courts except what he had picked up since he came into office. He was a sore trouble to the lawyers, for his rulings were pretty eccentric sometimes, and he stood by them with Roman simplicity and fortitude; but the people were well satisfied with him, for they saw that his intentions were always right, that he was entirely impartial, and that he usually made up in good sense what he lacked in technique, so to speak. He now perceived that there was likely to be a miscarriage of justice here, and he rose to the occasion.

'Wait a moment, gentlemen,' he said, 'it is plain that an assault has been committed—it is plain to anybody; but the way things are going, the guilty will certainly escape conviction. I cannot allow this. Now—'

'But, your honor!' said Wilson, interrupting him, earnestly but respectfully, 'you are deciding the case yourself, whereas the jury—'

'Never mind the jury, Mr Wilson; the jury will have a chance when there is a reasonable doubt for them to take hold of—which there isn't so far. There is no doubt whatever that an assault has been committed. The attempt to show that both of the accused committed it has failed. Are they both to escape justice on that account? Not in this court, if I can prevent it. It appears to have been a mistake to bring the charge against them as a corporation; each should have been charged in his capacity as an individual and—'

'But, your honor!' said Wilson, 'in fairness to my clients I must insist that inasmuch as the prosecution did not separate the—'

'No wrong will be done your clients, sir—they will be protected; also the public and the offended laws. Mr Allen, you will amend your pleadings, and put one of the accused on trial at a time.'

Wilson broke in: 'But, your honor! this is wholly unprecedented! To imperil an accused person by arbitrarily altering and widening the charge against him in order to compass his conviction when the charge as originally brought promises to fail to convict, is a thing unheard of before.'

'Unheard of *where*?'

'In the courts of this or any other State.'

The Judge said with dignity: 'I am not acquainted with the customs of other courts, and am not concerned to know what they are. I am responsible for this court, and I cannot conscientiously allow my judgment to be warped and my judicial liberty hampered by trying to conform to the caprices of other courts, be they—'

'But, your honor, the oldest and highest courts in Europe—'

'This court is not run on the European plan, Mr Wilson; it is not run on any plan but its own. It has a plan of its own; and that plan is, to find justice for both State and accused, no matter what happens to be practice and custom in Europe or anywhere else.' (Great applause.) 'Silence! It has not been the custom of this court to imitate other courts; it has not been the custom of this court to take shelter behind the decisions of other courts, and we will not begin now.

We will do the best we can by the light that God has given us, and while this court continues to have His approval, it will remain indifferent to what other organizations may think of it.' (Applause.) 'Gentlemen, I *must* have order!—quiet yourselves! Mr Allen, you will now proceed against the prisoners one at a time. Go on with the case.'

Allen was not at his ease. However, after whispering a moment with his client and with one or two other people, he rose and said:

'Your honor, I find it to be reported and believed that the accused are able to act independently in many ways, but that this independence does not extend to their legs, authority over their legs being vested exclusively in the one brother during a specific term of days, and then passing to the other brother for a like term, and so on, by regular alternation. I could call witnesses who would prove that the accused had revealed to them the existence of this extraordinary fact, and had also made known which of them was in possession of the legs yesterday—and this would, of course, indicate where the guilt of the assault belongs—but as this would be mere hearsay evidence, these revelations not having been made under oath—'

'Never mind about that, Mr Allen. It may not all be hearsay. We shall see. It may at least help to put us on the right track. Call the witnesses.'

'Then I will call Mr John Buckstone, who is now present, and I beg that Mrs Patsy Cooper may be sent for. Take the stand, Mr. Buckstone.'

Buckstone took the oath and then testified that on the previous evening the Count Angelo Cappello had protested against going to the hall, and had called all present to witness that he was going by compulsion and would not go if he could help himself. Also, that the Count Luigi had replied sharply that he would *go*, just the same, and that he, Count Luigi, would see to that himself. Also, that upon Count Angelo's complaining about being kept on his legs so long, Count Luigi retorted with apparent surprise, '*Your* legs!—I like your impudence!'

'*Now* we are getting at the kernel of the thing,' observed the Judge, with grave and earnest satisfaction. 'It looks as if the Count Luigi was in possession of the battery at the time of the assault.'

Nothing further was elicited from Mr Buckstone on direct examination. Mr Wilson took the witness.

'Mr Buckstone, about what time was it that that conversation took place?'

'Toward nine yesterday evening, sir.'

'Did you then proceed directly to the hall?'

'Yes, sir.'

'How long did it take you to go there?'

'Well, we walked; and as it was from the extreme edge of the town, and there was no hurry, I judge it took us about twenty minutes, maybe a trifle more.'

'About what hour was the kick delivered?'

'About thirteen minutes and a half to ten.'

'Admirable! You are a pattern witness, Mr Buckstone. How did you happen to look at your watch at that particular moment?'

'I always do it when I see an assault. It's likely I shall be called as a witness, and it's a good point to have.'

'It would be well if others were as thoughtful. Was anything said, between the conversation at my house and the assault, upon the detail which we are now examining into?'

'No, sir.'

'If power over the mutual legs was in the possession of one brother at nine, and passed into the possession of the other one during the next thirty or forty minutes, do you think you could have detected the change?'

'By no means!'

'That is all, Mr Buckstone.'

Mrs Patsy Cooper was called. The crowd made way for her, and she came smiling and bowing through the narrow human lane, with Betsy Hale, as escort and support, smiling and bowing in her wake, the audience breaking into welcoming cheers as the old favorites filed along. The Judge did not check this kindly demonstration of homage and affection, but let it run its course unrebuked.

The old ladies stopped and shook hands with the twins with effusion, then gave the Judge a friendly nod, and bustled into the seats provided for them. They immediately began to deliver a volley of eager questions at the friends around them: 'What is this thing for?' 'What is that thing for?' 'Who is that young man that's writing at the desk? Why, I declare, it's Jack Bunce! I thought he was sick.' 'Which is the jury? Why, is *that* the jury? Billy Price and Job Turner, and Jack Lounsbury, and—well, I never!' 'Now who would ever a' thought—'

But they were gently called to order at this point, and asked not to talk in court. Their tongues fell silent, but the radiant interest in their faces remained, and their gratitude for the blessing of a new sensation and a novel experience still beamed undimmed from their eyes. Aunt Patsy stood up and took the oath, and Mr Allen explained the point in issue, and asked her to go on now, in her own way, and throw as much light upon it as she could. She toyed with her reticule a moment or two, as if considering where to begin, then she said:

'Well, the way of it is this. They are Luigi's legs a week at a time, and then they are Angelo's, and he can do what ever he wants to with them.'

'You are making a mistake, Aunt Patsy Cooper,' said the Judge. 'You shouldn't state that as a *fact*, because you don't know it to *be* a fact.'

'What's the reason I don't?' said Aunt Patsy, bridling a little.

'What is the reason that you do know it?'

'The best in the world—because they told me.'

'That isn't a reason.'

'Well, for the land's sake! Betsy Hale, do you hear that?'

'*Hear* it? I should think so,' said Aunt Betsy, rising and facing the court. 'Why, Judge, I was there and heard it myself. Luigi says to Angelo—no, it was Angelo said it to—'

'Come, come, Mrs Hale, pray sit down, and—'

'Certainly, it's all right, I'm going to sit down presently, but not until I've—'

'But you *must* sit down!'

'*Must!* Well, upon my word if things ain't getting to a pretty pass when—'

The house broke into laughter, but was promptly brought to order, and meantime Mr Allen persuaded the old lady to take her seat. Aunt Patsy continued:

'Yes, they told me that, and I know it's true. They're Luigi's legs this week, but—'

'Ah, *they* told you that, did they?' said the Justice, with interest.

'Well, no, I don't know that *they* told me, but that's neither here nor there. I know, without that, that at dinner, yesterday, Angelo was tired as a dog, and yet Luigi wouldn't lend him the legs to go up stairs and take a nap with.'

'Did he ask for them?'

'Let me see—it seems to me somehow, that—that—Aunt Betsy, do you remember whether he—'

'Never mind about what Aunt Betsy remembers—she is not a witness; we only want to know what you remember yourself,' said the Judge.

'Well, it does seem to me that you are most cantankerously particular about a little thing, Sim Robinson. Why, when I can't remember a thing myself, I always—'

'Ah, *please* go on!'

'Now how *can* she when you keep fussing at her all the time?' said Aunt Betsy. 'Why, with a person pecking at *me* that way, I should get that fuzzled and fuddled that—'

She was on her feet again, but Allen coaxed her into her seat once more, while the court squelched the mirth of the house. Then the Judge said:

'Madam, do you know—do you absolutely *know*, independently of anything these gentlemen have told you—that the power over their legs passes from the one to the other regularly every week?'

'Regularly? Bless your heart, regularly ain't any name for the exactness of it! All the big cities in Europe used to set the clocks by it.' (Laughter, *suppressed by the court*.)

'How do you *know*? That is the question. Please answer it

plainly and squarely.'

'Don't you talk to me like that, Sim Robinson—I won't have it. How do I know, indeed! How do *you* know what you know? Because somebody told you. You didn't invent it out of your own head, did you? Why, these twins are the truthfulest people in the world; and I don't think it becomes you to sit up there and throw slurs at them when they haven't been doing anything to you. And they are orphans besides— both of them. All—'

But Aunt Betsy was up again now, and both old ladies were talking at once and with all their might; but as the house was weltering in a storm of laughter, and the judge was hammering his desk with an iron paper weight, one could only see them talk, not hear them. At last, when quiet was restored, the court said:

'Let the ladies retire.'

'But, your honor, I have the right, in the interest of my clients, to cross-exam—'

'You'll not need to exercise it, Mr Wilson—the evidence is thrown out.'

'Thrown out!' said Aunt Patsy, ruffled; 'and what's it thrown out for, I'd like to know.'

'And so would I, Patsy Cooper. It seems to me that if we can save these poor persecuted strangers, it is our bounden duty to stand up here and talk for them till—'

'There, there, there, *do* sit down!'

It cost some trouble and a good deal of coaxing, but they were got into their seats at last. The trial was soon ended now. The twins themselves became witnesses in their own defense. They established the fact, upon oath, that the leg-power passed from one to the other every Saturday night at twelve o'clock sharp. But on cross-examination their counsel would not allow them to tell whose week of power the current week was. The Judge insisted upon their answering, and proposed to compel them, but even the prosecution took fright and came to the rescue then, and helped stay the sturdy jurist's revolutionary hand. So the case had to go to the jury with that important point hanging in the air. They were out an hour and brought in this verdict:

'We the jury do find: 1, that an assault was committed, as charged; 2, that it was committed by one of the persons accused, he having been seen to do it by several credible witnesses; 3, but that his identity is so merged in his brother's that we have not been able to tell which was him. We cannot convict both, for only one is guilty. We cannot acquit both, for only one is innocent. Our verdict is that justice has been defeated by the dispensation of God, and ask to be discharged from further duty.'

This was read aloud in court and brought out a burst of hearty applause. The old ladies made a spring at the twins, to shake and congratulate, but were gently disengaged by Mr Wilson and softly crowded back into their places.

The Judge rose in his little tribune, laid aside his silverbowed spectacles, roached his gray hair up with his fingers, and said, with dignity and solemnity, and even with a certain pathos:

'In all my experience on the bench, I have not seen justice bow her head in shame in this court until this day. You little realize what far-reaching harm has just been wrought here under the fickle forms of law. Imitation is the bane of courts—I thank God that this one is free from the contamination of that vice—and in no long time you will see the fatal work of this hour seized upon by profligate so-called guardians of justice in all the wide circumstance of this planet and perpetuated in their pernicious decisions. I wash my hands of this iniquity. I would have compelled these culprits to expose their guilt, but support failed me where I had most right to expect aid and encouragement. And I was confronted by a law made in the interest of crime, which protects the criminal from testifying against himself. Yet I had precedents of my own whereby I had set aside that law on two different occasions and thus succeeded in convicting criminals to whose crimes there were no witnesses but themselves. What have you accomplished this day? Do you realize it? You have set adrift, unadmonished, in this community, two men endowed with an awful and mysterious gift, a hidden and grisly power for evil—a power by which each in his turn may commit crime after crime of the most heinous character, and no man be able to tell which is the guilty or which the innocent party in any case of them all. Look to your homes—look to your property—look to your lives—for you have need!

'Prisoners at the bar, stand up. Through suppression of evidence, a jury of your—our—countrymen have been obliged to deliver a verdict concerning your case which stinks to high heaven with the rankness of its injustice. By its terms you, the guilty one, go free with the innocent. Depart in peace, and come no more! The costs devolve upon the outraged plaintiff—another iniquity. The court stands dissolved.'

Almost everybody crowded forward to overwhelm the twins and their counsel with congratulations; but presently the two old aunties dug the duplicates out and bore them away in triumph through the hurrahing crowd, while lots of new friends carried Pudd'nhead Wilson off tavern-wards to feast him and 'wet down' his great and victorious entry into the legal arena. To Wilson, so long familiar with neglect and depreciation, this strange new incense of popularity and admiration was as a fragrance blown from the fields of paradise. A happy man was Wilson.

6

[A deputation came in the evening and conferred upon Wilson the welcome honor of a nomination for mayor; for the village has just been converted into a city by charter. Tom skulks out of challenging the twins. Judge Driscoll thereupon challenges Angelo (accused by Tom of doing the kicking); he declines, but Luigi accepts in his place against Angelo's timid protest.]

IT was late Saturday night—nearing eleven.

The Judge and his second found the rest of the war party at the further end of the vacant ground, near the haunted house. Pudd'nhead Wilson advanced to meet them, and said anxiously:

'I must say a word in behalf of my principal's proxy, Count Luigi, to whom you have kindly granted the privilege of fighting my principal's battle for him. It is growing late, and Count Luigi is in great trouble lest midnight shall strike before the finish.'

'It is another testimony,' said Howard, approvingly. 'That young man is fine all through. He wishes to save his brother the sorrow of fighting on the Sabbath, and he is right; it is the right and manly feeling and does him credit. We will make all possible haste.'

Wilson said:

'There is also another reason—a consideration, in fact, which deeply concerns Count Luigi himself. These twins have command of their mutual legs turn about. Count Luigi is in command now; but at midnight, possession will pass to my principal, Count Angelo, and—well, you can foresee what will happen. He will march straight off the field, and carry Luigi with him.'

'Why! sure enough!' cried the Judge, 'we have heard something about that extraordinary law of their being, already— nothing very definite, it is true, as regards dates and durations of power, but I see it is definite enough as regards to-night. Of course we must give Luigi every chance. Omit all the ceremonial possible, gentlemen, and place us in position.'

The seconds at once tossed up a coin; Howard won the choice. He placed the Judge sixty feet from the haunted house and facing it; Wilson placed the twins within fifteen feet of the house and facing the Judge—necessarily. The pistol-case was opened and the long slim tubes taken out; when the moonlight glinted from them a shiver went through Angelo. The doctor was a fool, but a thoroughly well-meaning one, with a kind heart and a sincere disposition to oblige, but along with it an absence of tact which often hurt its effectiveness. He brought his box of lint and bandages, and asked Angelo to feel and see how soft and comfortable they were. Angelo's head fell over against Luigi's in a faint, and precious time was lost in bringing him to; which provoked Luigi into expressing his mind to the doctor with a good deal of vigor and frankness. After Angelo came to he was still so weak that Luigi was obliged to drink a stiff horn of brandy to brace him up.

The seconds now stepped at once to their posts, half way between the combatants, one of them on each side of the line of fire. Wilson was to count, very deliberately, 'One—two—three—fire!—stop!' and the duellists could bang away at any time they chose during that recitation, but not after the last word. Angelo grew very nervous when he saw Wilson's hand rising slowly into the air as a sign to make ready, and he leaned his head against Luigi's and said:

'Oh, please take me away from here, I can't stay, I know I can't!'

'What in the world are you doing? Straighten up! What's the matter with you?—*you're* in no danger—nobody's going to shoot at you. Straighten up, I tell you!'

Angelo obeyed, just in time to hear:

'One—!'

'Bang!' Just one report, and a little tuft of white hair floated slowly to the Judge's feet in the moonlight. The Judge did not swerve; he still stood erect and motionless, like a statue, with his pistol-arm hanging straight down at his side. He was reserving his fire.

'Two—!'

'Three—!'

'Fire—!'

Up came the pistol-arm instantly—Angelo dodged with the report. He said 'Ouch!' and fainted again.

The doctor examined and bandaged the wound. It was of no consequence, he said—bullet through fleshy part of arm—no bones broken—the gentleman was still able to fight—let the duel proceed.

Next time Angelo jumped just as Luigi fired, which disordered his aim and caused him to cut a chip out of Howard's ear. The Judge took his time again, and when he fired Angelo jumped and got a knuckle skinned. The doctor inspected and dressed the wounds. Angelo now spoke out and said he was content with the satisfaction he had got, and if the Judge— but Luigi shut him roughly up, and asked him not to make an ass of himself; adding:

'And I want you to stop dodging. You take a great deal too prominent a part in this thing for a person who has got nothing to do with it. You should remember that you are here only by courtesy, and are without official recognition; officially you are not here at all; officially you do not even exist. To all intents and purposes you are absent from this place, and you ought for your own modesty's sake to reflect that it cannot become a person who is not present here to be taking this sort of public and indecent prominence in a matter in which he is not in the slightest degree concerned. Now, don't dodge again; the bullets are not for you, they are for me; if I want them dodged I will attend to it myself. I never saw a person act so.'

Angelo saw the reasonableness of what his brother had said, and he did try to reform, but it was of no use; both pistols went off at the same instant, and he jumped once more; he got a sharp scrape along his cheek from the Judge's bullet, and so deflected Luigi's aim that his ball went wide and chipped a flake of skin from Pudd'nhead Wilson's chin. The doctor attended to the wounded.

By the terms, the duel was over. But Luigi was entirely out of patience, and begged for one more exchange of shots, insisting that he had had no fair chance, on account of his brother's indelicate behavior. Howard was opposed to granting so unusual a privilege, but the Judge took Luigi's part, and added that indeed he himself might fairly be considered entitled to another trial, because although the proxy on the other side was in no way to blame for his (the Judge's) humiliatingly resultless work, the gentleman with whom he was fighting this duel was to blame for it, since if he had played no advantages and had held his head still, his proxy would have been disposed of early. He added:

'Count Luigi's request for another exchange is another proof that he is a brave and chivalrous gentleman, and I beg that the courtesy he asks may be accorded him.'

'I thank you most sincerely for this generosity, Judge Driscoll,' said Luigi, with a polite bow, and moving to his place. Then he added—to Angelo, 'Now hold your grip, hold your *grip*, I tell you, and I'll land him sure!'

The men stood erect, their pistol-arms at their sides, the two seconds stood at their official posts, the doctor stood five paces in Wilson's rear with his instruments and bandages in his hands. The deep stillness, the peaceful moonlight, the motionless figures, made an impressive picture and the impending fatal possibilities augmented this impressiveness to solemnity. Wilson's hand began to rise—slowly—slowly— higher—still higher—in another moment:

'*Boom!*'—the first stroke of midnight swung up out of the distance; Angelo was off like a deer!

'Oh, you unspeakable traitor!' wailed his brother, as they went soaring over the fence.

The others stood astonished and gazing; and so stood, watching that strange spectacle until distance dissolved it and swept it from their view. Then they rubbed their eyes like people waking out of a dream.

'Well, I've never seen anything like that before!' said the Judge. 'Wilson, I am going to confess now, that I wasn't quite able to believe in that leg-business, and had a suspicion that it was a put-up convenience between those twins; and when Count Angelo fainted I thought I saw the whole scheme—thought it was pretext No. I, and would be followed by others till twelve o'clock should arrive, and Luigi would get off with all the credit of seeming to want to fight and yet not have to fight, after all. But I was mistaken. His pluck proved it. He's a brave fellow and did want to fight.'

'There isn't any doubt about that,' said Howard, and added, in a grieved tone, 'but what an unworthy sort of Christian that Angelo is—I hope and believe there are not many like him. It is not right to engage in a duel on the Sabbath—I could not approve of that myself; but to finish one that has been begun—that is a duty, let the day be what it may.'

They strolled along, still wondering, still talking.

'It is a curious circumstance,' remarked the surgeon, halting Wilson a moment to paste some more court plaster on his chin, which had gone to leaking blood again, 'that in this duel neither of the parties who handled the pistols lost blood, while nearly all the persons present in the mere capacity of guests got hit. I have not heard of such a thing before. Don't you think it unusual?'

'Yes,' said the Judge, 'it has struck me as peculiar. Peculiar and unfortunate. I was annoyed at it, all the time. In the case of Angelo it made no great difference, because he was in a measure concerned, though not officially; but it troubled me to see the seconds compromised, and yet I knew no way to mend the matter.'

'There was no way to mend it,' said Howard, whose ear was being readjusted now by the doctor; 'the code fixes our place, and it would not have been lawful to change it. If we could have stood at your side, or behind you, or in front of you, it—but it would not have been legitimate and the other parties would have had a just right to complain of our trying to protect ourselves from danger; infractions of the code are certainly not permissible in any case whatever.'

Wilson offered no remarks. It seemed to him that there was very little place here for so much solemnity, but he judged that if a duel where nobody was in danger or got crippled but the seconds and the outsiders had nothing ridiculous about it for these gentlemen, his pointing out that feature would probably not help them to see it.

He invited them in to take a nightcap, and Howard and the Judge accepted, but the doctor said he would have to go and see how Angelo's principal wound was getting on.

[It was now Sunday, and in the afternoon Angelo was to be received into the Baptist communion by immersion—a doubtful prospect, the doctor feared.]

7

WHEN the doctor arrived at Aunt Patsy Cooper's house, he found the lights going and everybody up and dressed and in a great state of solicitude and excitement. The twins were stretched on a sofa in the sitting-room, Aunt Patsy was fussing at Angelo's arm, Nancy was flying around under her commands, the two young boys were trying to keep out of the way and always getting in it, in order to see and wonder, Rowena stood apart, helpless with apprehension and emotion, and Luigi was growling in unappeasable fury over Angelo's shameful flight.

As has been reported before, the doctor was a fool—a kindhearted and well-meaning one, but with no tact; and as he was by long odds the most learned physician in the town, and was quite well aware of it, and could talk his learning with ease and precision, and liked to show off when he had an audience, he was sometimes tempted into revealing more of a case than was good for the patient.

He examined Angelo's wound, and was really minded to say nothing for once; but Aunt Patsy was so anxious and so pressing that he allowed his caution to be overcome, and proceeded to empty himself as follows, with scientific relish:

'Without going too much into detail, madam—for you would probably not understand it, anyway—I concede that great care is going to be necessary here; otherwise exudation of the oesophagus is nearly sure to ensue, and this will be followed by ossification and extradition of the maxillaris superioris, which must decompose the granular surfaces of the great infusorial ganglionic system, thus obstructing the action of the posterior varioloid arteries, and precipitating compound strangulated sorosis of the valvular tissues, and ending unavoidably in the dispersion and combustion of the marsupial fluxes and the consequent embrocation of the bicuspid populo redax referendum rotulorum.'

A miserable silence followed. Aunt Patsy's heart sank, the pallor of despair invaded her face, she was not able to speak; poor Rowena wrung her hands in privacy and silence, and said to herself in the bitterness of her young grief, 'There is no hope—it is plain there is no hope;' the good-hearted negro wench, Nancy, paled to chocolate, then to orange, then to amber, and thought to herself with yearning sympathy and sorrow, 'Po' thing, he ain' gwyne to las' throo de half o'. dat;' small Henry choked up, and turned his head away to hide his rising tears, and his brother Joe said to himself, with a sense of loss, 'The baptizing's busted, that's sure.' Luigi was the only person who had any heart to speak. He said, a little bit sharply, to the doctor:

'Well, well, there's nothing to be gained by wasting precious time; give him a barrel of pills—I'll take them for him.'

'You?' asked the doctor.

'Yes. Did you suppose he was going to take them himself?'

'Why, of course.'

'Well, it's a mistake. He never took a dose of medicine in his life. He can't.'

'Well, upon my word, it's the most extraordinary thing I ever heard of!'

'Oh,' said Aunt Patsy, as pleased as a mother whose child is being admired and wondered at, 'you'll find that there's more about them that's wonderful than their just being made in the image of God like the rest of His creatures, now you can depend on that, *I* tell you,' and she wagged her complacent head like one who could reveal marvelous things if she chose.

The boy Joe began:

'Why, ma, they *ain't* made in the im—'

'You shut up, and wait till you're asked, Joe. I'll let you know when I want help. Are you looking for something, doctor?'

The doctor asked for a few sheets of paper and a pen, and said he would write a prescription; which he did. It was one of Galen's*; in fact, it was Galen's favorite, and had been slaying people for sixteen thousand years. Galen used it for everything, applied it to everything, said it would remove everything, from warts all the way through to lungs—and it generally did. Galen was still the only medical authority recognized in Missouri; his practice was the only practice known to the Missouri doctors, and his prescriptions were the only ammunition they carried when they went out for game. By and by Dr Claypool laid down his pen and read the result of his labors aloud, carefully and deliberately, for this battery must be constructed on the premises by the family, and mistakes could occur; for he wrote a doctor's hand—the hand which from the beginning of time has been so disastrous to the apothecary and so profitable to the undertaker:

'Take of afarabocca, henbane, corpobalsamum, each two drams and a half: of cloves, opium, myrrh, cyperus, each two drams; of opobalsamum, Indian leaf, cinnamon, zedoary, ginger, coftus, coral, cassia, euphorbium, gum tragacanth, frankincense, styrax calamita, celtic, nard, spignel, hartwort, mustard, saxifrage, dill, anise, each one dram; of xylaloes, rheum ponticum, alipta, moschata, castor, spikenard, galangals, opoponax, anacardium, mastich, brimstone, peony, eringo, pulp of dates, red and white hermodactyls, roses, thyme, acorns, pennyroyal, gentian, the bark of the root of mandrake, germander, valerian, bishop's weed, bay-berries, long and white pepper, xylobalsamum, carnabadium, macedonian, parsely-seeds, lovage, the seeds of rue, and sinon, of each a dram and a half; of pure gold, pure silver, pearls not perforated, the blatta byzantina, the bone of the stag's heart, of each the quantity of fourteen grains of wheat; of sapphire, emerald and jasper stones, each one dram; of hazel-nut, two drams; of pellitory of Spain, shaving of ivory, calamus odoratus, each the quantity of twenty-nine grains of wheat; of honey or sugar a sufficient quantity. Boil down and skim off.'

'There,' he said, 'that will fix the patient; give his brother a dipperful every three-quarters of an hour—'

—'while he survives,' muttered Luigi—

—'and see that the room is kept wholesomely hot, and the doors and windows closed tight. Keep Count Angelo nicely covered up with six or seven blankets, and when he is thirsty—which will be frequently—moisten a rag in the vapor of the tea-kettle and let his brother suck it. When he is hungry—which will also be frequently—he must not be humored oftener than every seven or eight hours; then toast part of a cracker until it begins to brown, and give it to his brother.'

'That is all very well, as far as Angelo is concerned,' said Luigi, 'but what am I to eat?'

'I do not see that there is anything the matter with you,' the doctor answered, 'you may, of course, eat what you please.'

'And also drink what I please, I suppose?'

'Oh, certainly—at present. When the violent and continuous perspiring has reduced your strength, I shall have to reduce your diet, of course, and also bleed you, but there is no occasion for that yet awhile.' He turned to Aunt Patsy and said: 'He must be put to bed, and sat up with, and tended with the greatest care, and not allowed to stir for several days and nights.'

'For one, I'm sacredly thankful for that,' said Luigi, 'It postpones the funeral—I'm not to be drowned to-day anyhow.'

Angelo said quietly to the doctor:

'I will cheerfully submit to all your requirements, sir, up to two o'clock this afternoon, and will resume them after three, but cannot be confined to the house during that intermediate hour.'

'Why, may I ask?'

'Because I have entered the Baptist communion, and by appointment am to be baptized in the river at that hour.'

'Oh insanity!—it cannot be allowed!'

Angelo answered with placid firmness:

'Nothing shall prevent it, if I am alive.'

'Why, consider, my dear sir, in your condition it might prove fatal.'

A tender and ecstatic smile beamed from Angelo's eyes, and he broke forth in a tone of joyous fervency:

'Ah, how blessed it would be to die for such a cause—it would be martyrdom!'

'But your brother—consider your brother; you would be risking his life, too.'

'He risked mine an hour ago,' responded Angelo, gloomily; 'did he consider me?' A thought swept through his mind that made him shudder. 'If I had not run, I might have been killed in a duel on the Sabbath day, and my soul would have been lost—lost.'

'Oh, don't fret, it wasn't in any danger,' said Luigi, irritably; 'they wouldn't waste it for a little thing like that; there's a glass case all ready for it in the heavenly museum, and a pin to stick it up with.'

Aunt Patsy was shocked, and said:

'Looy, Looy!—don't talk so, dear!'

Rowena's soft heart was pierced by Luigi's unfeeling words, and she murmured to herself, 'Oh, if I but had the dear privilege of protecting and defending him with my weak voice!—but alas! this sweet boon is denied me by the cruel conventions of social intercourse.'

'Get their bed ready,' said Aunt Patsy to Nancy, 'and shut up the windows and doors, and light their candles, and see that you drive all the mosquitoes out of their bar, and make up a good fire in their stove, and carry up some bags of hot ashes to lay to his feet—'

—'and a shovel of fire for his head, and a mustard plaster for his neck, and some gum shoes for his ears,' Luigi interrupted, with temper; and added, to himself, 'Damnation, I'm going to be roasted alive, I just know it!'

'Why, Looy! Do be quiet; I never saw such a fractious thing. A body would think you didn't care for your brother.'

'I don't—to *that* extent, Aunt Patsy. I was glad the drowning was postponed a minute ago, but I'm not now. No, that is all gone by; I want to be drowned.'

'You'll bring a judgment on yourself just as sure as you live, if you go on like that. Why, I never heard the beat of it. Now, there,—there! you've said enough. Not another word out of you,—I won't have it!'

'But, Aunt Patsy—'

'Luigi! Didn't you hear what I told you?'

'But, Aunt Patsy, I—why, I'm not going to set my heart and lungs afloat in that pail of sewage which this criminal here has been prescri—'

'Yes, you are, too. You are going to be good, and do everything I tell you, like a dear,' and she tapped his cheek affectionately with her finger. 'Rowena, take the prescription and go in the kitchen and hunt up the things and lay them out for me. I'll sit up with my patient the rest of the night, doctor; I can't trust Nancy, she couldn't make Luigi take the medicine. Of course, you'll drop in again during the day. Have you got any more directions?'

'No, I believe not, Aunt Patsy. If I don't get in earlier, I'll be along by early candlelight, anyway. Meantime, don't allow him to get out of his bed.'

Angelo said, with calm determination:

'I shall be baptized at two o'clock. Nothing but death shall prevent me.'

The doctor said nothing aloud, but to himself he said:

'Why, this chap's got a manly side, after all! Physically he's a coward, but morally he's a lion. I'll go and tell the others about this; it will raise him a good deal in their estimation— and the public will follow their lead, of course.'

Privately, Aunt Patsy applauded too, and was proud of Angelo's courage in the moral field as she was of Luigi's in the field of honor.

The boy Henry was troubled, but the boy Joe said, inaudibly, and gratefully, 'We're all hunky, after all; and no postponement on account of the weather.'

8

BY nine o'clock the town was humming with the news of the midnight duel, and there were but two opinions about it: one, that Luigi's pluck in the field was most praiseworthy and Angelo's flight most scandalous; the other, that Angelo's courage in flying the field for conscience's sake was as fine and creditable as was Luigi's in holding the field in the face of the bullets. The one opinion was held by half of the town, the other one was maintained by the other half. The division was clean and exact, and it made two parties, an Angelo party and a Luigi party. The twins had suddenly become popular idols along with Pudd'nhead Wilson, and haloed with a glory as intense as his. The children talked the duel all the way to Sunday-school, their elders talked it all the way to church, the choir discussed it behind their red curtain, it usurped the place of pious thought in the 'nigger gallery'.

By noon the doctor had added the news, and spread it, that Count Angelo, in spite of his wound and all warnings and supplications, was resolute in his determination to be baptized at the hour appointed. This swept the town like wildfire, and mightily reinforced the enthusiasm of the Angelo faction, who said, 'If any doubted that it was moral courage that took him from the field, what have they to say now!'

Still the excitement grew. All the morning it was traveling countrywards, toward all points of the compass; so, whereas before only the farmers and their wives were intending to come and witness the remarkable baptism, a general holiday was now proclaimed and the children and negroes admitted to the privileges of the occasion. All the farms for ten miles around were vacated, all the converging roads emptied long processions of wagons, horses, and yeomanry into the town. The pack and cram of people vastly exceeded any that had ever been seen in that sleepy region before. The only thing that had ever even approached it, was the time long gone by, but never forgotten, nor even referred to without wonder and pride, when two circuses and a Fourth of July fell together. But the glory of that occasion was extinguished now for good. It was but a freshet to this deluge.

The great invasion massed itself on the river bank and waited hungrily for the immense event. Waited, and wondered if it would really happen, or if the twin who was not a 'professor' would stand out and prevent it.

But they were not to be disappointed. Angelo was as good as his word. He came attended by an escort of honor composed of several hundred of the best citizens, all of the

Angelo party; and when the immersion was finished they escorted him back home: and would even have carried him on their shoulders, but that people might think they were carrying Luigi.

Far into the night the citizens continued to discuss and wonder over the strangely-mated pair of incidents that had distinguished and exalted the past twenty-four hours above any other twenty-four in the history of their town for picturesqueness and splendid interest; and long before the lights were out and burghers asleep it had been decided on all hands that in capturing these twins Dawson's Landing had drawn a prize in the great lottery of municipal fortune.

At midnight Angelo was sleeping peacefully. His immersion had not harmed him, it had merely made him wholesomely drowsy, and he had been dead asleep many hours now. It had made Luigi drowsy, too, but he had got only brief naps, on account of his having to take the medicine every three-quarters of an hour—and Aunt Betsy Hale was there to see that he did it. When he complained and resisted, she was quietly firm with him, and said in a low voice:

'No—no, that won't do; you mustn't talk, and you mustn't retch and gag that way, either—you'll wake up your poor brother.'

'Well, what of it, Aunt Betsy, he—'

"Sh-h! Don't make a noise dear. You mustn't forget that your poor brother is sick and—'

'Sick, is he? Well, I wish I—'

'Sh-h-h! Will you be quiet, Luigi! Here, now, take the rest of it—don't keep me holding the dipper all night. I declare if you haven't left a good fourth of it in the bottom! Come—that's a good boy.'

'Aunt Betsy, don't make me! I feel like I've swallowed a cemetery; I do, indeed. Do let me rest a little—just a little; I can't take any more of the devilish stuff now.'

'Luigi! Using such language here, and him just baptized! Do you want the roof to fall on you?'

'I wish to goodness it would!'

'Why, you dreadful thing! I've a good notion to—let that

blanket alone; do you want your brother to catch his death?'

'Aunt Betsy, I've *got* to have it off, I'm being roasted alive; nobody could stand it—you couldn't yourself.'

'Now, then, you're sneezing again—I just expected it.'

'Because I've caught a cold in my head. I always do, when I go in the water with my clothes on. And it takes me weeks to get over it, too. I think it was a shame to serve me so.'

'Luigi, you are unreasonable; you know very well they couldn't baptize him dry. I should think you would be willing to undergo a little inconvenience for your brother's sake.'

'Inconvenience! Now how you talk, Aunt Betsy. I came as near as anything to getting drowned—you saw that yourself; and do you call this inconvenience?—the room shut up as tight as a drum, and so hot the mosquitoes are trying to get out; and a cold in the head, and dying for sleep and no chance to get any on account of this infamous medicine that assassin prescri—'

'There, you're sneezing again. I'm going down and mix some more of this truck for you, dear.'

9

DURING Monday, Tuesday, and Wednesday the twins grew steadily worse; but then the doctor was summoned South to attend his mother's funeral, and they got well in forty-eight hours. They appeared on the street on Friday, and were welcomed with enthusiasm by the new-born parties, the Luigi and Angelo factions. The Luigi faction carried its strength into the Democratic party,* the Angelo faction entered into a combination with the Whigs.* The Democrats nominated Luigi for alderman under the new city government, and the Whigs put up Angelo against him. The Democrats nominated Pudd'nhead Wilson for mayor, and he was left alone in his glory, for the Whigs had no man who was willing to enter the lists against such a formidable opponent. No politician had scored such a compliment as this before in the history of the Mississippi Valley.

The political campaign in Dawson's Landing opened in a pretty warm fashion, and waxed hotter every week. Luigi's whole heart was in it, and even Angelo developed a surprising amount of interest—which was natural, because he was not merely representing Whigism, a matter of no consequence to him, but he was representing something immensely finer and greater—to wit, Reform. In him was centred the hopes of the whole reform element of the town; he was the chosen and admired champion of every clique that had a pet reform of any sort or kind at heart. He was president of the great Teetotalers' Union, its chiefest prophet and mouth-piece.

But as the canvass went on, troubles began to spring up all around—troubles for the twins, and through them for all the parties and segments and fractions of parties. Whenever Luigi had possession of the legs, he carried Angelo to balls, rum shops, Son's of Liberty parades, horse races, campaign riots, and everywhere else that could damage him with his party and the church; and when it was Angelo's week he carried Luigi diligently to all manner of moral and religious gatherings, doing his best to regain the ground he had lost before. As a result of these double performances, there was a storm blowing all the time, an ever rising storm, too—a storm of frantic criticism of the twins, and rage over their extravagant, incomprehensible conduct.

Luigi had the final chance. The legs were his for the closing week of the canvass. He led his brother a fearful dance.

But he saved his best card for the very eve of the election. There was to be a grand turnout of the Teetotalers' Union that day, and Angelo was to march at the head of the procession and deliver a great oration afterward. Luigi drank a couple of glasses of whisky—which steadied his nerves and clarified his mind, but made Angelo drunk. Everybody who saw the march, saw that the Champion of the Teetotalers was half seas over, and noted also that his brother, who made no hypocritical pretensions to extra temperance virtues, was dignified and sober. This eloquent fact could not be unfruitful at the end of a hot political canvass. At the mass meeting

Angelo tried to make his great temperance oration, but was so discommoded by hiccoughs and thickness of tongue that he had to give it up; then drowsiness overtook him and his head drooped against Luigi's and he went to sleep. Luigi apologized for him, and was going on to improve his opportunity with an appeal for a moderation of what he called 'the prevailing teetotal madness,' but persons in the audience began to howl and throw things at him, and then the meeting rose in wrath and chased him home.

This episode was a crusher for Angelo in another way. It destroyed his chances with Rowena. Those chances had been growing, right along, for two months. Rowena had partly confessed that she loved him, but wanted time to consider. Now the tender dream was ended, and she told him so the moment he was sober enough to understand. She said she would never marry a man who drank.

'But I don't drink,' he pleaded.

'That is nothing to the point,' she said, coldly, 'you get drunk, and that is worse.'

[There was a long and sufficiently idiotic discussion here, which ended as reported in a previous note.]

10

DAWSON'S LANDING had a week of repose, after the election, and it needed it, for the frantic and variegated nightmare which had tormented it all through the preceding week had left it limp, haggard, and exhausted at the end. It got the week of repose because Angelo had the legs, and was in too subdued a condition to want to go out and mingle with an irritated community that had come to distrust and detest him because there was such a lack of harmony between his morals, which were confessedly excellent, and his methods of illustrating them, which were distinctly damnable.

The new city officers were sworn in on the following Monday—at least all but Luigi. There was a complication in his case. His election was conceded, but he could not sit in the board of aldermen without his brother, and his brother could not sit there because he was not a member. There seemed to be no way out of the difficulty but to carry the matter into the courts, so this was resolved upon. The case was set for the Monday fortnight. In due course the time arrived. In the meantime the city government had been at a standstill, because without Luigi there was a tie in the board of aldermen, whereas with him the liquor interest—the richest in the political field—would have one majority. But the court decided that Angelo could not sit in the board with him, either in public or executive sessions, and at the same time forbade the board to deny admission to Luigi, a fairly and legally chosen alderman. The case was carried up and up from court to court, yet still the same old original decision was confirmed every time. As a result, the city government not only stood still, with its hands tied, but everything it was created to protect and care for went a steady gait toward rack and ruin. There was no way to levy a tax, so the minor officials had to resign or starve; therefore they resigned. There being no city money, the enormous legal expenses on both sides had to be defrayed by private subscription. But at last the people came to their senses, and said:

'Pudd'nhead was right at the start—we ought to have hired the official half of that human phillipene* to resign; but it's too late now; some of us haven't got anything left to hire him with.'

'Yes, we have,' said another citizen, 'we've got this'—and he produced a halter.

Many shouted: 'That's the ticket.' But others said: 'No—Count Angelo is innocent; we mustn't hang him.'

'Who said anything about hanging him? We are only going to hang the other one.'

'Then that is all right—there is no objection to that.'

So they hanged Luigi. And so ends the history of 'Those Extraordinary Twins'.

Final Remarks

As you see, it was an extravagant sort of a tale, and had no purpose but to exhibit that monstrous 'freak' in all sorts of grotesque lights. But when Roxy wandered into the tale she had to be furnished with something to do; so she changed the children in the cradle; this necessitated the invention of a reason for it; this, in turn, resulted in making the children prominent personages—nothing could prevent it, of course. Their career began to take a tragic aspect, and some one had to be brought in to help work the machinery; so Pudd'nhead Wilson was introduced and taken on trial. By this time the whole show was being run by the new people and in their interest, and the original show was become side-tracked and forgotten; the twin-monster, and the heroine, and the lads, and the old ladies had dwindled to inconsequentialities and were merely in the way. Their story was one story, the new people's story was another story, and there was no connection between them, no interdependence, no kinship. It is not practicable or rational to try to tell two stories at the same time; so I dug out the farce and left the tragedy.

The reader already knew how the expert works; he knows now how the other kind do it.

MARK TWAIN

The Man That
Corrupted Hadleyburg

I

IT was many years ago. Hadleyburg was the most honest and
upright town in all the region round about. It had kept that
reputation unsmirched during three generations, and was
prouder of it than of any other of its possessions. It was so
proud of it, and so anxious to insure its perpetuation, that
it began to teach the principles of honest dealing to its babies
in the cradle, and made the like teachings the staple of their
culture thenceforward through all the years devoted to their
education. Also, throughout the formative years temptations
were kept out of the way of the young people, so that their
honesty could have every chance to harden and solidify, and
become a part of their very bone. The neighboring towns
were jealous of this honorable supremacy, and affected to
sneer at Hadleyburg's pride in it and call it vanity; but all the
same they were obliged to acknowledge that Hadleyburg was
in reality an incorruptible town; and if pressed they would
also acknowledge that the mere fact that a young man hailed
from Hadleyburg was all the recommendation he needed
when he went forth from his natal town to seek for responsible employment.

But at last, in the drift of time, Hadleyburg had the ill luck
to offend a passing stranger—possibly without knowing it,
certainly without caring, for Hadleyburg was sufficient unto
itself, and cared not a rap for strangers or their opinions.
Still, it would have been well to make an exception in this
one's case, for he was a bitter man and revengeful. All
through his wanderings during a whole year he kept his injury
in mind, and gave all his leisure moments to trying to invent
a compensating satisfaction for it. He contrived many plans,
and all of them were good, but none of them was quite
sweeping enough; the poorest of them would hurt a great
many individuals, but what he wanted was a plan which would
comprehend the entire town, and not let so much as one

person escape unhurt. At last he had a fortunate idea, and when it fell into his brain it lit up his whole head with an evil joy. He began to form a plan at once, saying to himself, 'That is the thing to do—I will corrupt the town.'

Six months later he went to Hadleyburg, and arrived in a buggy at the house of the old cashier of the bank about ten at night. He got a sack out of the buggy, shouldered it, and staggered with it through the cottage yard, and knocked at the door. A woman's voice said 'Come in,' and he entered, and set his sack behind the stove in the parlor, saying politely to the old lady who sat reading the *Missionary Herald* by the lamp:

'Pray keep your seat, madam, I will not disturb you. There—now it is pretty well concealed; one would hardly know it was there. Can I see your husband a moment, madam?'

No, he was gone to Brixton, and might not return before morning.

'Very well, madam, it is no matter. I merely wanted to leave that sack in his care, to be delivered to the rightful owner when he shall be found. I am a stranger; he does not know me; I am merely passing through the town tonight to discharge a matter which has been long in my mind. My errand is now completed, and I go pleased and a little proud, and you will never see me again. There is a paper attached to the sack which will explain everything. Good night, madam.'

The old lady was afraid of the mysterious big stranger,* and was glad to see him go. But her curiosity was roused, and she went straight to the sack and brought away the paper. It began as follows:

TO BE PUBLISHED: or, the right man sought out by private inquiry—either will answer. This sack contains gold coin weighing a hundred and sixty pounds four ounces—

'Mercy on us, and the door not locked!'

Mrs. Richards flew to it all in a tremble and locked it, then pulled down the window shades and stood frightened, worried, and wondering if there was anything else she could do toward making herself and the money more safe. She listened awhile for burglars, then surrendered to curiosity and went back to the lamp and finished reading the paper:

I am a foreigner, and am presently going back to my own country, to remain there permanently. I am grateful to America for what I have received at her hands during my long stay under her flag; and to one of her citizens—a citizen of Hadleyburg—I am especially grateful for a great kindness done me a year or two ago. Two great kindnesses, in fact. I will explain. I was a gambler. I say I WAS. I was a ruined gambler. I arrived in this village at night, hungry and without a penny. I asked for help—in the dark; I was ashamed to beg in the light. I begged of the right man. He gave me twenty dollars—that is to say, he gave me life, as I considered it. He also gave me fortune; for out of that money I have made myself rich at the gaming table. And finally, a remark which he made to me has remained with me to this day, and has at last conquered me; and in conquering has saved the remnant of my morals: I shall gamble no more. Now I have no idea who that man was, but I want him found, and I want him to have this money, to give away, throw away, or keep, as he pleases. It is merely my way of testifying my gratitude to him. If I could stay, I would find him myself; but no matter, he will be found. This is an honest town, an incorruptible town, and I know I can trust it without fear. This man can be identified by the remark which he made to me; I feel persuaded that he will remember it.

And now my plan is this: If you prefer to conduct the inquiry privately, do so. Tell the contents of this present writing to anyone who is likely to be the right man. If he shall answer, 'I am the man; the remark I made was so-and-so,' apply the test—to wit: open the sack, and in it you will find a sealed envelope containing that remark. If the remark mentioned by the candidate tallies with it, give him the money, and ask no further questions, for he is certainly the right man.

But if you shall prefer a public inquiry, then publish this present writing in the local paper—with these instructions added, to wit: Thirty days from now, let the candidate appear at the town hall at eight in the evening (Friday), and hand his remark, in a sealed envelope, to the Rev. Mr. Burgess (if he will be kind enough to act); and let Mr. Burgess there and then destroy the seals of the sack, open it, and see if the remark is correct: if correct, let the money be delivered, with my sincere gratitude, to my benefactor thus identified.

Mrs. Richards sat down, gently quivering with excitement, and was soon lost in thinkings—after this pattern: 'What a strange thing it is! ... And what a fortune for that kind man who set his bread afloat upon the waters! ... If it had only been my husband that did it!—for we are so poor, so old and poor! ... ' Then, with a sigh—'But it was not my Edward; no, it was not he that gave a stranger twenty dollars. It is a pity, too; I see it now...' Then, with a shudder—'But it is *gambler's* money! the wages of sin: we couldn't take it; we couldn't touch it. I don't like to be near it; it seems a defilement.' She moved to a farther chair ... 'I wish Edward would come, and take it to the bank; a burglar might come at any moment; it is dreadful to be here all alone with it.'

At eleven Mr. Richards arrived, and while his wife was saying, 'I am *so* glad you've come!' he was saying, 'I'm so tired—tired clear out; it is dreadful to be poor, and have to make these dismal journeys at my time of life. Always at the grind, grind, grind, on a salary—another man's slave, and he sitting at home in his slippers, rich and comfortable.'

'I am so sorry for you, Edward, you know that; but be comforted: we have our livelihood; we have our good name—'

'Yes, Mary, and that is everything. Don't mind my talk—it's just a moment's irritation and doesn't mean anything. Kiss me—there, it's all gone now, and I am not complaining any more. What have you been getting? What's in the sack?'

Then his wife told him the great secret. It dazed him for a moment; then he said:

'It weighs a hundred and sixty pounds? Why, Mary, it's for-ty thou-sand dollars—think of it—a whole fortune! Not ten men in this village are worth that much. Give me the paper.'

He skimmed through it and said:

'Isn't it an adventure! Why, it's a romance; it's like the impossible things one reads about in books, and never sees in life.' He was well stirred up now; cheerful, even gleeful. He tapped his old wife on the cheek, and said, humorously, 'Why, we're rich, Mary, rich; all we've got to do is to bury the money and burn the papers. If the gambler ever comes to inquire, we'll merely look coldly upon him and say: 'What is this nonsense you are talking? We have never heard of you and your sack of gold before'; and then he would look foolish, and—'

'And in the meantime, while you are running on with your jokes, the money is still here, and it is fast getting along toward burglar-time.'

'True. Very well, what shall we do—make the inquiry private? No, not that: it would spoil the romance. The public method is better. Think what a noise it will make! And it will make all the other towns jealous; for no stranger would trust such a thing to any town but Hadleyburg, and they know it. It's a great card for us. I must get to the printing office now, or I shall be too late.'

'But stop—stop—don't leave me here alone with it, Edward!'

But he was gone. For only a little while, however. Not far from his own house he met the editor-proprietor of the paper, and gave him the document, and said, 'Here is a good thing for you, Cox—put it in.'

'It may be too late, Mr. Richards, but I'll see.'

At home again he and his wife sat down to talk the charming mystery over; they were in no condition for sleep. The first question was, Who could the citizen have been who gave the stranger the twenty dollars? It seemed a simple one; both answered it in the same breath.

'Barclay Goodson.'

'Yes,' said Richards, 'he could have done it, and it would have been like him, but there's not another in the town.'

'Everybody will grant that, Edward—grant it privately, anyway. For six months, now, the village has been its own proper self once more—honest, narrow, self-righteous, and stingy.'

'It is what he always called it, to the day of his death—said it right out publicly, too.'

'Yes, and he was hated for it.'

'Oh, of course; but he didn't care. I reckon he was the best-hated man among us, except the Reverend Burgess.'

'Well, Burgess deserves it—he will never get another congregation here. Mean as the town is, it knows how to estimate *him*. Edward, doesn't it seem odd that the stranger should appoint Burgess to deliver the money?'

'Well, yes—it does. That is—that is—'

'Why so much that-*is*-ing? Would *you* select him?'

'Mary, maybe the stranger knows him better than this village does.'

'Much *that* would help Burgess!'

The husband seemed perplexed for an answer; the wife kept a steady eye upon him, and waited. Finally Richards said, with the hesitancy of one who is making a statement which is likely to encounter doubt:

'Mary, Burgess is not a bad man.'

His wife was certainly surprised.

'Nonsense!' she exclaimed.

'He is not a bad man. I know. The whole of his unpopularity had its foundation in that one thing—the thing that made so much noise.'

'That 'one thing,' indeed! As if that 'one thing' wasn't enough, all by itself.'

'Plenty. Plenty. Only he wasn't guilty of it.'

'How you talk! Not guilty of it! Everybody knows he *was* guilty.'

'Mary, I give you my word—he was innocent.'

'I can't believe it, and I don't. How do you know?'

'It is a confession. I am ashamed, but I will make it. I was the only man who knew he was innocent. I could have saved him, and—and—well, you know how the town was wrought up—I hadn't the pluck to do it. It would have turned everybody against me. I felt mean, ever so mean; but I didn't dare; I hadn't the manliness to face that.'

Mary looked troubled, and for a while was silent. Then she said, stammeringly:

'I—I don't think it would have done for you to—to—One mustn't—er—public opinion—one has to be so careful—so—' It was a difficult road, and she got mired; but after a little she got started again. 'It was a great pity, but—Why, we couldn't afford it, Edward—we couldn't indeed. Oh, I wouldn't have had you do it for anything!'

'It would have lost us the good will of so many people, Mary; and then—and then—'

'What troubles me now is, what *he* thinks of us, Edward.'

'He? *He* doesn't suspect that I could have saved him.'

'Oh,' exclaimed the wife, in a tone of relief, 'I am glad of that. As long as he doesn't know that you could have saved him, he—he—well, that makes it a great deal better. Why, I might have known he didn't know, because he is always trying to be friendly with us, as little encouragement as we give him. More than once people have twitted me with it. There's the Wilsons, and the Wilcoxes, and the Harknesses, they take a mean pleasure in saying, "*Your friend* Burgess," because they know it pesters me. I wish he wouldn't persist in liking us so; I can't think why he keeps it up.'

'I can explain it. It's another confession. When the thing was new and hot, and the town made a plan to ride him on a rail, my conscience hurt me so that I couldn't stand it, and I went privately and gave him notice, and he got out of the town and stayed out till it was safe to come back.'

'Edward! If the town had found it out—'

'*Don't!* It scares me yet, to think of it. I repented of it the minute it was done; and I was even afraid to tell you, lest your face might betray it to somebody. I didn't sleep any that night, for worrying. But after a few days I saw that no one was going to suspect me, and after that I got to feeling glad I did it. And I feel glad yet, Mary—glad through and through.'

'So do I, now, for it would have been a dreadful way to treat him. Yes, I'm glad; for really you did owe him that, you know. But, Edward, suppose it should come out yet, some day!'

'It won't.'

'Why?'

'Because everybody thinks it was Goodson.'

'Of course they would!'

'Certainly. And of course *he* didn't care. They persuaded poor old Sawlsberry to go and charge it on him, and he went blustering over there and did it. Goodson looked him over, like as if he was hunting for a place on him that he could despise the most, then he says, "So you are the Committee of Inquiry, are you?" Sawlsberry said that was about what he was. "Hm. Do they require particulars, or do you reckon a kind of a *general* answer will do?" "If they require particulars, I will come back. Mr. Goodson; I will take the general answer first." "Very well, then, tell them to go to hell—I reckon that's general enough. And I'll give you some advice, Sawlsberry; when you come back for the particulars, fetch a basket to carry the relics of yourself home in."'

'Just like Goodson; it's got all the marks. He had only one vanity: he thought he could give advice better than any other person.'

'It settled the business, and saved us, Mary. The subject was dropped.'

'Bless you, I'm not doubting *that*.'

Then they took up the gold-sack mystery again, with strong interest. Soon the conversation began to suffer breaks—interruptions caused by absorbed thinkings. The breaks grew more and more frequent. At last Richards lost himself wholly in thought. He sat long, gazing vacantly at the floor, and by and by he began to punctuate his thoughts with little nervous movements of his hands that seemed to indicate vexation. Meantime his wife too had relapsed into a thoughtful silence, and her movements were beginning to show a troubled discomfort. Finally Richards got up and strode aimlessly about the room, plowing his hands through his hair, much as a somnambulist might do who was having a bad dream. Then he seemed to arrive at a definite purpose; and without a word he put on his hat and passed quickly out of the house. His wife sat brooding, with a drawn face, and did not seem to be aware that she was alone. Now and then she murmured, 'Lead us not into t—... but—but—we are so poor, so poor!...Lead us not into...Ah, who would be hurt by it?—and no one would ever know....Lead us...' The voice died out in mumblings. After a little she glanced up and muttered in a half-frightened, half-glad way:

'He is gone! But, oh dear, he may be too late—too late... Maybe not—maybe there is still time.' She rose and stood thinking, nervously clasping and unclasping her hands. A slight shudder shook her frame, and she said, out of a dry throat, 'God forgive me—it's awful to think such things—but...Lord, how we are made—how strangely we are made!'

She turned the light low, and slipped stealthily over and kneeled down by the sack and felt of its ridgy sides with her hands, and fondled them lovingly; and there was a gloating light in her poor old eyes. She fell into fits of absence; and came half out of them at times to mutter, 'If we had only waited!—oh, if we had only waited a little, and not been in such a hurry!'

Meantime Cox had gone home from his office and told his wife all about the strange thing that had happened, and they had talked it over eagerly, and guessed that the late Goodson was the only man in the town who could have helped a suffering stranger with so noble a sum as twenty dollars. Then there was a pause, and the two became thoughtful and silent. And by and by nervous and fidgety. At last the wife said, as if to herself:

'Nobody knows this secret but the Richardses...and us... nobody.'

The husband came out of his thinkings with a slight start, and gazed wistfully at his wife, whose face was become very pale; then he hesitatingly rose, and glanced furtively at his hat, then at his wife—a sort of mute inquiry. Mrs. Cox swallowed once or twice, with her hand at her throat, then in place of speech she nodded her head. In a moment she was alone, and mumbling to herself.

And now Richards and Cox were hurrying through the deserted streets, from opposite directions. They met, panting, at the foot of the printing office stairs; by the night light there they read each other's face. Cox whispered:

'Nobody knows about this but us?'

The whispered answer was:

'Not a soul—on honor, not a soul!'

'If it isn't too late to—'

The men were starting upstairs; at this moment they were overtaken by a boy, and Cox asked:

'Is that you, Johnny?'

'Yes, sir.'

'You needn't ship the early mail—nor *any* mail; wait till I tell you.'

'It's already gone, sir.'

'*Gone?*' It had the sound of an unspeakable disappointment in it.

'Yes, sir. Timetable for Brixton and all the towns beyond changed today, sir—had to get the papers in twenty minutes earlier than common. I had to rush; if I had been two minutes later—'

The men turned and walked slowly away, not waiting to hear the rest. Neither of them spoke during ten minutes; then Cox said, in a vexed tone:

'What possessed you to be in such a hurry, *I* can't make out.'

The answer was humble enough:

'I see it now, but somehow I never thought, you know, until it was too late. But the next time—'

'Next time be hanged! It won't come in a thousand years.'

Then the friends separated without a good night, and dragged themselves home with the gait of mortally stricken men. At their homes their wives sprang up with an eager 'Well?'—then saw the answer with their eyes and sank down sorrowing, without waiting for it to come in words. In both houses a discussion followed of a heated sort—a new thing; there had been discussions before, but not heated ones, not ungentle ones. The discussions tonight were a sort of seeming plagiarisms of each other. Mrs. Richards said:

'If you had only waited, Edward—if you had only stopped to think; but no, you must run straight to the printing office and spread it all over the world.'

'It *said* publish it.'

'That is nothing; it also said do it privately, if you liked. There, now—is that true, or not?'

'Why, yes—yes, it is true; but when I thought what a stir it would make, and what a compliment it was to Hadleyburg that a stranger should trust it so—'

'Oh, certainly, I know all that; but if you had only stopped to think, you would have seen that you *couldn't* find the right man, because he is in his grave, and hasn't left chick nor child nor relation behind him; and as long as the money went to somebody that awfully needed it, and nobody would be hurt by it, and—and—'

She broke down, crying. Her husband tried to think of some comforting thing to say, and presently came out with this:

'But after all, Mary, it must be for the best—it *must* be; we know that. And we must remember that it was so ordered—'

'Ordered! Oh, everything's *ordered*, when a person has to find some way out when he has been stupid. Just the same, it was *ordered* that the money should come to us in this special way, and it was you that must take it on yourself to go meddling with the designs of Providence—and who gave you the right? It was wicked, that is what it was—just blasphemous presumption, and no more becoming to a meek and humble professor of—'

'But, Mary, you know how we have been trained all our lives long, like the whole village, till it is absolutely second nature to us to stop not a single moment to think when there's an honest thing to be done—'

'Oh, I know it, I know it—it's been one everlasting training and training and training in honesty—honesty shielded, from the very cradle, against every possible temptation, and so it's *artificial* honesty, and weak as water when temptation comes, as we have seen this night. God knows I never had shade nor shadow of a doubt of my petrified and indestructible honesty until now—and now, under the very first big and real temptation, I—Edward, it is my belief that this town's honesty is as rotten as mine is; as rotten as yours is. It is a mean town, a hard, stingy town, and hasn't a virtue in the world but this honesty it is so celebrated for and so conceited about; and so help me, I do believe that if ever the day comes that its honesty falls under great temptation, its grand reputation will go to ruin like a house of cards. There, now, I've made confession, and I feel better; I am a humbug, and I've been one all my life, without knowing it. Let no man call me honest again—I will not have it.'

'I—well, Mary, I feel a good deal as you do; I certainly do. It seems strange, too, so strange. I never could have believed it—never.'

A long silence followed; both were sunk in thought. At last the wife looked up and said:

'I know what you are thinking, Edward.'

Richards had the embarrassed look of a person who is caught.

'I am ashamed to confess it, Mary, but—'

'It's no matter, Edward, I was thinking the same question myself.'

'I hope so. State it.'

'You were thinking, if a body could only guess out *what the remark was* that Goodson made to the stranger.'

'It's perfectly true. I feel guilty and ashamed. And you?'

'I'm past it. Let us make a pallet here; we've got to stand watch till the bank vault opens in the morning and admits the sack. . . . Oh dear, oh dear—if we hadn't made the mistake!'

The pallet was made, and Mary said:

'The open sesame—what could it have been? I do wonder what that remark could have been? But come; we will get to bed now.'

'And sleep?'

'No: think.'

'Yes, think.'

By this time the Coxes too had completed their spat and their reconciliation, and were turning in—to think, to think, and toss, and fret, and worry over what the remark could possibly have been which Goodson made to the stranded derelict; that golden remark; that remark worth forty thousand dollars, cash.

The reason that the village telegraph office was open later than usual that night was this: The foreman of Cox's paper was the local representative of the Associated Press.* One might say its honorary representative, for it wasn't four times a year that he could furnish thirty words that would be accepted. But this time it was different. His dispatch stating what he had caught got an instant answer:

Send the whole thing—all the details—twelve hundred words.

A colossal order! The foreman filled the bill; and he was the proudest man in the state. By breakfast time the next morning the name of Hadleyburg the Incorruptible was on every lip in America, from Montreal to the Gulf, from the glaciers of Alaska to the orange groves of Florida; and millions and millions of people were discussing the stranger and his money sack, and wondering if the right man would be found, and hoping some more news about the matter would come soon—right away.

II

Hadleyburg village woke up world-celebrated—astonished—happy—vain. Vain beyond imagination. Its nineteen principal citizens and their wives went about shaking hands with each other, and beaming, and smiling, and congratulating, and saying *this* thing adds a new word to the dictionary—*Hadleyburg*, synonym for *incorruptible*—destined to live in dictionaries forever! And the minor and unimportant citizens and their wives went around acting in much the same way. Everybody ran to the bank to see the gold sack; and before noon grieved and envious crowds began to flock in from Brixton and all neighboring towns; and that afternoon and next day reporters began to arrive from everywhere to verify the sack and its history and write the whole thing up anew, and make dashing freehand pictures of the sack, and of Richards's house, and the bank, and the Presbyterian church, and the Baptist church, and the public square, and the town hall where the test would be applied and the money delivered; and damnable portraits of the Richardses, and Pinkerton the banker, and Cox, and the foreman, and Reverend Burgess, and the postmaster—and even of Jack Halliday, who was the loafing, good-natured, no-account, irreverent fisherman, hunter, boys' friend, stray-dogs' friend, typical 'Sam Lawson' of the town. The little mean, smirking, oily Pinkerton showed the sack to all comers, and rubbed his sleek palms together pleasantly, and enlarged upon the town's fine old reputation for honesty and upon this wonderful endorsement of it, and hoped and believed that the example would now spread far and wide over the American world, and be epoch-making in the matter of moral regeneration. And so on, and so on.

By the end of a week things had quieted down again; the wild intoxication of pride and joy had sobered to a soft, sweet, silent delight—a sort of deep, nameless, unutterable content. All faces bore a look of peaceful, holy happiness.

Then a change came. It was a gradual change: so gradual that its beginnings were hardly noticed; maybe were not noticed at all, except by Jack Halliday, who always noticed everything; and always made fun of it, too, no matter what it was. He began to throw out chaffing remarks about people not looking quite so happy as they did a day or two ago; and next he claimed that the new aspect was deepening to positive sadness; next, that it was taking on a sick look; and finally he said that everybody was become so moody, thoughtful, and absent-minded that he could rob the meanest man in town of a cent out of the bottom of his breeches pocket and not disturb his revery.

At this stage—or at about this stage—a saying like this was dropped at bedtime—with a sigh, usually—by the head of each of the nineteen principal households: 'Ah, what *could* have been the remark that Goodson made?'

And straightway—with a shudder—came this, from the man's wife:

'Oh, *don't!* What horrible thing are you mulling in your mind? Put it away from you, for God's sake!'

But that question was wrung from those men again the next night—and got the same retort. But weaker.

And the third night the men uttered the question yet again—with anguish, and absently. This time—and the following night—the wives fidgeted feebly, and tried to say something. But didn't.

And the night after that they found their tongues and responded—longingly:

'Oh, if we *could* only guess!'

Halliday's comments grew daily more and more sparklingly disagreeable and disparaging. He went diligently about, laughing at the town, individually and in mass. But his laugh was the only one left in the village: it fell upon a hollow and mournful vacancy and emptiness. Not even a smile was findable anywhere. Halliday carried a cigar box around on a tripod, playing that it was a camera, and halted all passers and aimed the thing and said, 'Ready!—now look pleasant, please,' but not even this capital joke could surprise the dreary faces into any softening.

So three weeks passed—one week was left. It was Saturday evening—after supper. Instead of the aforetime Saturday evening flutter and bustle and shopping and larking, the streets were empty and desolate. Richards and his old wife sat apart in their little parlor—miserable and thinking. This was become their evening habit now: the lifelong habit which had preceded it, of reading, knitting, and contented chat, or receiving or paying neighborly calls, was dead and gone and forgotten, ages ago—two or three weeks ago; nobody talked now, nobody read, nobody visited—the whole village sat at home, sighing, worrying, silent. Trying to guess out that remark.

The postman left a letter. Richards glanced listlessly at the superscription and the postmark—unfamiliar, both—and tossed the letter on the table and resumed his might-havebeens and his hopeless dull miseries where he had left them off. Two or three hours later his wife got wearily up and was going away to bed without a goodnight—custom now—but she stopped near the letter and eyed it awhile with a dead interest, then broke it open, and began to skim it over. Richards, sitting there with his chair tilted back against the wall and his chin between his knees, heard something fall. It was his wife. He sprang to her side, but she cried out:

'Leave me alone, I am too happy. Read the letter—read it!'

He did. He devoured it, his brain reeling. The letter was from a distant state, and it said:

I am a stranger to you, but no matter: I have something to tell. I have just arrived home from Mexico, and learned about that episode. Of course you do not know who made that remark, but I know, and I am the only person living who does know. It was GOODSON. I knew him well, many years ago. I passed through your village that very night, and was his guest till the midnight train came along. I overheard him make that remark to the stranger in the dark—it was in Hale Alley. He and I talked of it the rest of the way home, and while smoking in his house. He mentioned many of your villagers in the course of his talk—most of them in a very uncomplimentary way, but two or three favorably; among these latter yourself. I say 'favorably'—nothing stronger. I remember his saying he did not actually LIKE any person in the town—not one; but that you—I THINK he said you—am almost sure—had done him a very great service once, possibly without knowing the full value of it, and he wished he had a fortune, he would leave it to you when he died, and a curse apiece for the rest of the citizens. Now, then, if it was you that did him that service, you are his legitimate heir, and entitled to the sack of gold. I know that I can trust to your honor and honesty, for in a citizen of Hadleyburg these virtues are an unfailing inheritance, and so I am going to reveal to you the remark, well satisfied that if you are not the right man you will seek and find the right one and see that poor Goodson's debt of gratitude for the service referred to is paid. This is the remark: 'YOU ARE FAR FROM BEING A BAD MAN: GO, AND REFORM.'

HOWARD L. STEPHENSON.

'Oh, Edward, the money is ours, and I am so grateful, *oh*, so grateful—kiss me, dear, it's forever since we kissed—and we needed it so—the money—and now you are free of Pinkerton and his bank, and nobody's slave any more; it seems to me I could fly for joy.'

It was a happy half-hour that the couple spent there on the settee caressing each other; it was the old days come again—days that had begun with their courtship and lasted without a break till the stranger brought the deadly money. By and by the wife said:

'Oh, Edward, how lucky it was you did him that grand service, poor Goodson! I never liked him, but I love him now. And it was fine and beautiful of you never to mention it or brag about it.' Then, with a touch of reproach, 'But you ought to have told *me*, Edward, you ought to have told your wife, you know.'

'Well, I—er—well, Mary, you see—'

'Now stop hemming and hawing, and tell me about it, Edward. I always loved you, and now I'm proud of you. Everybody believes there was only one good generous soul in this village, and now it turns out that you—Edward, why don't you tell me?'

'Well—er—er— Why, Mary, I can't!'

'You *can't? Why* can't you?'

'You see, he—well, he—he made me promise I wouldn't.'

The wife looked him over, and said, very slowly.

'Made—you—promise? Edward, what do you tell me that for?'

'Mary, do you think I would lie?'

She was troubled and silent for a moment, then she laid her hand within his and said:

'No ... no. We have wandered far enough from our bearings—God spare us that! In all your life you have never uttered a lie. But now—now that the foundations of things seem to be crumbling from under us, we—we—' She lost her voice for a moment, then said, brokenly, 'Lead us not into temptation. . . . I think you made the promise, Edward. Let it rest so. Let us keep away from that ground. Now—that is all gone by; let us be happy again; it is no time for clouds.'

Edward found it something of an effort to comply, for his mind kept wandering—trying to remember what the service was that he had done Goodson.

The couple lay awake the most of the night, Mary happy and busy, Edward busy but not so happy. Mary was planning what she would do with the money. Edward was trying to recall that service. At first his conscience was sore on account of the lie he had told Mary—if it was a lie. After much reflection—suppose it *was* a lie? What then? Was it such a great matter? Aren't we always *acting* lies? Then why not *tell* them? Look at Mary—look what she had done. While he was hurrying off on his honest errand, what was she doing? Lamenting because the papers hadn't been destroyed and the money kept! Is theft better than lying?

That point lost its sting—the lie dropped into the background and left comfort behind it. The next point came to the front: *Had* he rendered that service? Well, here was Goodson's own evidence as reported in Stephenson's letter; there could be no better evidence than that—it was even *proof* that he had rendered it. Of course. So that point was settled... No, not quite. He recalled with a wince that this unknown Mr. Stephenson was just a trifle unsure as to whether the performer of it was Richards or some other—and, oh dear, he had put Richards on his honor! He must himself decide whither that money must go—and Mr. Stephenson was not doubting that if he was the wrong man he would go honorably and find the right one. Oh, it was odious to put a man in such a situation—ah, why couldn't Stephenson have left out that doubt! What did he want to intrude that for?

Further reflection. How did it happen that *Richards'* name remained in Stephenson's mind as indicating the right man, and not some other man's name? That looked good. Yes, that looked very good. In fact, it went on looking better and better, straight along—until by and by it grew into positive *proof*. And then Richards put the matter at once out of his mind, for he had a private instinct that a proof once established is better left so.

He was feeling reasonably comfortable now, but there was still one other detail that kept pushing itself on his notice: of course he had done that service—that was settled; but what *was* that service? He must recall it—he would not go to sleep till he had recalled it; it would make his peace of mind perfect. And so, he thought and thought. He thought of a dozen things—possible services, even probable services—but none of them seemed adequate, none of them seemed large enough, none of them seemed worth the money—worth the fortune Goodson had wished he could leave in his will. And besides, he couldn't remember having done them, anyway. Now, then—now, then—what *kind* of a service would it be that would make a man so inordinately grateful? Ah—the saving of his soul! That must be it. Yes, he could remember, now, how he once set himself the task of converting Goodson, and labored at it as much as—he was going to say three months; but upon closer examination it shrunk to a month, then to a week, then to a day, then to nothing. Yes, he remembered now, and with unwelcome vividness, that Goodson had told him to go to thunder and mind his own business—*he* wasn't hankering to follow Hadleyburg to heaven!

So that solution was a failure—he hadn't saved Goodson's soul. Richards was discouraged. Then after a little came another idea: had he saved Goodson's property? No, that wouldn't do—he hadn't any. His life? That is it! Of course. Why, he might have thought of it before. This time he was on the right track, sure. His imagination mill was hard at work in a minute, now.

Thereafter during a stretch of two exhausting hours he was busy saving Goodson's life. He saved it in all kinds of difficult and perilous ways. In every case he got it saved satisfactorily up to a certain point; then, just as he was beginning to get well persuaded that it had really happened, a troublesome detail would turn up which made the whole thing impossible. As in the matter of drowning, for instance. In that case he had swum out and tugged Goodson ashore in an unconscious state with a great crowd looking on and applauding, but when he had got it all thought out and was just beginning to remember all about it, a whole swarm of disqualifying details arrived on the ground: the town would have known of the circumstance, Mary would have known of it, it would glare like a limelight in his own memory instead of being an inconspicuous service which he had possibly rendered 'without knowing its full value.' And at this point he remembered that he couldn't swim, anyway.

Ah—*there* was a point which he had been overlooking from the start: it had to be a service which he had rendered 'possibly without knowing the full value of it.' Why, really, that ought to be an easy hunt—much easier than those others. And sure enough, by and by he found it. Goodson, years and years ago, came near marrying a very sweet and pretty girl, named Nancy Hewitt, but in some way or other the match had been broken off; the girl died, Goodson remained a bachelor, and by and by became a soured one and a frank despiser of the human species. Soon after the girl's death the village found out, or thought it had found out, that she carried a spoonful of Negro blood in her veins. Richards worked at these details a good while, and in the end he thought he remembered things concerning them which must have gotten mislaid in his memory through long neglect. He seemed to dimly remember that it was *he* that found out about the Negro blood; that it was he that told the village; that the village told Goodson where they got it; that he thus saved Goodson from marrying the tainted girl; that he had done him this great service 'without knowing the full value of it,' in fact without knowing that he *was* doing it; but that Goodson knew the value of it, and what a narrow escape he had had, and so went to his grave grateful to his benefactor and wishing he had a fortune to leave him. It was all clear and simple now, and the more he went over it the more luminous and certain it grew; and at last, when he nestled to sleep satisfied and happy, he remembered the whole thing just as if it had been yesterday. In fact, he dimly remembered Goodson's *telling* him his gratitude once. Meantime Mary had spent six thousand dollars on a new house for herself and a pair of slippers for her pastor, and then had fallen peacefully to rest.

That same Saturday evening the postman had delivered a letter to each of the other principal citizens—nineteen letters in all. No two of the envelopes were alike, and no two of the superscriptions were in the same hand, but the letters inside were just like each other in every detail but one. They were exact copies of the letter received by Richards—handwriting and all—and were all signed by Stephenson, but in place of Richards' name each receiver's own name appeared.

All night long eighteen principal citizens did what their caste-brother Richards was doing at the same time—they put in their energies trying to remember what notable service it was that they had unconsciously done Barclay Goodson. In no case was it a holiday job; still they succeeded.

And while they were at this work, which was difficult, their wives put in the night spending the money, which was easy. During that one night the nineteen wives spent an average of seven thousand dollars each out of the forty-thousand in the sack—a hundred and thirty-three thousand altogether.

Next day there was a surprise for Jack Halliday. He noticed that the faces of the nineteen chief citizens and their wives bore that expression of peaceful and holy happiness again. He could not understand it, neither was he able to invent any remarks about it that could damage it or disturb it. And so it was his turn to be dissatisfied with life. His private guesses at the reasons for the happiness failed in all instances, upon examination. When he met Mrs. Wilcox and noticed the placid ecstasy in her face, he said to himself, 'Her cat has had kittens'—and went and asked the cook: it was not so; the cook had detected the happiness, but did not know the cause. When Halliday found the duplicate ecstasy in the face of 'Shadbelly' Billson (village nickname), he was sure some neighbor of Billson's had broken his leg, but inquiry showed that this had not happened. The subdued ecstasy in Gregory Yates's face could mean but one thing—he was a mother-in-law short: it was another mistake. 'And Pinkerton—Pinkerton—he has collected ten cents that he thought he was going to lose.' And so on, and so on. In some cases the guesses had to remain in doubt, in the others they proved distinct errors. In the end Halliday said to himself, 'Anyway it foots up that there's nineteen Hadleyburg families temporarily in heaven: I don't know how it happened; I only know Providence is off duty today.'

An architect and builder from the next state had lately ventured to set up a small business in this unpromising village, and his sign had now been hanging out a week. Not a customer yet; he was a discouraged man, and sorry he had come. But his weather changed suddenly now. First one and then another chief citizen's wife said to him privately:

'Come to my house Monday week—but say nothing about it for the present. We think of building.'

He got eleven invitations that day. That night he wrote his daughter and broke off her match with her student. He said she could marry a mile higher than that.

Pinkerton the banker and two or three other well-to-do men planned country-seats—but waited. That kind don't count their chickens until they are hatched.

The Wilsons devised a grand new thing—a fancy-dress ball. They made no actual promises, but told all their acquaint-anceship in confidence that they were thinking the matter over and thought they should give it—'and if we do, you will be invited, of course.' People were surprised, and said, one to another, 'Why, they are crazy, those poor Wilsons, they can't afford it.' Several among the nineteen said privately to their husbands, 'It is a good idea: we will keep still till their cheap thing is over, then *we* will give one that will make it sick.'

The days drifted along, and the bill of future squanderings rose higher and higher, wilder and wilder, more and more foolish and reckless. It began to look as if every member of the nineteen would not only spend his whole forty thousand dollars before receiving day, but be actually in debt by the time he got the money. In some cases lightheaded people did not stop with planning to spend, they really spent—on credit. They bought land, mortgages, farms, speculative stocks, fine clothes, horses, and various other things, paid down the bonus, and made themselves liable for the rest—at ten days. Presently the sober second thought came, and Halliday noticed that a ghastly anxiety was beginning to show up in a good many faces. Again he was puzzled, and didn't know what to make of it. 'The Wilcox kittens aren't dead, for they weren't born; nobody's broken a leg; there's no shrinkage in mother-in-laws; *nothing* has happened—it is an unsolvable mystery.'

There was another puzzled man, too—the Rev. Mr. Burgess. For days, wherever he went, people seemed to follow him or to be watching out for him; and if he ever found himself in a retired spot, a member of the nineteen would be sure to appear, thrust an envelope privately into his hand, whisper 'To be opened at the town hall Friday evening,' then vanish away like a guilty thing. He was expecting that there might be one claimant for the sack,—doubtful, however, Goodson being dead—but it never occurred to him that all this crowd might be claimants. When the great Friday came at last, he found that he had nineteen envelopes.

III

The town hall had never looked finer. The platform at the end of it was backed by a showy draping of flags; at intervals along the walls were festoons of flags; the gallery fronts were clothed in flags; the supporting columns were swathed in flags; all this was to impress the stranger, for he would be there in considerable force, and in a large degree he would be connected with the press. The house was full. The 412 fixed seats were occupied; also the 68 extra chairs which had been packed into the aisles; the steps of the platform were occupied; some distinguished strangers were given seats on the platform; at the horseshoe of tables which fenced the front and sides of the platform sat a strong force of special correspondents who had come from everywhere. It was the best-dressed house the town had ever produced. There were some tolerably expensive toilets there, and in several cases the ladies who wore them had the look of being unfamiliar with that kind of clothes. At least the town thought they had that look, but the notion could have arisen from the town's knowledge of the fact that these ladies had never inhabited such clothes before.

The gold sack stood on a little table at the front of the platform where all the house could see it. The bulk of the house gazed at it with a burning interest, a mouth-watering interest, a wistful and pathetic interest; a minority of nineteen couples gazed at it tenderly, lovingly, proprietarily, and the male half of this minority kept saying over to themselves the moving little impromptu speeches of thankfulness for the audience's applause and congratulations which they were presently going to get up and deliver. Every now and then one of these got a piece of paper out of his vest-pocket and privately glanced at it to refresh his memory.

Of course there was a buzz of conversation going on— there always is; but at last when the Rev. Mr. Burgess rose and laid his hand on the sack he could hear the microbes gnaw, the place was so still. He related the curious history of the sack, then went on to speak in warm tones of Hadleyburg's old and well-earned reputation for spotless honesty, and of the town's just pride in this reputation. He said that this reputation was a treasure of priceless value; that under Providence its value had now become inestimably enhanced, for the recent episode had spread this fame far and wide, and thus had focused the eyes of the American world upon this village, and made its name for all time, as he hoped and believed, a synonym for commercial incorruptibility. [*Applause.*] 'And who is to be the guardian of this noble treasure—the community as a whole? No! The responsibility is individual, not communal. From this day forth each and every one of you is in his own person its special guardian, and individually responsible that no harm shall come to it. Do you—does each of you—accept this great trust? [*Tumultuous assent.*] Then all is well. Transmit it to your children and to your children's children. Today your purity is beyond reproach—see to it that it shall remain so. Today there is not a person in your community who could be beguiled to touch a penny not his own—see to it that you abide in this grace. ['*We will! we will!*'] This is not the place to make comparisons between ourselves and other communities— some of them ungracious toward us; they have their ways, we have ours; let us be content. [*Applause.*] I am done. Under my hand, my friends, rests a stranger's eloquent recognition of what we are; through him the world will always henceforth know what we are. We do not know who he is, but in your name I utter your gratitude, and ask you to raise your voices in endorsement.'

The house rose in a body and made the walls quake with the thunders of its thankfulness for the space of a long minute. Then it sat down, and Mr. Burgess took an envelope out of his pocket. The house held its breath while he slit the envelope open and took from it a slip of paper. He read its contents—slowly and impressively—the audience listening with tranced attention to this magic document, each of whose words stood for an ingot of gold.

' "*The remark which I made to the distressed stranger was this:* "*You are very far from being a bad man: go, and reform.*" " ' Then he continued:

'We shall know in a moment now whether the remark here quoted corresponds with the one concealed in the sack; and if that shall prove to be so—and it undoubtedly will—this sack of gold belongs to a fellow citizen who will henceforth stand before the nation as the symbol of the special virtue which has made our town famous throughout the land—Mr. Billson!'

The house had gotten itself all ready to burst into the proper tornado of applause; but instead of doing it, it seemed stricken with a paralysis; there was a deep hush for a moment or two, then a wave of whispered murmurs swept the place—of about this tenor: '*Billson!* oh, come, this is *too* thin! Twenty dollars to a stranger—or *anybody*—Billson! Tell it to the marines!' And now at this point the house caught its breath all of a sudden in a new access of astonishment, for it discovered that whereas in one part of the hall Deacon Billson was standing up with his head meekly bowed, in another part of it Lawyer Wilson was doing the same. There was a wondering silence now for a while.

Everybody was puzzled, and nineteen couples were surprised and indignant.

Billson and Wilson turned and stared at each other. Billson asked, bitingly:

'Why do *you* rise, Mr. Wilson?'

'Because I have a right to. Perhaps you will be good enough to explain to the house why *you* rise?'

'With great pleasure. Because I wrote that paper.'

'It is an impudent falsity! I wrote it myself.'

It was Burgess's turn to be paralyzed. He stood looking vacantly at first one of the men and then the other, and did not seem to know what to do. The house was stupefied. Lawyer Wilson spoke up, now, and said:

'I ask the Chair to read the name signed to that paper.'

That brought the Chair to itself, and it read out the name:

' "John Wharton *Billson*." '

'There!' shouted Billson. 'What have you got to say for yourself, now? And what kind of apology are you going to make to me and to this insulted house for the imposture which you have attempted to play here?'

'No apologies are due, sir; and as for the rest of it, I publicly charge you with pilfering my note from Mr. Burgess and substituting a copy of it signed with your own name. There is no other way by which you could have gotten hold of the test-remark; I alone, of living men, possessed the secret of its wording.'

There was likely to be a scandalous state of things if this went on; everybody noticed with distress that the shorthand scribes were scribbling like mad; many people were crying 'Chair, Chair! Order! Order!' Burgess rapped with his gavel, and said:

'Let us not forget the proprieties due. There has evidently been a mistake somewhere, but surely that is all. If Mr.

Wilson gave me an envelope—and I remember now that he did—I still have it.'

He took one out of his pocket, opened it, glanced at it, looked surprised and worried, and stood silent a few moments. Then he waved his hand in a wandering and mechanical way, and made an effort or two to say something, then gave it up, despondently. Several voices cried out:

'Read it! Read it! What is it?'

So he began in a dazed and sleepwalker fashion:

' "*The remark which I made to the unhappy stranger was this: "You are far from being a bad man.* [The house gazed at him, marveling.] *Go, and reform.*" ' [*Murmurs:* 'Amazing! what can this mean?'] This one,' said the Chair, 'is signed Thurlow G. Wilson.'

'There!' cried Wilson, 'I reckon that settles it! I knew perfectly well my note was purloined.'

'Purloined!' retorted Billson. 'I'll let you know that neither you nor any man of your kidney must venture to—'

The Chair. 'Order, gentlemen, order! Take your seats, both of you, please.'

They obeyed, shaking their heads and grumbling angrily. The house was profoundly puzzled; it did not know what to do with this curious emergency. Presently Thompson got up. Thompson was the hatter. He would have liked to be a Nineteener; but such was not for him: his stock of hats was not considerable enough for the position. He said:

'Mr. Chairman, if I may be permitted to make a suggestion, can both of these gentlemen be right? I put it to you, sir, can both have happened to say the very same words to the stranger? It seems to me—'

The tanner got up and interrupted him. The tanner was a disgruntled man; he believed himself entitled to be a Nineteener, but he couldn't get recognition. It made him a little unpleasant in his ways and speech. Said he:

'Sho, *that's* not the point! *That* could happen—twice in a hundred years—but not the other thing. *Neither* of them gave the twenty dollars!'

[*A ripple of applause.*]

Billson. '*I* did!'

Wilson. '*I* did!'

Then each accused the other of pilfering.

The Chair. 'Order! Sit down, if you please—both of you. Neither of the notes has been out of my possession at any moment.'

A Voice. 'Good—that settles *that!*'

The Tanner. 'Mr. Chairman, one thing is now plain: one of these men has been eavesdropping under the other one's bed, and filching family secrets. If it is not unparliamentary to suggest it, I will remark that both are equal to it. [*The Chair.* 'Order! Order!'] I withdraw the remark, sir, and will confine myself to suggesting that *if* one of them has overheard the other reveal the test-remark to his wife, we shall catch him now.'

A Voice. 'How?'

The Tanner. 'Easily. The two have not quoted the remark in exactly the same words. You would have noticed that, if there hadn't been a considerable stretch of time and an exciting quarrel inserted between the two readings.'

A Voice. 'Name the difference.'

The Tanner. 'The word *very* is in Billson's note, and not in the other.'

Many Voices. 'That's so—he's right!'

The Tanner. 'And so, if the Chair will examine the test-remark in the sack, we shall know which of these two frauds— [*The Chair.* 'Order!']—which of these two adventurers—[*The Chair.* 'Order! Order!']—which of these two gentlemen— [*Laughter and applause*]—is entitled to wear the belt as being the first dishonest blatherskite* ever bred in this town— which he has dishonored, and which will be a sultry place for him from now out!' [*Vigorous applause.*]

Many Voices. 'Open it!—open the sack!'

Mr. Burgess made a slit in the sack, slid his hand in and brought out an envelope. In it were a couple of folded notes. He said:

'One of these is marked, 'Not to be examined until all

written communications which have been addressed to the Chair—if any—shall have been read.' The other is marked '*The Test.*' Allow me. It is worded—to wit:

' "I do not require that the first half of the remark which was made to me by my benefactor shall be quoted with exactness, for it was not striking, and could be forgotten; but its closing fifteen words are quite striking, and I think easily rememberable; unless *these* shall be accurately reproduced, let the applicant be regarded as an impostor. My benefactor began by saying he seldom gave advice to anyone, but that it always bore the hallmark of high value when he did give it. Then he said this—and it has never faded from my memory: "*You are far from being a bad man—*" ' "

Fifty Voices. 'That settles it—the money's Wilson's! Wilson! Wilson! Speech! Speech!'

People jumped up and crowded around Wilson, wringing his hand and congratulating fervently—meantime the Chair was hammering with the gavel and shouting:

'Order, gentlemen! Order! Order! Let me finish reading, please.' When quiet was restored, the reading was resumed, as follows:

' "*Go, and reform—or, mark my words—some day, for your sins, you will die and go to hell or Hadleyburg—*TRY AND MAKE IT THE FORMER." '

A ghastly silence followed. First an angry cloud began to settle darkly upon the faces of the citizenship; after a pause the cloud began to rise, and a tickled expression tried to take its place; tried so hard that it was only kept under with great and painful difficulty; the reporters, the Brixtonites, and other strangers bent their heads down and shielded their faces with their hands, and managed to hold in by main strength and heroic courtesy. At this most inopportune time burst upon the stillness the roar of a solitary voice—Jack Halliday's:

'*That's* got the hallmark on it!'

Then the house let go, strangers and all. Even Mr. Burgess' gravity broke down presently, then the audience considered itself officially absolved from all restraint, and it made the most of its privilege. It was a good long laugh, and a tempestuously wholehearted one, but it ceased at last—long enough for Mr. Burgess to try to resume, and for the people to get their eyes partially wiped; then it broke out again; and afterward yet again; then at last Burgess was able to get out these serious words:

'It is useless to try to disguise the fact—we find ourselves in the presence of a matter of grave import. It involves the honor of your town, it strikes at the town's good name. The difference of a single word between the test-remarks offered by Mr. Wilson and Mr. Billson was itself a serious thing, since it indicated that one or the other of these gentlemen had committed a theft—'

The two men were sitting limp, nerveless, crushed; but at these words both were electrified into movement, and started to get up.

'Sit down!' said the Chair, sharply, and they obeyed. 'That, as I have said, was a serious thing. And it was—but for only one of them. But the matter has become graver; for the honor of *both* is now in formidable peril. Shall I go even further, and say in inextricable peril? *Both* left out the crucial fifteen words.' He paused. During several moments he allowed the pervading stillness to gather and deepen its impressive effects, then added: 'There would seem to be but one way whereby this could happen. I ask these gentlemen—Was there *collusion?—agreement?*'

A low murmur sifted through the house; its import was, 'He's got them both.'

Billson was not used to emergencies; he sat in a helpless collapse. But Wilson was a lawyer. He struggled to his feet, pale and worried, and said:

'I ask the indulgence of the house while I explain this most painful matter. I am sorry to say what I am about to say, since it must inflict irreparable injury upon Mr. Billson, whom I have always esteemed and respected until now, and in whose invulnerability to temptation I entirely believed—as did you all. But for the preservation of my own honor I must speak—and with frankness. I confess with shame—and I now beseech your pardon for it—that I said to the ruined stranger all of the words contained in the test-remark, including the disparaging fifteen. [*Sensation.*] When the late publication was made I recalled them, and I resolved to claim the sack of coin, for by every right I was entitled to it. Now I will ask you to consider this point, and weigh it well: that stranger's gratitude to me that night knew no bounds; he said himself that he could find no words for it that were adequate, and that if he should ever be able he would repay me a thousandfold. Now, then, I ask you this: Could I expect—could I believe—could I even remotely imagine—that, feeling as he did, he would do so ungrateful a thing as to add those quite unnecessary fifteen words to his test?—set a trap for me?—expose me as a slanderer of my own town before my own people assembled in a public hall? It was preposterous; it was impossible. His test would contain only the kindly opening clause of my remark. Of that I had no shadow of doubt. You would have thought as I did. You would not have expected a base betrayal from one whom you had befriended and against whom you had committed no offense. And so, with perfect confidence, perfect trust, I wrote on a piece of paper the opening words—ending with "Go, and reform"—and signed it. When I was about to put it in an envelope I was called into my back office, and without thinking I left the paper lying open on my desk.' He stopped, turned his head slowly toward Billson, waited a moment, then added: 'I ask you to note this: when I returned, a little later, Mr. Billson was retiring by my street door.' [*Sensation.*]

In a moment Billson was on his feet and shouting:

'It's a lie! It's an infamous lie!'

The Chair. 'Be seated, sir! Mr. Wilson has the floor.'

Billson's friends pulled him into his seat and quieted him, and Wilson went on:

'Those are the simple facts. My note was now lying in a different place on the table from where I had left it. I noticed that, but attached no importance to it, thinking a draft had blown it there. That Mr. Billson would read a private paper was a thing which could not occur to me; he was an honorable man, and he would be above that. If you will allow me to say it, I think his extra word "very" stands explained; it is attributable to a defect of memory. I was the only man in the world who could furnish here any detail of the test-remark—by *honorable* means. I have finished.'

There is nothing in the world like a persuasive speech to fuddle the mental apparatus and upset the convictions and debauch the emotions of an audience not practiced in the tricks and delusions of oratory. Wilson sat down victorious. The house submerged him in tides of approving applause; friends swarmed to him and shook him by the hand and congratulated him, and Billson was shouted down and not allowed to say a word. The Chair hammered and hammered with its gavel, and kept shouting:

'But let us proceed, gentlemen, let us proceed!'

At last there was a measurable degree of quiet, and the hatter said:

'But what is there to proceed with, sir, but to deliver the money?'

Voices. 'That's it! That's it! Come forward, Wilson!'

The Hatter. 'I move three cheers for Mr. Wilson, Symbol of the special virtue which—'

The cheers burst forth before he could finish; and in the midst of them—and in the midst of the clamor of the gavel also—some enthusiasts mounted Wilson on a big friend's shoulder and were going to fetch him in triumph to the platform. The Chair's voice now rose above the noise.

'Order! To your places! You forget that there is still a document to be read.' When quiet had been restored he took up the document, and was going to read it, but laid it down again, saying, 'I forgot; this is not to be read until all written communications received by me have first been read.' He took an envelope out of his pocket, removed its enclosure, glanced at it—seemed astonished—held it out and gazed at it—stared at it.

Twenty or thirty voices cried out:

'What is it? Read it! Read it!'

And he did—slowly, and wondering:

' "The remark which I made to the stranger—[*Voices.*

'Hello! how's this?']—was this: "You are far from being a bad man. [*Voices.* 'Great Scott!'] Go, and reform." ' [*Voice.* 'Oh, saw my leg off!'] Signed by Mr. Pinkerton the banker.'

The pandemonium of delight which turned itself loose now was of a sort to make the judicious weep. Those whose withers were unwrung laughed till the tears ran down; the reporters, in throes of laughter, set down disordered pothooks which would never in the world be decipherable; and a sleeping dog jumped up, scared out of its wits, and barked itself crazy at the turmoil. All manner of cries were scattered through the din: 'We're getting rich—*two* Symbols of Incorruptibility!—without counting Billson!' '*Three!*—count Shadbelly in—we can't have too many!' 'All right—Billson's elected!' 'Alas, poor Wilson—victim of *two* thieves!'

A Powerful Voice. 'Silence! The Chair's fished up something more out of its pocket.'

Voices. 'Hurrah! Is it something fresh? Read it! Read! Read!'

The Chair [*reading.*] ' "The remark which I made," etc.: "You are far from being a bad man. Go," etc. Signed, Gregory Yates." '

Tornado of Voices. 'Four Symbols!' ' 'Rah for Yates!' 'Fish again!'

The house was in a roaring humor now, and ready to get all the fun out of the occasion that might be in it. Several Nineteeners, looking pale and distressed, got up and began to work their way toward the aisles, but a score of shouts went up:

'The doors, the doors—close the doors; no Incorruptible shall leave this place! Sit down, everybody!'

The mandate was obeyed.

'Fish again! Read! Read!'

The Chair fished again, and once more the familiar words began to fall from its lips—' "You are far from being a bad man—" '

'Name! name! What's his name?'

'L. Ingoldsby Sargent.'

'Five elected! Pile up the Symbols! Go on, go on!'

' "You are far from being a bad—" '

'Name! name!'

'Nicholas Whitworth.'

'Hooray! hooray! It's a symbolical day!'

Somebody wailed in, and began to sing this rhyme (leaving out 'it's') to the lovely 'Mikado' tune of 'When a man's afraid, a beautiful maid—'*; the audience joined in, with joy; then, just in time, somebody contributed another line:

'And don't you this forget—'

The house roared it out. A third line was at once furnished:

'Corruptibles far from Hadleyburg are—'

The house roared that one too. As the last note died, Jack Halliday's voice rose high and clear, freighted with a final line:

'But the Symbols are here, you bet!'

That was sung, with booming enthusiasm. Then the happy house started in at the beginning and sang the four lines through twice, with immense swing and dash, and finished up with a crashing three-times-three and a tiger* for 'Hadleyburg the Incorruptible and all Symbols of it which we shall find worthy to receive the hallmark tonight.'

Then the shoutings at the Chair began again, all over the place:

'Go on! Go on! Read! Read some more! Read all you've got!'

'That's it—go on! We are winning eternal celebrity!'

A dozen men got up now and began to protest. They said that this farce was the work of some abandoned joker, and was an insult to the whole community. Without a doubt these signatures were all forgeries—

'Sit down! Sit down! Shut up! You are confessing. We'll find *your* names in the lot.'

'Mr. Chairman, how many of those envelopes have you got?'

The Chair counted.

'Together with those that have been already examined,

there are nineteen.'

A storm of derisive applause broke out.

'Perhaps they all contain the secret. I move that you open them all and read every signature that is attached to a note of that sort—and read also the first eight words of the note.'

'Second the motion!'

It was put and carried—uproariously. Then poor old Richards got up, and his wife rose and stood at his side. Her head was bent down, so that none might see that she was crying. Her husband gave her his arm, and so supporting her, he began to speak in a quavering voice:

'My friends, you have known us two—Mary and me—all our lives, and I think you have liked us and respected us—'

The Chair interrupted him:

'Allow me. It is quite true—that which you are saying, Mr. Richards: this town *does* know you two; it *does* like you; it *does* respect you; more—it honors you and *loves* you—'

Halliday's voice rang out:

'That's the hallmarked truth, too! If the Chair is right, let the house speak up and say it. Rise! Now, then—hip! hip! hip!—all together!'

The house rose in mass, faced toward the old couple eagerly, filled the air with a snowstorm of waving handkerchiefs, and delivered the cheers with all its affectionate heart.

The Chair then continued:

'What I was going to say is this: We know your good heart, Mr. Richards, but this is not a time for the exercise of charity toward offenders. [*Shouts of 'Right! right!'*] I see your generous purpose in your face, but I cannot allow you to plead for these men—'

'But I was going to—'

'Please take your seat, Mr. Richards. We must examine the rest of these notes—simple fairness to the men who have already been exposed requires this. As soon as that has been done—I give you my word for this—you shall be heard.'

Many Voices. 'Right!—the Chair is right—no interruption can be permitted at this stage! Go on!—the names! the names!—according to the terms of the motion!'

The old couple sat reluctantly down, and the husband whispered to the wife, 'It is pitifully hard to have to wait; the shame will be greater than ever when they find we were only going to plead for *ourselves*.'

Straightway the jollity broke loose again with the reading of the names.

' "You are far from being a bad man—" Signature, Robert J. Titmarsh.

' "You are far from being a bad man—" Signature, Eliphalet Weeks.

' "You are far from being a bad man—" Signature, Oscar B. Wilder.'

At this point the house lit upon the idea of taking the eight words out of the Chairman's hands. He was not unthankful for that. Thenceforward he held up each note in its turn, and waited. The house droned out the eight words in a massed and measured and musical deep volume of sound (with a daringly close resemblance to a well-known church chant)—' "You are f-a-r from being a b-a-a-a-d man." ' Then the Chair said, 'Signature, Archibald Wilcox.' And so on, and so on, name after name, and everybody had an increasingly and gloriously good time except the wretched Nineteen. Now and then, when a particularly shining name was called, the house made the Chair wait while it chanted the whole of the test-remark from the beginning to the closing words, 'And go to hell or Hadleyburg—try and make it the for-or-m-e-r!' and in these special cases they added a grand and agonized and imposing 'A-a-a-a-*men!*'

The list dwindled, dwindled, dwindled, poor old Richards keeping tally of the count, wincing when a name resembling his own was pronounced, and waiting in miserable suspense for the time to come when it would be his humiliating privilege to rise with Mary and finish his plea, which he was intending to word thus: '. . . for until now we have never done any wrong thing, but have gone our humble way unreproached. We are very poor, we are old, and have no chick nor child to help us; we were sorely tempted, and we fell. It was my purpose when I got up before to make confession and beg that my name might not be read out in this public place, for it seemed to us that we could not bear it; but I was prevented. It was just; it was our place to suffer with the rest. It has been hard for us. It is the first time we have ever heard our name fall from anyone's lips—sullied. Be merciful—for the sake of the better days; make our shame as light to bear as in your charity you can.' At this point in his reverie Mary nudged him, perceiving that his mind was absent. The house was chanting, 'You are f-a-r,' etc.

'Be ready,' Mary whispered. 'Your name comes now; he has read eighteen.'

The chant ended.

'Next! next! next!' came volleying from all over the house.

Burgess put his hand into his pocket. The old couple, trembling, began to rise. Burgess fumbled a moment, then said:

'I find I have read them all.'

Faint with joy and surprise, the couple sank into their seats, and Mary whispered:

'Oh, bless God, we are saved! He has lost ours—I wouldn't give this for a hundred of those sacks!'

The house burst out with its 'Mikado' travesty, and sang it three times with ever-increasing enthusiasm, rising to its feet when it reached for the third time the closing line:

'But the Symbols are here, you bet!'

and finishing up with cheers and a tiger for 'Hadleyburg purity and our eighteen immortal representatives of it.'

Then Wingate, the saddler, got up and proposed cheers 'for the cleanest man in town, the one solitary important citizen in it who didn't try to steal that money—Edward Richards.'

They were given with great and moving heartiness; then somebody proposed that Richards be elected sole guardian and Symbol of the now Sacred Hadleyburg Tradition, with power and right to stand up and look the whole sarcastic world in the face.

Passed, by acclamation. Then they sang the 'Mikado' again, and ended it with:

'And there's *one* Symbol left, you bet!'

There was a pause; then:

A Voice. 'Now, then, who's to get the sack?'

The Tanner (with bitter sarcasm). 'That's easy. The money has to be divided among the eighteen Incorruptibles. They gave the suffering stranger twenty dollars apiece—and that remark—each in his turn—it took twenty-two minutes for the procession to move past. Staked the stranger—total contribution, $360. All they want is just the loan back—and interest—forty thousand dollars altogether.'

Many Voices [derisively.] 'That's it! Divvy! Divvy! Be kind to the poor—don't keep them waiting!'

The Chair. 'Order! I now offer the stranger's remaining document. It says: "If no claimant shall appear [*grand chorus of groans*], I desire that you open the sack and count out the money to the principal citizens of your town, they to take it in trust [*cries of 'Oh! Oh! Oh!'*], and use it in such ways as to them shall seem best for the propagation and preservation of your community's noble reputation for incorruptible honesty [*more cries*]—a reputation to which their names and their efforts will add a new and far-reaching luster." [*Enthusiastic outburst of sarcastic applause.*] That seems to be all. No—here is a postscript:

' "P.S.—CITIZENS OF HADLEYBURG: There *is* no test-remark—nobody made one. [*Great sensation.*] There wasn't any pauper stranger, nor any twenty-dollar contribution, nor any accompanying benediction and compliment—these are all inventions. [*General buzz and hum of astonishment and delight.*] Allow me to tell my story—it will take but a word or two. I passed through your town at a certain time, and received a deep offense which I had not earned. Any other man would have been content to kill one or two of you and call it square, but to me that would have been a trivial revenge, and inadequate; for the dead do not *suffer*. Besides, I could not kill you all—and, anyway, mad as I am, even that would not have satisfied me. I wanted to damage every man in the place, and every woman—and not in their bodies or in their estate, but in their vanity—the place where feeble and foolish people are most vulnerable. So I disguised myself and came back and studied you. You were easy game. You had an old and lofty reputation for honesty, and naturally you were proud of it—it was your treasure of treasures, the very apple of your eye. As soon as I found out that you carefully and vigilantly kept yourselves and your children *out of temptation*, I knew how to proceed. Why, you simple creatures, the weakest of all weak things is a virtue which has not been tested in the fire. I laid a plan, and gathered a list of names. My project was to corrupt Hadleyburg the Incorruptible. My idea was to make liars and thieves of nearly half a hundred smirchless men and women who had never in their lives uttered a lie or stolen a penny. I was afraid of Goodson. He was neither born nor reared in Hadleyburg. I was afraid that if I started to operate my scheme by getting my letter laid before you, you would say to yourselves, 'Goodson is the only man among us who would give away twenty dollars to a poor devil'—and then you might not bite at my bait. But Heaven took Goodson; then I knew I was safe, and I set my trap and baited it. It may be that I shall not catch all the men to whom I mailed the pretended test secret, but I shall catch the most of them, if I know Hadleyburg nature. [*Voices.* 'Right—he got every last one of them.'] I believe they will even steal ostensible *gamble*-money, rather than miss, poor, tempted, and mistrained fellows. I am hoping to eternally and everlastingly squelch your vanity and give Hadleyburg a new renown—one that will *stick*—and spread far. If I have succeeded, open the sack and summon the Committee on Propagation and Preservation of the Hadleyburg Reputation."'

A Cyclone of Voices. 'Open it! Open it! The Eighteen to the front! Committee on Propagation of the Tradition! Forward—the Incorruptibles!'

The Chair ripped the sack wide, and gathered up a handful of bright, broad, yellow coins. shook them together, then examined them.

'Friends, they are only gilded disks of lead!'

There was a crashing outbreak of delight over this news, and when the noise had subsided, the tanner called out:

'By right of apparent seniority in this business, Mr. Wilson is Chairman of the Committee on Propagation of the Tradition. I suggest that he step forward on behalf of his pals, and receive in trust the money.'

A Hundred Voices. 'Wilson! Wilson! Wilson! Speech! Speech!'

Wilson [*in a voice trembling with anger.*] 'You will allow me to say, and without apologies for my language, *damn* the money!'

A Voice. 'Oh, and him a Baptist!'

A Voice. 'Seventeen Symbols left! Step up, gentlemen, and assume your trust!'

There was a pause—no response.

The Saddler. 'Mr. Chairman, we've got *one* clean man left, anyway, out of the late aristocracy; and he needs money, and deserves it. I move that you appoint Jack Halliday to get up there and auction off that sack of gilt twenty-dollar pieces, and give the result to the right man—the man whom Hadleyburg delights to honor—Edward Richards.'

This was received with great enthusiasm, the dog taking a hand again; the saddler started the bids at a dollar, the Brixton folk and Barnum's representative* fought hard for it, the people cheered every jump that the bids made, the excitement climbed moment by moment higher and higher, the bidders got on their mettle and grew steadily more and more daring, more and more determined, the jumps went from a dollar up to five, then to ten, then to twenty, then fifty, then to a hundred, then—

At the beginning of the auction Richards whispered in distress to his wife: 'O Mary, can we allow it? It—it—you see, it is an honor reward, a testimonial to purity of character, and—and—can we allow it? Hadn't I better get up and—O Mary, what ought we to do?—what do you think we—'

[*Halliday's voice. 'Fifteen I'm bid!—fifteen for the sack!—twenty!—*

*ah, thanks!—thirty—thanks again! Thirty, thirty, thirty!—do I hear forty?—forty it is! Keep the ball rolling, gentlemen, keep it rolling!—fifty!—thanks, noble Roman! going at fifty, fifty, fifty!—seventy!—ninety!—splendid!—a hundred!—pile it up, pile it up!—hundred and twenty—forty!—just in time!—hundred and fifty!—*TWO *hundred!—superb! Do I hear two h—thanks!—two hundred and fifty!—'*]

'It is another temptation, Edward—I'm all in a tremble—but, oh, we've escaped *one* temptation, and that ought to warn us to—*['Six did I hear?—thanks!—six fifty, six f*—SEVEN *hundred!'*] And yet, Edward, when you think—nobody susp—*['Eight hundred dollars!—hurrah!—make it nine!—Mr. Parsons, did I hear you say*—thanks—nine!—this noble sack of virgin lead going at only nine hundred dollars, gilding and all—come! do I hear—a thousand!—gratefully yours!—did someone say eleven?—a sack which is going to be the most celebrated in the whole Uni—'*] O Edward' (beginning to sob), 'we are *so* poor!—but—but—do as you think best—do as you think best.'

Edward fell—that is, he sat still; sat with a conscience which was not satisfied, but which was overpowered by circumstances.

Meantime a stranger, who looked like an amateur detective gotten up as an impossible English earl, had been watching the evening's proceedings with manifest interest, and with a contented expression in his face; and he had been privately commenting to himself. He was now soliloquizing somewhat like this: 'None of the Eighteen are bidding; that is not satisfactory; I must change that—the dramatic unities require it; they must buy the sack they tried to steal; they must pay a heavy price, too—some of them are rich. And another thing, when I make a mistake in Hadleyburg nature the man that puts that error upon me is entitled to a high honorarium, and someone must pay it. This poor old Richards has brought my judgment to shame; he is an honest man. I don't understand it, but I acknowledge it. Yes, he saw my deuces *and* with a straight flush, and by rights the pot is his. And it shall be a jackpot, too, if I can manage it. He disappointed me, but let that pass.'

He was watching the bidding. At a thousand, the market

broke; the prices tumbled swiftly. He waited—and still watched. One competitor dropped out; then another, and another. He put in a bid or two, now. When the bids had sunk to ten dollars, he added a five; someone raised him a three; he waited a moment, then flung in a fifty-dollar jump, and the sack was his—at $1,282. The house broke out in cheers—then stopped; for he was on his feet, and had lifted his hand. He began to speak.

'I desire to say a word, and ask a favor. I am a speculator in rarities, and I have dealings with persons interested in numismatics all over the world. I can make a profit on this purchase, just as it stands; but there is a way, if I can get your approval, whereby I can make every one of these leaden twenty-dollar pieces worth its face in gold, and perhaps more. Grant me that approval, and I will give part of my gains to your Mr. Richards, whose invulnerable probity you have so justly and so cordially recognized to-night; his share shall be ten thousand dollars, and I will hand him the money to-morrow. [*Great applause from the house.* But the 'invulnerable probity' made the Richardses blush prettily; however, it went for modesty, and did no harm.] If you will pass my proposition by a good majority—I would like a two-thirds vote—I will regard that as the town's consent, and that is all I ask. Rarities are always helped by any device which will rouse curiosity and compel remark. Now if I may have your permission to stamp upon the faces of each of these ostensible coins the names of the eighteen gentlemen who—'

Nine-tenths of the audience were on their feet in a moment—dog and all—and the proposition was carried with a whirlwind of approving applause and laughter.

They sat down, and all the Symbols except 'Dr.' Clay Harkness got up, violently protesting against the proposed outrage, and threatening to—

'I beg you not to threaten me,' said the stranger, calmly. 'I know my legal rights, and am not accustomed to being frightened at bluster.' [*Applause.*] He sat down. 'Dr.' Harkness saw an opportunity here. He was one of the two very rich men of the place, and Pinkerton was the other. Harkness was proprietor of a mint; that is to say, a popular patent medicine. He was running for the Legislature on one ticket, and Pinkerton on the other. It was a close race and a hot one, and getting hotter every day. Both had strong appetites for money; each had bought a great tract of land, with a purpose; there was going to be a new railway, and each wanted to be in the Legislature and help locate the route to his own advantage; a single vote might make the decision, and with it two or three fortunes. The stake was large, and Harkness was a daring speculator. He was sitting close to the stranger. He leaned over while one or another of the other Symbols was entertaining the house with protests and appeals, and asked, in a whisper:

'What is your price for the sack?'

'Forty thousand dollars.'

'I'll give you twenty.'

'No.'

'Twenty-five.'

'No.'

'Say thirty.'

'The price is forty thousand dollars; not a penny less.'

'All right, I'll give it. I will come to the hotel at ten in the morning. I don't want it known; will see you privately.'

'Very good.' Then the stranger got up and said to the house:

'I find it late. The speeches of these gentlemen are not without merit, not without interest, not without grace; yet if I may be excused I will take my leave. I thank you for the great favor which you have shown me in granting my petition. I ask the Chair to keep the sack for me until tomorrow, and to hand these three five-hundred-dollar notes to Mr. Richards.' They were passed up to the Chair. 'At nine I will call for the sack, and at eleven will deliver the rest of the ten thousand to Mr. Richards in person, at his home. Good night.'

Then he slipped out, and left the audience making a vast noise, which was composed of a mixture of cheers, the 'Mikado' song, dog-disapproval, and the chant, 'You are f-a-r from being a b-a-a-d man—a-a-a a-men!'

IV

At home the Richardses had to endure congratulations and compliments until midnight. Then they were left to themselves. They looked a little sad, and they sat silent and thinking. Finally Mary sighed and said:

'Do you think we are to blame, Edward—*much* to blame?' And her eyes wandered to the accusing triplet of big banknotes lying on the table, where the congratulators had been gloating over them and reverently fingering them. Edward did not answer at once; then he brought out a sigh and said, hesitatingly:

'We—we couldn't help it, Mary. It—well, it was ordered. *All* things are.'

Mary glanced up and looked at him steadily, but he didn't return the look. Presently she said:

'I thought congratulations and praises always tasted good. But—it seems to me, now—Edward?'

'Well?'

'Are you going to stay in the bank?'

'N-no.'

'Resign?'

'In the morning—by note.'

'It does seem best.'

Richards bowed his head in his hands and muttered:

'Before, I was not afraid to let oceans of people's money pour through my hands, but—Mary, I am so tired, so tired—'

'We will go to bed.'

At nine in the morning the stranger called for the sack and took it to the hotel in a cab. At ten Harkness had a talk with him privately. The stranger asked for and got five checks on a metropolitan bank—drawn to 'Bearer'—four for $1,500 each, and one for $34,000. He put one of the former in his pocketbook, and the remainder, representing $38,500, he put in an envelope, and with these he added a note, which he wrote after Harkness was gone. At eleven he called at the Richards house and knocked. Mrs. Richards peeped through the shutters, then went and received the envelope, and the stranger disappeared without a word. She came back flushed and a little unsteady on her legs, and gasped out:

'I am sure I recognized him! Last night it seemed to me that maybe I had seen him somewhere before.'

'He is the man that brought the sack here?'

'I am almost sure of it.'

'Then he is the ostensible Stephenson, too, and sold every important citizen in this town with his bogus secret. Now if he has sent checks instead of money, we are sold, too, after we thought we had escaped. I was beginning to feel fairly comfortable once more, after my night's rest, but the look of that envelope makes me sick. It isn't fat enough; $8,500 in even the largest banknotes makes more bulk than that.'

'Edward, why do you object to checks?'

'Checks signed by Stephenson! I am resigned to take the $8,500 if it could come in banknotes—for it does seem that it was so ordered, Mary—but I have never had much courage, and I have not the pluck to try to market a check signed with that disastrous name. It would be a trap. That man tried to catch me; we escaped somehow or other; and now he is trying a new way. If it is checks—'

'Oh, Edward, it is *too* bad!' And she held up the checks and began to cry.

'Put them in the fire! Quick! We mustn't be tempted. It is a trick to make the world laugh at *us*, along with the rest, and—Give them to *me*, since you can't do it!' He snatched them and tried to hold his grip till he could get to the stove; but he was human, he was a cashier, and he stopped a moment to make sure of the signature. Then he came near to fainting.

'Fan me, Mary, fan me! They are the same as gold!'

'Oh, how lovely, Edward! Why?'

'Signed by Harkness. What can the mystery of that be, Mary?'

'Edward, do you think—'

'Look here—look at this! Fifteen—fifteen—fifteen—thirty-four. Thirty-eight thousand five hundred! Mary, the sack isn't worth twelve dollars, and Harkness—apparently—has paid about par for it.'

'And does it all come to us, do you think—instead of the ten thousand?'

'Why, it looks like it. And the checks are made to 'Bearer,' too.'

'Is that good, Edward? What is it for?'

'A hint to collect them at some distant bank, I reckon. Perhaps Harkness doesn't want the matter known. What is that—a note?'

'Yes. It was with the checks.'

It was in the 'Stephenson' handwriting, but there was no signature. It said:

I am a disappointed man. Your honesty is beyond the reach of temptation. I had a different idea about it, but I wronged you in that, and I beg pardon, and do it sincerely. I honor you—and that is sincere too. This town is not worthy to kiss the hem of your garment. Dear sir, I made a square bet with myself that there were nineteen debauchable men in your self-righteous community. I have lost. Take the whole pot, you are entitled to it.

Richards drew a deep sigh, and said:

'It seems written with fire—it burns so. Mary—I am miserable again.'

'I, too. Ah, dear, I wish—'

'To think, Mary—he *believes* in me.'

'Oh, don't, Edward—I can't bear it.'

'If those beautiful words were deserved, Mary—and God knows I believed I deserved them once—I think I could give the forty thousand dollars for them. And I would put that paper away, as representing more than gold and jewels, and keep it always. But now—We could not live in the shadow of its accusing presence, Mary.'

He put it in the fire.

A messenger arrived and delivered an envelope.

Richards took from it a note and read it; it was from Burgess.

You saved me, in a difficult time. I saved you last night. It was at cost of a lie, but I made the sacrifice freely, and out of a grateful heart. None in this village knows so well as I know how brave and good and noble you are. At bottom you cannot respect me, knowing as you do of that matter of which I am accused, and by the general voice condemned; but I beg that you will at least believe that I am a grateful man; it will help me to bear my burden.

[Signed]   BURGESS.

'Saved, once more. And on such terms!' He put the note in the fire. 'I—I wish I were dead, Mary, I wish I were out of it all.'

'Oh, these are bitter, bitter days, Edward. The stabs, through their very generosity, are so deep—and they come so fast!'

Three days before the election each of two thousand voters suddenly found himself in possession of a prized memento—one of the renowned bogus double eagles. Around one of its faces was stamped these words: 'THE REMARK I MADE TO THE POOR STRANGER WAS—' Around the other face was stamped these: 'GO, AND REFORM. [SIGNED] PINKERTON.' Thus the entire remaining refuse of the renowned joke was emptied upon a single head, and with calamitous effect. It revived the recent vast laugh and concentrated it upon Pinkerton; and Harkness's election was a walkover.

Within twenty-four hours after the Richardses had received their checks their consciences were quieting down, discouraged; the old couple were learning to reconcile themselves to the sin which they had committed. But they were to learn, now, that a sin takes on new and real terrors when there seems a chance that it is going to be found out. This gives it a fresh and most substantial and important aspect. At church the morning sermon was of the usual pattern; it was the same old things said in the same old way; they had heard them a thousand times and found them innocuous, next to meaningless, and easy to sleep under; but now it was different: the sermon seemed to bristle with accusations; it seemed aimed straight and specially at people who were concealing deadly sins. After church they got away from the mob of congratulators as soon as they could, and hurried homeward, chilled to the bone at they did not know what—vague, shadowy, indefinite fears. And by chance they caught a glimpse of Mr. Burgess as he turned a corner. He paid no attention to their nod of recognition! He hadn't seen it; but they did not know that. What could his conduct mean? It might mean—it might mean—oh, a dozen dreadful things. Was it possible that he knew that Richards could have cleared him of guilt in that bygone time, and had been silently waiting for a chance to even up accounts? At home, in their distress they got to imagining that their servant might have been in the next room listening when Richards revealed the secret to his wife that he knew of Burgess's innocence; next, Richards began to imagine that he had heard the swish of a gown in there at that time; next, he was sure he *had* heard it. They would call Sarah in, on a pretext, and watch her face: if she had been betraying them to Mr. Burgess, it would show in her manner. They asked her some questions—questions which were so random and incoherent and seemingly purposeless that the girl felt sure that the old people's minds had been affected by their sudden good fortune; the sharp and watchful gaze which they bent upon her frightened her, and that completed the business. She blushed, she became nervous and confused, and to the old people these were plain signs of guilt—guilt of some fearful sort or other—without doubt she was a spy and a traitor. When they were alone again they began to piece many unrelated things together and get horrible results out of the combination. When things had got about to the worst, Richards was delivered of a sudden gasp, and his wife asked:

'Oh what is it?—What is it?'

'The note—Burgess's note! Its language was sarcastic, I see it now.' He quoted: "At bottom you cannot respect me, *knowing*, as you do, of *that matter* of which I am accused'—oh, it is perfectly plain, now, God help me! He knows that I know! You see the ingenuity of the phrasing. It was a trap—and like a fool, I walked into it. And Mary—?'

'Oh, it is dreadful—I know what you are going to say—he didn't return your transcript of the pretended test-remark.'

'No—kept it to destroy us with. Mary, he has exposed us to some already. I know it—I know it well. I saw it in a dozen faces after church. Ah, he wouldn't answer our nod of recognition—*he* knew what he had been doing!'

In the night the doctor was called. The news went around in the morning that the old couple were rather seriously ill—prostrated by the exhausting excitement growing out of their great windfall, the congratulations, and the late hours, the doctor said. The town was sincerely distressed; for these old people were about all it had left to be proud of, now.

Two days later the news was worse. The old couple were delirious, and were doing strange things. By witness of the nurses, Richards had exhibited checks—for $8,500? No—for an amazing sum—$38,500! What could be the explanation of this gigantic piece of luck?

The following day the nurses had more news—and wonderful. They had concluded to hide the checks, lest harm come to them; but when they searched they were gone from under the patient's pillow—vanished away. The patient said:

'Let the pillow alone; what do you want?'

'We thought it best that the checks—'

'You will never see them again—they are destroyed. They came from Satan. I saw the hell-brand on them, and I knew they were sent to betray me to sin.' Then he fell to gabbling strange and dreadful things which were not clearly understandable, and which the doctor admonished them to keep to themselves.

Richards was right; the checks were never seen again.

A nurse must have talked in her sleep, for within two days the forbidden gabblings were the property of the town; and they were of a surprising sort. They seemed to indicate that Richards had been a claimant for the sack himself, and that Burgess had concealed that fact and then maliciously betrayed it.

Burgess was taxed with this and stoutly denied it. And he said it was not fair to attach weight to the chatter of a sick old man who was out of his mind. Still, suspicion was in the air, and there was much talk.

After a day or two it was reported that Mrs. Richards' delirious deliveries were getting to be duplicates of her husband's. Suspicion flamed up into conviction, now, and the town's pride in the purity of its one undiscredited important citizen began to dim down and flicker toward extinction.

Six days passed, then came more news. The old couple were dying. Richards' mind cleared in his latest hour, and he sent for Burgess. Burgess said:

'Let the room be cleared. I think he wishes to say something in privacy.'

'No!' said Richards: 'I want witnesses. I want you all to hear my confession, so that I may die a man, and not a dog. I was clean—artificially—like the rest; and like the rest I fell when temptation came. I signed a lie, and claimed the miserable sack. Mr. Burgess remembered that I had done him a service, and in gratitude (and ignorance) he suppressed my claim and saved me. You know the thing that was charged against Burgess years ago. My testimony, and mine alone, could have cleared him, and I was a coward, and left him to suffer disgrace—'

'No—no—Mr. Richards, you—'

'My servant betrayed my secret to him—'

'No one has betrayed anything to me—'

—'and then he did a natural and justifiable thing, he repented of the saving kindness which he had done me, and he *exposed* me—as I deserved—'

'Never!—I make oath—'

'Out of my heart I forgive him.'

Burgess's impassioned protestations fell upon deaf ears; the dying man passed away without knowing that once more he had done poor Burgess a wrong. The old wife died that night.

The last of the sacred Nineteen had fallen a prey to the fiendish sack; the town was stripped of the last rag of its ancient glory. Its mourning was not showy, but it was deep.

By act of the Legislature—upon prayer and petition—Hadleyburg was allowed to change its name to (never mind what—I will not give it away), and leave one word out of the motto that for many generations had graced the town's official seal.

It is an honest town once more, and the man will have to rise early that catches it napping again.

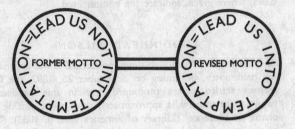

EXPLANATORY NOTES

Details of works referred to can be found in 'Further reading'; dates, where given, indicate the edition used.

PUDD'NHEAD WILSON

4 *the Villa Viviani*: 'Although much concerned about approaching bankruptcy, beginning on September 26, 1892, the Clemenses settled for a prolonged stay in this handsome, twenty-eight room villa approximately three miles outside the centre of Florence' (Library of America text, p. 1082). 'The square stone house [at Settignano] was so vast that he thought of setting a time and a room for the family to find each other once a day' (Kaplan, 316).

5 *Pudd'nhead Wilson's Calendar*: 'Clemens set down in notes and notebooks perhaps three hundred examples—most of them written during the 1890s and some in two or more versions—of aphoristic expressions such as were popularly used in Calendars and almanacs. During the serial publication of *Pudd'nhead Wilson* in the *Century Magazine*, the *Century* printed a miniature calendar with maxims from among those used as epigraphs at the head of each chapter. Early in 1894, after entering into an agreement (soon cancelled) with L. Prang & Co., an almanac maker, permitting the use of appropriate passages from his writings, Clemens spent several days composing compact witticisms, writing 'special squibs for 10 of the months & all the national holidays'. He later made use of previously unprinted maxims—over the inscription 'Pudd'nhead Wilson's New Calendar'—at the heads of chapters in *Following the Equator*' (Library of America text, p. 1082). Mark Twain is parodying a tradition that derives from the maxims that Ben Franklin introduced into *Poor Richard's Almanac*. Mark Twain's own want of sympathy with the kind of moralistic aphorism favoured by Franklin may be seen in his own review of a new edition of Franklin's *Autobiography*.

Dawson's Landing: i.e. Hannibal, Missouri, the village known as St Petersburg in *Huckleberry Finn*. Mark Twain lived in Hannibal as a boy, from the age of 3 to 17 (1839–53). It was a busy river port on the right bank of the Mississippi.

below St Louis: in fact Hannibal is just under 100 miles above St Louis.

1830: i.e. ten years prior to the dramatic date of *Huckleberry Finn*. During the period of Mark Twain's residence in Hannibal the village increased its population threefold, and this fact may be felt in *Pudd'nhead Wilson* in the difference between the sleepy, homogeneous little community described at the beginning of the novel, and the more unruly town involved in the political scenes toward the end of it. See the note on the population of St Louis (below, p. 268).

brick sidewalks: a sign of unusual prosperity and permanence, sidewalks (Eng. 'pavements') more normally being simple wooden planks.

6 *clear waters*: above St Louis the Mississippi is clear. It is the confluence with the Missouri that gives it the muddy appearance that proves so significant in ch. 16 of *Huckleberry Finn*. See *Life on the Mississippi*, ch. 2, p. 234: 'A short distance below 'a torrent of yellow mud rushed furiously athwart the calm blue current of the Mississippi . . .' This was the mouth of the Missouri . . .'; and ch. 22, p. 364.

Falls of St Anthony: at Minneapolis, Minnesota. cf. *Life on the Mississippi*, ch. 60, p. 582.

nine climates: the Mississippi passes through 9° latitude between Hannibal (Dawson's Landing) and New Orleans.

slaveholding town . . . grain and pork country back of it: Missouri was the northernmost slave state, and a 'border state' during the Civil War. The condition of slaves in these northerly climates, and in these agricultural conditions, was much easier than that of slaves working on cotton and tobacco plantations in the much less temperate climate of the deep South. Mark Twain's family had owned a slave.

old Virginia ancestry: the pseudo-aristocratic pretensions of southerners, supposed to have been derived from reading the novels of Sir Walter Scott, were a constant object of Mark Twain's satire.

7 *They ... free-thinker*: Mark Twain's mother was a Presbyterian, his father a 'free-thinker'. In his working notes for the novel, Mark Twain at first made the free-thinking Judge Driscoll the father of Roxy's child (Library of America, 1082).

First Families: the First Families of Virginia (FFV) were those claiming descent from Sir Walter Raleigh's original settlement. Hence the vaguely Elizabethan names with which the leading citizens of Dawson's Landing style themselves.

the 'code': that is, the 'code duello' governing the conduct of duels.

Percy Northumberland Driscoll: 'Percy Driscoll is more exemplary of the dehumanizing effect of slavery on slaveholders in the J. Pierpoint Morgan Library manuscript version of *Pudd'nhead Wilson* than he is in the published text. In the earlier version Percy Driscoll travels miles to collect a debt but lets it go uncollected because the debtor is in unfortunate circumstances. On the other hand, Driscoll sells a slave because the slave is a nuisance to travel with. This omitted episode parallels closely at key points an episode in the life of John Clemens [Mark Twain's father], who, when virtually bankrupt, made a long, expensive trip during the winter of 1841–42 trying to collect an old debt' (Library of America text, 1082).

Roxana: 'The name may come from Daniel Defoe's *Roxana, or the Fortunate Mistress* (1724), a novel urgently recommended to Clemens by William Dean Howells in 1885' (Library of America text, 1083).

8 *an Eastern law school*: in 1828 there were law schools at Litchfield, Conn., Harvard, William and Mary, Yale, and Virginia, and a private law college at Litchfield. Wilson was well ahead of his time in practising as a trained lawyer in a settlement so far west. In 1855, working as counsel in a patent suit in Cincinnati, Abraham Lincoln suffered the condescension of a college-trained senior counsel in the suit. During his return home to Illinois, he had the following conversation with Ralph Emerson:

LINCOLN: I am going home to study law.

EMERSON: You stand at the head of the bar in Illinois now.

LINCOLN: Oh, yes, I do occupy a good position there, and I

think I can get along with the way things are done there now. But these college-trained men, who have devoted their whole lives to study, are coming West, don't you see? And they study their cases as we never do. They have got as far as Cincinnati now. They will soon be in Illinois. I am going home to study law. I am as good as any of them, and when they get out to Illinois I will be ready for them.

(Nathaniel W. Stephenson, *An Autobiography of Abraham Lincoln*, 118)

'*I wish I owned half of that dog*': 'The witticism appears in many versions, including the story of Solomon as told in chapter 14 of *Huckleberry Finn* and the story of an elephant with two proprietors as recounted in *The Life of P. T. Barnum, Written by Himself* (1854), a book that Clemens read with pleasure' (Library of America text, 1083). Some critics have pointed out that the witticism was sufficiently within the traditions of southern and western humour to have been readily understood by the citizens of Dawson's Landing. See, for example, Jay B. Hubbell, *The South in American Literature* (Durham, NC, 1954), 835.

9 *lummox*: a stupid person.

labrick: 'US (Missouri) slang: a fool, an ass' (Library of America text, 1083).

11 *finger marks*: 'Clemens used the device of fingerprinting for the discovery of identity in ch. 31 of *Life on the Mississippi* (1883), but at that time little was accurately known about the regularity of these markings. In an earlier version of *Pudd'nhead Wilson*, he planned to use footprints as a means for establishing identity; then in 1892 Sir Francis Galton published *Finger Prints*, the first book on the subject, and Clemens requested a copy from his London publishers. Galton, he later declared, changed the whole plot and plan of his book. The use by Clemens of fingerprints for identification in 1830 has been questioned as an anachronism, but Galton refers to a university thesis on the subject in Breslau in 1823' (Library of America text, 1083).

16 *warm the end of a plank*: Mark Twain had first recounted this technique for stealing chickens in *Sketches, New and Old*, 81.

19 *bilin'*: lot.

20   *'like dey done in Englan' one time, long ago'*: evidently 'de preacher'
     had read *The Prince and the Pauper*, Mark Twain's earlier (1882)
     tale of changeling children.

22   *In the case of the children* . . . : see 2 Kings 2: 23–5.

24   *mush*: cornmeal boiled in water or milk to form a soft mass,
     or longer until it is firm enough to be formed into a loaf that
     can be sliced and fired.

     clabber: milk that has soured and thickened.

25   *Sir Kay*: 'Clemens knew Sir Thomas Malory's *Le Morte Darthur*
     in a printing of the Globe edition and in the version for boys
     edited by Sidney Lanier. Sir Lancelot takes the armor, shield,
     and horse of Sir Kay while Kay sleeps, leaving his own in
     their place. Upon waking, Kay says that knights will be bold
     against Lancelot, whereas because of Lancelot's armor and
     shield, he will ride in peace. (In the Globe text, London, 1868,
     bk. 6, ch. 11; in *The Boy's King Arthur*, New York, 1880, bk.
     2, ch. 8.)' (Library of America text, 1083).

30   *'conditions'*: his admission to Yale was made conditional upon
     his making up certain subjects in which he had failed to meet
     the required standards.

     He brought home . . . as well as he could: 'The passage is transcribed
     from memory of life in Hannibal. In "Villagers of 1840–3",
     written around 1897, Clemens describes an envied rich boy,
     Neil Moss: "Was sent to Yale—a mighty journey and an
     incomparable distinction. Came back in swell eastern clothes,
     and the young men dressed up the warped negro bell ringer
     in a travesty of him—which made him descend to village
     fashions" ' (Library of America text, 1083).

31   *St Louis*: see note to p. 5 above. St Louis, which stands at the
     confluence of the Missouri and the Mississippi, was the largest
     town on the Mississippi above New Orleans. In 1830 it had
     a population of 5,852, which by 1850 had grown to 77,860.
     See *Life on the Mississippi*, ch. 22.

33   *twins*: 'Clemens was acquainted with twins and doubles in
     literature ranging from Shakespeare to Charlotte M. Yonge
     and Sarah Grand. His interest in duality, disguises, and the
     problem of identity appears in his notes for writing and in
     his published works. Clemens' interest in Siamese twins was
     not new. Chang and Eng (1811–74), born in Siam of mainly

Siamese parentage, were exhibited in the United States, settled in North Carolina, and married sisters. In August, 1869, Clemens published 'Personal Habits of the Siamese Twins' in *Packard's Monthly*, and on September 2, 1869, he published in the *Buffalo Express* a sketch about a two-headed girl. The immediate suggestion for a tale about Siamese twins probably came from an article (with accompanying illustrations) in the *Scientific Monthly* for December 12, 1891, on the Italian twins, Giovanni and Giacomo Tocci, who had two heads, four arms, and one body. The Toccis were then appearing in the United States. In early versions of what became *Pudd'nhead Wilson*, the twins Luigi and Angelo are congenitally united. Clemens later separated them, but because his revising was inadequate, indications of their united origins remain in the published text' (Library of America text, 1083).

The boats were very uncertain in low water: the reason for this is made clear in ch. 12 of *Life on the Mississippi*.

34 *the West*: 'West' is a relative term. The first 'west' was the old Northwest Territory comprising what became the states of Ohio, Indiana, Illinois, Michigan, and Wisconsin. Cincinnati, 500 miles east of the Mississippi, is still sometimes called the Queen City of the West.

35 *we were their only child*: relic of the earlier text in which Luigi and Angelo were Siamese twins.

the war: presumably the uprising in Naples and Piedmont in 1820 and 1821 which marked the beginning of the *Risorgimento*.

placed among the attractions of a cheap museum: see first note to p. 35, and below, note to p. 252, 'The Man That Corrupted Hadleyburg'.

37 *a more than ordinarily friendly soul*: Mark Twain had already told the story of the garrulous man who hinders the procession in his *Galaxy* 'Memoranda'. See Bruce R. McElderry, Jun., *Contributions to 'The Galaxy', 1868–1871 by Mark Twain* (Gainesville, Ga.: Scholars' Facsimiles and Reprints, 1961), pp. 77–9.

38 *sunset seas of glory*: 'Possibly an allusion to a sonnet called "Miracles" by Clemens' friend Thomas Bailey Aldrich, published in his *Poems* (1865). The sonnet includes these lines (later revised): "The fading Alps, and archipelagoes, | And great cloud-continents of sunset-seas" ' (Library of America text, 1084).

42 *on a Cincinnati boat...Grand Mogul*: 'We took passage in a Cincinnati boat for New Orleans; or on a Cincinnati boat— either is correct; the former is the eastern form of putting it, the latter the western' (*Life on the Mississippi*, ch. 38, p. 457). Mark Twain describes such a boat later on in this chapter. The *Grand Mogul* is probably a fictitious name, though Mark Twain refers to a boat called the *Grand Turk* in *Life on the Mississippi*.

  winters on a Vicksburg packet: Vicksburg is a river port at the southern end of the Mississippi. Incorporated in 1825, it was a centre for cotton, timber, and livestock.

43 *amen corner*: a place in some Protestant churches, near the pulpit, occupied by worshippers who lead the responses.

56 *Krakatoa*: volcanic island between Java and Sumatra. In 1883 there was an eruption so explosive that it caused a tidal wave, threw up enough ash and lava to create new islands, and scattered debris across the Indian Ocean as far as Madagascar.

57 *curse of Ham*: '...Cursed be Canaan [Ham]; a servant of servants shall he be unto his bretheren' (Genesis 9: 25).

66 *I saved my own life*: another relic of the Siamese origins of the twins.

  Gaikowar of Baroda: Baroda was a native state, adjacent to Bombay, the ruler of which was titled the Gaekwar.

69 *powerful intoxicants of America*: 'Heavy drinking... became increasingly common in the early nineteenth century, the per capita consumption of spirits rising threefold between 1792 and 1823. Foreign visitors marvelled at the amount Americans drank... Ardent spirits, especially rum, corn whiskey, and hard cider were cheap and plentiful and were popularly regarded as conducive to hard work and as a preventative to disease' (Maldwyn Jones, *The Limits of Liberty*, Oxford, 1983, p. 167).

70 *'no heel taps!'*: i.e. drink to the bottom. A heel-tap is a small portion of liquor left in a glass after drinking, or in a bottle after decanting.

  human philopena snip: 'In the Morgan Library manuscript of *Pudd'nhead Wilson*, Clemens wrote "human pair of scissors" because of the visual image presented at the moment by the (still Siamese) twins. After deleting the image and separating the twins, he revised the description to "human philopena", referring to the twin kernels of a nut, but neglected to change the no longer appropriate "snip" ' (Library of America text 1084).

73 *Missouri ... Old Virginia*: see note on p. 6 above. Mark Twain's father had emigrated from Virginia to Kentucky to Tennessee, before settling in Missouri.

76 *'you have challenged him?'*: duels continued to be fought, particularly in the South, up to the time of the Civil War. Andrew Jackson, part southerner, part frontiersman, fought several in the earlier part of his life. Mark Twain, who heretofore had regarded the sham aristocratic pretensions of Southern gentlemen adumbrated in this chapter with contempt, seems here near to suggesting that they represent a civility to which Tom cannot aspire. Cf. Henry James in *The American*, where Christopher Newman, upon hearing that his friend Bellegarde as accepted a 'gentleman's challenge', exclaims: 'Your duel ... is a scene of the most flagrant description. It's a wretched theatrical affair ... It's G—d—barbarous, yet it's G—d—effete' (ch. 17). See also Henry Adams in ch. 7 of *The Education of Henry Adams*: 'The old and typical southern gentleman ... had nothing to teach or give, except warning. Even as an example to be avoided, he was too glaring in his defiance of reason to help the education of a reasonable being ... The whole field of instruction south of the Potomac . . . was overshadowed by the cotton planters, from whom he could learn nothing but bad temper, bad manners, poker, and treason.'

cartel: written challenge to a duel (Middle French; cf. Italian *cartello*, letter of defiance).

80 *jack-pair*: 'Perhaps two meanings are intended: a pair of rascals [knaves]; and (Siamese) twins, like the reversible figure of a jack, or knave, in a deck of playing cards' (Library of America text, 1084).

89 *ole Cap'n John Smith*: 'In an early draft Clemens wrote: "My father en yo gran'father was old John Randolph of Roanoke, de highes' blood dat ole Virginny ever turned out . . ." The revision was probably made to spare the feelings of existing Randolphs' (Library of America text, 1084).

finger-nails: 'It has been widely believed that Negro blood in a
person who otherwise appears to be white may be detected
in the distinctive appearance of his fingernails. About 1884
Clemens made notes for a story about a mulatto who decides
to pass for white: "At last, seeing even the best educated
negro is at a disadvantage, besides always being insulted, clips
his wiry hair close, wears gloves always (to conceal his telltale
nails,) & passes for a white man, in a northern city "' (Library
of America text, 1094).

95   *still-hunt*: a hunt for game, carried on stealthily as by stalking,
or under cover of an ambush.

102 '*Ain't you my chile?*': cf. Shylock's 'I am a Jew. Hath not a Jew
eyes?' speech, *Merchant of Venice*, III. i. 61 ff.

103 *Arkansas*: the state in which working conditions for slaves was
reputed to be worst.

104 *Michelangelo*: cf. *Innocents Abroad*, chs. XXV–XXVIII.

     side-show riff-raff, dime-museum freaks: another relic of the Siamese
origins of the twins. Cf. the 'King' and the 'Duke' in *Huckleberry Finn*.

105 *back-alley barbers disguised as nobilities*: cf. *The Gilded Age*, ch.
XXXIII, where Mark Twain complains about marriages in
Washington, DC.

108 *his wife she was a Yank... overseer wuz a Yank... outen New
Englan'*: northerners transplanted to the South were thought
to treat slaves with greater cruelty than native southerners.
See *Uncle Tom's Cabin*, ch. XIX.

111 *bitts*: thick posts for securing cables on a steamboat. They
stood in pairs.

121 *telegram*: this is a-historical. The first telegraph message was
sent from Washington to Baltimore in 1844, and the first use
of the word 'telegram' was in 1852.

     lynched: lynchings were not common in the South until after
the Civil War. Mark Twain had an abiding hatred of lynch-
law, and wrote a furious attack on it after a lynching in
Missouri in 1903 ('The United States of Lyncherdom', in
Europe and Elsewhere, ed. Albert Bigelow Paine, published by
the Mark Twain Co., 1923).

137 *Wilson stopped*: cf. the audience's reaction among a crowd of Vassar girls in Mark Twain's ghost story 'The Golden Arm'.

145 *sold him down the river*: 'In an earlier version Tom, instead of being sold down the river, makes use of his suspenders to hang himself' (Library of America text, 1084).

THOSE EXTRAORDINARY TWINS

150 *jack-leg*: southern-American dialect for a person unskilled or untrained for his work; an amateur.

a youthful Italian 'freak'—or 'freaks': the physical model for Mark Twain's twins were the Tocci brothers, late-nineteenth-century 'Siamese' twins. Like Angelo and Luigi they had two legs, four arms, and two heads. But in 1868 Mark Twain had written a comic sketch about Chang and Eng (1811–74), the most famous of all Siamese twins because they had for several years been exhibited in P. T. Barnum's circus. They married English sisters, settled on a farm in North Carolina, fathered twenty-two children, and owned slaves. See above, note to p. 33 of *Pudd'nhead Wilson*.

158–9 *Paine's 'Age of Reason'*: *The Age of Reason* (1793–5) was Tom Paine's attack on the Bible and his defence of Deism.

159 *'Whole Duty of Man'*: a devotional work, probably written by Richard Allestree (1619–81), setting out man's duty toward God and his fellow men.

'From Greenland's Icy Mountains': an Anglican hymn, written by Bishop Heber in 1819. There are two tunes, one by Thomas Clark (1828) and one by S. S. Wesley (1864).

160 *'Old Bob Ridley'*: a song by Charles A. White (1830–92), composer of minstrel songs. 'Old Bob Ridley' is a deliberately simplistic song, intended to portray the virtuous stability and order of life among 'the darkies' on pre-war Southern plantations.

175 *without change of cars*: without having to change from one train carriage to another in order to avoid the conductor.

198 *Galen*: (*c*.130–*c*.200), Greek physician who practised in Rome. His work influenced and dominated medical thought in Europe until the Renaissance.

205 *Democratic party*: formed in 1828 by Andrew Jackson, it was originally the party of farmers, mechanics, artisans, and small businessmen, and favoured states' rights.

      Whigs: formed in 1834 to oppose Andrew Jackson and 'Jacksonism', it disintegrated in the early 1850s.

208 *phillipene*: for fillipeen, or philopena. A philopena is a double almond.

THE MAN THAT CORRUPTED HADLEYBURG

214 *mysterious big stranger*: the 'mysterious stranger' in Mark Twain's tale of that name (first published posthumously in 1916) is Satan.

225 *Associated Press*: founded in 1827, it was by 1860 the most powerful news-gathering agency in the world.

240 *blatherskite*: a person given to empty talk.

246 *'Mikado' tune of 'when a man's afraid, a beautiful maid'*: See *The Mikado*, Act II, where Pitti-Sing, one of the wards of Ko-Ko, Lord High Executioner of Titipu, sings, in reply to Ko-Ko's description of an execution:

> He shivered and shook as he gave the sign
>   For the stroke he didn't deserve;
> When all of a sudden his eye met mine,
>   And it seemed to brace his nerve;
> For he nodded his head and kissed his hand,
>   And he whistled an air, did he,
>   As the sabre true
>   Cut cleanly through
>   His cervical vertebrae!
> When a man's afraid,
>   A beautiful maid
> Is a cheering sight to see;
>   And it's oh, I'm glad
>   That moment sad
> Was soothed by sight of me!

tiger: an additional cheer (often the word 'tiger' itself) after a round of cheering.

252 *Barnum's representative*: P. T. Barnum bought Scudder's American Museum in 1841 and turned it into the most successful collection of curiosities in the country. 'The transient attractions of the Museum were constantly diversified, and educated dogs, industrious fleas, automatons, jugglers, ventriloquists, living statuary, tableaux, gipsies, albinos, fat boys, giants, dwarfs, rope-dancers, live "Yankees", pantomime, instrumental music, singing and dancing in great variety, dioramas, panoramas, models of Niagara, Dublin, Paris, and Jerusalem; Hannington's dioramas of the Creation, the Deluge, Fairy Grotto, Storm at Sea; the first English Punch and Judy in this country, Italian fantoccini [puppets worked by concealed wires or strings], mechanical figures, fancy glassblowing, knitting machines and other triumphs in the mechanical arts; dissolving views, American Indians, who enacted their warlike and religious ceremonies on the stage—these, among others, were all exceedingly successful' (*The Life of P. T. Barnum, Written by Himself*, ed. G. S. Bryan, 2 vols., New York, 1927, i. 195).

THE WORLD'S CLASSICS

A Select List

The Two Drovers and Other Stories
Edited by Graham Tulloch
Introduction by Lord David Cecil

SIR PHILIP SIDNEY:
The Countess of Pembroke's Arcadia (The Old Arcadia)
Edited by Katherine Duncan-Jones

TOBIAS SMOLLETT: The Expedition of Humphry Clinker
Edited by Lewis M. Knapp
Revised by Paul-Gabriel Boucé

ROBERT LOUIS STEVENSON: Treasure Island
Edited by Emma Letley

ANTHONY TROLLOPE: The American Senator
Edited by John Halperin